HarperMonogram is pleased to present a unique selection of "keepers." Throughout this year we will bring back enduring romances that readers have told us they will always remember. Here is another chance to discover these gems—sizzling, tender, charming, passionate, captivating romances that you will want to have on your bookshelves and by your bedside forever. Written by some of romance's bestselling and most popular authors, these are heartfelt stories of hearts broken and sins forgiven, lost love found, and new love discovered. HarperMonogram knows that romance readers want only the best. So here is your chance to discover why the best deserves to be kept in your hearts and your homes always.

"A true Beauty and Beast romance . . . the sensual moonlight interplay will leave the reader breathless."
—*Gothic Journal*

Books by Terri Lynn Wilhelm

Shadow Prince
Fool of Hearts
A Hidden Magic
Storm Prince*

Published by HarperPaperbacks

*coming soon

SHADOW
PRINCE

Terri Lynn Wilhelm

HarperPaperbacks
A Division of HarperCollinsPublishers

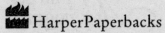 HarperPaperbacks
A Division of HarperCollins*Publishers*
10 East 53rd Street, New York, N.Y. 10022-5299

This is a work of fiction. The characters, incidents, and
dialogues are products of the author's imagination and are not to
be construed as real. Any resemblance to actual events or
persons, living or dead, is entirely coincidental.

ISBN 0-06-108551-0

Cover illustration by Pino Daeni

First printing: November 1994
Special edition printing: May 1997

Printed in the United States of America

Visit HarperPaperbacks on the World Wide Web at
http://www.harpercollins.com/paperbacks

❖ 10 9 8 7 6 5 4 3 2 1

*To my critique group, Ann Bair, Lori Harris,
Kathleen Pynn, and Lyn Welch, united in our
love of writing, the sharing of our rejections and joys,
and our constant quest to understand
what really makes men tick.*

ACKNOWLEDGMENT

The author's deepest appreciation to Dr. Richard O. Gregory, who took time from his pressing schedule to answer so many questions.

1

The wide, wrought iron gates clanged shut behind her.

A moment of panic seized Dr. Ariel Denham, and she longed to apply the brakes. Quickly she looked into her car's rearview mirror. The uniformed guard in his hut on the outside of the gate regarded her through the glass of his window and the black, ornately curved iron that separated them. Then he accorded her a curt nod and returned his attention to the outside world.

The gates had sealed her into this place where she did not want to be. How easily would they open for her if she chose to leave?

"Welcome to Fountainhead," Robert Maitland said, settling back into the passenger seat next to her.

The administrator of the Fountainhead Foundation had met her at the gate.

"Thank you." She couldn't bring herself to infuse the words with any warmth or enthusiasm.

Maitland smiled. The craggy good looks of the tall, middle-aged man prompted Ariel to think of the Marlboro Man in a custom-tailored suit.

"Did you have any trouble finding Fountainhead Valley?" he asked.

She shifted in her seat, trying to ease stiff back muscles. "No. The directions in your letter were easy to follow."

"Good."

She stared out the windshield at the rolling green parkland surrounded by dark, heavy forest. The smooth expanse of the lawn was broken by a dense line of towering sycamores and tulip trees, dogwoods, rhododendrons, and azaleas that meandered, like some strange barricade, the length of the park. Only her high vantage point at this narrow mountain pass allowed her to see that on the other side of that leafy rampart flowed a stream, which disappeared into the shadows of the forest.

"Did you have a pleasant drive?" Maitland inquired.

"Quite pleasant."

"Run into much traffic?"

"Not once I left Atlanta."

Ariel tapped her thumbs on the steering wheel as she proceeded on what appeared to be the sole road in or out of Fountainhead. She was a rising star in the heaven of cosmetic surgery. She should be back in Atlanta, nipping and tucking her way to fame and fortune instead of entering a year of indentured servitude in this isolated, privately owned valley in the Great Smoky Mountains.

But as her father had pointed out, she was his only hope, and certainly she owed him. Ariel had been a toddler when her mother had died, and Gerald Denham had raised his daughter by himself. He'd kept her fed and clothed and had even paid for some of her medical school expenses. Then, as now, she'd always striven to please him, always worked to gain his love. So when he'd pleaded with her to get him the position T. J. Renard had offered, she couldn't refuse him.

"Is there something wrong, Dr. Denham?" Maitland asked quietly.

"Nothing is wrong."

He lifted a skeptical eyebrow.

"All right," she said briskly, "there is something that's bothering me."

"Please, tell me what it is."

She set her teeth, then, catching the movement, unclenched her jaw. "I just don't see why Mr. Renard wouldn't talk with me."

Maitland regarded her for a moment. "As I told you last month, Mr. Renard travels a great deal. His business concerns are worldwide. He has generously endowed the Fountainhead Foundation, and he takes time from his pressing schedule to ensure that we engage only the finest medical staff, but that is where his involvement with this organization ends. I am the administrator. I do have the time to address your concerns. Talk with me."

Lord High and Mighty Renard, she thought.

"Am I the only person under contract to the Foundation who wanted to speak with him before signing?" She doubted it.

"No," he said mildly, "but you are the only person who seems to doubt my authority."

She frowned at the road ahead of them, then slanted him a glance. "I don't doubt your authority."

"I'm pleased to hear that."

She drove in silence for a moment. When she spoke, she was careful to make her question sound casual. "Whose idea was it to offer my father the job?"

"Mr. Renard's."

"Is it customary for him to offer managers' positions at his stores as part of the Fountainhead contracts?"

"Customary? No."

Of course not, she thought resentfully. And certainly not to someone like her father. No sane businessman took such a risk.

"But he's done so before?" she asked, unable to prevent the spurt of hope she felt.

Maitland slowly shook his head. "Not to my knowledge."

"I see." Not for one second did she believe Renard to be ignorant of her father's lousy credit history. Business empires weren't built by missing such details. He had to know no one else would even hire Gerald Denham, much less offer him a management position, complete with all the benefits.

"Mr. Renard can be . . . quite generous," Maitland said.

Her fingers tightened around the steering wheel. "I'm sure." She was sure, all right. She'd turned down his first proposal for her to work at Fountainhead; she'd had plans, which did not include the Foundation. Then Renard had struck again, and this time he had aimed at Ariel's weakest point—her father. He'd included Gerald Denham in his second offer. It was crazy. It was blackmail.

One by one, she loosened the grip of her fingers. It was pointless to object now. The damage had already been done. Like it or not, Fountainhead was her home for the next twelve months. Bitterly, Ariel regarded the surrounding parkland.

Everywhere she looked, verdant leaves glistened, plump with their daily libation of rain. Moisture-blackened trunks and branches slashed in stark contrast against the emerald veil. Like carelessly strewn moonstones and garnets, delicate white dogwood blossoms and showy blood-purple rhododendron blooms were scattered throughout the greenery. As she followed the road toward the main facilities of the Foundation, she couldn't remember ever before seeing a place that appeared so peaceful.

"Does the wall go all the way around Fountainhead?" she asked. It had probably been constructed to protect the privacy of the patients, yet there was about the high, unadorned stone structure a vaguely forbidding aura. She shook her head. It was the fairy garden atmosphere of this place. If she wasn't careful, she'd soon be imagining all sorts of silly things.

"The wall surrounds the entire valley," Maitland said.

As her car crested a small hill, she caught sight of the medical facility. It stood in the center of a group of buildings, which formed the hub of a spoked wheel. The spokes were walkways that radiated from the core buildings, out to clusters of what she guessed might be individual living quarters. Each bungalow was decently spaced from its neighbor.

The sharp *beep-beep* of a pager drew Ariel's attention back to Maitland. He withdrew a small unit from the inside pocket of his jacket.

"You're welcome to use my car phone," she said.

"Thank you, but I'm afraid cellular telephones don't work here. Something to do with the mountains. If you don't mind, I'd like to stop at my office for a minute, before we go to your quarters."

Following his directions, Ariel made her way into the parking lot next to the administration building.

She switched off the ignition, picked up her purse, and climbed wearily out of the car. "Please go on," she said when it appeared that Maitland was waiting for her. It had been a long drive from Atlanta and she welcomed the chance to stretch her legs.

After he strode off to answer the pager's call, Ariel paused to study the two-story, Greek Revival–style building, which was distinguished by towering, white columns that marched along the front. Hanging baskets filled with jewel-toned petunias festooned the lower portico above flower beds that glowed with color. A May breeze rustled through the trees that flanked the Foundation's main offices.

It certainly wasn't what she expected from the ruthless, conniving Renard. He was founder and primary funder of the Fountainhead Foundation, so she had expected Fountainhead to be, well, stark concrete and sharp steel. What she found here was all pleasing symmetry and soothing color, and this small surprise irked her. Then she remembered that there was always a sprinkling of the rich and famous among the patients at the clinic. Ariel doubted they'd come to a place that wasn't aesthetically appealing.

Inside the building, she introduced herself to the young man behind the desk, who smiled and invited her to have a seat. "Mr. Maitland will be with you in a moment," he assured her.

Ariel nodded in acknowledgment, but declined to sit. She'd been sitting for the past four hours. Her beige linen slacks and jacket were a mass of wrinkles, and her white, silk top looked little better.

She found her way to the ladies' room, where she discovered her hair was windblown, and that she'd fretted off her lipstick.

Staring into the mirror, she told herself that Maitland was the last person on earth she cared about impressing. No, make that second to the last. Robert Maitland wasn't responsible for Ariel's situation. He was only an instrument of the real culprit.

Wearily she released the remnants of her chignon and worked a comb through her long, light blond hair. She gathered it back in a ponytail with a lint-covered hair elastic she scavenged from the bottom of her purse.

She regarded the results of her hasty handiwork. Oh, yeah. That made a *big* difference. With a small sigh, she left the rest room.

Maitland was already in the lobby when she returned. Seeing him so impeccable in his well-pressed suit made Ariel feel even more rumpled.

His smile struck Ariel as surprisingly sincere. "Are you ready to see your quarters?" he asked.

"You bet."

"After you have a chance to freshen up, I'll give you a tour of the clinic."

She restrained a self-conscious urge to smooth her palm over wrinkled linen. "Sounds fine."

"Here's a map of the grounds," Robert Maitland said, offering her a clearly marked diagram. "If you'll follow me in your car, I'll show you the way."

When she'd learned that the clinic's remote location required patients and medical staff to be housed on premises, Ariel had assumed she would be given a room in a dormitory. Ten minutes later, she learned her error.

Living quarters, Maitland informed her as he swung open the front door of the bungalow, were designed for maximum privacy. The staff's were separate from the patients', which in turn were separate from the visitors'.

Ariel's bungalow stood apart from her neighbors', and its luxury astounded her. It possessed a state-of-the-art kitchen, a Jacuzzi in the rose marble bathroom, and a large bedroom with a draped, four-poster bed. A set of French doors opened onto a flagstone terrace, which, in turn, opened onto the park.

Her gaze lingered on the breathtaking view. Maybe her stay here wouldn't be so bad after all. Certainly this had not been what she'd expected. She turned to her guide. "Does everyone at Fountainhead have a place like this?"

"Not everyone. All accommodations are comfortable, of course."

"Of course," she murmured.

"Plastic surgeons of your caliber are not easy to come by, Dr. Denham, and we make a special effort to ensure their time at Fountainhead is as enjoyable as possible." His eyes twinkled. "We always hope the contract renewal option will be picked up."

Hope springs eternal, she thought darkly. "I see."

"There's a brochure on the kitchen counter that gives the schedules for the cafeteria, the gymnasium, and the different activities. There's a sunset curfew. After dark, you must keep strictly to the well-lit areas between the bungalows and the community center."

Ariel frowned slightly. "Why?"

"Insurance purposes. There were a few accidents. People stumbling in the dark, hurting themselves. We're a nonprofit organization, Dr. Denham, and we can't afford steep premiums."

She nodded wearily.

Maitland glanced at his wristwatch. "I'll be back in an hour to take you on your tour of the rest of the facilities. Is that agreeable?"

An hour? Ariel stifled a yawn. She'd been up since five that morning, attending to details incurred by this move. Now all she wanted to do was to take a shower, curl up on that lovely big bed, and sleep. "An hour's fine."

After he left, Ariel walked back to stand at the French doors and gaze at the dramatic vista.

The parkland rolled out like an emerald carpet, studded with the deeper verdure of trees and shrubs, encircled by ancient, deep-shadowed forest. Beyond, majestic peaks towered.

She heard the musical laughter of flowing water, and decided to investigate. Leaving the house, she wandered down the grassy slope, toward the dense bank of azaleas. After she had slipped through a narrow space in the hedge, Ariel discovered the clear brook that ran its course down the valley, into the forest. It was bordered by a footpath. For a moment she stood there, enjoying the peace. Until a dark thought intruded. Abruptly she turned back to the house.

So Renard believed he could soften his victim with luxury, seduce her with serenity. Well, he was wrong. She'd accept the amenities he afforded—she might even enjoy them—but she still loathed him, loathed the methods of recruitment he used for his pet project. Ariel closed the French doors behind her.

The man behind the heavy, hand-carved desk answered the telephone. "Renard here."

"This is Robert. Our new addition has arrived."

Renard slowly smiled, satisfied. "Excellent."

"I still think she will be the one."

Renard's smile vanished. "We'll see."

"I've taken her to her bungalow and will pick her up in an hour for a tour of the hospital."

"Any problems?"

"No, sir. But she did seem somewhat reserved."

"Did she?"

"She's unhappy because you wouldn't speak with her."

Renard chuckled. "But not so unhappy she refused to sign the contract. And now we have her for a year."

Exactly one hour after he'd departed from Ariel's apartment, Robert Maitland returned.

She was ready, tired but immaculate in a navy raw silk coatdress.

As they walked, the Foundation spokesman directed them past the visitors' quarters, past the patients' quarters, and on to the hospital.

The clinic's facilities and equipment were all first-rate. The cheerful pastels of the interior were repeated in the comfortable-looking furniture, the carpet and flooring, and the striped walls. Clearly, the Foundation was well funded.

But neither the decor, the facilities, nor the equipment gripped Ariel's attention like the patients.

"My god," she whispered. She looked up at Maitland. "I had no idea."

"I doubt anyone has, until they arrive at Fountainhead. Most of our patients seldom left their houses before they came here. Public reaction, ridicule, and shame have kept them living on the fringes of society." Maitland shook his head sadly. "Such a terrible waste."

She found their numbers vaguely disturbing. Here, she and the rest of the clinic staff—far in the minority—might well be the deviant ones. In the lobby and the halls, in the waiting rooms and the cafeteria, she observed every craniofacial abnormality she had ever read or heard about. It was difficult to remember not to stare when what she really wanted to do was to get a closer look. To examine. In her mind ran the techniques she would use to solve this problem or that. Some of the afflictions she encountered were completely outside her experience, and she regarded them as interesting professional challenges.

"These are the lucky ones," Maitland explained as the two of them rode the elevator up to the second floor operating rooms. "These patients have all been carefully screened by the Foundation. Unhappily, not all applicants can be accepted. Some cases are just plain impossible—neither the technology nor the medical data are sufficient yet. And, of course, like every other nonprofit organization, Fountainhead Foundation does have limits to its resources."

While she looked around she reminded herself that for the first time in her memory, her father had a respectable job. He now had secure employment with health insurance and a pension plan.

The purchase of that security, however, had cost her dearly. She'd had to turn down the offer from Bendl and MacDaid M.D., P.A. Even now it made her a little sick to think of what she'd had to refuse. A partnership in the prestigious, lucrative practice had been more than even she'd expected at this stage in her career. It had been the opportunity of a lifetime.

"And finally," Maitland said as they turned into a short hall off a waiting room, "your office."

He opened a door and led her into a small room painted a light, cheerful yellow. Everything was arranged in an orderly, logical fashion. Stainless steel and porcelain gleamed. The white paper that covered the top of the examining table looked as crisply clean as new-fallen snow.

"You're truly needed at this clinic, Dr. Denham," Maitland said softly

She sighed. "Yes, I saw."

He looked down at the floor, as if ordering his words, then met her gaze. "I know you could have commanded considerable fees, and what the Foundation will be paying you is . . . well, it's not comparable. All I can say is that you'll be serving a worthy cause."

She looked at Maitland. For the first time she noticed the lines across his forehead, around his eyes. She saw the first tinges of gray in the brown hair at his temples. As she met his eyes she glimpsed a quickly shuttered hope in their depths, and realized that he cared, really *cared* about the people here. In that moment Ariel believed him innocent of Renard's machinations. "I know," she said. "I'll do my best."

Ariel opened her eyes on a night-filled room. Moonlight streamed in through the open window, touching with pale silver an upholstered chair, a dressing table, the corner of the four-poster bed.

Not her furniture. Every sensor in her body registered *unfamiliar*. The quilted texture of the bedspread under her cheek was different from the cutwork comforter she was used to. She heard silence punctuated by the call of night birds where there should have been an air conditioner's whisper. Instead of the spicy fragrance of her favorite perfume, it was the moist, earthy scent of a rain-washed garden that permeated the air. Everything was different.

Still muzzy with the remnants of sleep, she struggled up far enough to lean back on her elbows. Where—?

Realization came to her. She was in the bungalow at Fountainhead, not in her bedroom in Atlanta. In fact, she no longer even had a bedroom in Atlanta. She hadn't liked her condo well enough to keep the unit for the time she'd be at Fountainhead, so she'd sold it and put her furniture into storage.

Ariel sat up, pushing her hair out of her face, as memories flooded back. She looked at the clock. Eleven.

Climbing off the bed, she walked down the hall toward the living room. The bungalow was as quiet as a mausoleum.

She went directly to the French doors and flung them open. The perfume of a mountain night swirled in to enfold her, and she breathed deeply, drawing in the freshness. She stood there a moment, her eyes closed as she listened to an owl's throaty warning, the murmurous sigh of the trees.

This valley held a certain magic for her. She had the oddest feeling that this place was an ancient living entity which did not hold itself bound by the strictures of man.

Ariel rubbed her palm across her forehead. There were those fanciful thoughts again. How unlike her pragmatic, practical self. Tension, that was the problem. She needed to work it off before she ended up with stress-cramped muscles.

She looked out over the night-darkened park and

smiled. It was a lovely evening. A brisk walk was just what the doctor ordered. Then she remembered the curfew.

Defiantly, she changed into a sweatshirt and shorts, then she snatched up her socks and walking shoes and tugged them on.

After locking the door behind her, she suddenly felt more carefree than she had in weeks. Across the terrace she strode, down the grassy slope beyond, to cut between enormous azalea bushes.

The little footpath she'd found earlier was dimly illuminated by tiny mushroom-shaped lamps. The light was just enough to let her see where she set her feet. Exhilaration lifted her spirits as she set a brisk pace. Glorious! The cool damp of late spring misted her skin, soothing her. It was so peaceful here. So tranquil. She was alone with the crescent moon.

Ariel pushed herself, striding just below a jog. She'd been at it for almost thirty minutes when she heard footfalls in the regular cadence of a runner. Abruptly she came to a halt and listened. The sound was moving toward her. She was alone, out of earshot of the bungalows. Nervousness seized her.

Eager not to be detected, curious to see who else was breaking the curfew, she ducked into the deep shadow of the thick foliage that followed the stream.

The runner was tall, and swift, and powerfully lean. Of his face she could see nothing, but as he flashed through shadow and moonlight on the opposite bank of the brook, she caught glimpses of broad shoulders and muscular arms. Sweatpants did nothing to conceal lean hips, long legs, and the hard curve of masculine buttocks. His breathing was harsh and deep. Sweat glistened on his skin.

Ariel watched. So much for the sacred curfew. This man moved with a confidence that came of familiarity, and she guessed he'd run this route before. Likely one of the staff, tired of restriction.

Something skittered across her foot. Instantly she danced back. She lost her balance and crashed down, with a squawk, into the bushes. Anxious and disgusted, she struggled to right herself. Twigs scratched her. Leaves slithered down the neck of her sweatshirt. At least she *hoped* they were leaves.

By the time she regained her feet, the runner had vanished.

Grumbling, Ariel brushed herself off. She held the bottom of her shirt away from her waist and shook. To her relief, three small leaves drifted to the ground.

She decided she'd done enough walking for tonight. As she headed back in the direction of her bungalow, she found herself wishing she'd been able to watch the runner until he'd disappeared from sight. For a moment, she hadn't felt so alone.

She didn't like that thought and determinedly established a rhythmic, demanding pace. There was nothing wrong with being alone. She'd been alone a lot during her life, and it hadn't killed her. But the soft thud of each footfall seemed to taunt her. *Alone . . . Alone . . . Alone.*

"What are you doing out here?" demanded a deep, masculine voice from the shadows beneath the trees, next to her.

Startled, she stumbled, but she quickly managed to

recover her balance. Her heart pounded as she turned and tried to establish the exact location of the voice. She finally focused on the darker, man-shaped density.

"You are the noisiest woman," the stranger observed dryly. "Now, I asked you what you're doing out here."

It was the runner. It had to be. Didn't it? She squinted into the dark, but glimpsed only the dim curve of what she thought might be a shoulder.

"Step out where I can see you," she countered.

"I'm quite comfortable where I am, thank you. Answer my question," he commanded.

Ariel scowled. "Don't take that tone with *me*, fella."

"My pardon," he drawled. "I had no idea I was in the presence of greatness." Like a fine, rich cognac, his baritone voice was deeply mellow while possessing an underlying fire.

And clearly he found her amusing. That thought rankled.

"Obviously much greater than you deserve," she muttered and turned on her heel to continue her walk. She wished he'd just go away.

"What are you doing out here?" he repeated, this time in a more conversational tone. He moved beside her, keeping to the shadows.

Ariel sighed. He really was annoyingly persistent. But that didn't mean she owed him any answers. "What does it look like I'm doing?"

"Walking." The single, clipped word bore a wealth of disapproval.

"Precisely. Walking. Just walking. Minding my own business," she added pointedly.

"You have no business out now," he informed her.

"Neither do you. Besides, who died and made you guardian of the grounds?"

For a long moment, he didn't speak. Well, no loss. Who wanted conversation with a pushy critic, anyway? Especially some night creeper, lurking in the shadows.

Her tread faltered fractionally. Night creeper. Wasn't there an old movie about a night creeper? A huge, misshapen creature who strangled people? Maybe this guy wasn't one of the hospital staff just out for a run, Ariel thought, casting a nervous glance into the shadows. Why wouldn't he come out where she could see him? She quickened her pace.

"Weren't you told about the curfew?" he demanded.

Ariel jumped, then glared into the shadows. "Will you *stop* that!" She pressed a hand over her chest, as if the gesture could calm her racing heart.

"Well, weren't you?"

"Yes! I was told about the curfew. Look, I know you were running earlier." She swept out her arm in a grand gesture. "Don't let me keep you." She stood where she was for a moment, but he seemed to make no move. Drat those shadows. She resumed her walk, forcing herself to a slower speed than she'd have liked, trying to give the appearance of nonchalance. Why couldn't she hear his footfalls? Nobody could be that quiet.

"If you were told about the curfew, then why are you out here?" he asked.

Irritation nudged against her nervousness. "For exercise."

"There's a gymnasium for that."

"So there is. Why aren't you in it?"

"Because I want to be outside," he said simply.

"Well, so do I. I *don't* want to be confined to a well-lit beehive. When I signed up for my stint here, no one said anything about a curfew."

"Do you plan to continue your evening walks?" A twig cracked on the ground close to her.

Ariel ran her tongue over dry lips. She edged toward the far side of the walkway, toward the stream, away from the shadows. "I don't know."

Dark humor colored his words. "How cautious you are."

Here the moonlight filtered though the trees. Faint silver touched broad shoulders in a tank top, and long legs in sweatpants. With his back to the moon, his face remained in darkness. Then he shifted, and she lost sight of him. She scanned the area.

"Do I make you nervous?" he asked, startlingly near to her.

Yes. Stubbornly, she lifted her chin. "Isn't that what you're trying to do?"

His soft laughter surprised Ariel. It held an intimate, sensual quality that slipped over her like a warm hand. "Perhaps."

Ariel swallowed. As far back as she could remember, she'd been left to face life's monsters on her own. And she'd been scared by some of the best. But they had been creatures of flesh and blood, not some shadowy mountain phantom. "Don't bother. It won't work." What was she supposed to do, admit that his tactics were working quite well? Wouldn't he just love that?

She tried to estimate how much farther she had to

go until she reached the break in the azalea hedge near her bungalow.

"Will you please step out where I can see you?" she coaxed.

"As I said before, I'm comfortable here."

"Well, listen, it's been great talking with you," she told him with patent insincerity. It wasn't much farther . . .

She looked straight ahead, frowning. Try as she might, she couldn't hear his footfalls, though she knew from his voice that he was moving along with her. It was unnatural for anyone to walk that quietly. But then, this whole scenario was more than a little eerie. Maybe he wasn't walking. Maybe he was floating.

"Aren't you afraid of being out in the park at night?" he asked.

At the same time she chided herself for allowing her imagination to run wild, Ariel looked in his direction, uncertain. "Why should I be afraid? This place has a wall around it and a guard at the gate. Besides, who'd want to get in? It's not exactly Disneyland."

He didn't respond.

She found she couldn't help asking. "Why should I be afraid?"

"This place is haunted." There was no smile in his voice.

Earlier, her first inclination might have been to laugh. North Carolina had its share of ghostly legends, but she'd never heard of a remote hospital and its grounds being haunted. Now she thought, what better place could there be for unhappy spirits to roam? If one believed in that sort of thing. Which, of course, she didn't.

She couldn't decide whether he was just jerking her chain, or was, in fact, a lunatic. Ariel cleared her throat and asked, "If it's haunted, what are *you* doing here? Aren't you afraid?"

"I'm not afraid," he answered. His next words held a brooding, faraway quality. "Ghosts are my constant companions."

His reply settled Ariel's indecision, a conclusion which came just as the break in the hedge appeared. Recklessly, she plunged across what must have been the stranger's path, directly into the small space between the old azaleas, sending leaves showering. Thin, skeletal branches plucked at her clothing, caught in her hair. Heedlessly, she tore free.

She bolted up the incline to her terrace, his soft, taunting laughter following her. Fumbled keys miraculously opened the lock, and she whirled into the living room, sweeping the doors closed behind her. She shot the bolt and jerked shut the drapes. Quickly she turned on the light.

Long moments passed as she stood panting, gulping air. Gradually, her brain cleared. Her breathing eased. The knot of panic in her chest evaporated and in its wake came such searing chagrin that she burned with it.

A fool. She'd been a silly fool. There were no such things as ghosts. She knew that, absolutely, for a fact. Long ago she'd outgrown most of her childish fears. That shadow being was nothing more than a man, a man who didn't want her in the park.

She shivered even as she briskly rubbed her palms up and down her arms. It was this valley. The place bred fanciful thoughts. She would have to stay on her guard against them.

She hurried through the house turning on all the lights. Then she showered and climbed into bed, all the while, trying to work out who—not what—the runner was.

A member of Fountainhead's staff? Probably. But why would someone from the staff behave toward her in such a manner? He could see clearly that she, too, was one of the staff. They might have enjoyed a nice walk together, conspirators in a lovely evening, if he hadn't insisted on testing her. If he hadn't refused to leave the shadows as though—as though he had something to hide from her.

Suddenly, the pieces slipped into place, and Ariel stared up at the ceiling with wide eyes. That man wasn't a member of the Foundation hospital staff.

He was a patient.

2

It was early when Ariel left her bungalow the next morning. The mountain air was cool but she knew it would warm pleasantly as the sun rose higher. Mist hung over the parkland like a delicate shroud, but all the buildings were situated on this low hill, and here only wisps of gray vapor remained.

She'd risen early to have extra time to familiarize herself with the layout of the clinic. Maitland's tour had given her a general idea, but there had been too much to absorb at one time. She wanted to learn her way around a little better before she officially started her day.

Motion detectors went into operation, and a pair of the clinic's glass doors slid open to admit her. On the other side of the glass vestibule another pair of doors rolled back, and she entered the main lobby.

Again she was struck by the care that had gone into the planning of the clinic. The floor coverings, and walls, and the comfortable furniture were all done in bright, cheerful colors, the predominant one being clear, true yellow. A happy tone, she thought, nodding to the attendants at the front desk as she passed, on her way to the elevators.

Before she reached them, she was greeted in the quiet hall by a smiling woman who looked for all the world like a redheaded pixie.

"Good morning, Dr. Denham."

Ariel was thirty-three, and she estimated the other woman's age to be about the same. "Good morning." She searched her memory for a name.

"Doris," the woman supplied. "Doris Farmer."

Ariel drew a blank, unable to place the name or the sunny, elfin face.

Doris laughed. "We didn't actually meet yesterday. I'm the supervisor of Patient Records. There's a good chance you'll never need to come back to the area where I work. But I saw Mr. Maitland escorting you around and knew you had to be the new surgeon. Have you had your morning coffee yet?"

"I had some at . . . home." It was difficult to accept, but the bungalow was her home now, at least for the next year.

"Oh."

"But I'd love another cup," Ariel hastened to assure her.

Doris brightened. "Come on."

As they made their way through gleaming corridors, Doris continued. "You'll usually take your coffee from the doctors' lounge, which is more convenient to your office, but I just finished brewing a fresh pot, and we're already here." She pushed open a door bearing a sign reading Patient Records and went straight to a vintage coffeemaker, which seemed to be holding court over an orderly, if mismatched, collection of ceramic mugs. It was early yet, and it appeared Doris was the first in her department to arrive.

She poured and handed Ariel a steaming cup. "So, how do you like it here, so far?"

"Well, I've been here less than twenty-four hours, but it seems okay."

"Fountainhead's really pretty, don't you think? I mean, with the mountains and all?"

"Gorgeous," Ariel agreed wholeheartedly. She took a sip of coffee, considering. "Doris," she said hesitantly. "What do you think about the curfew?"

"They're really strict about it. The park is mostly for patients. Oh, the staff is allowed to go there during the day, but we're usually at work then. Besides, on our days off most of us want to get away."

"Where is there to go, around here?"

"There's a little town—Farley—about an hour's drive from here. It has some shops, a couple of restaurants. There's an old, Gothic-looking mansion that's been made into an inn. I've never stayed there, but I have a friend who has. She said all the place needs is Bela Lugosi in a black cloak."

"Sounds interesting." Atlanta it wasn't.

"It's okay. The people are friendly. Doris continued, "Have you been to the gym yet? Actually, it's more like a health spa, but it's listed as a gym."

"Not yet."

"It's very nice. If I was back at my old job in New Bern, I'd never be able to afford a club as nice as the one here. But this one is open to all staff, and at a reasonable rate."

They chatted for a few minutes more, Doris listing some of the activities sponsored by the community center.

"Everything here in the clinic looks top-notch," Ariel commented, hoping to steer the conversation into more useful areas.

"Oh, it is," Doris stated proudly. "The equipment, the facilities, the surgeons—only the best."

"What prompted you to come to work here, Doris? Fountainhead's a long way from New Bern. What was it about the clinic that lured you away to the mountains?"

Doris frowned absently at her manicured nails, then opened a desk drawer and withdrew a bottle of tangerine-colored nail polish and unscrewed the lid. "Well," she said as she carefully dabbed color on a chipped edge of one forefinger, "I had a cousin who came to work here four years ago. She met a doctor, and they got married after his contract was up. When she left, she recommended me for her position. They checked me out, and offered me the job." She blew lightly on the new paint. "And here I am today."

"Checked you out?"

Doris waved her finger. "Oh, sure. Maitland says Renard is *very* particular about who works for him. Everyone is checked out. But he offers his employees a lot. Good pay. Benefits. All the perks I told you about." Suddenly she grinned, and her face looked more impish than usual. "One of those perks is all the doctors. My cousin got one. Why not me?"

Ariel didn't approve of such dated thinking, but she couldn't help but chuckle at Doris's outrageous honesty. "Why not indeed?" She swallowed the last sip of coffee in her mug. "Tell me, why doesn't the outside world ever hear of Fountainhead? I mean, the work done here is such a worthy cause, you'd think they'd want to get their names out in front of everyone to raise money, or to let people know there's help available."

The other woman shifted in her chair. "Want another cup of coffee?"

"No, thanks." She waited patiently for her answer.

Doris stood and went to the coffeemaker where she filled her cup. She dumped in nondairy creamer and sugar, then stirred. "Well, certain people in the outside world do know about Fountainhead. But the last thing our patients want is publicity. Most of them have been stared at too often as it is. And I've heard that Renard also wants Fountainhead to keep a low profile." She hesitated. "Seems he thinks some doctors grandstand. He believes they get so carried away with their own glorification that they forget their patients' needs." Doris ducked her head and needlessly stirred her coffee. Dark color flagged her cheeks.

Renard is even weirder than I believed, Ariel thought disgustedly. Most of the physicians she knew preferred to conduct their practices with quiet decorum. "Well, I'm sure he has his reasons. I was just curious."

She took her cup to the small sink, where she washed it out and set it upside down on a terry tea towel. Then she remembered the time. She glanced at her watch. So much for scouting the layout of the clinic. Oh, well. She'd have a year for that. With a sincere smile, she thanked Doris for the coffee.

"Come back any time," Doris offered. "I always have coffee ready at this hour."

Ariel felt warmed by the invitation. "Thanks. I appreciate that." With a wave, she left.

She found her way to the elevators and pressed the up button. Grandstanding surgeons indeed! What a creep.

There was no one in the waiting area yet, nor was the receptionist anywhere to be found. She hoped someone had thought to leave her patients' files out for her.

When she opened her office door, she discovered a single, long-stemmed rose lying on her desk. Accompanying the flower was a plain white card with one word scrawled across it: Welcome.

She picked up the bloom and drew in its sweet perfume. Voluptuous, satin petals of a tender, first-love pink cupped one another in perfect symmetry. On the delicate curve of an outer petal poised a single, crystalline droplet.

This was no florist's flower, Ariel decided. It was more fragrant, more delicate. She wondered who'd been so thoughtful. Who did she know here? Robert Maitland?

Or what about that other little guy, Kerwin Sprague? The anesthesiologist with the toupee and the snub nose? He'd been all blushing courtesy and helpfulness when they'd been introduced yesterday. Someone had told her that he was a rosarian, and—this spoken with a sly wink—that he'd probably never been as passionate about a woman as he was about roses. She'd thought the remark cruel. Kerwin hadn't seemed indifferent. Just shy.

Well, Ariel wanted to thank whoever had left the gift, but for now, she needed to put it in water and get to work. She walked back out to the reception area where four patients now sat. One man's face had been badly burned over the right half. The face of the African-American man sitting across from him was crisscrossed by the stiff ridges of keloid formations. That was to be expected. Injured black skin often developed keloids. A woman, who looked to be in her late fifties, lacked a mandible—probably the result of cancer. Where once there had been a chin and a jaw-line, now only slack folds of skin hung at her upper throat. Problems, Ariel thought. A jaw could be reconstructed for her, but the patient would probably always have difficulty chewing. Still, at least she'd look human again.

The fourth patient, a girl, sat with a woman Ariel guessed was her mother. Around six or seven years of age, the child had a double cleft lip, and in all likeli-hood, a cleft palate. The fact that the lip had not already been fixed surprised Ariel. Usually a cleft lip was repaired in the first year, and the cleft palate in the second. Even if both the soft and the hard palates were cleft, at least the lip should have been taken care of by now. Then she noticed the wash-faded garments worn by both woman and child, and the cheap quality of their polished shoes.

Ariel accorded the waiting patients a friendly greeting and a pleasant smile, noting which ones responded to her with lowered eyes.

She stopped at the desk of Toby Kearns, the strapping young man who served as the receptionist-secretary for her and two other doctors. He reminded her of a Minnesota farm boy. "Do you know who left this in my office? There's a card, but it's unsigned, so I don't know whom to thank."

Toby shook his blond head. "No, ma'am, I don't. It sure is pretty, though." Genuine delight danced in his cornflower-blue eyes. "Guess you already have an admirer."

"More likely someone just being nice. The flower needs water. Is there a container I can use?"

"I'll find one for it," the young man said. He handed her a file folder with records and test results neatly clipped inside. "Your first patient is here."

The girl with the cleft lip turned out to be Ariel's first patient. She clutched the woman's hand, and kept her head lowered.

Ariel gave the girl and her mother a friendly smile. "Hello. I'm Dr. Denham." The other woman introduced herself, as she reassuringly stroked her daughter's brown hair. Ariel turned to her patient. "And you're Sara, aren't you?"

Sara nodded, unwilling to speak. She bravely tried a smile, but it faded quickly.

"Sara, I need you to open your mouth," Ariel told the girl sitting on the examining table. "I'm going to be as gentle as I can, but I need to look inside, okay?"

Sara hesitated, then nodded and opened her mouth.

Ariel's examination verified what she'd read in the patient's file: Sara's soft and hard palates suffered from a double cleft, as did her lip. Both the muscular tissue and the bony inverted bowl that formed the roof of the girl's mouth were divided, with the split going into the upper jaw.

Ariel studied Sara's downcast face for a moment. Why hadn't this problem been taken care of before now? she wondered indignantly. Weren't there public agencies that dealt with these things?

She scribbled out her notes. In the past, she had performed the procedures this girl would need, though usually the patients had been younger by several years. While she was confident of her skill, this was not the sort of work she did nowadays. Correction, she thought dryly. It would be exactly the sort of work she'd be doing *nowadays*.

Completing her notes, she again scanned the file, noting the names and specialties of the other doctors who would be involved in this case. Then she swiveled on her stool to face Sara and her mother, who sat quietly waiting. As she ordered her thoughts, Ariel absently slipped the pen into the top pocket of her white lab coat.

"Sara," she said, "you're an important young lady. You're so important to us that we have a team of doctors to take care of your needs."

The girl blinked but did not speak. Ariel knew that under her present circumstances Sara would likely not be willing to speak unless absolutely necessary. The garbled sound caused by her cleft would by now have marked her as "different," and brought her shame and frustration.

"You're going to have me as your surgeon, but you're also going to have an orthodontist, a speech therapist, a psychologist, an audiologist, and an otolaryngologist."

Sara looked uncertainly at her mother, who smiled. Then, facing Ariel once more, Sara raised her eyebrows in question.

"Well, let's see," Ariel said. She held up six fingers, ticking one off for each doctor. "I'll correct the cleft lip and palates. Your orthodontist will take care of straightening your teeth, and will make any appliances necessary. A speech therapist will help you with your . . . well, your speech." Ariel grinned at Sara, who, despite the travesty of her top lip, grinned back. "A psychologist will be there for you to tell your troubles to," Ariel continued. "An otolaryngologist will be checking to make sure you don't get any more of those middle ear infections, and because you've had so many of them in the past, an audiologist will see if you might need a little hearing aid." Ariel softly tapped the tip of the girl's nose. "You're a regular star now, Sara."

The little girl's face glowed and she turned her bright eyes to her mother, who hugged her. The woman looked at Ariel.

"Thank you, Dr. Denham," she said softly. "Thank you very much."

°   °   °

At noon Ariel saw Robert Maitland and asked him about the rose, thinking it might be a welcome gesture extended to every new member of the staff.

He frowned slightly. "Rose?" He spotted the flower in its place of honor at the corner of her desk. Toby had scrounged up a disposable plastic water carafe to serve as a vase. Maitland regarded the rose for a moment, his expression unreadable. Then he smiled. "I wish I could take credit, but I'm afraid I can't. I don't know who left it."

She also wanted to talk with him about the runner in the park, but decided to hold her tongue. Doris had said the Foundation was strict about the curfew. Why make things more difficult than they already were? Especially since she'd decided not to give up her own evening walks in the park. From now on, she'd simply time her forays a little differently. That way she was bound to miss the runner. He'd be happier, and so would she.

Besides, if she said anything to Maitland, the runner might also be deprived of something he clearly enjoyed. She didn't want that. If he was a patient here, it was because he'd already been deprived of a normal life. He probably felt more at ease at night, free from the judgment of others. Ariel understood only too well the need to be free.

During the course of the morning, the stranger in the park had haunted her thoughts, and she'd come to the conclusion that he wasn't crazy at all. He'd just been trying to discourage her from intruding on his territory. So for now, she mentioned nothing about the park.

"I assumed my lovely rose was a traditional welcome from Fountainhead," she said. "Guess not."

"I'm glad to see you've settled in," he told her. "Let me know if you need anything." Pausing at the doorway, he looked back at her and smiled. This time it reached his eyes. "Welcome to Fountainhead, Dr. Denham." With that, he left.

A half hour later, she went through the line at the cafeteria, then took her tray to an empty table and sat down. The food looked surprisingly appealing, an unusual experience for her with hospital cafeteria food.

"May I j-join you?"

Ariel looked up to find Kerwin Sprague, clutching his tray with a white-knuckled grip. His toupee had slipped slightly to one side and color was high in his face.

"Certainly."

Ariel pretended not to notice his flustered awkwardness as he took a seat across from her. She realized that it must have cost him considerable anxiety to work up the nerve to approach her, even for something as inconsequential as sharing a table for lunch.

They ate in silence for a few minutes, but she sensed a growing tension in him. Perhaps a little conversation would put him more at ease. And maybe she could find the answer to her question.

"I understand, Dr. Sprague, that you're interested in roses."

He cast her a look of bright relief. "Oh, yes! Yes. The rose is truly the queen of flowers. Do you grow them, Dr. Denham?"

"No, I'm afraid not. I've never had time to spare for a garden. But I love roses," she added quickly. "They're so perfect and so elegant. I've never known a rosarian before." She hoped she wasn't being too obvious.

Under her enthusiasm, the anesthesiologist's narrow chest visibly expanded. "If you're interested in roses, you might find my latest project of interest. I'm in the process of developing a perfect mauve tea. It must be perfect, you see, because it is to bear the name of my mother. 'Madame Enid Sprague.' It has a dignified ring to it, don't you think?"

"Oh, yes. It certainly has a ring to it."

He smiled proudly. "She likes it, too."

How to broach the subject of her mystery rose? She recalled the flower's delicate scent, the perfection of its pink petals. As she took a swallow of tea she planned her words. "Uh, Dr. Sprague—"

"Please, call me Kerwin. And may I call you Ariel?"

She nodded. "Of course. Kerwin, I found a rose on my desk this morning."

He beamed. "Lovely ladies deserve roses."

To her surprise, Ariel felt a blush rising in her cheeks. "Well, uh, thank you. Do you know—"

"Yes. I dropped by your office early this morning to wish you well on your first day, but no one was in yet. The rose on your desk is an American Beauty, a hybrid perpetual. It was once what a man would give the woman he admired. At the turn of the century, American Beauties were the most popular florist's flower."

"Yes. Well. What a fascinating history for such a

beautiful rose." It was clear to Ariel who had left the flower on her desk.

The rest of the day was filled with patients. Always the problems were severe enough to have profoundly affected the patient's life. Many had lived years, some all of their lives, with craniofacial abnormalities so extreme that they would shock an unwary passerby.

There was little time to think of anything but the disfigurement, deformity, or the result of disease before her at the moment. By the time she'd finished seeing her last patient for the day, and labored through some of the paperwork, she was exhausted. The thought of a light dinner and the quiet of her comfortable bungalow had all the prospects of heaven.

She ate her meal in blessed silence, at a table by herself. Tomorrow she would pay a visit to the Fountainhead medical library to do some research. She jotted down in her ever-present planner additions to her list of things she needed to do, both personal and professional. How long would it take to get her mail forwarded to Fountainhead? She particularly wanted the journals she subscribed to. The kitchen needed to be stocked with food. Where could she buy groceries? And of course she needed to call her father.

After she finished her meal, she strolled the long sidewalk to her bungalow, which was set away from its neighbors. By the time she opened her front door it was dusk, and the tall, photoelectric lights that lined the walks and the central square were growing bright. Everywhere, shadows deepened.

So far so good, she thought as she stepped out of her dress in the spacious bedroom, then pulled on a pair of shorts and a T-shirt. She'd survived her first day at Fountainhead. Actually, she grudgingly admitted to herself, it had been interesting. She'd even been presented with a few cases that intrigued her. Odd. It had been a long time since she'd felt that *thrill*.

She slathered some lotion on her hands, then picked up the journals she'd brought with her from Atlanta. With a satisfied sigh, she curled up on the couch to read.

When the clock on the mantel struck ten, Ariel closed the journal. It was almost an hour earlier than she'd seen the runner last night. With luck, tonight he wouldn't be out yet.

With exuberant pleasure, she jogged down the grassy slope from her terrace and slipped through the narrow space in the high, thick hedge, into the forbidden park.

Clouds that had brought an early evening rain still filled the dark sky with billowing shapes of somber gray, partially edged in silver by the crescent moon. The crystal stream murmured next to the path she followed.

She relaxed and lost herself in the rhythm of her gait, in the beauty of the park. Fireflies came out to play.

"I see you're not afraid of ghosts," a familiar baritone said from the shadows.

Ariel jumped, barely managing to strangle the cry of surprise in her throat. She staggered to a halt. "What are you doing here?" she demanded breathlessly.

"The same as you, it would appear. Enjoying the night."

"*I'm* exercising."

"You don't like the evening?"

"No. I mean, that's not it at all." She shifted her weight to the other foot. Out here, they were beyond the azalea hedge. They now stood behind the living rampart of sycamores and tulip trees, dogwood, and rhododendron she had noticed on her drive through the valley. From here she couldn't see the bungalows, and she knew no one there could see her. Faint uneasiness rippled through her.

Moonbeams filtered through branches and leaves to brush across tousled hair, the strong column of a neck, a wide shoulder, a slim hip, a long, muscular leg. Ariel could see he wore jogging shorts and running shoes. Judging by her own five feet nine inches, she guessed he stood about six-foot-three. The contours of his body were superbly male.

He deftly kept his face cloaked by the dark and she found that frustrating. She wanted to see what he looked like.

"I just prefer daylight," she told him. Bright, clear light.

"But you work during the day, so the evenings are all you have," he said.

"How did you know?"

A shadowed shoulder lifted and dropped. "It's not difficult to tell staff from patients at Fountainhead."

Ariel could think of nothing to say to such an obvious, awkward truth.

"Your face is unblemished," he elaborated. "It is, in fact, beautiful."

To cover her nervousness, she retorted lightly, "I don't see how you can know that. It's dark." *What do you look like?* She didn't know why it should matter to her. She only knew it did.

He started walking at a comfortable pace, continuing in the direction she'd been headed, deeper into the park. Unwilling to end the conversation there, she walked, too.

When he spoke, his voice held that brooding tone she'd heard him use once last night. "My eyes have become accustomed to the night."

She plucked a leaf from a rhododendron bush as she passed it, launching a spray of gathered rain droplets across her face and shoulder. She licked the moisture from her lips. It seemed to her that he was less intent on driving her away tonight. Had he accepted the fact that ghost stories wouldn't scare her off? She found she was glad he was no longer trying to make her leave. "I'm Ariel Denham. May I know your name?"

He paused before answering. Deciding whether or not to tell her? Finally he said, "Jonah. I'm Jonah."

"Jonah what?" With a last name she could trace his patient records.

"Just Jonah will do."

Damn. Well, he'd given her at least one name. It was a start. "How do you do, Jonah?"

"Just peachy." Sarcasm marked his reply.

"Excellent," she replied brightly, ignoring his display of bad grace. "So. Jonah." She cast about looking for a topic of conversation. "When did you arrive at Fountainhead?" That seemed neutral enough.

"You don't need to know that."

"All right then," she persisted with dogged patience, despite her rising irritation, "would you like to know when I arrived?"

"Not especial—"

"Yesterday," she informed him firmly. "I arrived yesterday. From Atlanta. Where are you from?"

He remained silent.

Her irritation won out. "He's the strong silent type," she announced to the air. "He's so silent, I think he's trying to pretend he isn't here."

"No," he said, "I'm trying to pretend *you're* not here. But you talk so much it's hard."

Ariel halted abruptly. The darker shape in the shadows that was Jonah stopped, too.

"Are we back to that?" she snapped. "Look, fella, neither one of us is supposed to be out here now, so I have just as much right to be in this park as you do." Wait a minute. That didn't sound right. She frowned.

When he didn't comment, she continued. "How do you think *I* feel being around some strange guy who won't come out of the shadows? It's a little creepy."

She regretted her words as soon as they were out of her mouth. His insistence on staying in the shadows was creepy, but she needed to remember that Jonah was a Foundation patient. He required—no, *deserved*—consideration. And her words had been heedlessly insensitive.

With every passing second of his silence, Ariel felt worse.

A sliver of silver through the branches revealed that his head was turned toward her, but she couldn't make out his features. She took a step closer. "Jonah—"

"Don't." The warning was sharply spoken.

But she thought she detected something else. Threaded through that curt order, like an invisible thread, she thought she heard anguish. Neither of them spoke, and a second later, she wasn't certain if it had been her imagination.

"Jonah," she said, using her most gentle professional voice, "you don't need to hide from me. I'm a plastic surgeon."

"Thank you for sharing that with me, Dr. Denham. Star light, star bright," he said, sneering, "please give me a surgeon to make me right."

"So you are a patient," Ariel said quietly.

He didn't answer.

"Jonah, I'm not your enemy."

He remained silent.

She turned, and as she did, Ariel glimpsed him in partial silhouette. He lifted an arm as if he were running his hand through his hair. But he made no attempt to stop her, so she walked away.

Disappointment cut through her as she headed back toward the distant lights of the community. She'd had quite enough for tonight. So much for stress reduction.

"Wait."

She heard Jonah's single word close to her shoulder, but she stubbornly kept walking.

"Wait, damn you!"

A warm, firm grip took hold of her left upper arm. Her head snapped down to see a strong, long-fingered hand tugging her to a stop. She noticed the ridged scar that slashed across the back of his hand, up his long-muscled arm, into the shadows that concealed the rest of him. A sprinkling of dark hair dusted light skin.

Once she was stopped, he released her. She turned quickly, but he stepped back into the heart of the shadows before she could glimpse him. She stood there, glowering at him, refusing to speak first.

"You shouldn't have run away," he finally said.

"Run—!" Indignation nearly robbed her of speech. "I did *not* run away. But it's no business of yours if I choose to run, walk or—or—" she tried to think of something other than crawl "—*fly*."

"On your broom, no doubt. But you're wrong about it not being my business. You've insisted on making it my business."

She glared at him. "*I've* made it your business? I don't think so. I was just trying to be civilized. I'm sorry if that bothers you. But just in case, by some far stretch of the imagination, I have somehow given you the impression that what I do is any of your concern whatsoever, let me just lift that burden right off your shoulders. I hereby free you."

Ariel strode off.

"This is my park!" he told her fiercely. "*Mine.* You're the intruder here, but you think you deserve answers to all your questions. I've given you answers. But that's not enough, is it? You're trying to push your way into my life as well."

Something in Jonah's voice—an undertone, a certain note, Ariel wasn't sure what it was—reached out and prevented her from walking away and leaving him behind. There had been indignation, yes, and anger. But there'd been something else, something elusive, something wistful.

Could Jonah be lonely? A stranger in this isolated mountain valley? Like her?

She looked down at her shoes, dimly revealed in the faint lantern light. "No, I'm not, " she whispered. "I'm not trying to push into your life." Was that what he really thought? That she was pushy?

But what was one defensive man in the grand scheme of things, anyway? she asked herself, setting her jaw. *She* didn't need to spend her time in the dark. She didn't like the dark.

Robert Maitland's words regarding the curfew echoed in her mind. *There have been accidents.*

She looked up to discover that the rampart obscured the lights she used as a guidepost. Was Jonah behind the accidents? Had he violently defended what he considered his domain against other trespassers?

She didn't believe that. He'd had the opportunity to do her harm, but had made no move against her. The accidents were probably caused by people bumbling around in the dark, just as Maitland had said.

She released a harsh sigh. "Jonah?" she called softly.

Seconds ticked past.

"What?" The single, sullen word rumbled with wariness.

Ariel retraced her steps to stand on the path and

face his shadowy form. "Do you want me to leave?"

He made no reply.

She took a breath. "If you don't want me to walk in your park, I'm sure I can find someplace else."

When still he didn't answer, Ariel felt a sharp stab of disappointment. She had her answer.

His voice broke the silence. "It's a matter of indifference to me whether you stay or leave." The flat cadence of boredom rode his words. "But I wouldn't advise you to exercise outside of the park, if you refuse to go to the gym. The park is the safest place for you."

She felt relief blossom inside her, out of all proportion to logic. She carefully smothered the smile that tugged at her mouth. At that moment Jonah might mistake such a reaction for gloating or derision. "I noticed you usually run," she said.

"Sometimes."

They started walking again, the pace set at a stroll.

"I don't want to keep you from it," she volunteered. She didn't really want him to go bounding off, but she felt courtesy required something be said.

"Are you trying to get rid of me, Ariel?"

A shiver ran through her body at the sensual caress his mouth made of her name.

"No," she assured him."I just—"

"If I want to run, I will," Jonah told her dryly.

"All right," Ariel said. "Now that you've established your rightful ownership of the park, your absolute lack of interest in me and what I do, and your unrestricted freedom to do whatever you want to do, when you want to do it, what shall we talk about?"

"I—" The word was a bitten-off protest.

"Yes?" she prompted sweetly.

"I didn't say it like that."

"No, you didn't."

"There, see—

"Your tone of voice made what you said much more insulting." She edged toward him as he walked in the shadows, but she did not leave the path. Maybe it was the brighter moon. Maybe her eyes were becoming more accustomed to the dark. Whatever the reason, she could see his shadowed form striding along beside her. "You have a very rich, expressive voice, Jonah. It magnifies your meaning."

"I do, huh?"

"Do what?"

"Have a good voice."

Ariel permitted herself a small smile. Male vanity.

"Yes," she said. "You have a very"—*sexy*—"warm, rich voice. It's deep and masculine."

Jonah did not speak for a moment. "I never thought the voice was one of the things a woman noticed about a man."

"Not just a woman. Anyone. A beautiful voice is a pleasure to listen to." She slid her finger along the neckband of her T-shirt. When had it become so warm outside?

"Pleasure." He infused the simple word with husky eroticism.

Ariel thought of Jonah's finely honed body, of his powerful shoulders and arms, of his lean hips and long legs. She glanced quickly toward him, and saw stray moonbeams flash across a bare, ridged abdomen.

Carefully, she schooled her gaze back to what lay

before them. She'd never thought of it before, but what would a man with a ruined face do about sex? Singles bars and dating services would be out of the question for a man unwilling to leave the dark. A man like Jonah.

If a woman cared deeply about such a man, if she really loved him, would his face matter? Or would she have to close her eyes and fantasize?

"Are you married, Jonah?" The question popped out before she realized she even wanted to ask. Instantly, she wished it back. What had possessed her to ask such a personal question? And just when they had reached a sort of truce.

"No." His word was clipped. It invited no further questioning in that direction.

He didn't ask if she was married. Apparently he wasn't curious about her at all. Good, she told herself.

They walked in silence for a while. An owl called its haunting question from a nearby tree.

"Who-o-o do you think?" Jonah returned lightly.

Ariel smiled. "Don't confuse the poor bird, Jonah. It might think it's found dinner."

Jonah chuckled. "Not very flattering, to be mistaken for a field mouse."

"Think of the owl's surprise if it were to swoop down and try to snatch you up." She imagined the raptor doing a double take and laughed.

"The field mouse from hell." Ariel heard the warmth of a smile in his rich, mellow-fire voice.

"And what would he tell his indignant mate when he arrived home empty-taloned?"

"'Sorry, dear, but you should have seen the one that got away'?"

"Oh, but would she believe that old saw?" Ariel smiled, pleased that Jonah was offering the olive branch of humor.

"Females believe pretty much what they want to believe." There was challenge and amusement in his words.

"On behalf of all my gender, I thank you, Sir Chauvinist." She bowed slightly to him without breaking her stride. "The power of belief can work miracles." She'd seen belief turn the tide for one of her patients, years ago. But it hadn't worked that way in her own life. Despite all her girlhood prayers, there had been a marked absence of miracles.

When he spoke, she heard the amusement. "Are you saying that women have to arm themselves with miracles in order to deal with men?"

She laughed. "Of course. It's a miracle they ever come together at all."

At that moment, Ariel sighted the small space in the hedge she used to slip through to make her way to her bungalow.

She stopped. "Well, I must say good-night, here, Jonah."

Silence answered her.

"Jonah?"

But Jonah wasn't there.

He observed her from a distance as she strode to her bungalow, making certain she passed through her terrace door safely.

Not that he was aware of any present danger. The

valley was one of the safest places on earth. No, it was the woman. Beneath all her sharp bristles, all her careful armor, he'd glimpsed elusive flashes of . . . what? Uncertainty? A cautiously concealed vulnerability? Jonah shook his head. He should have taken her up on her offer to leave the park. After all, that's what he'd wanted from the start, wasn't it? With her out of the way, the park would belong to him again.

Doctor Denham. Ariel Denham. Yes, he liked that better. Ariel. He knew he had made her nervous last night. In fact he'd gloated over it. Or tried to. His victory had been like ashes in his mouth.

Jonah felt his mood lighten as he thought about her. She was a sassy little thing. Even when she'd been afraid, she'd refused to let him off uncontested. She possessed a sort of defiant courage that intrigued him.

Which was foolish. Very foolish. If she ever got a clear look at him, she'd be a lot less than intrigued. Or because she was a plastic surgeon she might be even more intrigued. He'd be reduced to the status of an interesting case. A damned lab rat. To hell with that. If only . . .

Hadn't he learned yet, after all these years? He had no hope of ever leading a regular life. Foolish to think that could change. Hadn't he already tried? Jonah turned his face up to the night sky. He dragged in a deep draught of air and shuddered. God, he still had nightmares of that moment when, after several operations, after the pain and all that fierce hope, the surgeon's bandages finally had been peeled away. In the mirror, Jonah had seen what he'd become.

Nightmares. Jonah shared his bitter laughter with the moon. He *was* a nightmare. A monster. A repulsive beast. Enough to frighten not only small children, but adults. So he tried to avoid them.

Except Ariel Denham. There was something about her. She was so lovely, so graceful. But it was more than that. She seemed willing to talk to him, to treat him like an ordinary man, despite the bizarre circumstances surrounding their encounters. He decided it was that very willingness that drew him to her. Jonah smiled in faint self-mockery. Or maybe he was just hoping for sex.

Well, he'd been careless to let her find out about him, but, for now, he didn't regret it.

For now, it was worth the risk.

3

The next morning when Ariel swung open her office door, she found another American Beauty rose sitting in the center of her desk blotter, surrounded by her piles of paperwork. Today the disposable water carafe wouldn't be necessary. This flower came in a simple crystal vase. There was, however, no note. But then, Kerwin really didn't need to leave one. Ariel smiled as she deposited her purse in the narrow yellow locker and withdrew her lab coat.

"Knock, knock."

She turned to find Doris Farmer standing at the office doorway. "Come on in."

Doris nodded toward the flower. "Gorgeous. From a boyfriend back home?"

"No. There is no boyfriend back home. I didn't have time for a social life, much less a love life."

"Well, then, who?" Doris leaned over and sniffed. "Mmm. Heavenly. This guy knows his roses."

"Kerwin Sprague, I think. Isn't it sweet of him? He knows I'm new here. Yesterday he left a card that said 'welcome.'"

A speculative look drifted over Doris's face. "Kerwin Sprague, eh? Who would ever have suspected the heart of a romantic beat beneath *that* lab coat? Love with the proper anesthesiologist."

"Not love, Doris, and don't you say anything about this to anyone. He's just a thoughtful man who's shy with women. He knows I like roses, so maybe he feels more comfortable with me. And he hasn't come right out and admitted to leaving the roses—"

"You mean there've been others?"

"Just one. Yesterday. With the card."

Doris slowly shook her head. "Still waters run deep, don't they? You know, I've always thought Dr. Sprague was kind of cute."

"It's a friendly gesture, nothing more," Ariel insisted, afraid her new friend might be jumping to wrong conclusions. "Two innocent roses."

Doris beamed. "Oh, I know you're not interested in him. He's too short for you and you've got lots of other options. I saw Dr. Perry giving you the eye yesterday. I'd watch out for him, though," she confided. "I hear surgery isn't the only thing he saves his hands for."

"Doris," Ariel said, her tone mildly admonishing.

"What?" she asked innocently.

"Didn't you come to see me about something?"

"Oh, yes. Want to have breakfast together tomorrow in the cafeteria?"

"I can't," Ariel said as she pulled on the white jacket. "I have surgery all tomorrow morning. What about lunch today?"

"Sounds great. One o'clock?"

Ariel quickly checked her patient appointments, then agreed. Doris waved as she hurried off.

"Dr. Perry, indeed," Ariel muttered, as she picked up her coffee mug. She took a sip of the tepid stuff and made a face.

Had Douglas Perry, the oncologist in the office four doors down from hers, really ogled her? Naaw. There'd probably been a wall mirror on the other side of her, and he was merely admiring his golden tresses. Even in a breeze, his hair never moved. He must buy styling mousse by the truckload.

Suddenly Ariel remembered what she wanted to ask Doris. She quickly set down her cup and hurried out the door.

"Doris," she called. "I have a favor to ask."

"Oh?"

Ariel grinned. "Don't sound so cautious. It's nothing illegal. Really. When you get a free minute, I'd appreciate it if you'd look up a patient named Jonah, and see who his doctor is."

"Okay. What's his first name?"

"Uh, well, that's the problem. All I know is Jonah. It could be either his first name or his last."

"You're not in a hurry for this, I take it?" Doris asked.

"Just when you can get to it." Her curiosity prompted her to hope that was soon.

"Don't get me wrong—I'll be happy to do it. But

there are many patient files I can't access. The records of our paying customers are absolutely classified. Only Maitland knows the real names. A PC file bears an alias, and that's what the patient is known as while he or she is connected with Fountainhead."

"Oh."

"I don't suppose I should ask why you're interested in this Jonah?"

"It's not a state secret or anything. I've run across him a couple of times, and he looks like an interesting case." It wasn't a complete lie, Ariel told herself, but she didn't like even partially deceiving Doris. Still, she must consider the fact that she was nightly breaking what she'd been told was an important Fountainhead rule.

Doris shook her head. "Boy, you really love your work, don't you?" she said.

"Thanks, Doris. I'll see you at lunch." With that, Ariel hastened back the way she'd come, unwilling to think about the real reasons behind her request for information on Jonah.

She made a detour into the empty doctor's lounge, to the snack machine. Until she made it to Farley to do some grocery shopping, her selection of snack foods was limited to the contents of vending machines; the refrigerator and cupboards of her new whiz-bang kitchen were bare.

She shoved two quarters into the machine and pressed the button for a granola bar. Stuffing it into the pocket of her lab coat, Ariel hurried around the corner to her office, where, right on schedule, she greeted her first patient of the day.

*   *   *

After examining patients who were variously shy, eager, or defensive, working through a ton of paperwork, a research expedition to the medical library, discussions with other surgeons, and finally, a walk-through of the operating rooms and an examination of the equipment that would be available to her tomorrow, Ariel was ready for the day to end.

She took a light dinner at the community cafeteria, then trudged back to her bungalow, where she settled down with the journals and books she'd checked out of the library.

The moon was high when she finally pushed her chair back from the kitchen table that she was using as a desk. The serenity of the park at night beckoned her. She jogged down the grassy slope to slip through the hedge. As she stood on the path by the stream, she saw him. Jonah was there, in the shadows.

More clearly than before, she could discern his shape. Subtle, muted shadings of gray and black merged to endow him with dimension. Now she could see the darkness of his hair surrounding the lighter area of his face, though the features were still too shadowed to make out.

"Hello, Jonah. Are you waiting for me?" she asked, pleased to finally see him even this well.

She was greeted by a second's hesitation. "Hello, Ariel."

She smiled to herself. "Have you been waiting long?"

"What makes you think I was waiting?" he asked a little too casually.

Her smile deepened into a grin, and she didn't care if he could see it. "I guess it's just fate then."

He made a noncommittal sound.

"Let's take a different route, tonight, shall we?" she suggested. "Just to keep things interesting."

"It might rain, and you'd have no lighted footpath to follow."

"You could help me."

"Possibly," he said softly.

She sighed. "Okay, we'll stick to this route. For now." She started walking.

After they'd left the area near the bungalows, Ariel thought she'd try a simple conversational gambit that might net her some information about him. "What did you do today, Jonah?"

Seconds passed before he answered. "Why do you ask?" The tone of his words carefully echoed her own, and she knew he was on to her ploy.

"It's called conversation," she said patiently. "You may have heard of it before. I ask you a question, and you answer it. Then you ask me a question, and I answer it. Then we discuss the answers."

"Ah."

She waited for him to continue, but he offered nothing else.

"Well?" she prompted.

"It sounds more like an interrogation to me." The amusement in his voice was almost effectively muffled.

"No, an interrogation is when only one of us asks questions." Questions she doubted he'd be willing to answer. And it was becoming rapidly apparent that if

Jonah didn't want to do something, that was that. "Civilized people converse. Now, shall we try again? What did you do today, Jonah?"

"Oh, slew a few dragons, saved a kingdom, searched for the Holy Grail. The usual."

"No, really," she said. "I mean it. What did you do?"

"What did *you* do today?"

"I asked first."

He chuckled. "I didn't realize we had to take a number," he said.

"You aren't going to tell me."

"No."

She looked over into the shadows that bordered the path. The half-moon's light flickered through the foliage as he moved, dancing across him. He held his head subtly angled, so that not even his profile was visible to Ariel.

A gust of wind rustled the leaves of the trees, stirred the bushes. Here in this valley the elements were so close at hand. It seemed to Ariel that the whisper of restlessness that shivered through her was no more than an echo of the realm. She breathed in the moist air.

"I'd like to hear about your day," Jonah said.

She wanted to ask him why he wouldn't tell her about *his* day. Why was it necessary for him to hide not only his face, but also his life from her? But Ariel suspected she already knew the answer: pride.

She sensed that prodding him would only snap the tenuous thread spinning between them.

"I'm meeting my patients now," she told him.

"Determining what needs to be done. Scheduling for surgery. Reading medical journals—always reading. My days are very full. Tomorrow I'll be in surgery all morning."

"Do you like your work here?"

"It's too early to tell," she hedged. "I've only been here two full days. Ask me that again in a couple of months."

They'd gone yards before he said in a low voice, "I thought I could expect an honest answer from you."

She flinched inside, knowing she'd deserved that. But wait a minute, she thought indignantly. At least he was getting answers from her. That was more than she was getting from him.

Ariel reminded herself that this man was a patient. He was preparing for an important change in his life, and his surgeon would play a crucial role. Perhaps he was casting about, looking for a touchstone. Or seeking reassurance.

"Jonah, I haven't done anything yet. I've just arrived at Fountainhead." She stopped and faced him, unable to see his expression. "I'll certainly do my best."

Ariel frowned as she tried to dredge up the words to express the burden that had descended on her when she'd taken the tour of the clinic with Maitland. There were so many needy here. Even when they tried to conceal their feelings, she sensed the hopeful desperation of each of her patients. Of every patient she met. Until all that bleeding, shining emotion threatened to overwhelm her. "I'll do what is in my power to help my patients, Jonah. But I won't try to fool myself into thinking better-looking faces will solve all their problems. There are scars that I can't reach with my scalpel."

When Jonah remained silent, Ariel felt uncomfortably awkward. So much for her truth. Then she realized she hadn't actually answered his question. She took a deep breath, then told him what she thought he needed to hear. "When I can see that I'm making a real difference in the lives of my patients, then I'll like my work at Fountainhead."

A bank of clouds moved across the sky, blotting out the moon and the stars, stealing the argent light.

"And do you think you'll ever know for certain that you've made a difference in their lives?" he asked, a peculiar, hard edge to his voice slicing through the night. "Do you expect fan mail from them after they've left Fountainhead? 'Dear Dr. Denham, thanks to you I've had my first date. He took me to our high school prom. Signed, your adoring patient, etc. etc. etc.'?"

Drops of rain stung her bare skin. Barely aware of the wetness, Ariel stared in Jonah's direction, stunned by his words, and oddly hurt.

"Get out of the rain, Ariel," Jonah ordered gruffly. "Get under the trees."

She ignored him, ignored the spring shower that quickly soaked her hair and clothes. Instead she thought about what had brought her here. Fan mail? She wanted to laugh, but the joke was too cruel.

Her pain sparked into anger. "What gives you the right to accuse me of such despicable vanity?" she demanded. Impatiently, she scraped her wet hair back from her cheek.

"Come, Ariel. Get out of the rain." His order had softened to cajolery. "Please."

"Is that what you really think of me, Jonah?" She blinked, dislodging droplets from her lashes. "That I feed my ego on the misery of others? That all I want is power?"

"Ariel—"

"Go back to your old schedule of running, Jonah. I prefer to walk by myself." She turned on her heel, ready to continue in the direction they had been headed.

His hand shot out from the shadows and captured her arm, pulling her into the shelter under the trees. Just as quickly, he released her.

She whirled around to face the dark shape of him. "Don't touch me," she snapped.

"I didn't mean to hurt you," Jonah said softly, and Ariel knew he wasn't talking about his brief grasp.

"Go to hell."

His laugh was hollow, devoid of humor. "I probably will."

There it was again. That note in his voice. That aching, distant note.

Against her will, it pierced her and hid under her heart like something wounded. The more often she heard that note, the more impossible it grew to ignore. And right now Ariel badly wanted to ignore it.

She inhaled a few long, calming breaths. Finally, she asked, "Jonah, did you once have a doctor like the one you described?"

He didn't answer.

"Did you have a doctor who disappointed you?"

A moment passed. "Yes."

She wanted to comfort him. "Will you tell me about it?"

"No."

She squeezed her eyes shut and massaged her forehead. Why was it that when she was with this man, her emotions simmered so close to the surface? She found it unnerving. "Jonah, we can't seem to communicate very well. You won't talk—"

"Not always."

"Not ever."

She heard the rustle of his tread in the wet humus and looked up. He was close to her, so close she could feel the heat of him along the length of her body. Her eyes were level with his chest. To see his face, she'd have to step back, and she suspected if she did that, he would turn away from her. So she took in those aspects of him that were available to her. His glorious height and lean strength. The powerful column of his throat. Her eyes followed a jagged scar up to the left side of his jaw, to discover the firm, squared curve, and the puckered, discolored skin. She breathed in the earthy, male scent of him.

It would be so easy to touch him now. To reach out and reassure herself that this man who kept to the shadows, who kept his face from her, wasn't just a haunting spirit, or her imagination run wild. But she couldn't bring herself to extend her fingers to the warmth of his flesh.

"Ariel." His voice was low and husky. She felt his warm breath sighing over the crown of her head. "Why can't you just accept things as they are? The past can't be changed. The future is uncertain. Talking about them will change nothing. But here in the park, at night, we have our own little world. Can't that be enough?"

"Jonah." What was it about this man that made him impossible for her to leave? Why couldn't she just walk off and put him from her mind as she had done with men before?

"I want to hear about your work, about the things that are important to you. Just don't expect too much from me," he said hoarsely, and she saw his throat work. "I'm not sure what I have to give."

For a moment she thought Jonah might take her into his arms. The notion thrilled and frightened her. Her heartbeat leapt into a gallop. Then he moved away, leaving her faintly disappointed, vaguely relieved.

"Sounds"—she cleared her dry throat—"sounds like rather a one-sided deal to me."

"Yes. Yes it does." He stood several feet away, looking out onto the park. The mottled shadows and moonlight made it impossible for her to find the clarity of his profile.

As she studied his solitary figure, it came to her why she was so drawn to him. This was a man who truly understood what it was to be lonely. Without knowing why, she was certain he'd faced abandonment, just as she had. Of course, she hastened to amend her traitorous thought, her father had always eventually come back.

Ariel swallowed hard and turned away. Loneliness. Enough of it inevitably hollowed out a chunk of your soul. It frightened you and crippled you until pride was all you had left. Until pride became your gleaming armor against the world.

"So"—she cleared her throat—"that's that."

He continued to face the park. "It's all I can offer."

She nodded slowly. Maybe that was for the best. If he set limits, she could, too.

She reminded herself that their lives were set on different courses, accidentally brushing together at this one, brief point. Jonah's time here would probably be limited to a matter of months at most, before he was released as an outpatient. She would leave when her contract was up. And she'd learned from Vickie's experience that when patients who'd suffered severe trauma were finally made presentable again, they wanted to forget their unhappy ordeal. Their surgeons were part of that ordeal.

Ariel said resolutely. "I understand. There can be no demands or expectations."

"No."

"From either of us." Though she spoke quietly, her words issued a challenge. The gate must swing both ways.

He turned his head toward her, but did not answer immediately. Seconds passed, as if he weighed her statement. "Understood."

Gradually, the rain let up. As the clouds drifted clear of the moon, Ariel stepped determinedly back out onto the path.

If she walked fast enough, maybe she could lose the unreasonable sadness that clung to her.

✿   ✿   ✿

From a distance, Jonah watched as, one by one, the lights in Ariel's bungalow winked out.

After they had left the shelter of the trees, they had found little to say to one another. Conversation had been sporadic, as if they'd each felt an obligation to fill the silence that grew between them.

He plucked a leaf from the hedge and worried it between his fingers. Again, he cursed himself for the lapse, earlier, in the usual control he so carefully exercised over his emotions. She had that effect on him.

This time an old, painful ghost had slipped through, and he feared he'd hurt Ariel. His fingers traced the ribbing of the azalea leaf.

Damn her, why couldn't she have abided by the curfew like everyone else? But no, she had to invade his park, insisting on acting as if there was nothing wrong with him. Granting him the personhood that he'd lost so long ago. And that hurt. It threatened to tear apart all his carefully constructed defenses. Because he wanted to reach past them to take hold of the fiction she'd created.

Fool. He knew he should put a stop to their evening encounters. What was the point anyway? Nothing could ever come of them. He was . . . well, what he was. And Ariel . . .

He closed his eyes, summoning her image in his mind. Her hair, caught up in a jaunty ponytail, pale in the moonlight. Her large, light eyes so expressive. He suspected they gave more away than she realized. He liked her mouth. He liked it a lot. Her lips were full and enticing. If everything had been different, if he'd been—his mind shied away from the word, but ruthlessly he forced himself to use it—*normal*, he would have kissed her by now. Several times. Jonah smiled faintly.

He imagined taking a willing Ariel into his arms. She'd slip her hands through his hair. Her lips would be soft and moist. They'd part for him, and with his tongue he'd penetrate her. He'd taste her. Their tongues would stroke against each other. Her sweet breath would hasten. Her fingers would tighten. . . .

Jonah's eyes flew open, and he broke free of his imaginings as his body clenched hard with desire. Sharply, he breathed in cool air. *Oh, God. What madness.*

He knew Ariel was not for him. He knew it but still he couldn't bring himself to relinquish the moments he spent with her. Not now. Not yet.

Ariel peeled off her bloody latex gloves and dropped them into the waste can in the scrub room. Then she rolled her head back on her neck, trying to ease the muscles that had grown rigid.

"So how do you think it went?" Kerwin Sprague asked, as he removed his own, more pristine gloves.

Sticking her hands and arms under the hot water running in the sink, she jabbed the dispenser and lathered with the antiseptic soap. "Well, there wasn't a hitch with the surgery itself. Everything went well. If nothing unexpected happens, Mr. Zaleski should look like a new man."

Actually, she thought, nineteen-year-old Billy Zaleski had barely had time to look like the "old" man before the motorcycle accident that had smashed his nose and left his young face covered with burns three years ago.

Kerwin nodded. "I've watched many surgeons work," the anesthesiologist said solemnly, "and in these past two weeks, I've come to the conclusion that you're quite incredible, Ariel. Such skill. Such artistry."

Heat bloomed in her cheeks. She was confident of her expertise, and she knew she could be considered an outstanding surgeon. Still, hearing such praise from soft-spoken Kerwin, who seldom gave professional accolades of any kind unless he was satisfied they were justified, made her feel curiously humble.

"Why, uh, thank you, Kerwin." She smiled. "Well, Billy's parents are waiting."

Kerwin gave her his shy smile in return. "See you later."

Without taking time to change from her blue scrubsuit, Ariel strode down the corridor to the waiting room. She found the middle-aged couple sitting huddled together close to the door. The man wore an out-of-date, dark brown suit and the woman had donned a faded green cardigan over a plain print dress. From her conversations with Billy, Ariel knew them to be hardworking farmers from Indiana.

"Billy made it through surgery with no problems," she told them, hoping she didn't look as fatigued as she felt. How much confidence would a wiped-out–looking surgeon inspire? Fortunately, she was finished with surgery for the day.

"The Lord be praised," Mrs. Zaleski breathed, tears gathering in her eyes.

Mr. Zaleski nodded emphatically. "Amen," he murmured. "How is our son?"

"He's still under the effects of the anesthesia."

"Doctor, when can we see our boy?" Mrs. Zaleski wanted to know.

"He's being monitored in recovery right now. Why don't you go over to the cafeteria and have lunch? Give it about an hour. He should be in his room by the time you get back. Check with the nurses' station then and someone will be able to give you his room number."

"Is . . . is everything going to be all right?" the older woman asked.

"As I said, he came through surgery like a champ. But we'll know more in about a week. Remember we discussed that his bone had collapsed?" She gestured with a finger along the facial bone under her right eye.

"Yes, ma'am," Mr. Zaleski said. "And you said as how you'd have to rebreak that bone, which would require a little rebuilding."

"Right. And that's what I did. For the next several days, Billy's going to look as if someone beat him up. Expect swelling. Some discoloration. That's not unusual."

After directing the Zaleskis to the cafeteria, she headed toward the locker room to change out of her scrubs. Then she grabbed a quick lunch and began her patient rounds.

As she walked through the corridors, from one

patient's room to another's, she remembered that today marked the second full week since she'd first donned the blue scrubs of a Fountainhead Foundation surgeon. She'd come to appreciate having the finest equipment at her command and working with other skilled, often extraordinarily gifted, professionals.

Each morning, an American Beauty rose had appeared in the vase on her desk until she'd begun to look forward to it. The flower's scent and the perfection of the pink petals gave her moments of respite from dealing with the severity of her patients' needs.

Each evening she walked with Jonah.

After the strained moments they'd shared under the trees during the summer shower fifteen days ago, their evening walks were just that—walks. Exercise. Oh, they exchanged a few meaningless amenities. But they didn't really talk. And she could feel tension building between them. It all but crackled. Ariel had grown increasingly dissatisfied with the arrangement.

Now, she returned to her office to go through her patient files for tomorrow. At Fountainhead, on the days when doctors were in surgery, they didn't see new patients.

The last file in the stack was that of Michael Corey. He'd been transferred to Fountainhead from Chattalogh.

Ariel glanced briefly at the history form on the new patient. "This can't be right," she said to Toby, who had just walked into her office with workup reports on three patients. "Chattalogh is a mental hospital."

"Read further," Toby suggested grimly. "What this kid's been through is unbelievable."

Six-year-old Michael Corey, Ariel learned, had been an inmate of Chattalogh since the age of ten months, when his mother had applied a piece of burning kindling to his face. Before the neighbors could stop her, she'd managed to take her own life. Michael's father had never been found. The infant had, surprisingly, survived, only to be condemned to existence in Chattalogh, a mental hospital Ariel knew to be desperately understaffed, underfinanced, and hopelessly outdated. His relatives had refused to take Michael into their own families, but they were willing to pay for his basic upkeep in that miserable institution.

Michael had been, according to the tests, endowed with normal intelligence. Unfortunately, a child learned what he lived with. The latest diagnostic tests revealed that Michael's language skills were appallingly below the norm for his years. His motor skills seemed adequate, but his social skills were almost nonexistent.

Ariel closed the file after reading the lab reports and the screening results. This child had suffered pain most people could only imagine, and enough rejection to bring even an adult to his knees.

Tight-mouthed, she drummed the end of her cheap pen against the desk blotter, her sense of justice burning with outrage. Michael had lived a horror story.

How could she fix this?

His medical history and the lab reports in the file suggested that there would likely be complications. If everything turned out all right, it would be just shy of a miracle. While Ariel believed in miracles—and what physician didn't?—she knew never to count on them.

That evening, the gibbous moon painted the park with fine strokes of silver and splashes of shadow, creating a haunting wonderland.

Ariel quickened her steps as she approached their rendezvous point and smiled when she saw Jonah's denser, darker form in the night shade under the sycamores and tulip trees. She stopped in front of him, but remained on the path.

"Good evening, Jonah."

"Ariel." His voice touched her with an intimate sensuality, like trailing fingers down the skin on her back.

He waited for her here every night. She'd never asked him to; it was something he'd chosen to do. He'd had two weeks to get used to her. Two neutral weeks.

In unspoken agreement, they started along the familiar route.

"Your day, how was it?" he inquired.

She wanted to tell him about Michael Corey, but hesitated. It wasn't that she doubted Jonah's discretion. His whole life appeared to be discreet. It was just that she wasn't ready to speak of the disturbing case. And, after all, Jonah had problems of his own.

Ariel said, "One of my patients wants me to make her look like Marilyn Monroe." She remembered the portly sixty-year-old walking into the office. The short, platinum hairstyle, and the bright red lips declared the woman a devoted fan of the sexy, fifties film star.

Jonah cleared his throat. "Is the lady, uh, *built* like Marilyn Monroe?"

"Let's just say she's of a certain age and believes in the beauty of a healthy appetite."

From the shadows came a choking sound. "I don't suppose she wants to look like Marilyn would have looked today?"

"Nope."

Ariel smiled as she remembered the eight-by-ten glossy the patient had whipped out of her purse and held in front of Ariel's nose. "If I get to have a new face," the patient had declared, "I want *this* one."

It had taken Ariel a while to convince her patient that an entirely new face wasn't called for in her instance, and that plastic surgery wasn't a matter of one face fits all.

She turned her head to speak to Jonah, but her words never formed. She blinked. Was it her imagination or could she see him better?

She glanced up at the moon. It was fuller, brighter tonight. Of course! The moon had entered another phase.

Jonah's hair had wave—though it stopped short of being curly—and was so inky dark she was sure it must be black. His profile possessed a startling beauty, which surprised her. The moon's kindness to Jonah, however, stopped there. Its cold light also revealed the peculiar discolored, rippled, ridged scars that covered the side of his face turned to her. The corner of his eye was pulled down slightly by the taut way the tissue had healed. The scars were like nothing she'd ever seen before, and she wondered what had made them.

Ariel suspected that whatever could do such damage to a face would also have affected some of its structure. The nose, at least, which was primarily formed by cartilage. If that was so, she felt certain Jonah must have been through surgery before, and she was impressed with the skill that had built the elegant, straight nose. But why hadn't the surgeon also done something about the rest of Jonah's face? Was he the same one Jonah had mentioned last night?

She looked at him again. There was something oddly familiar about that elegant profile, but when she couldn't put her finger on where she might have seen him before, she shook it off as a product of her imagination.

If Jonah realized she could see him, even this well, he gave no sign, and she thought he probably didn't know. He'd made it clear that he didn't want her to see him. So, she decided, she would try to abide by his wish. Perhaps he would someday willingly step into the light.

"I finally have some time, next week, to go into Farley," she said. "I'm going to take the entire weekend off and spend Saturday night at that inn—you know, the old mansion."

"The Black Tupelo."

"Yes, that's the name. I've already made my reservation."

Jonah chuckled. "You've probably made Beryl's week."

"Beryl?"

"Beryl Jenkins. She runs The Black Tupelo."

"I didn't know you were acquainted with anyone in Farley. Are you from this area?" She concealed her excitement that he'd actually volunteered information.

There was a pause. "I'm familiar with it."

Damn. For a moment, she'd thought she might learn something about him. Maybe about how he spent his days.

She worried her bottom lip between her teeth as she wondered how to approach the challenge of finding out more about Jonah. So far, nothing had worked. He kept his life a bigger secret than the recipe for turning base metal into gold. Might as well try the direct approach. What did she have to lose?

"So you've been to Farley before?" she asked.

"Yes."

Elated with her small triumph, she forged ahead. "I've never been there. Will you tell me about it?"

"Some people find it not to their liking. It's small, and there isn't much in the way of entertainment. The movie theater was closed down years ago. I think there's a video rental place in town now, though. And of course some shops. It's picturesque, but not fussy."

"Is the town very old?"

He cocked his head to one side as he considered. She found his gesture endearing.

"About a hundred and fifty years old," he said.

"I imagine I'll have quite a bit of spare time on my

hands when I'm finished with my grocery shopping. What would you suggest I do?"

"Hike. Fish. Read. Watch TV."

She nodded. It was what she expected of a tiny, isolated burg. Dullsville. "Do you find Farley to your liking?"

There was a slight pause—slighter than usual. "Yes."

"Why?" Would he answer? He'd already shared more with her than ever before. To her surprise, he responded.

"The people. They're generous with what little they have, and they're loyal to one another."

So he was familiar enough with the town to know at least some of the people. "Have you ever stayed at The Black Tupelo? What's it like?"

At that instant, the toe of her athletic shoe stubbed against a rock, sending her off-balance.

Jonah's arm shot out to block her fall. Instinctively, she clutched it. He held firm as she regained her balance. But when she again stood evenly on the path, she found herself reluctant to release his arm. Her fingers remained curled over the curve of warm skin, which was dusted sparsely with smooth, dark hair. Beneath that, she felt the shift and ease of steelstrong sinews. She wanted to slide her hand all over Jonah's beautifully masculine arm, acquainting herself with the silkiness of hair, with the graceful swell of hard muscle, and the smooth, tender skin at elbow and wrist. She wanted—

Slowly, as if giving her a chance to withdraw, Jonah curved his arm and drew her into the shadows with him. He stood close to her—too close for her to see his face. But in that moment, as she shared the night shade space with him under the trees, Ariel cared only that Jonah was here. And that he wanted her here, too. Hesitantly, she lifted one hand and rested it against his chest. Through the skin-warmed cloth of his tank top, she felt the steady, accelerated beat of his heart.

His arms tightened slightly, moving her closer to him, so that she touched his body, but was not forced to press against him. Her bare thighs brushed his.

She stood perfectly still and wished she could breathe more calmly. Could he tell the difference? Could he hear how her breath trembled in her throat?

Jonah lowered his head and in a movement that was almost uncertain, almost shy, he softly rested his cheek against the hair over her temple.

Ariel forgot all about breathing. All that mattered was Jonah, and that he wanted to hold her. And perhaps, just perhaps, he might trust her a little. That thought brought a gladdened skip to her heart.

Finally, Jonah eased away, deeper into the shadows. "It's getting late," he murmured.

Longing swept through her. Must their moment together end so soon? She caught sight of the moon, low in the night sky, and knew he was right. It was late. "Yes." She resisted the urge to sigh.

They didn't speak during the short remainder of their walk. At the space in the hedge, they stood apart, as ever.

When he made no move to leave, she asked, "What is it?"

He didn't answer immediately. She counted several heartbeats, each heavier than the one before.

"When you go for your walk tomorrow night," he said, "I won't be here."

4

Jonah sat on the edge of his bed in the darkened room and savored the memories of his hours with Ariel. It still surprised him when she laughed with him. Her laughter was wonderfully real, lacking that brittle, nervous edge he'd heard so often from others. Too often. He stared out the open window at a black sky littered with stars. A whisper of breeze stirred the heavy draperies.

Now he must give up Ariel's company for a few days. He couldn't risk being with her.

Tomorrow night there would be a full moon.

A child's scream echoed in the corridors outside Ariel's office. The high, piercing sound carried a burden of frenzied anguish and fear.

Ariel hurried out of her office and down the short

hall to the waiting area. She was just in time to see Toby relieve a nurse of her struggling charge. The stocky young man used his greater strength with surprising gentleness, cradling the small boy against him in a way that deftly restrained thin, flailing arms and legs.

"There now," he crooned to the child. "What's all this about? Nobody's going to hurt you, champ."

Ariel approached her secretary and the wailing boy. "Michael Corey?" she quietly asked Toby.

"In person."

She looked at her new patient. Brown eyes were wide with terror in the small, disfigured face that was wet with tears.

"Poor little thing," the nurse said, brushing her hair back into place with her fingers. "Away from everything familiar to him."

Ariel could only guess what that might have been in an ancient, understaffed mental hospital. "Bring him into my office, please."

She went ahead of Toby and the nurse. From a drawer in her desk she retrieved a chocolate bar she'd bought from the vending machine that morning. She plucked a lancet from the top drawer of the white metal cabinet, then sliced a small piece from the bar. She held it within the child's reach. "Do you like candy, Michael?"

He twisted away from her, in Toby's arms, making a grunting noise in his throat.

"I wonder if he's ever had any candy," the nurse murmured.

Ariel noticed the name on the other woman's badge.

Lucy Norton. "I hope that's not the case, Lucy." It seemed too cruel that this boy, who had led such a harsh existence, should also have been deprived of something as basic to childhood as candy.

Finally Michael turned around. His sobs had dwindled to hiccups. He stuck a fist to his trembling mouth and regarded the bit of chocolate with an unwavering gaze.

Again she offered him the treat.

Carefully, he took it from her, greed momentarily overcoming caution. His small, warm hand grasped the tidbit and immediately popped it in his twisted mouth. He warily watched the three adults as he chewed.

"I think the question has been answered," Ariel said, smiling. "He's had candy before."

Succumbing to the bribery of chocolate pieces, Michael was gradually coaxed out of Toby's arms and onto the examining table. He perched on the edge like a wild fledgling, ready to attempt flight at the first unexpected noise or movement. Ariel thought he might object when Toby left to return to his own work, but the boy remained where he sat, munching.

Moving slowly, careful not to startle him, Ariel was able to examine Michael's face. She was appalled at the damage that had been left uncorrected. True, the medical personnel who had attended the him had done well to save his life. The trauma of such an injury would have been catastrophic for an infant. Loss of fluids, shock, infection—all so much more life-threatening for a baby weighing under twelve pounds.

And from the looks of the scarring, that's all that had been done. There was no evidence that any attempt had been made to correct the damage created by the burns. Part of the scalp had been seared away by the kindling, leaving a shiny bald patch near the forehead. The scar tissue had contracted, but Michael had grown. Now his left eye was pulled down in a manner that the reports in his file indicated was impairing his vision. The left nostril and the corner of his mouth were also drawn taut, contorted into a gruesome sneer that affected both his breathing and his speech. Keloids had grown rampantly across the injury site.

She studied her patient. There was too much damage to be approached all at once. The most immediate problem, she decided, was that eye. That would have to top her list of tasks.

She gave him a reassuring smile. "Michael," she said, "do you know my name?"

He regarded her steadily, but made no effort to reply.

"I'm Dr. Denham. Can you say that? Dr. Denham?"

"Dar-dinamm." He tried to echo her inflection, but his pronunciation was slurred. His gaze slid away from hers, and he stared down at his sneaker-clad feet, dangling so high above the linoleum. Her heart went out to him.

"Very good," she told him. "We'll be seeing a lot of each other now. Do you have anything you'd like to ask me?"

He regarded her a moment. Then, slowly, he opened his mouth. "Unnh. Unnh."

She'd been dismayed to learn from Lucy, earlier, that this primitive noise was his request for food. Ariel found the sound unnerving. This child of normal intelligence appeared to be emulating Down's Syndrome children. She knew such unfortunates inhabited Chattalogh, where Michael would have found limited choice for his selection of role models.

Ariel cautiously reached out her hand and was pleased when he allowed her to stroke his fine brown hair. "We've got to keep you out of that place, kiddo," she murmured.

"It's not fair, is it?" Lucy asked. "Children should be cherished."

Ariel studied the disfigured face before her. It *wasn't* fair. No one could ever deserve this, especially not an innocent child.

She gave him the last of the candy, and lifted him off the examining table. "You're not afraid of me, are you, Michael?"

He cocked his head and looked at her from the corners of his eyes.

"Michael? Do you understand what I'm asking you?"

He hesitated, then nodded.

"Are you afraid of me?"

A few seconds trickled by before he slowly shook his head.

To her surprise, something inside her eased. She smiled at him again. "Good."

After Michael left with Lucy, the day seemed to go downhill. Several of her patients were fractious. The lab lost a report she needed. The vending machine ate her quarters, but refused to deliver her bag of M&M's. By the end of the day, Ariel was ready to call it quits.

In her bungalow, she kicked off her shoes, headed for the living room, and, with a drawn-out sigh, slumped into the upholstered embrace of a comfortable chair.

The telephone in the kitchen jangled, severing her moment of peace.

"Ariel, hi!" a familiar voice said when she answered.

"Nelson, what a surprise."

Nelson Herrick laughed. "Why? Did you think I'd forget my sponsor?"

She supposed she was his sponsor. But the only reason she'd suggested him to Bendl and MacDaid when she'd had to turn down their offer was to put him in her debt. A debt she planned to call when her sentence at Fountainhead was finished.

She considered his skills as a plastic surgeon to be quite adequate, but it was his access to important contacts that had prompted her to recommend him. The old money tentacles of the Herrick family reached from coast to coast.

"Not at all," she said smoothly. "I knew you'd be busy."

"I am! This place is incredible, Ariel. I've been stripping fat and lifting fannies out of sight this month." He laughed again, and she could see in her mind's eye his white teeth flashing in his handsome face, the perfect Golden Boy, complete with a cellular phone in his custom-made golf bag. "I wish you were here, Ariel. You're really missing out on all the action. You wouldn't *believe* the people who come here. Movie stars. Business moguls."

Ariel opened the refrigerator and poured herself a glass of cold water. She didn't want to hear this. It was bad enough having had to turn down the position. "I know. The patients make up a kind of *Who's Who* of Hollywood."

"So, how are you doing?" Nelson asked. "What's it like there?"

Ariel refused to tell him that she didn't want to be at Fountainhead. She glanced outside. Dusk was closing in, the sinking sun swathing the sky in pink and purple and orange. "It's beautiful, Nelson. The clinic is in a valley surrounded by forest and mountains. The air is clean. The water is so pure it's actually sweet. All the clinic's equipment is first-rate—"

"But are you making any money?"

She flinched with embarrassment. She'd feel too stupid having to admit that she was making very little money after turning down the lucrative position he now filled. "I'm making enough," she hedged.

"Enough? Is there such a thing?"

She could hear his grin through the telephone lines. "I stand corrected." Could there ever be a point where she felt as if she were making enough? It would take an awful lot to make up for a lifetime of poverty.

"I was worried there for a minute," he said. "I thought maybe the Ariel Denham I know had been kidnapped and an imposter substituted."

"No. Same old me."

"I tell you, Ariel, if people think they can look better, especially if it doesn't require any effort or discipline, they can't open their wallets fast enough. It's amazing. But, hey, you're not surprised, are you? You're a woman, right?"

"Last time I looked," she said dryly.

He had the grace to sound chagrined. "What I mean is, women have seen how vanity works in the marketplace. My sister has been spending a fortune on cosmetics since she turned thirteen. Forty dollars for makeup—foundation, she calls it. Fifteen bucks for a lipstick that she'll never use up."

Forty-dollar foundation and fifteen-dollar lipsticks. Ariel had been lucky to afford dime store cosmetics. In med school she'd given up wearing makeup entirely, using the excuse that she didn't have time to fool with face paint. Which was, of course, the truth, or at least part of it. But she had no intention of mentioning this to Nelson.

"Not everyone is as naturally beautiful as you are, Dr. Herrick."

There was a pause on the line, a hesitation, as if he debated sharing some terrible secret. Then: "I wore braces."

The grave confession caught Ariel by surprise, and she laughed. "Braces! Egad! What shame you must feel."

"I should have known better than to tell you," he said stiffly.

"At least a quarter of the kids in the country have probably had some sort of orthodonture. And another quarter would like to have, but can't afford to." She'd make certain that her children didn't grow up as she had. They'd have braces if they needed them. They'd have hot meals and clothes that fit.

"You're right about vanity paying off," she said.

"No doubt about it. Cosmetic surgery is a growth industry."

And Ariel was determined to get her share of that growth. She'd learned the hard way that being poor was an unforgivable sin in this world. Poverty made you an acceptable target for violence and neglect.

She shook her head, trying to cast off the memories. "Was there a particular reason you called, Nelson?"

There was a slight pause. "No special reason. I just hadn't talked to you in a long time."

"Oh. Well, it was good to hear from you," she said absently, thinking about getting a glass of iced tea.

"Let's keep in touch, Ariel."

"Good idea. Let's do keep in touch." She'd have to go to the cafeteria for the tea. She still hadn't gotten any groceries.

After they said good-bye, she decided to forget the tea. Instead, she poured herself another glass of ice water. As she leaned against the sink and drank, she thought about their conversation.

Money. It was a magic spell backed by the full faith and credit of the U. S. government, and it gave you control over your life. Barring Fate and Mother Nature, nothing else conferred that kind of power.

She wanted that power. And she would have it.

The fanciful wooden sign creaked as it swung from its post, tugged by the twilight breeze. Ariel read the words that were painted in rose, outlined in black: Welcome to Farley.

There at the crossing point of two country roads, the sign stood with a handful of other signs, advising the traveler of the existence of the VFW, the First Baptist Church, the First Methodist Church, and the Chamber of Commerce.

She reread the directions that she'd received from the manager of The Black Tupelo. The road she needed to take angled away from the town.

She'd intended to leave Fountainhead Valley in the early afternoon, but a missing serum chemistry report had delayed her. Now it was twilight and the heavy moisture in the air presaged rain.

Spicy scents of the surrounding forest filled her car and she eagerly breathed them in, making a game of identifying each note. Pine and oak and wet green fern. The tranquilizing burble of water tumbling over rocks eased away the tension of her day.

Ariel found the entrance to the property, which was marked by a tall masonry arch. According to her conversation with Beryl Jenkins, 140 years ago the mansion had been part of a large estate, a summer retreat belonging to a wealthy tobacco planter. Over the years bits and pieces of the land had been sold off, until only the present ten acres remained.

The main drive to the inn wound through a stand of tall black tupelos, their thick brown bark deeply furrowed, their glossy, oblong leaves shifting and whispering in the breeze.

The road took a turn around a hillock of azalea bushes, and for the first time she saw The Black Tupelo.

It looked like a Gothic castle. Constructed of gray stone, the mansion lacked only a moat and a drawbridge to complete the impression of a late medieval citadel.

Set in a deep stone porch that was topped by a crenellated battlement and flanked by a tower on each side, the elaborately carved double front doors towered to a gracefully curved point. Behind the front porch, more battlements and towers were accompanied by ornate finials, an abundance of stone tracery, and foliated windows, which Ariel thought any medieval lady would have coveted for her bower.

Her gaze soared up the uncompromising stone walls. Jonah had said he was familiar with Farley. Had he stayed at The Black Tupelo?

She parked her car in the circular drive in front of the hotel, then went to register.

When she walked through the etched glass doors of the vestibule, Ariel felt as if she'd stepped into another, more luxurious century. Everything from the sumptuously draped windows to the black walnut fireplace mantelpiece spoke of the gilded age of Queen Victoria.

An orange tabby cat glided out from behind the gleaming front desk of mahogany to sniff delicately at her ankles.

"Well, hello there," Ariel said.

For a moment, the cat regarded her with unblinking green eyes. Then it stretched and leisurely rubbed up against her legs, caressing her calves with its tail. She leaned down to scratch behind furry orange ears and was rewarded with a low rumble signifying feline pleasure.

"Selene usually ignores people." The woman's voice startled Ariel.

A woman who appeared to be in her fifties had quietly entered the room through the door behind the desk. She was of medium height, solidly built, and her silver-streaked brown hair was twisted up into a knot high at the back of her head. Ariel thought she wouldn't have looked out of place attired in a nineteenth century dress rather than the pink cotton blouse and mauve slacks she wore.

"I don't know why, but cats have always seemed to like me," Ariel said. She scratched Selene's jaw and the purr grew louder. "And I like them."

"I'm Beryl Jenkins. You must be Dr. Denham." Beryl nodded toward the tabby that contentedly sat on Ariel's foot. "You've already met Selene."

Beryl assisted Ariel through the check-in process. "What floor would you prefer?" she asked. "There are three, and you're the only guest tonight."

The only guest? How odd. The mansion was enormous, and appeared to be meticulously maintained. That would cost money, a lot of money. Ariel briefly considered asking if this was the off-season, but decided against it. If The Black Tupelo was going through financial hard times, the last thing Beryl would want to hear was any inquiry in reference to her lack of guests.

Instead, Ariel looked at the magnificent staircase with its beautifully turned banister, its intricate wood tracery, and solid, dignified finials. A path of crimson carpet flowed down the middle of the steps, held in place by brass carpet rods. "I'd feel like the belle of the ball, coming down those stairs."

"Yes, the staircase is rather dramatic. The rooms on the third floor offer an especially nice view."

Ariel chose a room there, and Beryl's nephew Chuck brought her suitcase up to the room, then left to park her car in the guest lot.

"The bathroom is down the hall," Beryl said after checking to make certain everything was satisfactory. "The library and game room are on the first floor. Would you like me to send tea up to you?"

"Yes, thank you." A glass of iced tea did sound rather nice. Ariel was impressed with the thoughtful gesture.

Beryl left, and Ariel walked over to the window and drew aside a heavy drapery to look out. The sun was sinking behind the dark mountains.

Had Jonah ever watched the sun set out of a window in this inn? Perhaps on vacation? Had he been just an average man, content with his life, before the accident that had left him disfigured?

Ariel absently brushed her fingertips back and forth over the rose-colored velvet as she tried to imagine Jonah checking into The Black Tupelo, exchanging pleasantries with Beryl, patting Selene. Somehow, she couldn't focus that scene. It was difficult to think of Jonah as ever having been average.

She released the drapery, and its long silk fringe shivered. Where did he go during the day? What did he do?

A knock sounded at the door. "Room service," Beryl's nephew announced, then grinned widely. The boy was tall, but still retained his youthful gangliness. The tray that he set on the desk contained not the glass of iced tea that Ariel had expected, but a flowered porcelain teapot snuggled under a lace-trimmed cozy, a matching cup and saucer, a folded linen napkin, and a crystal plate bearing several small cakes and bonbons.

"This is really lovely, Chuck," Ariel said, delighted. It was much nicer than she'd expected. How could Doris's friend have thought The Black Tupelo was creepy?

"Yeah." His pride was clear to see. "Aunt Beryl does everything like it should be done. Oh, she said to tell you that she made you Earl Grey tea, because it goes well with sweet things, but that she's got some very nice Ceylon, if you'd prefer, or some Lapsang souchong."

Ariel tipped the teenager. "Tell Beryl that I'll trust in her expertise. The Earl Grey will be perfect, I'm sure."

After Chuck left, she drank a cup of tea while she unpacked her clothes into the dresser and armoire. Then she ate a bonbon and went downstairs to investigate the library and the game room.

The first thing that struck her was the silence. As she descended the stairs, the only sound she heard was the sonorous *tock* of the grandfather clock in the entrance hall.

Gloom hovered in the corners of the rooms, and clung to the high ceilings. Every heavy piece of furniture proved a haven for shadows. Several lamps provided oases of illumination, reminding Ariel of so many round stones forming a way across dark water.

"Hello?" she called softly. No one answered. Feeling a little edgy, she tried again.

"Yes?" Beryl walked out onto the landing of the second floor, holding what looked to be a bunched-up sheet. She started folding it. "Are you finding everything all right?"

Suddenly Ariel felt foolish. After all, Beryl had told her she was the only guest. "Uh, yes. I just . . . It's so quiet," she finished lamely.

Beryl completed folding the sheet, then smiled at Ariel. "There's no one here but you and me. It's all these shadows, I think. Don't worry, though. I have the security system on."

As Ariel searched the paperback titles on the "lending" shelves in the library, the first drops of rain splattered against the windowpanes. Minutes later, a deep rumble of thunder rolled out over the mountains.

Failing to find a book that caught her interest, she decided to get ready for bed and curl up with her latest issue of *Plastic and Reconstructive Surgery*.

By the time she reached the third floor, the rain hammered the house with heavy violence.

She'd been wrong, Ariel admitted to herself, glancing down the long shadowy hallway. She could definitely understand why Doris's friend had said that all The Black Tupelo lacked was Bela Lugosi. If he'd appeared at that moment, in his persona as vampire, he would not have been out of place. She found herself hurrying to her door.

She grabbed her nightgown from the armoire, snatched up her cosmetics case, and hastened down the corridor. She quickly passed a hall table bearing a bronze statue of Athena with a clock set in her belly and a collection of colorful Majolica plates, and a little farther down the hall, a pedestal supporting a white plaster bust of Theodore Roosevelt.

The lights went out.

Ariel stopped in her tracks and squeezed her eyes shut. "It's okay," she told herself unsteadily. "Everything is going to be just fine. All she had to do was go back to her room and light the emergency candles she'd seen in the drawer of the nightstand.

She turned slowly. There were no windows in the hall, and when she opened her eyes, she saw no difference from having them closed. The darkness was thick and absolute. Inching over to the wall, she began feeling her way back to her room. The dark wouldn't last. In a minute the lights would come back on. It was only an unreliable transformer. Everyone around here knew this frequently happened during storms.

Finally she made it back to her room, and when one of the matches she found in the drawer caught, and the flame burst into life, Ariel felt a rush of relief—then disgust at her earlier anxiety.

With three candles stuck in a brass candelabrum that had been placed on the lower shelf of the nightstand, she marched back down the hall, determined to take the power outage in her stride. As she passed under a false doorway, she felt a soft gust of air. The damask portieres shifted. The candle flames fluttered. Ariel drew a shaky breath. These old houses probably had a million places drafts could get in. She hurried on.

The candlelight illuminated the bathroom with subdued golden light as Ariel stopped the drain of the claw-footed bathtub and turned the brass faucets to release a flow of hot water. She added a few drops of her favorite bath oil, and was rewarded when the scents of violet, heliotrope, and juniper filled the room.

The fragrance still lingered in the air when she stepped out of the tub. As she had leisurely bathed, the storm outside had passed, taking the rain with it. Except for the soft gurgling of draining bathwater, the house was silent.

She brushed her hair, then drew on her nightgown, settling the spaghetti straps into place on her shoulders. She caught a glimpse of herself in the steamed cheval mirror and smoothed a hand down her side, enjoying the feel of the pink silk. Silly to take such pleasure in pretty lingerie.

She picked up her cosmetics case and looked around for her bathrobe, then realized she'd forgotten to bring it and her slippers. Who would see her, anyway? Opening the bathroom door, she looked out into the hall.

The doors to all the empty guest rooms stood open. Moonlight spilled into the corridor, punctuating the length of black with wedges of silver.

She frowned as she lifted the candelabrum and turned into the hall. Surely Beryl could do better than this. It seemed to Ariel that anyone living in an area where the power was unreliable would be better prepared, especially an innkeeper. Where were her hurricane lamps or propane lanterns?

She walked slowly toward her bedroom, pausing now and then to peer into rooms. None were alike, yet each held the charm of a bygone era.

As she stepped from a patch of moonlight into dark, the flames of her candles flickered wildly and went out.

Uneasy, she hurried into the next bit of moonlight. She stood there a moment, clutching her bundle of clothes to her chest with one hand, her useless candelabrum in the other. There was no more moonlight in this section of the hall. About twelve feet of blackness separated her from her door. She dropped her clothes and fumbled in her cosmetics case for the matches. Her sense of urgency grew more intense when the hairs on the back of her neck began to prickle. She struck a match.

It blew out.

Her fingers tightened around the base of the brass candelabrum. She swallowed hard.

A man spoke from the stygian shadows. "Don't light the candles."

5

She whirled toward the voice. "J—Jonah?"

"Yes."

Relief flooded her, but she refused to admit to him how frightened she'd been. "What are you doing here?"

Amusement warmed his tone. "Watching you."

Embarrassment heated her cheeks. She didn't want him to know how cowardly she was. "I hope you're satisfied," she said waspishly.

"Very." His voice grew slightly rough. "You look good in moonlight and silk."

Suddenly she remembered that she was wearing only a thin nightgown. Self-consciously she pulled a fallen spaghetti strap back onto her shoulder. "I, uh—"

"Do you always walk the halls of hotels wearing only a nightgown?"

"Do you always sneak around the halls of hotels at

night?" she demanded as she crouched to gather up the clothing she'd dropped. She stood, clutching the wad of garments in front of her like a shield, uncomfortably aware of how the silk clung to her.

"No."

"Well, neither do I." She stalked toward her room. "What are you doing here, anyway?" she snapped. "Creeping around in the dark like the bogeyman."

As soon as the words were out of her mouth she realized how cruel they sounded. She turned abruptly to face the shadow-presence near her door. "I didn't mean that, Jonah. Not like it sounded. I mean . . ." Oh, hell, she was only making it worse. She reached out toward him, expecting him to avoid her touch. To her surprise, her fingertips met with the rough cloth of a chambray sleeve, warmed by the muscular arm wearing it.

"Are you going to put on your robe, or are you planning to stand there and grope me?" he said. Strong fingers encircled her wrist. They slid slowly upward, caressing the inside of her bare arm, sending an electrifying tingle through her body. Then the touch was gone.

Somehow she managed to get the door to her room open. She stood there gripping the embossed doorknob, stalling for time while her heart rate returned to normal. "I'm certainly not planning to grope you."

"Pity." She could hear the smile in his voice.

"Why have you left Fountainhead, Jonah?"

"Why not? Aren't I allowed to leave when I choose?" He leaned slightly closer, yet remained far enough away that she could not distinguish his features. "Or is it that you're afraid I won't make it back to my coffin before the sun rises?"

A tiny chill went up the back of her neck. "Oh, very funny." Her voice came out a little higher pitched than she intended. "But you haven't answered my question."

"You know," he said casually, "with the moonlight from your window behind you like that, I fully realize just how . . . delicate . . . that nightgown is. You have such a small waist, Ariel."

She hadn't realized he could even see her. Quickly she stepped all the way behind the door. Briefly she debated closing and locking it.

"I thought you'd enjoy a tour of The Black Tupelo," he continued in a more conversational tone. "It's an interesting old house, and Beryl won't mind."

She frowned. "A tour? You came here to give me a tour? *Now?*"

"I'm sorry. Is now not a good time for you?" His voice was all innocence.

Ariel knew that was as close as she was going to get to an answer. Was he here because he'd missed her? She'd missed him. But as she slipped her robe off the hanger and drew it on, she knew she wouldn't admit that to him anymore than he was likely to admit it to her.

Pride. It always came down to cautious, isolating, lonely pride. She stepped into her slippers, trying to ignore the faint, familiar ache of longing.

"Okay," she said, walking back out into the hall. "I'm ready for the tour. If you're sure it's all right with Beryl."

"No problem there."

He guided her down the moonlight-dappled corridor, staying so close to her that she couldn't see his face. He smelled of the forest, that sharp green scent of growing things.

"How did you get here?" she asked.

He opened a door. "I came through the woods." He preceded her up the unvarnished oak stairs.

"Is this the attic?"

"Once it was the servants' quarters, but those days are long gone. The fourth floor has served as the attic for years."

Here, too, there were windows, scattered throughout a warren of small rooms. Hatboxes and trunks and crates were stored everywhere. Ariel spied a wooden rocking horse almost hidden behind an old dress form. The moonlight revealed that, beneath a thick coat of dust, the paint was unscratched, the colors barely faded, as if long ago the toy had been put away new.

He led her back down the stairs. "What did you think of the bathroom? Did you enjoy your bath?"

"It's a very old-fashioned–looking bathroom. And that big claw-footed tub is kind of charming."

Out of the corner of her eye, she thought she glimpsed the pale flash of a grin. "There's a story about that bathroom."

"Okay. I'm game. Tell me."

They walked toward the big, Victorian bathroom, she through the stepping-stone path of moonlight, he through the flowing shadows. At the door, he turned her so that she looked into the room. He stood close behind her, a warm, solid presence. She resisted the urge to lean back.

Here the stained glass window tinted the tile and porcelain, and the walnut cabinetwork in haunting blue, deep purple, blood-crimson and amber. Ariel thought that if she'd just awakened in this place, she would have thought she was still dreaming.

"The story's happy, right?" She tilted her head back a little, favoring the underside of his chin with an exaggerated scowl.

He gently tugged a lock of her hair forward, and she lowered her head again. "There was an old maid who lived here. Her sisters, all younger than she, had been married for years and had thriving families of their own. Only poor, plain Vesta remained unwed."

"This doesn't sound happy," she accused.

"Hush."

Jonah told Ariel how the new plumber in town had fallen in love with Vesta at first sight, and how he contrived to install a new bathtub in her third-floor bathroom. The entire town was scandalized when word got out about the laughter—both a man's and a woman's—that the servants heard behind closed doors in that bathroom.

Ariel smiled, happy for lonely Vesta. "But it would have ruined her reputation," she said. "How did she handle it?"

Jonah placed his palm at the small of her back, and nudged Ariel into the bathroom, until she stood in front of him, at the foot of the large bathtub, facing the ornate brass faucets at the other end. "She didn't have to handle it," he said. "He married her."

"Oh." Thoughts of Vesta scattered like leaves caught in a spring wind. All Ariel could think of was Jonah's hand at the small of her back.

"According to her diary, they made love in this tub every night of their honeymoon," Jonah whispered in her ear. His warm breath sent a frisson of sensation through her, leaving her a little breathless . "Sometimes they even filled it with water."

"How adventurous of them," she managed.

"It's a large tub."

Suddenly, Ariel saw a shadowy man and woman lying naked in the tub. Their limbs were feverishly tangled, their bodies wet and straining. The room echoed with their short, labored breathing, their increasingly urgent murmurs.

"Ariel?"

With a dizzying lurch, she felt sensation and perspective shift abruptly. Confused, she stood still for a few seconds. Her heart pounded. Her body felt flushed.

In front of her, the bathtub stood dry and empty.

Jonah laid his hand on her shoulder. His fingers tightened slightly. "Ariel? What is it?"

She didn't want to talk about the erotic, spectral scene she'd witnessed. She *couldn't* talk about it— what would she say? But the episode had left her shaken.

Ariel turned her head slightly, unable to see Jonah, who still stood behind her.

His voice was quiet when he spoke again. "You saw them, didn't you?"

His question caught her off guard. "Them?" she echoed stupidly.

"Vesta and Thomas."

The lovers. But had it been Vesta and Thomas? Ariel felt as if she had been the one lying beneath what had seemed like the very real weight of her lover.

Abruptly, she moved away from Jonah and walked out of the room. He returned to the hall more slowly. She sensed him, standing there in the shadows. She could feel him watching her.

"Why didn't you warn me?" she said chokingly.

"They haven't been seen for years. No one knows why they appear."

A hiccup of near-hysterical laughter escaped the control she was struggling to maintain. "Oh, swell! I'm staying in a hotel with a haunted bathtub."

Jonah didn't reply immediately. "What did you see?"

"You tell me. You're the one who knows the story." She could hear her voice rising. She jumped when she felt his hand touch her nape.

His strong fingers massaged the back of her neck and her shoulders. "Keep your voice down. You'll wake Beryl."

"I'd think Beryl would be used to hysterical guests by now."

"Maybe. Beryl hasn't seen the ghosts."

She drew in a deep, steadying breath. "Have you?" she asked.

"No. I don't know anyone who has. Until now. Are you all right, Ariel?" The touch of his fingers softened, offering assurance.

She stared up at the ceiling, at a chandelier farther down the hall, and told herself that she certainly hoped what she'd seen had been ghosts. "I'm fine."

"So, what did Vesta and Thomas look like?" Jonah's deep voice carried his interest.

Ariel eased away from his touch. What she'd seen were only ghosts, she told herself sternly. Just old, household-variety ghosts. *Not* some deep-seated fantasy lurking in her subconscious.

"It's a little embarrassing," she said. The understatement of the century.

"Ah." That one word conveyed his instant attention. "That sounds promising. After all, what could embarrass a doctor?"

She glared in his direction. "How about a naked man and woman making love in a bathtub not two feet away?"

Jonah's bark of surprised laughter was instantly suppressed into a coughing sound.

"I'm glad you're amused," she said stiffly and started to walk off.

Still laughing, he took her arm in a light hold. "I'm sorry. It just caught me off guard. Who'd ever expect two Victorian ghosts to be exhibitionists?"

Ariel recalled the soaring joy she'd sensed. "No," she said slowly. "I don't believe they appear that way for, uh, prurient reasons."

"Oh? What makes you say that?"

"Just a feeling I got."

"Then why do they appear in flagrante delicto? Could it be some ghostly sense of humor? Maybe they intended to embarrass you."

"Maybe . . ." She groped for a reason that might make at least a modicum of sense. Then it came to her. "Maybe that was their happiest moment."

Jonah steered her toward the grand staircase. "A lonely spinster and a lonely immigrant find true love in a bathtub," he said as they took the steps down. "Well, stranger things could happen."

"Yes," Ariel agreed solemnly. "They could."

Only the heavy *tock, tock* of the grandfather clock in the entry hall penetrated the silence of the house as Jonah and Ariel descended the carpeted stairs to the first floor.

Moonlight poured through the tall windows. Ariel remembered that all the draperies had been closed before she went to bed.

"Jonah, who opened the drapes?"

He continued to shepherd her through the rooms. "I did."

"And you're sure it's all right with Beryl for us to tour the house?"

"I said so, didn't I?"

"Yes, you did. She frowned. "Does Beryl even know you're here?"

"Don't worry about it."

Her frown intensified. "I'm asking you."

"Why?"

She halted in the middle of the parlor, noticing that the large mirror over the mantel had been covered. "Because I want to know."

He urged her back into motion again, maneuvering her into the library. "What does it matter?"

"Don't you think Beryl has a right to know if someone enters her house? Especially after she's closed for the night?" Did Jonah hide from Beryl, too?

And then she remembered Beryl had said The Black Tupelo had a security system that was turned on at night. Suddenly a chill passed through Ariel.

"You think she'd be upset if she knew I was here." It wasn't a question.

Ariel nodded. Then, uncertain he could see her clearly, she said, "I think she might be, yes." She turned toward him and found that he'd moved into deeper shadow.

"So you think I'm lying to you." There was an underlying tightness in his voice.

"I didn't say that, exactly."

"Not exactly." Sarcasm fairly dripped from each word.

Ariel lifted her chin. "Well, I'm not happy about wandering around the woman's home unless I'm certain she approves. And just how did you get past the security system?"

She saw the black-on-black shadow of his head turn sharply in her direction. He didn't speak for long seconds. "I see I made a mistake in coming here tonight. Can you find your own way back to your room? I won't trouble you further." He suddenly blended back with the rest of the dark and disappeared.

"Just why did you come, Jonah?" she asked.

She received no answer.

"That's right," she muttered. "Pull your vanishing act." A sense of loss welled up inside her. "Damn you, Jonah, whoever you are." Her fascinating, eerie tour of this strange house was at an end. Her self-appointed guide had left her. "Damn you."

"Save your breath, Ariel. That job has already been done."

She spun around to find his tall, shadow-figure leaning against the doorframe, arms crossed. She wanted to be angry, but all she could feel was a ridiculous relief. "I thought you'd gone."

"It would seem," Jonah said quietly, "that you're not an easy woman to walk away from."

"Oh."

"But let's get one thing straight. I'm not a liar, Ariel. I said it would be all right with Beryl for me to take you through the house. It will be."

Before she could question him on his relationship with Beryl, he said, "Did you know a man was murdered in this room?"

"Murdered?" Were there more ghosts? She scanned the moonlit library uneasily. One brush with phantoms was more than enough.

Jonah pushed away from the doorway and strolled out of the room, deftly managing to keep her from getting a clear view of him.

He showed her the rooms on the ground floor—all but one. Beryl's room. They passed quietly by her door.

Finally, he brought Ariel to an unimportant-looking door in the modernized kitchen.

"What does that lead to?" she asked.

"The cellar."

Irrational panic clutched at her. She couldn't go down there! Cellars were dark. Dark and close. Things lived in them.

She wanted to refuse, to tell Jonah no, absolutely

not. But if she did that, she'd be caving in to weakness and cowardice.

"What's in the cellar?" she asked, trying hard to sound unconcerned.

"Lots of things."

"Oh."

He opened the door. Slowly, it swung wide, and Ariel stared at what lay beyond.

Impenetrable darkness.

Fear surged through her. She backed away from the door, into Jonah's chest. "I can't go in there," she insisted.

Jonah chuckled. "It's pitch-dark. Of course you can't go in there, not without light." He opened his hands, revealing a candle and a book of matches. "But you've got to promise me . . ." His voice died away. He cleared his throat and tried again. "You've got to promise me not to look at me."

Something in his voice tore at her. She forgot her fear as she thought about how carefully he always concealed his face from her. How clearly important it was to him that she think of him as if he were a normal man. But he wasn't a normal man. Fallen angels could never be just normal men.

She wanted to tell him that she could cope with seeing his face. It wasn't his face that touched something deep within her, but rather his spirit. "I won't look," she promised.

Ariel lit a match and touched it to the wick. Cupping her hand around the flame, she took a deep breath and stepped forward.

The steep, narrow steps seemed to go on forever

into an ominous black netherworld. Only the golden halo of light that surrounded the tip of the candle protected her. Her heart hammered.

The cellar expanded before her like a vast cavern. Candlelight danced across floor-to-ceiling shelves stocked with jars of homemade pickles, peaches, and jams. Bunches of fragrant dried herbs hung from racks. White wicker furniture cloaked in dustcovers came into sight, and beyond that were stacked wooden crates bearing black Chinese characters on their sides.

"What's in those boxes?" she asked, glad of the distraction.

"I think that's the porcelain dinner service for twenty," he replied. "It was brought out of China just before the Boxer Rebellion."

"Of course."

Ariel struggled not to think about the darkness that surrounded her. Something brushed her shoulder. She let out a strangled shriek.

Jonah's deep voice reassured her. "It's just me." He chuckled. "Come over here."

Speech was beyond her capability at that moment. She followed him to a brick wall that ran the length of the cellar.

Ariel watched as Jonah counted six bricks up the wall from the floor. Then he pried out the old brick above that. To her astonishment, a knob was revealed. After several twists, he tugged. A small door, covered with half-cut bricks to disguise it, scraped opened.

Jonah held his hand out to her. "Come on."

Ariel ignored his hand and inched only slightly closer. Close enough to see that the door opened into a tiny room. It was as dark and airless as a sealed coffin.

Panic swelled inside her, blotting out everything else. She drew back abruptly. "No!" She had to get out of there, out of that hellish cellar, and she had to get out *now*.

"My god, you're shaking." He reached for her.

Blindly, she dodged his hand. She had to get out, *out*. She stumbled into one of the crates. The candle flew from her hand. With a faint *thunk* it hit the floor, and the only light in the cellar went out.

Darkness was instant and absolute.

Ariel moaned and huddled down. She knew she needed to exert control, but somehow she couldn't summon any.

"Stay where you are," Jonah commanded. His voice cut through her fear like a beacon of hope.

"Jonah, I'm here!"

"I'm coming, Sunshine. Don't move, okay?" He spoke firmly, but his tone was reassuring. "Talk to me. I'll follow your voice."

She sucked in a deep breath. "Please hurry."

Warm fingers closed around her calf. "Don't be frightened, it's only me, Sunshine."

She launched herself at that wonderful, reassuring voice. Instantly, strong arms went around her, gathering her against the solid wall of his body as he crouched there on the floor with her. She clung to him, sobbing in relief and fear and shame.

He rocked her. "I'm here, Ariel," he said soothingly. "It's all right now. Everything is okay."

She shook her head vigorously, keeping her face buried against his chest.

He stopped rocking. "It's not?"

"We're still here, in the dark."

Jonah sighed heavily. "Yeah. Look, I'm going to search for the candle." He unwound her arms from around his chest. "You stay right here—"

"Don't leave me!" She gripped his arm with the tenacity of a terrier.

"I'm only—"

"No!"

He brushed his fingertips along her tear-dampened cheek, smoothing her hair back. "We won't have any light unless I find that candle."

Deeply ashamed of her craven display, Ariel forced herself to fall back on her most plentiful reserve: pride.

She managed to uncurl her fingers from their death grip on his arm. "Of course."

"Here." He felt around for one of her hands, which he slipped beneath his belt at his back. "Hold on. I don't want to lose you."

They crawled on their hands and knees, Jonah feeling around for the candle, Ariel clutching onto his belt. She heard a thump, and he stopped suddenly. He cursed under his breath.

"What is it?" she hissed, fighting against threatening hysteria.

"I ran into one of these crates." He muttered another oath.

"I thought you could see in the dark," she accused.

"I'm not a damned bat, for chrissake," he shot back crossly.

A few minutes later Jonah found the candle. She

heard the scratch of the striking match, then felt as well as saw the bloom of light.

Jonah stood and helped her up. "C'mon. Let's get out of here."

She didn't need his urging to hurry up the stairs, back into the kitchen, where moonlight splashed counters and cabinets. With a long sigh of relief, she collapsed into a straight-backed chair at the oak trestle table.

Gradually, her heartbeat slowed, her breathing calmed. The silence between Ariel and Jonah grew with every second that passed.

"Why didn't you tell me?" he asked roughly.

She couldn't bare to have him see her face. Embarrassment burned her cheeks. Shame tore at her pride.

Out of the corner of her eye she saw his movement as he took a step closer to her. He didn't leave the shadows. "I think I rate an answer, don't you?"

"I'm sorry," she said, her voice little more than a whisper. She wanted to vanish, to be out of his sight. What contempt he must have for her now.

"Sorry?" he echoed incredulously. "More like crazy! Why didn't you say you're afraid of the dark? I'd never had taken you down there if I'd known."

As if by magic, the flame on the candle went out. From behind her, Jonah clasped her arms and persuaded her to stand. He turned her around and tucked her cheek against his shoulder, the top of her head fitting comfortably just below his chin. "Now, tell me why."

She still couldn't see his face, but neither could he

see hers, and for that she was thankful. It felt so good to stand there, listening to his steady heartbeat, surrounded by his capable strength. "I've been able to control it, mostly. After all, I'm a big girl now." Her attempt at levity was spoiled by the tremble in her voice.

He lightly rubbed his jaw against her temple. "Most children outgrow their fear of the dark. Unless they have cause."

When he didn't say anything else, she knew he was giving her a chance to talk about the source of her fear. She never had before. She'd learned to conceal her anxiety. And she'd been successful. Until tonight.

After the display Jonah had just witnessed, he was entitled to think she was a coward. But she found she didn't want him to.

"When I was little, we lived in . . . well, not very nice apartments, in neighborhoods that tended to have high crime rates. At night there were always sirens going off. Often there was shouting—fights, you know—and crying. Sometimes you could hear a gun go off. My father was gone a lot at night." She took a deep breath and let it out. "The light bill didn't always get paid on time, so the power company would turn off the electricity. And then . . . and then the rats would come."

"How old were you?" She heard the hard edge in his voice.

"For as far back as I can remember, it was always like that."

"What about your mother?"

"My mother died when I was nineteen months old. Dad raised me alone."

Jonah was silent. Then: "Sounds as if the one alone was you."

"He did the best he could," she said defensively.

"Did he work at night?" Jonah asked, ignoring her testiness.

"He was an entrepreneur. He worked when opportunities presented themselves." But she knew what her father had been doing most of those nights; and she knew that dice didn't constitute business opportunities—at least not for her father.

She was surprised when Jonah's arms gathered her to him a little bit more firmly. He nuzzled the hair at side of her head. "You've come a long way," he told her, the words rumbling in his chest.

Seeing he didn't mean to pursue the subject of her father, she relaxed a little. "But I'm still afraid of the dark."

"All things considered, I'd say you're doing damn well. Look at us. We're standing in the dark. Are you afraid?"

She would have preferred to be standing in a room with all the lamps blazing, or—better yet—brilliant with daylight, but the terrible fear had eased. And, although there was moonlight where she was standing, the rest of the room was dark. "No," she said softly. "I guess not." *Not with you.*

His thumb smoothed slowly back and forth against her neck. The light, intimate friction sizzled down her spine. "You should know you're safe, even in the dark," Jonah said; his mellow-fire voice was low, and carried a faint note of humor.

She wanted to see his face, to look into his eyes.

She imagined how they would look, reflecting that humor. They would light with warmth, maybe crinkle a little at the corners. "Why should I know that?"

"What bogeyman with any sense would dare approach the indomitable Dr. Denham? He'd end up with a pretty face. Then who could he frighten?"

Ariel giggled. The sound was foreign to her. Giggling was undignified. Silly. "That's ridiculous," she said gruffly, but didn't bother to control the smile that took over.

What color were his eyes, she wondered. Green? Blue? No, brown, she decided. Brown eyes were so expressive.

He lifted his hand, palm out, as if he were taking an oath. "Word of honor. I have it on the best authority that you've got bogeymen everywhere very nervous. "

Her smile grew with her delight at seeing this unexpected, teasing side of him. "That's crazy." Unthinkingly, she raised her face.

Immediately his hand blocked her vision. It settled lightly across her eyes. Fingertips stroked her eyelids, and she closed them. When he took his hand away, she kept them closed. She sensed he was studying her upraised face. The feeling left her oddly breathless.

"Yes," he murmured. "Crazy."

6

His lips brushed hers, gently, almost tentatively. Then they were gone. Ariel kept her eyes closed, despite the thundering of her heart.

Jonah kissed her again, his mouth firmly over hers. His tongue traced the sealed line of her lips, and she parted them for him.

His hand moved up from her nape, burying itself in her hair. His arms tightened around her, pressing her close to his body.

Ariel's blood sang through her veins like potent wine. She clasped his shoulders, feeling the tense sinews through his shirt. Then she slid her palms up his neck, feeling a line of rough flesh on one side. She twined her arms around him, needing to get closer, closer to his strength and heat.

His mouth moved on hers, open and demanding. There, in the moonlit room, Ariel felt released from gravity, rocketing with dizzy sensation. Without thinking, she raised her hand to his cheek. She'd barely touched Jonah's skin when he suddenly stiffened.

He tore his mouth from hers, and his fingers caught her wrist in a steel grip. "Don't."

He released her wrist. When she opened her eyes, she found he'd returned to the shadows.

She stood in the patch of moonlight, alone again. The warmth of his arms, of his lips lingered on her, like the passing caress of the sun on a winter's day.

The only sound in the room was the rasp of their labored breathing.

"I'm sorry," she said. "I forgot."

"No," he said softly. "*I* forgot."

Seconds passed.

"It's late. I'll show you back to your room." His level tone gave no clue to what he was thinking.

He guided her directly to the staircase. They ascended two flights of stairs, and walked down the hall to her room. Not one word was spoken between them.

At her door, she turned, searching the darkness in vain.

"Sweet dreams, Ariel," he said.

She went into her room, quietly closed the door, and slumped back against it. How could a few passionate kisses affect her so strongly? They had shaken her more than her experience with the ghosts. But then, the ghosts hadn't rocked her in their arms, trying to ease her fear.

No, Jonah was very real. He was strong, and tender, and full of fire—a fire that he had shared with her.

Ariel slowly straightened and glanced at the clock on the mantel. It was now early morning. Her hours with Jonah had sped by faster than she'd realized.

Suddenly, the lamps in her room came on, flooding the room with bright light.

She regarded them for a moment, then, with a smile, she went around and turned each of them off.

Jonah sat on the stone bench and absently rolled the leaf between his fingers. The moon highlighted with silver the old sundial, the statues, the granite benches, and each lush rosebush.

He knew that in going to The Black Tupelo he had taken a foolish risk, but it had been nights since he'd seen her. It had been too long since he'd been enfolded in the spell of normality she seemed to cast over him. He'd delighted in showing Ariel the old mansion that had been a special place to him since he was a boy. Jonah leaned back on his hands and gazed up at stars. Christ, that seemed like aeons ago.

The Black Tupelo would always remind him of his uncle. Jonah smiled faintly. He allowed the familiar warm affection that always accompanied thoughts of his uncle to flow through him. Jonah felt certain that, had the old gentleman still been living, he would have found it in his heart to forgive his nephew.

Jonah expelled a harsh sigh. Whom was he trying to kid? How could anyone forgive him when he couldn't even forgive himself? No one who had committed the act he had, with such horrifying results, deserved forgiveness.

Deliberately, he turned his thoughts aside from their dark, tortured path. Tonight he'd brought back from his excursion a memory more precious than gold.

For one clear, sweet moment, Ariel had needed him.

She had trusted him. She'd seemed so fragile, so heartbreakingly vulnerable that he had wanted to hold off the world for her.

She'd accepted the comfort he'd offered her as if he were a normal man. For a moment he had been able to forget that he was not.

He longed to howl at the moon with his frustration, with his regret, because he'd forgotten also why she'd been brought to Fountainhead.

That was a mistake he could not afford to make.

The next morning, Ariel dragged herself out of bed when what she really wanted to do was to snuggle back under the covers and sleep all day. There wasn't time for that, though. She had to drive into Farley to get her shopping done before the shops closed at noon so that she could be back here in time to pack and check out. What barbarian had come up with an eleven o'clock checkout hour anyway?

Thirty minutes later, she silently agreed with Jonah—Farley was definitely a small town. Actually, Ariel thought as she parked her car on the main street and got out, the place was more a village than a town, having maybe twenty streets in all.

Tidy clapboard buildings lined First Street. She

could see at a glance that this was Farley's financial, business, and shopping districts all rolled into one. She could also see that the residents took pride in their town. Jewel-colored clouds of begonias, petunias, and impatiens filled window boxes. Sidewalks and porches had been swept. The glass in windows and doors sparkled. Here and there park benches had been set in the shade of the graceful potted trees.

Ariel went into the drugstore, and the bell above the door tinkled cheerfully. She smiled at the man behind the counter, who looked up from unpacking bottles of after-shave and placing them in the display case. He appeared to be about fifty years old. Gray touched his faded auburn hair at each temple.

The man gave Ariel an answering smile. "May I help you with anything?"

"I'm just stocking up," Ariel told her.

The man laughed. "Stocking up, huh? You must be from Fountainhead." He offered his hand. "I'm Howard Adams."

Ariel took his hand and shook it. "Ariel Denham. *The* Adams of Adams Pharmacy?"

Howard Adams spread his arms wide as if to embrace the entire store. "The one and only. I'm usually the pharmacist only, but my daughter—she's my clerk—is running late. Her son is teething and he's giving her such a fit, the little demon." From the man's beaming expression, Ariel knew that the little demon was the apple of his eye. "So, if you need any help, just let me know."

"Thank you." Still smiling, Ariel went off in search of the items on her list. She stifled a yawn. She wouldn't get here often, so she needed to make certain she bought everything she'd need for at least the next month.

By the time she'd worked her way to the bottom of her list, she'd nearly filled the basket she'd picked up at the door.

As she stood in the checkout line, she noticed a few curious glances from the other patrons. Not unusual when one was a stranger in a small town. Finally, it was her turn.

"Sorry about the wait," Howard said. "Usually it's not a problem."

Ariel said good-naturedly, "Usually you have help."

Howard nodded. "That's true. Did you find everything all right?"

"Yes, and lots of other things not on my list. Your store is extremely well stocked."

He beamed at the compliment. "I try. We do a lot of business with the people who work at Fountainhead, so I make an effort to keep the things they ask for. You know, like a certain brand of candy bar, or a particular shade of lipstick. A wide array of stuff for contact lens wearers."

Ariel began emptying the contents of her basket onto the counter. "So you see quite a few people from Fountainhead?"

Howard rang up a package of dental floss. "I'd say so."

Ariel's fingers paused over a bottle of shampoo in the basket. "Do many Fountainhead patients come here?"

"A few. Not many, though. Most prefer to use our

delivery service. It's something we offer the patients because, well, because most of them don't want to go out into public."

A box of tissues followed the shampoo onto the old laminated counter. "Does Jonah come here?" she asked casually, trying to look as if she were interested in the moisturizer or the plastic shower cap still left in the basket.

"Jonah?" Howard sounded puzzled.

"He's a patient at Fountainhead. But I thought he might be one of the patients who come here."

"What's his last name?"

Annoyance flashed through Ariel. Darn that man. "I don't know."

Slowly Howard shook his head. "Sorry I can't help you. Jonah is an old-fashioned name. Kinda unusual. I'd remember it, I'm sure. I haven't done business with him."

Despite her disappointment, Ariel noticed that two more customers had stepped into line behind her, so she unloaded her remaining items. Howard promptly totaled the purchase.

The next stop was the grocery store, where Ariel loaded up for the coming month. No more vending machines for her, she thought as she rolled her shopping cart down the snack and cookie aisle. She also stocked up on fruits and vegetables, pasta, frozen dinners, and frozen yogurt. She bought ice for the ice chest she'd brought, mindful of the trip back to Fountainhead.

The clerk claimed to know nothing of a Fountainhead patient named Jonah, last name unknown. Not surprising, Ariel thought as she settled the frozen items into the ice-filled chest. How would a grocery store clerk know him, when Jonah refused even to leave the shadows?

All the way back to The Black Tupelo, Ariel considered possibilities, but common sense kept returning her to two possible conclusions. The first one was that Jonah had not given her his real name. Maybe Jonah was the name he'd use only as long as he was at Fountainhead.

She sighed as she turned into the inn's main drive. The second possibility—the one she was inclined to believe—was that he'd visited Farley before his disfigurement and been intrigued by the town, especially the old mansion. If he'd stayed even one night, he would have met Beryl, but not necessarily anyone else in town. Maybe. Maybe. Maybe.

After Ariel packed, she made arrangements for Beryl's nephew to take her luggage to her car. Meanwhile, she went downstairs to check out.

"I hope you enjoyed your stay with us," Beryl said as she slid the folio across the marble countertop toward Ariel for her approval.

"Yes, very much." Ariel scanned the charges, then nodded as she smothered a yawn. She returned the bill to Beryl. "Perhaps you'd tell me something."

"Certainly." Beryl tore the guest copy from the three-part form.

"Do you know a man named Jonah?"

Beryl stiffened. She stared at Ariel, the separated guest folio forgotten in her hand. "What is his last name?" she asked.

Ariel studied the older woman. "I don't know it."

"I'm sorry, I don't know anyone by that name," Beryl said, a little too quickly.

And pigs can fly, Ariel thought. Beryl should stick to the truth; she made a really lousy liar. Another thought occurred to Ariel: Had the others been lying, too?

She directed a bland look at the hotel manager. "Really? I guess I misunderstood him. My mistake." She smiled. "Well, good-bye."

As she drove the winding mountain road back to Fountainhead Valley, she replayed her conversations with the pharmacist and the clerk. They might have told the truth. Or maybe not. But Beryl Jenkins definitely had lied.

Ariel decided that if she was going to discover anything about Jonah, she must start at the most logical place: The Black Tupelo.

Her conscience gave her a momentary twinge. It was clear that Jonah didn't want her to know about him. The noble thing to do would be to respect his wishes.

But she wasn't noble. Neither was Jonah for that matter. And she was tired of playing by his rules.

Ariel arrived back at her bungalow a little past one o'clock, and put away the groceries. She'd just stretched out on the bed to take a nap when the phone rang with a call summoning her to the hospital. One of her patients had fallen and rebroken the nose she had just fixed, as well as tearing open a myriad of painstakingly placed sutures.

By the time she left the hospital, Ariel felt as if

she'd been on a forced march for two days. She didn't bother to stop in the cafeteria to eat dinner, never mind the lunch she'd missed. Instead, she went directly to her quarters and fell onto the bed. After setting the alarm to wake her in time for her walk with Jonah, Ariel closed her eyes and plummeted into sleep.

Jonah stood at the azalea hedge. He looked up at the moon, which was already high in the night sky. Where was Ariel? She was more than an hour late.

Since last night he had looked forward to seeing her again, even knowing that there might be an awkward moment or two between them. After all, she had revealed a secret fear to him. He had held her in his arms. They had kissed.

Jonah couldn't recall ever before having experienced that powerful mixture of wonder, protectiveness, and raw carnal need that had surged through him when Ariel's lips had parted for him. It had been so long since a woman had wanted to be close to him.

Ariel had wanted to touch him, and he had reveled in that discovery. She had pressed close to him, and the breath had strangled in his throat. Hot blood had pounded through his veins.

It had all come crashing to an end when she'd tried to touch his face, the simple gesture of a woman with her lover. But he had not responded in a loverlike way.

Where was she? The moon had begun its descent

and she still wasn't here. A cold knot twisted inside him.

She wasn't coming.

After one last fruitless look through the space in the hedge, Jonah began to walk, heading farther into the park.

Of course, he was glad she'd decided to end their time together. Damned glad. It was the smart thing to do.

He gathered speed. His long legs stretched out to eat up the distance until sweat rolled down his ribs. His lungs pumped like a bellows and his breath sounded harsh in his own ears. Faster and faster he ran. He'd work loose this damn pain. It was nothing. Nothing. He cared nothing.

Ariel woke to find the first light of morning illuminating her bedroom. Disoriented, she fumbled for the alarm clock. She'd set it to wake her in time for her walk with Jonah. Struggling up in bed, she flopped back against the headboard and examined the clock.

The alarm had gone off. Ariel frowned. How could that be? She'd never slept through an alarm.

But then, it had been a long time since she'd been as exhausted as she was yesterday. She'd been up all the night before, her emotions set at high charge. Then she'd come back to Fountainhead, where she'd been greeted by emergency surgery. Dear lord! The clock rolled out of her hands, onto the blankets.

Jonah.

He had expected her. She'd told him she would

meet him for their walk. Had he waited for her at the hedge?

She threw the covers aside and ran through the house to the French doors. She flung them open. Still clad in her nightgown, she crossed the terrace, the flagstones damp with dew and rough under her bare feet.

The park was shrouded in gray mist. Here and there a tall tree rose above the curtain. She saw nothing moving, nothing the size and shape of a man.

Reluctantly, she withdrew into the house and closed the glass-paned doors. "Oh, Jonah," she murmured, filled with regret. She could imagine what had gone through his mind. And it wasn't true! She'd intended to meet him. She'd meet him now if there was any way.

But there wasn't. She had no way to contact him.

She sighed and scraped her hair back, away from her face. The kimono sleeve of her gown fell to her upraised elbow, baring her arm. She caught sight of her pale wrist.

Two nights ago, when Jonah had caught her wrist, preventing her from touching his face, his grasp had been firm enough that she'd expected to find a bruise the next day, but the skin had remained smooth and fair. Even in his moment of fierce distress, he had not harmed her.

When she'd failed to meet him for their evening walk, after their evening together, after their kiss, had she hurt him?

Slowly she walked back to her bedroom and began to get ready for work.

Thirty minutes later, Ariel entered the hospital and

headed toward her office. "Good morning," Doris sang, falling into step with her. "How was your weekend away from home?"

Ariel managed a smile. "Interesting."

"You stayed at The Black Tupelo, didn't you?" Doris asked. "What did you think? Was it creepy?"

On the receiving end of Doris's cheerfulness, Ariel felt her spirits lighten. "It's really a fascinating old mansion. Full of antiques." She hesitated. "I saw a ghost."

"No!" Doris gave her a look of squint-eyed skepticism. "Really?"

Ariel nodded. "Really."

"Well, don't just stand there, tell me about it!"

Unwilling to think about, much less discuss, the transformation she had experienced, Ariel concentrated instead on the story of the lovers, and told her friend what she had seen.

"You're kidding!" Doris accused, her eyes wide.

Ariel sketched an imaginary X over her chest. "Cross my heart, it's the truth."

"In the *bathtub?* I thought all those Victorians were stuffy and proper."

"Have you ever seen any of the books of their erotica? The Victorians were sensualists. Even the strait-laced ladies surrounded themselves with fine linen and lace, and scented creams."

Doris grinned. "I feel as if I've been missing out on something wonderful. I'll just have to make a reservation for the weekend at The Black Tupelo."

"Don't miss out on Beryl's tea," Ariel advised. "She makes the most wonderful little bonbons. And everything is served on delicate china, with ornate silver utensils. It's really quite lovely."

"The Black Tupelo sounds as if it's a perfect get-away for lovers." Doris waited while Ariel unlocked her office door. "I wish I had one."

Ariel fingers jerked and she dropped her key. "Yes," she mumbled, bending to retrieve it. A lover. "Don't we all."

She opened the door. There on her desk, in the crystal vase, stood a single perfect rose.

It was a clear medium pink and its numerous satiny petals were cupped and slightly globular. Its leaves were dark green.

"Aloha," said a voice behind them. Ariel turned to see Kerwin standing there. She didn't know how he'd managed to get her roses past locked doors, but she'd stopped worrying about it weeks ago. She'd come to know Kerwin as an honorable man. If it gave him plea-sure to play this little game, she would play, too. She smiled at him. Besides, she enjoyed receiving the roses.

"Aloha to you, too," Doris said.

He smiled and shook his head. "Aloha is the name of the rose. It's a climbing hybrid tea, you know."

"No, I didn't know that," Ariel said. The gorgeous flower is what impressed her.

"The bloom has a strong fragrance for a hybrid tea," Kerwin went on. He squeezed by the two women and sniffed the bloom.

Each of them, in turn, dutifully sniffed and agreed with the anesthesiologist.

"I read somewhere that Aloha means good-bye as well as hello," Doris said. "I think that's strange, don't you?"

"Maybe it's considered bad luck to say good-bye," Kerwin offered, his gaze fixed on the rose.

"Are you ready?" Ariel asked him. "We have Michael this morning." This would be the first of a series of operations on the child. Ariel viewed it as the initial step toward a better life for him.

"Ready, able, and willing," Kerwin answered. He cast a shy glance at Doris and quickly looked back at Ariel.

Ariel checked the clock on the wall above her desk. "Let's get going."

The operation went smoothly, though Ariel found that the damage was slightly more extensive than she'd expected. It looked to her as if there had been infection that had either been left unattended for a while, or perhaps the patient had not responded quickly to whatever treatment he'd been given. Understandable, considering what shape he must have been in at the time.

As she worked, at the back of her mind she held an image of Michael with a relatively smooth face, smiling. She set a graft in place on his forehead, wishing the research laboratories would perfect the artificial skin they'd experimented with for so many years. As well as she could, she'd matched the texture of the graft to the skin surrounding the site, but her experienced eyes told her it wasn't perfect.

When she finished, she looked down at her patient, and refocused on him as a child, as Michael. Under the effects of the anesthesia, he lay unnaturally still. His narrow chest rose and fell with regularity. The undamaged side of his face possessed a cherubic beauty.

"It seemed to go well," Kerwin commented as they scrubbed their hands a few minutes later.

"Yes," Ariel agreed. She reached for a paper towel. "If his body accepts the graft, if the graft attaches, if the vessels grow . . ."

He pulled the loose blue shirt over his head and tossed it into a hamper. "You aren't God, Ariel. You're only a surgeon—an excellent surgeon, admittedly, but still a long way from divinity."

She squeezed a dab of hand cream into her palm and began massaging it into the chapped skin. "There are those who believe we consider ourselves gods."

"Huh. You mean like Renard?" Kerwin's tone held amusement. "There are those who believe Elvis is alive and well and living in the Amazon forest. That doesn't make it true."

Ariel kept her back turned to the anesthesiologist, who, in turn, politely kept his back to her as they changed clothes.

She grinned. "The Amazon forest? I thought he'd last been spotted working at a Dairy Queen in Mobile." She pulled on a fresh set of scrubs.

Kerwin laughed. "Who can keep track? The guy has moved around more since he died than when he was alive."

The rest of the day was spent between operating rooms, recovery, and making the rounds to check on her patients' progress.

She took her dinner in the cafeteria, then went back to her bungalow, where she put on her walking clothes. She began to mark time. Would Jonah be at their rendezvous place tonight?

Gradually, her nerves wound tighter and tighter. She couldn't concentrate on the article in her journal. Trying to plow through her stack of correspondence proved hopeless.

The telephone jangled loudly, shattering the quiet. Even as she caught herself hoping it was Jonah, she knew that it was not.

"Hello, Ariel," her father said.

"Hi, Dad!"

"Whatever happened to 'daddy'?" he objected jovially.

Ariel's excitement plummeted. Whenever Gerald Denham went into his "daddy" mode he wanted something. She should have known.

"How are you doing?" she asked cautiously, trying to suppress her disappointment.

"Me? Oh, fine, fine. I was calling to see how *you* were doing? What is Fountainhead like? Is it nice?"

"It's nice."

"Good, good. I'm glad you like it there. See? I knew this would work out for the best."

Bitterness welled up in Ariel, nearly choking her.

He didn't seem to notice her silence. "It will be good experience for you," he went on. "It will look good on your résumé. So, how are you feeling?"

"Fine," she said. She knew better than to tell him something he didn't want to hear. He'd only get upset, then find some way to twist her words around to make her sound ungrateful.

"Now aren't you glad you listened to your old dad? You've got a secure position that has benefits and pays you on time. They do pay you on time, don't they?"

So that was why he was calling. Money.

The old familiar hurt returned, filling her with a hollow ache. Always, she hoped . . . "Yeah," she said dully. "They pay me on time."

He cleared his throat. "Well, I was wondering if I could borrow three hundred dollars. Just to tide me over to my next paycheck, you understand."

Gerald's own paycheck was generous. Ariel knew this because it had been a stipulation in the terms of her signing of her own contract.

"You know, Dad, you never needed to take that job in the first place." Numerous times she had offered to support him. At what she was making before, she could have provided nicely for them both.

"I want my own life," he said impatiently. "I've told you that before. I need a little help getting on my feet right now, that's all. But a man doesn't want to be dependent on his daughter. I just need a little loan."

"I'll put a check in the mail to you tomorrow," she said.

"I appreciate that."

She didn't want to talk any more about this latest request for money. "How do you like your new job?" she asked. "Are you learning the ropes easily?"

"Ropes?" Gerald echoed sharply. "There's so much rope to this job I wouldn't be surprised to find the previous manager hung himself just to be free of it. That damn Renard certainly expects a lot for his money. Slave wages, that's what he pays," he declared indignantly. "No one could get all this work done. It's impossible."

Ariel's fingers tightened on the telephone handset. "I'm sorry to hear that," she said.

Would her father never be satisfied? She'd sold herself for a year, given up a once-in-a-lifetime opportunity to get him that job—the job of his dreams, he'd told her. The job he had to have, or she was no daughter of his.

Suddenly she realized she was angry at her father. So angry that her muscles were bunched into knots in her arms and shoulders. Horrified, she immediately tried to deny her feelings.

"That just goes to show how wrong you can be about someone," Gerald fumed. "That bastard Renard. He sure had me fooled. I thought he was a good man, but he's nothing but a con artist."

Ariel latched onto that name. Renard. Yes, all of this was *his* fault. He was responsible for this whole mess, not Gerald Denham. Her father had merely wanted a good job. That's what Renard had promised him. But look what had been delivered, and at what cost.

"I'm sorry you don't like your job, Dad. Maybe it will get easier when you've been there a while and know more," she said soothingly.

"Are you insinuating that I'm ignorant?" he demanded. "That I don't know an impossible work load when I'm faced with one?"

"No, not that—"

"I should hope not." His voice softened. "You're all I have, Kitten. You're the only one I can count on."

Ariel tried to swallow around the lump in her throat. He was right, of course.

Before they said good-bye, he reminded her to send the check.

By the time she dropped the handset into its cradle, Ariel felt as if her emotions had been put through a mangler. She looked at her watch. An hour until she went into the park. An hour until she could be with Jonah. The prospect brought a smile to her lips. Her heart lightened. Somehow, she was certain he would understand about the confused emotions her father always stirred up in her.

Not that she planned to tell Jonah. The subject was much too personal. It was bad enough that she'd spilled her guts to him about her fear of the dark. Worse, she'd cried. God, she'd lost all control.

But instead of the contempt she'd expected, he'd given her comfort. He'd held her in his arms, trying to shield her from her fears.

Then he'd kissed her.

Ariel closed her eyes for a moment, remembering.

When the time finally arrived, Ariel flew out the French doors and across the terrace. Down the grassy knoll, she sped, slowing to ease through the hedge.

No one was there. She stood still for a moment, hoping to sense Jonah nearby, as she'd so often done. Tonight his presence eluded her.

"Jonah?" she called softly. "Jonah, are you there?"

Her only answer was the soft sad call of a chuck-will's-widow.

"Jonah," she tried again. But she knew that, after she hadn't shown up last night, he might have decided to go on, to stop meeting her at the hedge. Her pace quickened. "Jonah, if you're there, wait up."

She completed the circuit they usually made together, calling his name frequently. At first she was hopeful, but as the distance grew, her hope dwindled. While she walked alone through the moonlit park, she recalled what he'd told her the night she'd discovered him running. *This place is haunted.*

This whole mountain range must be haunted, she thought. Too clearly she remembered the ghosts making love in the bathtub. Despite the warm evening air, Ariel shivered. She wished she could find Jonah. In a low-pitched, urgent voice, she resumed calling his name.

By the time she came back to the space in the hedge, her feet moved heavily. Disappointment weighed on her. Jonah had not shown up for their walk.

She stood there a moment, listening to the burbling water of the stream, wishing for a miracle to guide him to her. After a few minutes, she slipped back through the hedge.

Who could blame him? she thought miserably. He'd kissed her, and the next thing he knew she was standing him up. It didn't take a psychiatrist to guess what must have gone through his mind when she didn't show. Tonight she had a pretty good idea.

7

Ariel handed Doris a glass of wine, then picked up her own glass and the platter containing crackers, cheese, and an apple. She led the way through the living room to the wrought-iron table and chairs on the terrace.

"Boy," Doris said, "the powers that be must really think a lot of you. This is a great place. And what a view!" She sipped her wine.

Ariel looked out over the parkland, to the deep forest beyond. Jonah had walked miles through that forest to get to her at The Black Tupelo. Just to tell her an outrageous story and guide her through the lovely but eerie old mansion. With him she'd seen ghosts and revealed a dark, mortifying secret. With him, she'd shared passion.

Doris harrumphed loudly. "I said, they must want you to renew your contract very badly."

"I'm sorry. I didn't hear you. Robert Maitland did say something about that when he showed me around on my first day." She gestured toward the chair closest to Doris. "Please, make yourself comfortable and have something to eat."

They sat and kicked off their shoes.

"This is such a beautiful valley," Doris said dreamily. "So serene." She picked up a cracker. "Owls live in the tree outside my bedroom window. I like to listen to them at night."

Ariel smiled as she spread Camembert on a slice of apple. "Yes, it is lovely here."

Doris sighed contentedly.

Ariel remembered that Jonah had answered an owl shortly after she'd arrived. *Whooo do you think?* It was the first evidence she'd seen that he had a lighter-hearted side to him than the somber, cynical one she'd seen.

"Hello in there? Is anyone home?" Doris asked.

Ariel blinked. "I don't know what is the matter with me. What did you say?"

"Don't worry about it." Doris leaned forward, closely examining Ariel's face. "You know, you have two very dark circles under your eyes, m'dear. Are you having trouble sleeping?"

Ariel lowered her gaze to her wine. Absently, she moved the glass around and around in a circle. "Maybe just a little."

"Is everything all right with your work?"

She looked up to see concern in her friend's eyes. "Yes. Yes, everything is fine."

"Could it be the change in altitude? You know, a sort of delayed reaction?"

Ariel wanted to tell Doris what was really bothering her. It might feel good to pour her heart out to someone. But a lifetime of learning the hard way to keep her own counsel cautioned her against confiding. It was bad enough that she had blubbered her most embarrassing secret to Jonah. If that ever got around, she'd find herself extremely embarrassed, but that was the worst that could happen. If it got out that Jonah was running in the park, Maitland would stop him, and Jonah would lose something he treasured. Ariel couldn't chance that.

"Probably the combination of all this fresh mountain air and the cafeteria's meat loaf."

Doris chuckled. "Could be. Don't let this go, though, okay? If it continues, have it checked." She grinned. "See a doctor."

Ariel laughed. "I'll do that."

Twenty minutes later, Doris wished Ariel a good night and left. Ariel cleaned up the dishes and glasses, but returned to the terrace to watch the last streaks of purple and pink in the sky darken into night.

Thoughts of Jonah had haunted her all day. It had never occurred to her before how many memories they shared. She'd never realized that slowly, quietly, she'd come to care for him. She cringed inside whenever she thought about him standing there alone at the hedge.

Oh, she knew there was a chance that two nights ago he hadn't shown up either, but she doubted that. Ariel stood on the terrace a moment, her arms folded across her chest. A breeze caught at her hair, teasing a tendril loose from her single braid. No, she felt certain that Jonah had come to the hedge and waited for her. Now she must find him and explain.

When she entered the park, her heart fell. There was no sign of Jonah. Taking a deep breath, she rolled back her shoulders and set off.

As she strode along she called his name in a loud whisper. A voice at the back of her mind told her that even if he heard her, he would refuse to answer. He'd had the good sense to put a stop to their meetings. After all, he'd be eager to leave Fountainhead by the time his surgery was complete. She'd be a mere sentence in a chapter of his life he'd be all too ready to forget, just as Patrick had forgotten Vickie.

Vickie Granfield and Ariel had served their residency together, and had grown to be sisters in spirit. Then Vickie had fallen deeply in love with a badly scarred patient, an army officer who'd taken shrapnel in his face. After several operations, she had restored Patrick's face enough for him to lead a normal life again.

First he'd stopped calling Vickie. Then he'd stopped writing her. His answering machine's recorded tape was as close as Vickie could get to hearing his voice, and her desperate letters were returned unopened. Through the grapevine she had learned that he was seeing someone new, and she'd never been the same after that.

His abandonment had destroyed Vickie.

But despite the logic of going back to her bungalow and forgetting Jonah, Ariel continued walking, calling his name.

He staggered to a stop when he heard the sound. He stood there, panting, damp with sweat, as he listened. Every cell in his body strained to pick up that vibration again.

"Jonah!"

His head jerked in the direction of the voice. It was Ariel.

She was trying to find him.

He wanted to run to her as fast as he could, but he knew he should stay where he was, keeping his silence until she gave up and went home. That would be the smartest course.

"Jo-naah!"

He headed toward her voice, restraining himself to a dignified walk. That lasted for three steps. Then he broke into an all-out, leg-stretching run, tearing through the shadows beneath the trees.

He saw her standing on the path. One of her white socks drooped around an ankle. Locks of her hair waved in the breeze. She'd never looked more beautiful to him.

"What are you trying to do?" he said gruffly. "Wake up the whole valley?"

She gasped and spun around to search the shadows. She took two steps in his direction, then halted. "Jonah." Her lips seemed to imbue his name with a soft magic.

He wanted to hold her, to wrap her in his arms and never let her go. With a will, he kept his hands at his sides. He reminded himself that she'd hurt him. It had been years since he'd allowed anyone close enough to do that.

"Jonah . . . I . . ."

He maintained his silence.

She tried again. "I wanted you to know . . ."

"Yes?" he asked politely.

Ariel drew in a deep breath. "The other night I didn't meet you for our walk."

"Really?"

"You're not making this easy."

"Should I?"

Her eyes widened. Quickly, she turned her face away. "I slept through the alarm. I didn't get much sleep the night before. When I got back to the clinic, I walked into an emergency situation."

"What kind of emergency situation?"

"One of my patients fell. He'd gone through surgery less than forty-eight hours before and his fall did quite a lot of damage." She sighed.

"You had to operate?"

"Yes."

"Is he going to be all right?"

She looked in his direction, and, if he didn't know better, Jonah would have thought she could see him. That uneasy thought prompted him to step farther back in the shadows.

"I believe so," she said.

Everything sounded so logical that Jonah's anger began to lose its steam.

"And you slept through your alarm."

Her mouth tightened. "That's what I said."

His conscience nipped at him. He hadn't wanted to go to their meeting place at the hedge again; he had not been able to stay away. Jonah's mouth twisted into a bitter facsimile of a smile.

She plucked at the small pocket in her shorts. "I came out last night, but you never showed up. I thought you might have gone back to the schedule you seemed to be keeping before we started walking together. So I came out later tonight."

Silence drifted in to separate them. For a moment they stood there, each in his own place—Jonah in the shadows, Ariel in the moonlight.

He had reacted strongly when she had failed to meet him. Too strongly. Jonah's gut knotted with the realization of what that meant. From now on, he'd have to be more careful. Exercise better judgment.

With a sweep of his arm, he indicated the path that stretched before them. "Do you wish to continue?"

Ariel felt certain that Jonah hadn't meant to make any confessions. And as confessions went, his out-of-breath respiration rate, his short, sharp questions, and the way he was keeping his distance weren't definitive, but their meaning was clear enough.

Jonah cared about her.

She felt as if she were glowing inside, all bright energy and soaring light. Words deserted her as she stared at him, easily picking his form out in the shadows. Proud, stubborn Jonah.

"It's getting late," he pointed out, his voice possessing an unusual roughness. "I'll see you back to the hedge."

Ariel started walking, wondering that she didn't

feel the ground beneath her feet. She tried to tell herself that she was being silly. "Are our walks back on?"

"If you like."

His apparent unconcern pricked her, but failed to deflate her euphoria.

"You'll meet me at the hedge at the usual time," he said casually. Then, a little less casually: "Right?"

"If you like."

There was a pause. "I like," he said softly.

Ariel didn't even try to hide her smile as she looked at him. Filtered moonlight formed a faint nimbus around him, exposing slight waves in his longish hair, outlining the breadth of his shoulders, the narrowness of his hips, the muscular conformation of arms and legs as he strode the darkness beneath the trees.

He turned his head, and the beauty of his profile pierced her with its sad cruelty. It mocked the disfigured flesh Jonah tried so hard to conceal, the face that drove him to live in a dark world.

But that would soon change, she reminded herself. He would undergo the series of operations to transform him. Then he would leave Fountainhead.

Quickly she shunted the thought away. She didn't want to think of that.

"Is Jonah your real name?" she asked.

He turned his head to look at her. "I told you my name is Jonah."

"That doesn't answer my question."

"It damned well should."

"So you're saying Jonah *is* your name?"

"I don't lie, Ariel."

She nodded. "What is your last name?"

He expelled a harsh sigh of impatience. "We've been through this already. Jonah is enough."

Oh, really? "Why?"

A feminine giggle sounded from ahead of them on the path. It was followed by a masculine voice, though the words were indistinguishable to Ariel.

"What—?" she began indignantly, then remembered that neither she nor Jonah was supposed to be in the park, either. Instantly she scurried under the umbrella of the trees, taking cover behind the rough column of a trunk. When she looked around, she discovered she was alone. Jonah had vanished.

A man and a woman strolled down the path, speaking to one another in soft tones. They stopped almost in front of Ariel's hiding place, and she cursed her bad luck. Didn't these people pay attention to Foundation rules?

The woman reached up and plucked a leaf from the tree next to the one that concealed Ariel.

Ariel set her teeth in frustration. No one would ever call her Lucky Ariel.

When the woman turned back to the man and spoke to him, Ariel made her escape. As quietly as she could, she dashed through the shadows. As she rounded a bend, she stumbled and nearly fell when the toe of her shoe caught a gnarled root. Regaining her balance, she staggered to a stop. For a moment she bent forward at the waist, palms pressed against her thighs, and dragged in a lungful of sweet mountain air.

"It's disgraceful the way people ignore rules around here." Jonah clucked his disapproval. "A crying shame."

Ariel started at his voice. She glared at him, but she doubted he could see. "And just where did you disappear to?"

In what Ariel thought must be a creditable Transylvanian accent he said, "Every twenty-four hours I must return to my native soil."

"Would you cut the vampire humor?" she asked, shifting her weight from one foot to the other. "It's not all that funny and, frankly, I find it a little . . ." Her voice died as she realized how ridiculous what she'd been about to say sounded.

"You find it a little what?" he prompted. She could hear the grin in his voice.

She answered his question in a mutter.

"Speak up, Dr. Denham."

She looked away, trying to think up a nice lie, something that would do her credit, something that would make her sound less foolish.

"Ariel?"

"Creepy. Okay? Happy? It's *creepy* when you pretend to be a vampire."

She felt like an idiot.

Embarrassment burned her cheeks as she waited for him to laugh. Wind sighed through the boughs of the ancient hickories. A dark cloud trailed across the moon, dimming its radiance.

"Who said I was pretending?" he asked softly.

Ariel didn't know which was worse: her fertile imagination or his bizarre sense of humor. "Of course you're pretending," she insisted. But her chuckle sounded as hollow as her amusement. After all, Jonah seemed to come out only at night. He'd covered the mirrors when he'd given her the tour of The Black Tupelo. He refused to meet her at all during the full moon.

Wait a minute. Full moons were when werewolves transformed, not vampires. Ariel clenched her teeth as she considered her own stupidity. The very idea of Jonah being a vampire *or* a werewolf was ludicrous.

"There are no vampires," she declared stoutly.

"Just as there are no ghosts?"

Blood drained from Ariel's face.

His smoky golden voice said, "'There are more things in heaven and earth, Horatio, than are dreamt of in your philosophy.'"

She nervously twisted a stray wisp of hair around her forefinger. "So you're saying you *are* a vampire?"

"Did I say that?"

"No, but—"

"Really, Ariel. Such an imagination." He shook his head. "Someday it will get you in trouble."

"It's already gotten me in trouble," she muttered.

"What?"

She cleared her throat and in a slightly louder voice told him, "I said you've really broken my bubble."

He began to walk, and she fell into step with him, separated from him only by shadow and a couple of yards of lawn.

"How disappointed you must feel." His words rumbled with his amusement.

She thought of how he'd called encouragement to her as he'd worked his way across the pitch-dark cellar. How he'd held her as if he were determined to keep her fear at bay. And later, how he'd kissed her.

"No," she said. "I'm not disappointed, Jonah."

She longed to give him the encouragement he had given her, but she sensed he wasn't ready to accept it. Not yet.

Before she could think of anything to say to bridge the awkward silence between them, they arrived at the space in the hedge.

She turned to Jonah. "Here we are."

He seemed to be staring at his feet. "So. We meet tomorrow?"

She nodded emphatically. "Right. Absolutely. The usual time."

"Good." He shifted his shoulders, as if their muscles had drawn uncomfortably tight. "Well."

She waited for him to make the first move.

"I'll see you tomorrow then." He took a step backward, apparently getting ready to leave.

Wrong move. Wrong direction.

Ariel knew she was going to have to take matters into her own hands. She swallowed dryly. "Jonah, would you please kiss me?"

He stopped in his tracks. "What?" he asked, as if he couldn't believe what he'd just heard.

"Would you please kiss me?" It came more easily the second time.

"Ariel." His voice was a croak.

"Yes, Jonah?"

"I don't think that's such a good idea."

She eased a short step toward him. "I do."

"No."

"Just a small kiss." She took another step, careful to keep her gaze focused on his throat. "We'll keep it short." A third step. "And very"—another step—"sweet."

She didn't know who crossed the distance between them. All that mattered was that she was in his arms, feeling his heart pounding against hers, his arms hard around her. She closed her eyes and lifted her face.

His lips strummed across hers, as soft as a mystical sigh, leaving a tingling trail of sparks.

The edges of Ariel's reality grew misty as other sensations swept in. The warm, lean solidity of his body pressed against hers. His fingertips tight against her scalp. The uneven clamor of his breathing. The earthy perfume of rain-swept earth and foliage mingled with the heated musk of healthy male.

He put her from him, holding her upper arms. She felt a tremor pass through his hands, heard him draw in a deep, sharp breath. She barely managed to keep her eyes closed.

"Jonah?"

"Don't ask this of me again, Ariel."

"But—"

"Just don't."

Pride rose up in her, pushing aside her humiliation. She stepped back. His fingers hesitated before they released her. She took another step and opened her eyes, staring at his left shoulder.

"I'm sorry you find kissing me such an unpleasant ordeal," she said stiffly.

He gave a short bark of humorless laughter. "Is that what you think? That I find kissing you *unpleasant?*"

"Then why?"

"Because it's unwise. Because— Ariel, please. Honor my request."

She turned to leave, but stopped. She didn't look

back at him. "All right, Jonah. I'll honor your request."

Ariel pushed past the leaves and branches and ran up the slope to her bungalow. She closed the French doors with a resounding thud.

Damn him. Damn, damn, damn him.

In the bathroom, she wrenched on hot water for a shower. As the room filled with steam, she tried to calm her rocketing emotions and regain her reason.

She had no business damning Jonah. He already lived in hell. Besides, he wasn't the one acting foolishly.

She was the doctor. Jonah was a patient. Soon his body would be called upon to perform the miracle of healing. The last thing he needed was stress.

She wished his surgeon would get started. Once the operations began, running in the park would be out of the question for Jonah.

The thought of not walking with Jonah, not hearing his voice or even seeing his shadowy form filled her with a yearning emptiness. Ruthlessly, she tried to push the feeling aside. What was the holdup on Jonah's surgery, anyway? she thought savagely.

Ariel quickly finished undressing and stepped under the hot spray. She slapped a glob of shampoo into her wet hair and mercilessly worked the lather through.

Jonah was one hundred percent correct in not wanting to become emotionally involved with her. As she rinsed her hair, she reflected on her transgression. She found it humiliating that she, a doctor, had so completely lost her professional distance. Never before had that happened to her.

She'd make certain it did not happen again.

8

The following evening, Ariel opened the door to Michael's room to find Lucy keeping vigil. Infection had sent the child's temperature soaring early in the morning, but antibiotics and cooling ice baths had brought it under control. His fever had broken an hour ago.

Ariel automatically checked his pulse, then, assured that it remained within normal limits, smoothed the sleeping boy's silky hair. So young to have already gone through so much.

She smiled at a tired-looking Lucy. "I thought I'd find you here. Did you have dinner?"

The nurse shook her head. "No. I didn't want to leave him alone."

"Why don't you go get something to eat? I'll stay with him until you get back."

"Okay. Thanks." Lucy pushed herself out of the chair and leaned over the still child. She tucked the covers around his narrow shoulders, then slipped silently out the partially open door.

Ariel took the chair Lucy had vacated. Outside it would be twilight now. Here in this room, with the lined drapes drawn, it was dark except for the wedge of light that shone in from the hall.

"You scared us today, scout," she murmured to her small patient. "I think Lucy's been crying."

Michael's only response was a faint sigh as he turned in his sleep.

"I wish your life could always be this peaceful." She dropped her head back against the high, cushioned chair and echoed his sigh.

A tall figure blocked the light in the doorway for a second, then seemed to flow into the dark room.

"Jonah?" she asked, surprised.

He came around to the back of her chair, bracing his hands on the top. "I heard there was a little kid in trouble." His shadow-face was turned toward Michael. "How is he doing?"

"His fever broke about an hour ago. He's sleeping now."

"Will he get better?"

"I believe so. He's responding to medication."

Jonah went to the bed. "He's so small."

"Yes, he is. And he's had a tough life."

She smiled at the angelic side of Michael's face that was turned toward her, careful not to look at Jonah. "He's got the heart of a lion, this one."

Jonah tentatively reached toward the boy, barely

touching Michael's relaxed hand. Childish fingers curled around Jonah's much larger ones.

"He needs a teddy bear," Jonah said in a low, oddly rough voice.

"He has one. It's being cleaned."

"Oh."

Jonah stood by the bed, apparently unwilling to break the anchor of Michael's light grasp. "You said he's had a tough life."

Ariel stretched cramped muscles. "He's endured more than his share of hardship." She checked Michael's temperature. "His mother is responsible for the damage to his face. Afterward she killed herself. The father apparently never was in the picture. His mother's family has kept him in a mental hospital." Ariel still found it difficult to keep her anger down.

"Is there something wrong with his brain?"

"There's been no indication of brain damage."

Jonah remained silent.

"It doesn't seem fair, does it?" she asked. "I believe that there must be people out there who would just love to have a child as sweet-natured as Michael. But he's been written off, stuck in an institution where no one would think to look."

"Do you plan to just fix him up and send him back?" There was a hard edge to Jonah's words.

"No. Lucy and Kerwin and I have already talked to the other members of our medical team. We're going to try to convince Michael's relatives to put him up for adoption."

"Surely his people would be willing at least to do that."

"I don't know, Jonah. From what I can gather, they believe Michael is God's retribution for their having raised a daughter who was a loose woman. They've been hiding him in Chattalogh for years. They're ashamed of what they think he represents."

"That's sick!"

"Guilt isn't ruled by logic." But she could never forgive them for what they'd done to Michael.

Ariel and Jonah fell quiet again, separated by the sleeping boy. Finally Ariel said, "Lucy will be coming back any minute now."

With obvious reluctance, Jonah slipped his fingers from Michael's hold. "I'll see you in a little while," he told Ariel. Then he walked to the door, where he turned. All Ariel could see was his jet black silhouette. "You didn't have to do this, did you?" It was more statement than question.

"Do what?" she asked.

"Stay by Michael."

"No."

Jonah stepped out the door and vanished from her sight.

Later that evening Ariel had a new agenda planned.

"Let's change our route tonight," she suggested.

Jonah stood in the shadows beside the path, a few feet from her. "All right," he said slowly.

She sensed his reluctance. "You know this park better than I do. Why don't you be the guide?"

He turned and headed in the opposite direction, following the line of trees and shrubs. "What prompted this decision?"

She kept pace with him. "I just thought it was time for a change." Something to take their minds off what had happened between them last night. They'd start all over again, only this time she'd remain a doctor so Jonah could remain a patient.

"I see."

"Good," she said, but she doubted he really did see. Not yet.

She smiled at him and chose a neutral subject. "You know, I've been here several weeks, but I've never been over to the patients' quarters. Are they comfortable?" Her smile vanished. Wait a minute. That had come out wrong. Now he might think—

"Are you angling for an invitation?" he asked wryly.

Warmth tinged her cheeks. "Not at all," she assured him. "It's just that I haven't found time to visit that part of the complex yet. Everything in Fountainhead seems to be first-rate, so I assumed the patients' living quarters were, too, but I haven't seen them." She brushed back a nonexistent strand of hair. "I haven't seen the inside of the gym, either, for that matter."

She was almost relieved when he didn't answer. As the heat faded from her face, she turned her attention to their surroundings.

This direction would take them to the edge of the forest, to the wall that encompassed the park and all the Foundation's buildings. Directly ahead of her, the lit path ended. She would be left in the dark. Her tension eased as she passed the last mushroom-shaped lantern, and she found she could see by the moon's light well enough to walk.

"Are you okay, Ariel?" Jonah asked softly.

His concern stroked past the protective barrier she was attempting to maintain, and touched a neediness in her that she abhorred. Instinctively she drew back.

"I'm all right." She smiled stiffly. "Thank you."

She was the physician, the strong one, she reminded herself. *He* was a patient. And she'd better start remembering that.

Ariel could feel his gaze boring into her, and she flushed. "Have you been out this way before? In this direction, I mean." Even to her own ears her voice sounded falsely cheerful.

"Yes." The single word sliced between them like a knife.

She tried again. "It seems you've been all over the park."

"So it seems."

The rough stone wall that encircled the valley towered a dozen yards ahead of them. Here and there a wildflower vine clung to it.

"I wonder how high that thing is," she murmured.

"Twelve feet."

"How do you know?"

"I just know."

How precise he must be, she thought. Maybe he was an architect or an engineer. "Twelve feet. What is it supposed to keep out? The Mongol Hordes?" She glimpsed his shoulder rise and fall in a beam of moonlight, then returned her gaze to the wall. "I wonder if Renard built this."

"Renard? The guy who founded Fountainhead?"

"Yeah." The guy who had blackmailed her into

putting her career on hold for a year. "It seems like the sort of thing he'd do."

"What makes you say that?"

"Oh, come on. A twelve-foot-high stone wall around the base of an entire valley? Having such a thing built is nothing but an ostentatious exercise in power, or, at the very least, a tasteless display of wealth."

They reached the barrier, and Ariel saw that a morning glory vine, its trumpet flowers closed now, had found a toehold in the mortar and stones. Ariel ran her fingertips lightly over the granite. Maybe she was wrong. Standing this close, even at night she could see how time and the elements had weathered the surface. This wall had been standing long before the advent of Fountainhead Clinic.

"You really don't like Renard, do you?" Jonah asked.

She looked at him, at his tall, ink-dark form standing there beneath the last tree in the rampart. "No," she said. "I don't."

"Why? What did he do to you?"

This direction of conversation was getting much too personal, Ariel decided. "I have my reasons."

She turned away, her gaze following the line of the wall. It formed a wide arch over the stream, apparently allowing for spring thaw, when the brook would swell with melted snow from the higher elevations. "I wonder what's on the other side."

"Let's climb over and find out."

She looked up at the top of the wall. "Climb this? Unh-uh. No way." She was a thirty-three-year-old plastic surgeon, not a mountain climber.

"Chicken."

That one word stung her pride as sharply as the flick of a whip. She knew that, after what he'd witnessed, he probably did think she was a coward, and it bothered her.

"Am not," she countered, with a forced attempt at humor.

"Don't you want to see what's on the other side?"

"Of course."

"C'mon," he cajoled. "I'll help you."

She smiled sweetly. "I'll make a deal with you. I'll try to climb over the wall, but if I get hurt, you have to explain to my patients why they have to wait for their operations. Maybe they won't mind too much. After all, most of them have already waited years."

He held up his hands. "I get the point."

To her surprise, he dashed out of his cover and grabbed her hand as he passed. His longer, more powerful legs made it impossible for her to catch all the way up with him. They ran to the arched opening where the wall spanned the stream. He ducked under, and Ariel followed.

She emerged into a ravine. Trees and shrubs and ferns jostled for space. Enormous oaks, yellow poplars, silver bells, and sugar maples populated the deeply cut gorge. Giant hemlocks wept gracefully on the banks of the crystal stream that splashed and sang over mossy rocks. Ariel thought the only thing missing was a host of sparkling fairies.

She slowly turned, trying to take it all in. At that moment she didn't know if the wall she had just squeezed under had been built to keep outsiders from Fountainhead, or the inhabitants of Fountainhead from this magical place.

"What do you think?" Jonah's low voice behind her didn't even startle her.

"It's beautiful," she said simply. She knew mere words would prove inadequate. "Any minute now I expect Titania or Oberon to appear."

He chuckled. "What's a doctor doing reading Shakespeare? Do you believe in magic?"

She looked around her, drinking in the mystical beauty of the place. "I believe in miracles."

The ravine was darker, much darker, than the park. Yet somehow it wasn't. Treetops blocked out much of the moon's light, but that which managed to filter through glimmered on the water, reflected off the myriad droplets of moisture in the air, creating a soft, shifting glow, filled with stygian shadows that seemed to have a life of their own. Ariel knew that, logically, she should be experiencing fear, or at the least, anxiety. Instead, peaceful acceptance settled over her.

Perhaps it was because the events in her own life dimmed in significance when measured against the cove's scale of aeons. Here, even the memory of the ghosts she'd seen took on a curious normality.

"You've been here before," she said. It wasn't a question.

Faint light touched the top of his head as he nodded. The dark hair was ruffled, slightly mussed. Absently Ariel wondered if he'd brushed against the wall as he'd passed under.

"It's one of my favorite places." His head turned,

and she knew he was looking around. "As you pointed out, there's magic here."

"But you weren't going to bring me here."

"No."

She tried to push aside the small hurt his admission brought her. "Why? Because it's a private place for you? A special place?"

"The Black Tupelo is special to me," he said.

And he had shared its secrets with her. He had hiked through the forest at night, had found his way into the house, and shown it to her. Jonah had delighted in bringing the old mansion to life for her.

"Why is the inn special to you?" she asked. Maybe he would give her an answer this time, a clue to the identity of the real Jonah. She caught herself holding her breath.

"You wanted to know why I didn't plan to bring you here," he said.

She sighed. She'd take what she could get. "Yes."

He paused. "You don't like the dark."

"So? Has that ever stopped me from walking with you?"

"No. But this cove is beyond the lanterns. In the past, you've had trouble walking without light."

She longed to reach out and brush her fingers down his upper arm. She wanted the reassurance she found in the subtle swell of his firm muscles, in his warm skin.

"I didn't have any trouble tonight," she pointed out. "The moon seemed to provide enough light." She watched him as she spoke her carefully chosen words. "Or maybe my eyes are just becoming accustomed to the dark."

His head snapped around to face her.

So. He still worried that she could see him. Ariel felt a small stab of disappointment. Why couldn't he accept that his face wasn't that important to her? She'd seen faces more disfigured than his. Here at Fountainhead, she saw them every day.

"I can't see you, Jonah," she assured him. At least not now.

He seemed to relax a little then, the stiffness in the position of his shoulders lessening somewhat.

"Jonah, why won't you let me see you?"

Stony silence met her question.

She tried again. "Jonah, I'm a plastic surgeon."

"I know what you are," he said flatly.

"Then surely you understand that an imperfect face doesn't bother me." But his did. Because it hurt him. Because it drove him into the dark where she couldn't reach him.

"So gratifying to hear," he drawled, his voice hard-edged with sarcasm. "Because you know I'd never want to *bother* you."

"You know what I mean."

His harsh laugh sent a horned owl from its perch. The nocturnal hunter cruised away on silent wings.

"Never fear, good doctor. I know exactly what you mean."

"I doubt you do," Ariel said, her temper rising.

"Oh? Then, by all means, please explain to me what you did mean."

Absently she studied a hemlock. One side of its bottom branches draped out over the water. "I meant that I won't be shocked, if that's what you're worried about."

"How can you be sure?"

"Not being shocked is part of my job." As soon as the words were out of her mouth, Ariel knew she'd said the wrong thing. Jonah's posture grew ramrod straight. She could almost hear his inner fortress doors clang shut as she sensed his withdrawal. Frustration clawed at her. Quickly she tried to clarify her meaning. "After all, I see severe cases many times a day. When I look at a patient, I don't think in terms of ugly or handsome. I analyze and determine which procedures will be most effective in solving his particular problems."

"I'm not your damned patient," Jonah said tightly, anger thrumming through every syllable. "And I'm sure as hell not some jigsaw puzzle for you to *analyze*." He fairly spit the last word.

Miserably, Ariel realized she had only succeeded in making the matter worse by trying to explain. She suspected that anything she said now would only fuel his fury, like pouring gasoline on fire. So instead of replying, she strolled over to the stream. She sat down on a rocky outcrop and untied her shoes.

"What are you doing?" he demanded.

"What does it look like I'm doing?" she asked mildly, allowing him time to cool down. Somewhere in his past, a plastic surgeon had left scars on Jonah that went deeper than skin. He refused to tell her the story, and it was futile to speculate. She knew Jonah would welcome a fight right now, and she was not inclined to oblige him. If he was determined, he'd just have to try harder.

"Is this ravine public land?" she asked as she pried

off her walking shoes and peeled away her socks.

"No. It's owned by the same man who owns everything around here."

"Renard?"

"Yeah."

"That figures." She lowered her feet into the chill rushing water. The current rippled between her toes, causing her to smile with pleasure. "C'mon in," she called. "Get your feet wet." She didn't turn to see if he was still there, but she listened so intently she held her breath. There was only the sound of the water. Then she heard a heavy sigh.

"I'm glad we came here, Jonah," she told him.

When he spoke again, he was at her shoulder, apparently sitting behind her. "I thought you would be," he said softly. His breath stirred the tendrils of hair at her nape. "I think you're just a sucker for beauty." While his words were spoken jokingly, Ariel heard a hidden, faraway note of wistfulness.

She turned her head slightly, not enough to catch sight of him, just enough to let him know that she listened to what he said. "Guess that makes two of us, huh?"

Jonah was closer when he answered her. "Yeah. I guess it does." He lightly touched one of wisps of hair at the back of her neck. She went still, waiting. Hoping.

"When was the last time you sat by a stream and dangled your feet in the water?" he asked, his voice lower, more intimate.

Ariel's breath nearly caught in her throat. Her heart began a crazy tap dance in her chest. "Long ago."

"How old were you?"

"Ten. I was ten." She was afraid he'd hear her struggling to draw enough of the oxygen-rich air into her lungs.

"Were you camping?" he asked.

Would these questions never end? Why didn't he just take her in his arms and kiss her? Dimly she recalled her vow to act more like a physician. Where was her distance? She should pull away now.

"No," she murmured. "I've never been camping. My father and I were on our way to another town where he'd found a job. Our car overheated, and he pulled into a little park at the side of the road. There was a stream. The day was hot."

Jonah moved away from her, and she struggled to swallow her disappointment.

"You've never been camping?" he asked, sounding somewhat incredulous. "You've really missed something. It's great. Tim and I used to go camping a lot."

Immediately Ariel forgot her disappointment. Who was Tim? A friend? A relative? Where did they go camping? Maybe the site was close to Jonah's home.

"Who's Tim?" she asked casually.

He hesitated, and she thought that, once again, he would refuse to answer.

"My kid brother."

Ariel pounced on that crumb of knowledge. His brother. Somehow, the fact that Jonah had a brother, one with whom he was close, made him seem so . . . normal.

"When I was little, I always wanted a brother," she confided. Or a sister. Someone to share the dark with. A friend who would move with her each time Gerald Denham decided to pull up stakes.

When Jonah spoke, the direction of his voice revealed him to be under a tree to her right.

"You would have wanted one like Tim, then," he said, his smoky voice suffused with warmth.

"Not one like you?" she teased.

"Good God, no. Tim was the good brother."

She tilted her head and regarded Jonah. "What were you? The bad brother?"

"Some think so."

Her smile faded. "Maybe you just had a lot of energy you didn't know what to do with." She didn't like the idea that someone believed Jonah was bad.

He shifted his weight from one leg to the other. "Are we going to hang around here all night, or are we going to get some exercise?"

She shook her feet off and pulled on her socks. "Where did you go camping?"

"Forget it, Ariel."

"I don't see what it would hurt to tell me where you went camping."

"Forget it, Ariel."

She cut him a look. "I don't appreciate being manipulated, Jonah."

"I'm not manipulating you," he said curtly. "I'm not trying to get you to do a damned thing. Except maybe get your shoes on so we can get going."

Her mouth set, she shoved her shoes on and jerked the laces tied. She rose to her feet and turned an expressionless face to Jonah.

Without a word, he started off through the ravine. Ariel said nothing as she kept the undemanding pace he set.

They hiked for thirty minutes. Ariel kept her silence, stewing. Maybe she should be just as unforthcoming as Jonah, she thought pettishly. What was he hiding anyway? Or hiding from?

"Beaver Dam," Jonah said.

Ariel looked over at him, and in doing so, nearly tripped over a rock. "What?"

"Beaver Dam. That's one of the places where Tim and I used to camp."

The name was unfamiliar to her. "Where's Beaver Dam?"

"I knew it would mean nothing to you. But you asked. And I answered."

"You're being clever, Jonah."

"It's the best I can do."

"I don't buy that." Not for a minute did she believe that. What possible reason could he have for keeping everything about himself a secret?

Suddenly, like the answers in a glass mystery ball, reasons floated to the top of her mind. *Jonah is wanted by the police. He's wanted by the federal government. He's a secret agent.*

The last thought made the most sense to her. She knew the damage his face had suffered, and she'd heard that the CIA was always involved in dangerous activities. Perhaps he'd been caught in an explosion.

What were the chances Jonah was an agent? Slim to none! Ariel felt silly even considering such a possibility. Still . . .

"Do you work for the government?" she asked.

He shook his head. "Christ. Well, I guess at least you don't think I'm a vampire anymore."

Her cheeks blazed with embarrassment. "I didn't say what I was think—"

"I can guess."

"For all I know, you might be both."

"Sort of a double-oh-seven with a taste for O negative?"

She rolled her eyes. "Ha, ha."

"You're right. It is a ridiculous theory."

They left the misty world of the ravine behind and entered the forest proper. Here the trees were of normal size. Ariel followed the moonlight. Jonah kept to the shadows.

"Okay," she conceded grudgingly, "maybe you're not a spy."

Jonah was quiet a moment. "Just a vampire?"

"It would explain your night sight."

"Some people have good night vision."

True, she thought. But his was *very* good.

Before he replied, Ariel spotted a building through the trees, off to their right. "Look. Is that a cabin?" She struck off in that direction.

"Ariel."

His voice at her back gave her a start. She hadn't heard his steps.

"Just what do you think you're doing?" he asked in an urgent whisper.

"I'm investigating," she informed him.

"I don't think that's wise."

She stopped short. "Why? Who lives here?" Up close the place looked deserted. When he didn't answer, she approached the cabin.

A stone had tumbled down from the top of the

chimney of the log cabin, and pine needles and dead leaves cloaked the wood shingle roof. Ariel peered into the dim interior through one of the grimy, broken windows. It appeared to her that the only inhabitants this cabin had seen for years had either four legs or wings.

She stepped up onto the porch, avoiding a board that had collapsed. Then she turned around to repeat her last question to him, but her surprise silenced her.

He'd followed her to the edge of the porch, and now stood outside of the deepest shadow. Had he decided to risk revealing himself to her? She searched his face for her answer, but his gaze was locked on the cabin.

Scarred, discolored skin stretched over high cheekbones, a straight, elegant nose, and an even, angular jaw. One of his eyebrows was partially missing, but to Ariel, it was more intriguing than defacing. Miraculously, his eyelashes appeared to be intact. In fact, from what she could see in the moonlight, they were long and thick, and possessed a slight curl. Something crashed throught the leaves near the side of the house, and a raccoon scurried for cover. Jonah started at the noise, as if breaking from a trance. In a fluid movement, he disappeared back into the shadows.

Quickly she looked away. If he'd meant for her to see him, he would have remained where he'd stood.

"Hello," she called toward the cabin. Carefully she picked her way across the porch. "Is there anyone here?" The sagging door stood ajar. Hinges shrieked as she slowly pulled it open.

The flapping of wings told her she'd disturbed a tenant. A large bird swooped out the door, and she ducked aside to avoid a head-on collision.

"Ariel," Jonah called. He hadn't followed her. "Don't go in there."

"It looks as if it's been abandoned for years. I just want to look. Why shouldn't I go in?" she said. She waited several seconds.

"Just don't."

She studied his dark, rigid form. "Not good enough, Jonah." She opened the door wider and cautiously stepped inside.

She stood in a single, large room. It smelled of damp wood and decaying vegetation. A soft breeze slipped through the broken windows to send dead leaves whispering across the debris-strewn plank floor.

Moonlight lit half the room, leaving the other half in darkness. She knew she should get out now. She waited for the familiar tightening in her stomach, the unreasoning panic, but her only reaction to this room was uneasiness. She put that down as an echo of Jonah's reluctance to approach the cabin. But as usual, he would give her no reasons. Annoyance and curiosity won out, and she took another step into the room. Maybe she'd be all right as long as she didn't try to go into the dark end.

A rustic stone fireplace dominated one side of the room. Two upholstered chairs, now ragged and filthy, sat in front of the hearth. The seat of one chair held an abandoned nest. On the other side of the room was the kitchen, comprised of a narrow stove, a chipped and

stained sink, counter and cupboards, an old refrigerator, and a table and four chairs. Next to the kitchen
stood a nightstand and a set of bunk beds. Rotting
leaves, twigs and dirt lay everywhere, blown in through
the windows and door.

Ariel walked over to the cupboards. The floorboards
creaked under her feet. Spiderwebs and a squirrel's
nest covered cans of soup, Spaghettios, Vienna
sausages, and baked beans. There were jars of peanut
butter, mustard, catsup, and pickles. She glanced
toward the refrigerator. Who knew what moldering
staples she'd find in there? She decided to pass on the
refrigerator and went to the bunks. On the bottom one
lay a dusty canvas duffel bag. She tugged at the rusted
zipper.

"Please come out of there."

He stood in the doorway, backlit by the moon like a
dark angel surrounded by celestial radiance. He cast
an eerie shadow across the room.

The further darkening of the room brought an
instant panic in Ariel. "Get away from the door," she
ordered in a strangled voice.

Immediately, he entered and moved to one side,
out of the path of the moonlight. "This is ridiculous,
Ariel," he said. "You're afraid of the dark, for chrissake. You shouldn't be in here."

"I'm a little better, I think," she told him. "And now
you're here. . . ."

He made a rude noise in his throat.

She turned back to the duffel bag. The zipper
wouldn't budge.

"What's so important about this place, anyway?" he

asked. He remained where he was, standing just inside the door.

"I've never been in a cabin before. Will you see if you can unjam this zipper?"

"No."

Next to the bunks was a nightstand. She pulled open the top drawer and peered inside. Protected from the elements, a cassette tape player seemed to be in good condition. She picked it up.

"You're trespassing."

"No one has been here in years, Jonah. Besides, I'm not going to take anything. I'm just curious."

He turned his head, and she knew he was looking directly at her. "About what?"

"About the people who stayed here. Look around you. Someone took the trouble to make this a snug, comfortable little retreat. Or home. Maybe they lived here. And then they just left. They never even came back for their things. Don't you wonder what happened? Aren't you at all interested in their lives?"

"You've already seen two ghosts," he said in a low, flat voice. "Are you looking for another?"

Ariel shivered. "No." But she couldn't help wondering: where had the occupants of this cabin gone?

She looked down at the small machine she held in her hand. Why had the owner left it behind?

"We need to get back."

She nodded absently. Then she noticed there was a tape in the cassette player. She depressed the play button.

Nothing happened.

"Ariel." Jonah's voice held a note that told her the little patience he'd possessed had run out.

The batteries were probably dead, she thought. Disappointed, she set the player back down in the drawer.

She glanced at Jonah, who was staring at the fireplace. Quickly she slipped the tape out of the player and into her shorts pocket. Then she closed the nightstand drawer.

"Okay," she said. "Let's go."

Jonah shut the cabin door behind them. "Ariel, I think you might be too curious for your own good."

9

Doris made a face at the contents of her lunch tray as she and Ariel wound their way among the cafeteria tables to the first empty one they saw. "Hamburgers. I wish they wouldn't serve hamburgers."

"They offered other things," Ariel pointed out as they sat down. "There were salads."

"Oh sure. Offer a low-calorie salad at the same time hamburgers are available. It's sadism, that's what it is. They know what a weak person I am." She glanced up in time to see a man wave to her from behind the counter. "See how that Arno is grinning," she said indignantly.

Ariel looked up to see the cook still smiling. "Doris, Arno has a crush on you. Just look at him. Is that love or what?"

Doris waved back. "That's not love, that's glee. He's gloating."

Ariel shook her head as she spread mustard on the inside of her hamburger bun. "I don't see why you worry about eating hamburgers, anyway. You certainly don't need to lose weight."

"Not now, maybe, but a few of these babies, and I'll be moving up to the next dress size. I can't afford a whole new wardrobe." Doris took a bite of her hamburger. A blissful expression settled over her face. "Mmmm."

Ariel enjoyed each bite of her own hamburger. Arno and his crew really knew how to make them.

"Between the snacks and the hamburgers, I don't understand how you keep your weight down," Doris observed. "You look great. How do you do it?"

"I—" Ariel caught herself. She'd been about to say "I exercise," but Doris regularly went to the gym and knew that Ariel didn't. "I have an exercise tape I use. And there's the stress. Stress really burns the calories, you know."

"I'm stressed, and I don't look like you," Doris grumbled good-naturedly.

"Why would you want to? Doris, every man in the valley thinks you're a knockout. They practically fall over each other trying to get to you." Ariel nipped off a bit of carrot stick. "You should be satisfied. Even happy. You'll have your wish before you know it. Doris the Doctor's Wife."

Doris waved away Ariel's pep talk with a ripple of her fingers. "Not likely."

"I thought you wanted to marry a doctor. Just like your cousin."

Swallowing the last mouthful of hamburger, Doris sank back against her chair. "Yeah. A doctor. But it seems like all the good ones are already taken. And I want the same thing my cousin found. Love."

"Well, aren't you picky?"

But Doris didn't seem to hear. Her eyes were focused on something across the room.

Curious, Ariel looked to see what occupied Doris's attention.

Across the cafeteria, alone at a table, sat Kerwin Sprague.

"I think Kerwin is very much a 'good one,'" Ariel said quietly.

Doris looked at her, then quickly away. Color tinged her cheeks. "He's not interested in me."

"How do you kno—" Two and two clicked together in her brain. "Wait a minute. You think that because he gives me roses, Kerwin has a thing for me?"

"Well, duh."

"It's just not so," Ariel said firmly.

Doris seemed to find her tangerine fingernail polish of riveting interest. "I've seen how his face lights up when he sees you. I could be wallpaper for all that he notices me."

Ariel genuinely liked and respected Kerwin. He was an excellent anesthesiologist, a conscientious man. He was generous to a fault with his friends, which, admittedly, were few at Fountainhead Clinic, but she knew that was because he was shy.

In fact Dr. Kerwin Sprague was so painfully shy that it was a wonder he'd survived medical school and residency. And Kerwin had mentioned that his mother tended to be overly protective of him—something he often found annoying. Ariel believed he needed—and deserved—a wife who would help him to stand on his own.

She studied Doris for a moment. "The woman who marries Kerwin will have a loyal, thoughtful, intelligent husband," she said. "But that woman won't be me, Doris. Kerwin and I are friends, not lovers."

Lovers. Like vaporous genies escaping a lamp, impressions of Jonah curled into her conscious. The heart-quickening sound of his mellow-fire voice. The warmth of his body standing so close behind her. The silken feel of his hair as it slipped through her fingers.

Her blood warmed, carrying a pulse that beat just a little bit heavier, just a fraction faster. Thankful that Doris was still distracted, Ariel took a deep swallow from her glass of ice water.

"When we're not talking about our work, Doris, Kerwin and I talk about roses," Ariel offered. "Why don't you try roses? He has a passion for them."

Doris sighed. "This table knows more about roses than I do."

"Tell him you want to learn. Give him the pleasure of teaching you. He's such a generous man."

Ariel managed to smother a smile when she saw the light of speculation ignite in Doris's eyes.

"Now that I've shared my deep insight into Kerwin's psyche," Ariel said, "I need a favor from you."

"I haven't found anyone by the name of Jonah in my patient files."

"Yes, I know, you told me already. What I want is to borrow your tape player." Doris had told her she'd bought a new one on her last trip to Asheville. "I promise I'll treat it with great care. I'll give it back tomorrow."

"Of course you can borrow my tape player. You can borrow some tapes, too, if you like."

After they deposited their trays and dirty dishes on the cafeteria's conveyor belt, they walked to Doris's apartment. Ariel accepted the player, but declined borrowing from the extensive tape collection. Saying good-night quickly, she hastened back to her bungalow.

From a kitchen drawer she retrieved the tape that she had taken the night before. It bore the label of an unfamiliar recording company, nor had she heard of any of the titles listed. She slipped it into the player, arranged the headset, and pressed the play button.

At first there was no sound. Then, before disappointment could take hold, she heard the faint static that indicated the recording was progressing.

Suddenly there was a waterfall of crystal notes. Harp and hammered dulcimer wove a spritely melody that Ariel thought might be an Irish or Scottish folk tune. She found herself lifted into the music.

The next piece was a waltz. The artists played their instruments with such finesse that the piercingly delicate notes wove together like gossamer lace. Ariel closed her eyes and allowed her imagination to sweep her into a ballroom paved with polished marble and illuminated by Waterford crystal chandeliers. Light glinted off the gold braid and silver metals on the men's military uniforms. The sumptuous, wide skirts of the women belled out as the couples glided around the room in perfect tempo. *One*-two-three, *one*-two-three. Music from another age, a different world. Haunting. Ethereal. It was the most beautiful waltz she'd ever heard.

The rest of the tape was entertaining, though it could not compare to the second piece. When she finished listening, Ariel took out the tape and tried to find the name of the composer, but only the titles were given. Number two was listed simply as "April Waltz."

She changed into her shorts and knit top, slid the tape into one pocket. She hesitated, then went to the kitchen drawer where she kept the batteries she'd bought in Farley and selected four of the AA cells. She felt a little silly, but her guilt at taking the tape prompted her to make a small offering to the owners.

She headed back to the cabin. She retraced her way through the park, under the wall, past the ravine, and into the forest.

It was dusk when she arrived. The partial light was cruel to the abandoned shelter, stripping it of any pretense that the owners had only temporarily vacated. Twigs stuck out the top of the chimney, and Ariel thought a bird or squirrel had probably built a nest. Several wood shingles were missing. The broken windows stared into the forest like haunted eyes.

She crossed the porch and entered. An air of melancholy pervaded the place. Ariel tried to shake off the feeling.

She walked through the room to the nightstand, layers of dead leaves crunching beneath the soles of her sneakers.

Quickly she put the tape back into the drawer. She took the old batteries out of the player, and deposited the new ones in the drawer.

Conscious of the fleeting time, she turned to leave. Out of the corner of her eye she saw the duffel bag. She stopped. What if there was something inside to give her a clue about the owners' identity, or why they had not returned? The tape had told her only that someone had a taste for obscure music played on stringed instruments. She went back to the bunk beds. She brushed off more caked dirt and moldering vegetation and tried again to dislodge the rusted zipper. Carefully, she worked at it, nudging and tugging until her patience wore thin. Then, just when she was ready to quit in disgust, the pull grated down the corroded metal teeth.

She hesitated, suddenly uneasy about delving into the bag. Yes, she was curious about the people who had abandoned this cabin. She wanted to know more about them. But now, the thought of rummaging through the long-untouched duffel bag seemed like . . . well, like opening a grave. A cool breeze wafted through the shattered windows. Ariel shivered.

"What are you doing here?" a man's voice demanded from the doorway behind her.

Startled, her heart jolted to a stop. For the first time, she noticed that the sun had disappeared. Slowly she turned.

He stood in the shadows. Moonlight gilded his tall, obsidian form with an outline of molten silver. Wavy hair. Masculine columnar neck. Broad, square shoulders. Slim hips. Long, muscular arms and legs.

"Jonah," she managed breathlessly. "It's early yet. I didn't expect you. How did you know—"

"I followed you."

Ariel blinked. "Followed me? Why?"

"I saw you leave the park and thought you didn't know your way around the forest. Apparently I was wrong." His voice hardened. "What are you doing here, Ariel?"

She was recovered from her fright well enough to take exception to his question, his tone—his whole attitude. "I don't see that that's any of your business."

He took a step inside. The silver outline vanished as he blended easily into shadow. "It *is* my business."

She tensed, feeling exposed. She knew he could see her, but even squinting, she could barely make out his shape. "Oh, really?" she challenged more bravely than she felt. "How so?"

"I'm making it my business."

Alone, living in run-down apartments on the poor side of town, Ariel had learned early to stick up for herself. She'd had more than one bloody nose in her life. Still, she found Jonah thoroughly intimidating. He was big. He was superbly developed. And he was angry as hell.

"I may swoon," she said in defiance.

To her dismay, he crossed the room until he stood toe-to-toe with her. Even if she craned her neck back, she couldn't look him in the eye. She couldn't even see his face. So she glared at his clavicle. She only hoped he couldn't hear her heart crashing like a kettledrum.

"I asked you not to come in here."

"No," she snapped. "You *told* me not to come in here. But, as usual, you wouldn't tell me why. I'm getting sick of it, Jonah."

"I explained to you."

"No, you didn't. All you said was that you can't tell me about yourself. I can think of only a few reasons good enough for that. Are you an undercover agent, Jonah? Are you in the witness protection program? Is your life in jeopardy?"

His bitter laughter rang hollowly in the small cabin. "My life in jeopardy? God, that would be a kindness." Pain, raw and ragged, permeated his voice. "A swift, unknown assassin—it would be an act of mercy."

Ariel's anger vanished. She gripped his upper arms, felt the coiled tension in his muscles. "Don't talk like that! Jonah, you've been screened and tested and admitted to Fountainhead," she reminded him urgently, looking up at him. His scarred jaw was clenched. She tried to shake him and found him jarringly immovable. "Soon you may *want* to walk into the daylight."

"You know nothing about it."

She wanted to make him promises, to tell him whatever he wanted to hear in order to banish his torment. But she couldn't. That would only add to the cruelty fate had dealt him. "I know the world can be a very nasty place. You've held on this long, don't give up now, not when you're so close."

"Yeah. So close," he said, his low-spoken words almost lost to her.

He remained silent for a moment. Then he stepped back, sinking farther into shadow.

Unconsciously she moved in his direction. Her foot bumped something solid among the moldering leaves on the floor, and she looked down just in time to see a snake slither away.

Ariel instantly recoiled. "Ugh!"

"It's only a corn snake," Jonah said.

"A snake is a snake. They're all creepy."

"Don't be afraid. That snake isn't poisonous."

"I'm not afraid," she said quickly. "It's just that the thing is so . . . different. So *alien*."

Jonah broke the quiet with two words. "I'm different."

Ariel caught her breath at the pain that echoed in that softly spoken revelation. Desperately she searched for words to help heal his wound.

"Am I alien, too, Ariel?"

"No!" She stepped into the pitch-darkness of the shadows in which he hid, stretching her arms out to him. Suddenly she felt his hands on her shoulders. He pulled her to him and wrapped his arms around her in a fierce embrace.

She clung to him tightly. "Never think such a thing!" She pressed her cheek against his chest and felt his heart hammering. Tears for Jonah welled in her throat and burned behind her eyes. "You are as human as I am." *And you are dear to me*. "What's more, you're a beautiful man, Jonah. You're tall, and straight, and you have a body other men can only envy."

"The surgeons did their jobs well," he said, bitterness saturating each syllable.

"Good! Be glad! And be glad when your next surgeon—"

"It's time to go back, Ariel," he said, his voice flat and dull. "It's getting late."

When he started to put her away from him, she clutched him tightly. "I'm not finished," she said stubbornly.

"I know what you're going to say, so you don't need to repeat it."

"Well, clearly someone needs to. Fountainhead is about changes, Jonah. Life-shaking changes. None of them are easy. None of them." She drew a sharp, steadying breath and somehow managed to keep the ache from her voice. "Not for any of us."

She let him go then and stepped back, into the moonlight. As she stood there, Ariel knew that she was going to pay a hard price for breaking her resolution against getting involved with a patient. She knew it as surely as she knew the tide followed the moon.

This time, it was the doctor, not the patient, who might not recover.

"You never answered my question," he said. "What are you doing here?"

Ariel regarded the darkness that was Jonah. He had drawn the line. They had gone as far as he would allow. "I was putting the tape back," she said.

"The tape?"

"The, uh, one in the drawer, here." If only she hadn't stayed to open the duffel bag.

"I see."

She shifted uncomfortably where she stood.

"Did you listen to it?" he asked quietly.

Ariel nodded.

"What—" He broke off, as if he wasn't sure he wanted to ask the question. "What was it?"

She fitted the batteries into the old cassette player. "Music," she said and turned it on, praying it still worked.

A cascade of harp and dulcimer notes filled the cabin, flowing into the folk tune Ariel remembered.

Jonah listened until the first piece came to an end. "I've heard enough," he said in curt dismissal. But there was something in his voice. . . .

"No," Ariel said as she walked over to the deep shadows to face him, remaining in the moonlight. "Not yet."

The waltz began to play, shimmering through the cabin like an invisible mist of magic.

"Dance with me," she said softly, holding out her arms to him. "Dance with me, Jonah."

He remained where he was for several beats. "I trust you not—"

"—to look. I understand."

He waited until she lowered her gaze to his throat then stepped into the moonlight.

He took her in his arms as if she were the most delicate of ladies, and together they danced around the filthy plank floor. But to Ariel, the floor was polished marble. And for this moment, Jonah was her prince.

She felt his gaze on her, and she wanted to lift her eyes and look at him. She wanted to see the height of his forehead, the shape of his eyebrows, the contour of his mouth.

He drew her a little closer and her heart beat a little faster.

The waltz ended.

Without releasing Ariel, Jonah walked over to the cassette player and pressed the rewind button. Neither spoke as they waited, as if by speaking they would break the spell that lay over the cabin. Then Jonah tested the tape and found the place he sought. He pressed another button. The waltz began to play and he swept her into the dance.

"Tim loved 'April Waltz,'" Jonah said in a low voice.

"It's beautiful. Before today, I hadn't heard it before."

"Most people haven't."

Ariel glanced toward the duffel bag on the bottom bunk bed. Someone had.

Jonah was silent for a few seconds. "Tim had a real gift for music."

She was surprised at his offering. Trying to sound casual, she tried for another piece to the puzzle that was Jonah. "What kind of music?"

"Classical. R and B. Folk. His tastes were eclectic. He had a scholarship to Juilliard," he added proudly. "He . . . died before he could finish it."

"Did he make this tape?"

"No. He played several different instruments, but harp and dulcimer weren't among them."

His bare thigh brushed hers. Awareness shot through her, making her more sensitive than ever to the warmth of his palm where it pressed gently against the small of her back. She could feel each finger through the thin cotton knit of her top. In his other hand he clasped hers. As she looked at their joined hands now, she realized just how much larger his was than her own. His fingers were long, tapered, blunt-tipped, the clean fingernails clipped short, just as she thought a man's should be.

"Do you have any sisters, or other brothers?" she asked. Her voice seemed unusually loud to her ears.

He surprised her by answering her question. "No. There was only Tim."

She wanted to know how Tim had died, how long ago, how old he had been, but she sensed in Jonah a sorrow that was still too raw, so she remained silent.

"My mother didn't want to have any more children than she felt she could support on her own, in case something happened to my dad."

"She sounds like a practical woman. Was your father's health in question?"

"You could say that. He was a firefighter." She heard the smile in his voice.

"Well, then, I'd say your mother was eminently sensible." Were his parents still alive? "Is your father still a firefighter?"

"No. He retired years ago. Now he can devote himself full-time to developing the perfect barbecued hamburger."

A stab of envy flashed through Ariel. "Did your family have barbecue parties?"

He chuckled. "Oh, yeah. Dad presided over his grill as if it was a rare instrument that only he knew how to play. He made the grill. It was stone. The thing even had a chimney." He chuckled again. "It was quite a sight. Dad in his special apron, overseeing the hamburgers, and Mom fussing over everything else." He shook his head. "The queen of coleslaw."

The perfect family, Ariel thought, remembering all the times she'd wept alone in her bed, aching for a mother, for a father who would want to be with her as much as she wanted to be with him. "Sounds like you've had some wonderful times."

Jonah tilted his head back, as if he were staring at the ceiling. She saw his throat work.

"Yeah," he said in a voice so low she barely heard. "Wonderful." There it was again. That faraway note in his voice.

"Jonah?"

The tape came to an end, and dimly Ariel realized they'd been waltzing long after the waltz had ended, paying no attention to the music.

They slowed to a stop, but made no attempt to move apart. Jonah seemed to fill her world as they stood there in the abandoned cabin. She wanted to remain in his embrace forever.

Softly, softly, he skimmed his fingertips across her forehead. She held her breath. He stroked her eyebrows with his thumb, his hesitant grace making the simple movement impossibly erotic. Beneath his hand her skin tingled with life.

His fingertips lit on her eyelids, which drifted closed. He touched her eyelashes, and she shivered with wanting. The light pressure of his fingers trailed to her cheekbones. He traced the length and slant of them, then moved to her nose, her cheeks, her jaws. Finally he reached her lips.

It was as if she'd been waiting for him, her body filled with an ineffable yearning.

She touched the tip of her tongue to his fifth finger.

Jonah went as still as a statue. She took his finger into her mouth. Lightly, she sucked.

A groan tore from the depth of his throat. His arm tightened around her waist. She felt the hard power of his arousal. Boldly she swirled her tongue around the base of his finger.

He jerked his finger from her mouth. "Close your eyes," he ordered.

She obeyed, her body heavy with needful heat. He tangled his hands in her hair, tilted back her head. Then he took her lips by storm, possessing them with a fierce intensity, a burning desperation. He pressed and softened, teased with the tip of his tongue. He drew her bottom lip between his and sucked lightly.

She curved into his warm steel body, reaching up to twine her arms around his neck. The thick silk of his hair flowed through her fingers. She wanted to get closer, much closer.

His tongue slipped into her mouth, sliding across her teeth. It flicked against her tongue, flirting, tempting. When she answered, she was rewarded with a sensual thrust and rub that sent fire shimmering through her veins.

He left her mouth to glide his lips softly over her face, to her jaw, to the sensitive spot just behind it. Ariel moaned, her fingers tightening in his hair.

His muscles were hard with tension, his breathing short and rapid. She kissed him at the base of his throat, just above the neckline of his cut-off T-shirt. With the tip of her tongue she traced a delicate pattern on his hot, damp flesh. She felt a tremor go through him.

Ariel clung to him. At last he was so close, so wonderfully close. She could feel the beat of his heart. Could he feel hers?

"I want you, Ariel. God, I want you so badly." His breath was hot in her ear.

"Yes," she whispered earnestly. "Jonah, I want you, too."

He took her hand and strode quickly from the cabin. When the structure was obscured from their sight by the trees, he stopped. She leaned back against the trunk of an oak, admiring him as he stood before her, partially bathed in moonlight.

In a single swift motion, Jonah stood over her, hemming her in against the tree by the simple expedient of placing one arm on either side of her, pressing his palms against the rough bark of the oak. He kept his face well above her head until she closed her eyes.

Then he kissed her with engulfing passion. As his mouth moved on hers, his need burned into her, searing through to lock with her own.

She felt his hand cover her breast and she pressed against his warm palm. For an instant, his hand left her. Before she could voice her protest, he pushed up her knit top and shoved aside her bra, to claim her breast again, this time feverish flesh to flesh. He plucked gently at her nipple, which hardened into a sensitized pearl. She heard his growl of masculine satisfaction, then felt the wet heat of his mouth as he covered the tip of her breast. He kneaded her with his tongue. With his teeth he teased her with quick, light bites, barely glancing her flesh. As if not wishing to miss a single tempting dish at a banquet, he moved to her other breast, licking, sucking, biting.

Desire raged through her like an electric storm, crackling around them both. She anchored her fists in his hair on either side of his head, wanting him to continue his ministrations, wanting him to kiss her mouth again, wanting . . .

She felt him straighten. When he came back to her, his T-shirt was up, baring his chest to her breasts. With a whimper she released his hair and wrapped her arms tightly around his torso, wanting him closer. She wanted to draw him into herself, into her soul, where he would see she cared nothing for the way his face looked. She pressed against him. "Jonah."

He fit his hips to hers. "Oh, God." He groaned. "Ariel."

Through the double layers of their shorts, his thick, hard arousal ignited her. Fever claimed her senses.

She wanted Jonah. She wanted his beautiful man's body in the most elemental way a woman could want a man.

But she also wanted . . . something more.

Suddenly, she was gripped by a yearning, a gut-deep longing. Lifting her hand, she softly traced the angular line of his jaw. She held her breath, expecting him to stop her before her fingers touched the area of puckered flesh she knew was there. To her surprise, he made no move to catch her hand. Instead, he stood still. The only sound she could hear was the soughing of their mingled breath. Carefully, lightly, her fingertips rode over the irregular surface of disfigurement.

His hand flashed up to stop her exploration. "No." His voice was unsteady. "Don't, Ariel."

"Do you think it matters to me?" she asked.

"It matters to me."

Deep aching sorrow poured into her. He still didn't trust her. Even for so small a thing as to acquaint her fingertips with his face he still didn't trust her. Maybe he never would.

Reluctantly, she tugged her hand from his and straightened her clothing.

Silently, Jonah stepped back, away from her. The dark form of his head turned away. "It's better this way."

She didn't believe him. "Is it?"

"Yes," he said flatly.

She stuffed her shaking hands into her pockets. "I thought you wanted to make love." Ariel knew his body had been ready. He'd said he wanted her. What had been going through his mind? Did he truly feel nothing for her? Had she been seeing something that really wasn't there?

"Make love?" he said, his voice harsh. "Is that what you call what we were about to do? Here? Against this tree? I can think of several words to describe it, but none of them involve love."

The lash of his sarcasm left her stunned. She stared at him in disbelief, her thoughts disjointed as she tried to make sense of his words. Was this the same man . . . ? She'd thought . . . They'd been about to . . .

Suddenly, it all came together with a savage jolt that left Ariel feeling exposed and dirty. Shame expanded in her chest, pressed against her lungs.

She turned on her heel and blindly strode away. All she wanted was to be out of Jonah's sight, to have him out of hers. Misery churned in her. She wanted to run, but her shredded pride wouldn't allow her to humiliate herself further.

"Stop," Jonah called. "You're going in the wrong direction."

She kept walking. She didn't care where she was going, as long as it was away from him.

A strong hand caught her arm. "Ariel."

She halted, but refused to turn and face him. "Take your hand off me," she snapped. Fury at herself, at Jonah, howled inside her like a tornado.

"You're going in the wrong direction," he repeated stubbornly, retaining his hold on her.

"From here on out, what I do is none of your business." She jerked free from his relaxed grip. Without so much as a backward look, she spun around and marched away from him. This time in the right direction, she hoped.

Silently, he kept pace with her, blending with the forest shadows. "Ariel, listen to me—"

"You have nothing to say that I want to hear," she informed him. To her burning mortification, she felt herself perilously close to tears. She clamped her jaw shut and dragged in a deep breath through her nostrils.

"Please stop and listen to me," he said quietly.

Certain that he wouldn't leave her alone until she allowed him to say what was on his mind, Ariel came to a halt. She swallowed hard, not trusting herself to try to speak.

He moved from behind her to face her, stopping

just within the edge of the shadow that concealed him. "Ariel." His voice trailed off.

She turned away from him.

"I'm sorry," he said.

Ariel squeezed her eyes shut, wishing she could also shutter her ears against the almost-pleading note in his voice. "You hurt me," she told him tightly. The muscles of her throat ached.

For a moment, there was only the rustle of the night breeze through the leaves. "God, I'm so sorry," he whispered hoarsely.

His fingers gently closed around hers and coaxed her into the stygian shade. Tentatively, he touched her bare upper arm. She moved her arm away, and he dropped his hand to his side.

"I know I hurt you," he said. "I— What I did was inexcusable."

"Do you know how you made me feel?" she demanded flatly.

He moved fractionally closer. "I lied, Ariel."

She started to move farther from him, but his words stopped her. "Lied?" she echoed.

His hands cupped her shoulders, as if he needed an anchor before he could continue. He hesitated before he went on. Finally he spoke. "I wanted to make love to you."

"You told me that you could think of several other words that would better apply to what you were feeling," she said, her words barely audible.

"That was the lie. I want the bond, the connection I believe I could have with you. Don't get me wrong—I want the sex, too." He released a harsh breath that stirred her hair. "Christ, I really want sex with you. But it's more than that."

Her throat clogged with emotion. "Then why . . . ?"

His fingers tightened slightly. "It scares me. The wanting. It scares me more than you can ever realize. Because it's impossible."

"Why?"

His harsh crack of laughter sent a shiver through her. "For more reasons than you want to know."

"That's a stupid answer."

But she could think of at least one very real reason. Jonah would forget her when the doctors of Fountainhead finished their job, and he went back out into the world. He would want a new life where nothing would remind him of all that he'd suffered.

She'd tracked Patrick down, when it had become clear that Vickie wasn't going to recover from her heartbreak on her own. Ariel had pleaded with him to go back to her friend. Then she'd seen the torment in his eyes. He'd told her that he couldn't go back to Vickie, that the old nightmares returned when he was with her.

It still hurt to remember how one afternoon Vickie had just walked out of the hospital where they were working, and vanished.

Ariel felt Jonah move. "Name me one intelligent thing about this whole situation," he said. "Nothing is normal in our little world. Maybe that's why it works for us."

"But it doesn't work for us anymore," she observed sadly.

"It could. We could go back to the way we were before."

She shook her head. "That would never work."

"Yes it would," he whispered in her ear, his breath making her shiver. "We can make it work. Tonight never happened. There is only tomorrow night, and the nights that follow."

She allowed him to seduce her into believing. But some small insistent voice inside her required that she at least acknowledge the inevitable. "Until we part ways."

"Yes," he said softly, his voice vibrating with an odd undernote. "Until we part ways."

10

Jonah strode away from the grassy hillock where he'd stood and watched Ariel disappear into her bungalow.

He'd almost ruined everything tonight. Clumsy. Greedy. He'd lost control. Savagely, Jonah tore a leaf from a dogwood tree he passed. *Idiot!*

He should have insisted they leave as soon as the waltz ended. He should have— The leaf tore like tissue between his fingers. Hell, he'd babbled about his family. And she'd listened to every word he said. She'd been *interested*, though only God knew why. He'd told her what were probably the most mundane facts in his entire life, yet she'd appeared to be pleased, almost envious.

It felt good to be the center of a beautiful woman's attention. No, he corrected himself. To be the center

of Ariel's attention. With Ariel, he knew she was
interested in him as a man, not as an object of horrified fascination.

And he'd responded to her as a man. A man who
ached to hold her in his arms, to press himself into
her welcoming body, to sleep beside her through the
night.

She'd touched him softly, with caring. His thorny
protective shield had buckled under her tenderness.

Jonah stopped and turned to look back in the direction of Ariel's quarters. Trees obscured his vision. But
he knew she was there.

She frightened him.

While she hadn't said she loved him, she'd spoken
the word. *That* word no one had spoken to him in
years. A word he'd dreamed of hearing from her lips
in a different phrase.

But it was just a dream, a tormenting dream. Only
a miracle could make it come true once she saw him
in the light. Once she saw his face.

Oh, he knew she wouldn't scream or faint. She
wouldn't even cringe. He knew this because she was a
goddamned plastic surgeon.

Once Dr. Ariel Denham clearly saw him, he would
cease to be a man to her. She would examine the tension and color of his skin, and ask questions, lots of
questions, about how this had happened, and how
long ago. And she'd forget that she'd ever found him
attractive or interesting as a man.

He'd been reduced to the status of patient, of *thing*
before. He would occupy that status again. But for
now, with Ariel, he had something precious, some-

thing he might never find again. He wanted to hold on to it for as long as possible.

So he would keep his face hidden from her.

That meant they could never make love; he couldn't risk her seeing him. His mouth twisted with the bitter irony of the situation, even as the knowledge filled him with sharp regret.

He couldn't make love to the only woman who treated him as a man, a man she could love. The only woman who wouldn't treat him as what he had become. A monster.

The next morning Jonah was very much on Ariel's mind as she walked through the hospital to her office.

Tonight they wouldn't walk together. While he'd never mentioned why, Ariel knew the cause was the full moon that would rise in this evening's sky. Three days would pass before she'd meet him again.

She unlocked her office to find her rose-of-the-day waiting for her in its crystal vase. This was not one of the pink ones, nor was it like the Aloha rose. Although every bit as perfect as the others, the petals of this flower were purest white with only a breath of pink tinting the edges. She leaned close and sniffed. The perfume of this blossom was faint, elusive.

Doris walked into the small office. "What kind of rose did you get this morning?" she asked. She studied the flower. "You haven't had one like this before, have you?"

Ariel shook her head.

Kerwin appeared at the door. "That's a Pristine. A perfect example of a classic hybrid tea shape."

"Ah," Ariel said.

Doris nodded sagely.

He came closer, bending over the slender vase and its contents. Like a gourmet sampling the steam from a rare coffee, Kerwin inhaled deeply of the rose's scent. His eyes drifted closed.

Ariel looked over at Doris, who looked back at her. It seemed insensitive to disturb his reverie with mere conversation.

Kerwin opened his eyes and smiled. "What do you ladies think?" He waved his slim hand in the direction of the rose.

"I think it's beautiful, as always, Kerwin," Ariel said. "It will certainly brighten my day." She hoped he wasn't getting a crush on her. Surely not. They were just good friends, right? "You know, Doris is interested in roses."

Doris smoothly picked up on her impromptu cue. "You know, Doctor," she said to Kerwin, "I really would like to know what makes a classic hybrid tea shape. Do you think that maybe someday, when you have a few minutes . . ."

Kerwin's eyes lit. "I'd be delighted. In fact, I was on my way to get some coffee."

"Oh, why don't you come to my office? I've just made a fresh pot."

Ariel caught the look Doris sent her and answered her with a wink. Atta girl, Ariel thought.

After Kerwin and Doris left, a few minutes remained before Ariel's first appointment. The pale rose in front of her seemed to command her attention.

Pristine. Innocent. Pale. The way Jonah wanted to keep their relationship. Her eyes narrowed as she stared at the bloom, consideringly.

She picked up the telephone handset and dialed Doris's number in patient records. "Doris, I hate to disturb your fascinating lesson on hybrid tea shapes, but I'm going into Reavesboro tomorrow, and I thought you might like to go with me. I've got some boring stuff to do, but maybe we could have fun on the ride."

Doris sounded puzzled. "Reavesboro. You mean the county seat? What's in that little old town?"

"The courthouse."

"Hmm. Sounds intriguing. Count me in. But promise me we'll have lunch someplace good."

Ariel had never been to the county seat but had heard it was even smaller than Farley, having steadily lost population since the War Between the States. "I promise we'll have lunch at the best place in Reavesboro."

Doris settled for that, and they hung up.

Ariel went to her locker and pulled on her lab coat. She was finished following Jonah's rules. If he thought he could freely manipulate their relationship to his convenience or comfort level, he was in for a surprise.

"So this is Reavesboro," Doris observed the next day as she looked out the car window.

The small frame houses with their covered verandas gave way to a few streets of old warehouses, many of which were boarded shut. Next came the stolid buildings that housed offices, stores and, from the looks of it, a couple of restaurants.

"Yep," Ariel said without taking her eyes from the view through the windshield. "Ah, here it is."

On the main street, surrounded by a manicured green lawn and wide-spreading oaks, stood a three-storied brick structure, fronted by a march of towering, white Ionic columns. Between the courthouse and the sidewalk along the street, next to the bronze statue of the Confederate soldier was a sign that read: Marwood County Courthouse.

"You really are determined to find out who this Jonah fellow is," Doris said as she got out of the car and shut the door.

"It's just about all I can think of these days."

"If you ask me, you're obsessing. I wish you'd tell me why a patient you don't even know is so important to you," Doris grumbled.

"I want to find out who he is."

"Yes, I *know* that. But why?"

"Because I think I know him." She wished Doris would drop the subject. Guilt nibbled at her. Ariel hated deceiving her friend.

"Why do you think that?"

"His voice. I heard him say something, and his voice sounded familiar." There was an iota of truth in that.

Doris airily waved a hand, as if to dismiss such an insubstantial observation. "Voices change. Especially when someone has been through the kind of trauma many of Fountainhead's patients have." She frowned slightly. "You know that. Besides, if he wanted a reunion with you, he'd have told you who he was before now."

"Yeah, yeah. I know."

They climbed the broad white concrete steps of the courthouse. Suddenly, Doris brightened. "Is this unrequited love?"

Ariel's cheeks heated. "Of course not."

But Doris had seen the color in Ariel's face. "It is!" she crowed. "You're in love with this Jonah person, aren't you?"

"Certainly not! What a ridiculous idea."

Love Jonah? It was a thought that hadn't occurred to her. But the words echoed in her mind as she and Doris entered the building and their footfalls rang on the polished granite. Love? Ariel scowled.

"May I help you?" the woman at the information desk asked warily.

Ariel realized she was frowning and eased into a smile. "Yes, please. I'm trying to find a little history on a piece of property."

"You need the Register of Deeds." The woman gave directions.

When they located the right room, Ariel was told she needed to take a number. All the clerks were busy. Ariel took a plastic card from the hook indicated.

"This promises to be very dull," Doris observed.

"It does indeed," Ariel agreed. "You don't need to wait with me, Doris. Why don't you do some shopping while I take care of this? When I'm finished, I'll go sit on that bench by the statue of the soldier. You can probably see that from just about any of the shops."

Doris left gratefully, and Ariel sat down on one of the hard, heavy wooden chairs to wait her turn.

Finally, her number was called. She moved to another hard, heavy wooden chair across the counter from the clerk, a stocky woman in her fifties who wore her thick salt-and-pepper hair cropped short. Ariel crossed her legs, and explained what she was looking for.

"Do you know when the present owners took title?" the woman asked.

"No."

"What is the name of the present owner?"

"I'm afraid I don't know."

"What about the legal description of the property? Do you have that?"

"Uh, no." Ariel recrossed her legs.

"What *do* you have?"

At last, something she could answer. "The street address."

"Then you'll need to go to Mapping. They can help you find the name of the present owner and the legal description. Once you have that, I can tell you how to look up the names of the previous owners." She jotted down the room number of the Mapping and Appraisal Department on a slip of paper and handed it to Ariel.

At the Mapping and Appraisal Department Ariel took another number and sat waiting on another hard wooden chair.

Forty-five minutes later she learned that the book containing the microfiche records she needed was missing. The clerk who informed her appeared to be genuinely distressed.

"We can't have our records disappearing," he said,

removing his spectacles and vigorously rubbing the lenses with his handkerchief. "That information is very important."

"Of course it is," Ariel sympathized, wondering how she should proceed from this point.

"We've got a new person here. Maybe the volume has just been misplaced. If you come back after lunch, I may have located it by then."

Fifteen minutes after Ariel sat down on the bench by the statue, Doris arrived, carrying a bag bearing the name of a dress shop.

"What did you get?" Ariel asked.

"A yellow sundress." Doris opened the bag and showed her. "All I can say is thank God you got done in there." She nodded her head in the direction of the courthouse. "Otherwise I would have done something foolish, like buy more clothes. This place has the best sale going on. It was all I could to do resist spending more money."

"I have to go back for one more try after lunch. The records are missing."

Doris brightened immediately. "Oh, good! Then I can buy those shoes."

Ariel laughed. "That's right. Be strong. Resist that temptation. Come on, let's go eat." She started off in the direction of the cafe the woman at the information desk had recommended.

Doris automatically walked with her. "Everyone needs shoes," she insisted.

"Thirty pairs of them?"

"I never should have told you that!"

They debated the need for a large shoe wardrobe

over an enjoyable lunch in a small restaurant adorned with country decor. Then Doris headed back toward the shoe store, and Ariel returned to the Mapping and Appraisal Department, where she found the clerk she'd talked with earlier bristling with righteous outrage. The microfiche log had not been found. Heads would roll, he assured her sternly as he adjusted his wire-rimmed glasses on his nose. Heads would certainly roll.

Now what was she supposed to do? Because she didn't know anyone else to ask, she returned to the Register of Deeds and spoke with a clerk.

"A Mapping log is missing?" the clerk responded. "I must say, I've never heard of that happening before."

Just her luck it would happen now, Ariel thought sourly. "Could I pay someone to find the information I need?" Ariel inquired. "I'm afraid I don't live close by and it's difficult for me to take time off to come here."

"There are people who do that. For a fee they search the chain of title for you and send you a report."

From the clerk, Ariel obtained the names of three title searchers. She went to a pay phone and finally engaged the services of a Mrs. Lambert, who sounded as if she were a bit on the officious side. Relieved not to have to go through this bureaucratic musical chairs again on her next day off, Ariel arranged to have Mrs. Lambert look up what she wanted to know about The Black Tupelo.

As she headed toward the shoe store where Doris had said she intended to buy a certain pair of yellow shoes, Ariel reflected on how much of the day had been wasted. Discovering what should be a matter of public record about the inn had proved to be more trouble than she'd expected.

"How did it go?" Doris asked as she handed the shoe salesman the cash for her purchase.

"They didn't find the microfiche log, so I'm having a title searcher find what I need."

Doris thanked the salesman and accepted the bag containing her new shoes. A small bell over the shop's door tinkled as Ariel and she left.

As they strolled down the street toward Ariel's car, Doris said, "The Mapping and Appraisal Department must really be messed up to lose something like a log."

"The clerk in Deeds said she'd never heard of that happening before. My luck." Ariel unlocked the car doors, then slid behind the wheel.

"Yeah." Doris shook her head. "That's weird. Really weird."

Ariel thought so, too.

11

Jonah sat on the side of his bed, studying the life-size portrait that hung on the wall. The important artist who had painted it had captured her subject's likeness with an almost eerie touch. She had also managed to reveal the subject's inner spirit.

Arrogance. In the lift of the young man's perfect eyebrow, in the curl of his perfect lips, in the tilt of his perfectly proportioned head, arrogance came screaming forth.

The young man painted on the canvas had been one of the handsomest men in the world, so the critics had said. In fact, they had refused to use the term handsome, claiming to find it too limiting, too insipid to describe his marveled-at good looks.

Beauty. That had been the word they'd used to describe him. Incredible beauty. Jonah stared at the portrait that he kept as a merciless reminder. As punishment.

Once he'd had it all. A loving family. Talent. Success. He'd been the crown prince of his world. His fault. It was all *his fault*. He'd held everything a man could want in the palm of his hand, and he'd carelessly thrown it away. He'd destroyed everything he'd ever cared about. And now. He dropped back to lean against the wall. He squeezed his eyes closed.

Now his only kingdom was the night. He was only a shadow prince.

Michael chewed his treat contentedly while Ariel examined his latest set of grafts.

"They're healing well, don't you think, Doctor?" Lucy Norton asked.

Ariel nodded in answer to the nurse's question. The color was good. The fine lines of the incisions were smooth and pink. If the process continued to go this well, the tracery web of the cuts would fade and, with the grace of God, vanish.

As if sensing opportunity, Michael looked up at Ariel. "Candy?" he asked in his child's bell-like voice. Scar tissue no longer pulled his expressive brown eye down at the corner.

"What do you say, Michael?" Lucy admonished gently.

"Please," he said promptly.

Ariel smiled, delighted. "What a polite young gentleman you're becoming," she told him, pulling one of the gaily wrapped fruit-paste-and-nut treats she'd brought for him from the pocket of her lab coat. She handed it to him and watched as he adroitly removed the paper and put the goody in his mouth.

"He really shouldn't have much refined sugar," Lucy said softly. She accepted the piece of colored paper from him.

Ariel emptied the contents of her pocket into Lucy's hand. "You'll be pleased to hear that I found these candies in a reliable natural foods catalog. Not a bit of refined sugar in them. They use fruit juices instead. The nutritionist has okayed them for his diet, but not too many of them." She lightly tapped Michael on the tip of his nose, and he giggled. "Only good stuff for our boy."

Lucy beamed. "Excellent."

Ariel smoothed Michael's hair. He gave her a wide grin, which tugged at her heart. She grinned back.

"I hear felicitations are in order," she told Lucy. "Have you set the date yet?" Through the hospital grapevine she'd learned that Lucy had become engaged to a physical therapist who also worked at Fountainhead.

Pleased color tinted Lucy's cheeks. "We're still trying to decide. Either October or December."

"Both sound good to me. In October you can be a harvest bride. In December you can wear white velvet." Ariel walked to the door, aware of the other patients left to see on her rounds. She raised her hand to Lucy as if in benediction. "You have my blessings either way."

Lucy laughed. "Oh, thank you, Mother Bountiful."

"Anytime, kid."

As Ariel strode down the busy corridor on the way to her next patient's room, she heard her name paged over the public address system. She stopped at the wall phone a few yards away. The operator connected her to the sentry at the Fountainhead's main gate.

"There's a man here who says he's come to visit you, Dr. Denham. His name is Nelson Herrick, Dr. Nelson Herrick, but he's not on the guest list."

Ariel frowned. Nelson Herrick? What was he doing here? "I'm in the middle of rounds now, Jack," she explained. "I can't come to the gate."

"Not necessary, Dr. Denham. I'll fax you a photo of him, and you can fax your approval to me. Then I'll call administration, and they'll send a host or hostess here to see him to guest quarters."

"Great. Thanks." She gave the sentry the location of the nurses' station closest to her.

Why was Nelson here? Fountainhead was a long way from Beverly Hills.

When she finished with her rounds, Ariel dialed Nelson's guest quarters extension. He answered on the second ring.

"There you are, Ariel," he said. "I'll bet you're surprised to have me drop in like this."

Drop in? Fountainhead was close to nothing. If he'd come directly from California, it was one hell of a drop.

"I'm somewhat surprised," she admitted dryly. "To what do I owe the honor?"

"It was time to talk with you."

"Oh?"

He failed to elaborate. "I didn't realize your new position involved such high security."

So that was it. Nelson was curious about Fountainhead and her work here. After all, it had "enticed" her away from the very lucrative position he now held. Maybe he wanted to know what she'd found that was even better than Bendl and MacDaid. Ha. What a joke. But her pride demanded he not find that out.

"Privacy is important here," she said smoothly. "How long do you plan to stay?"

"Just tonight. I hope we can have dinner together and reminisce. I'll tell you what's happening in Beverly Hills. And Hollywood. I'm really plugged into what's going on in Tinsel Town now."

Unwilling to prepare a meal for Nelson at her bungalow, Ariel agreed to meet him for dinner at Fountainhead's finest restaurant—the cafeteria. Afterward they would go to his quarters to share the bottle of wine he'd brought, while they "reminisced." Over what, Ariel couldn't imagine. They hadn't really shared much history. As she recalled, in medical school they'd existed in two different worlds.

She didn't want to hear him go on and on about being a partner in Bendl and MacDaid. The last thing she needed was confirmation of her lousy career move.

For the rest of the day her reasons to wish Nelson elsewhere accumulated, and as she walked back to her bungalow she added another important one. Because of him, she would miss her time with Jonah tonight. That was special time, and she resented relinquishing it.

After she showered, Ariel decided against taking

the trouble to pull her hair back into the chignon which was its customary daytime style. Instead, she brushed it out and left it to drape about her shoulders. With a light hand she applied makeup, than changed into a jade blue sueded silk top, jacket, and slacks.

Then she quickly walked down the incline and went into the park. She tied the envelope to an eye-level branch in the hedge, where it would be hard to miss.

The envelope bore only one word. *Jonah*. Inside was her note explaining that unexpected company had arrived, so she'd be unable to join him that evening. She hadn't signed the note in case someone else intercepted it.

Nelson stood waiting for her in front of the cafeteria. He was of medium height, with a squarish athletic build, and possessed the kind of wholesome, California-blond good looks that had kept songmeisters and Madison Avenue photographers busy since the sixties. When he spied her, his handsome face broke into a smile that Ariel had seen women turn silly over.

"Ariel!" He swept toward her. "You're looking lovelier than ever." She was startled when he kissed her cheek.

"You look good, too, Nelson," she said. "Beverly Hills seems to agree with you."

"Oh, it does! It really does." As they walked into the cafeteria, he started to put his arm around her shoulders, then, to her relief, he seemed to think better of the move.

"I think you'll find the food is quite good," she told him as she picked up a tray and placed it on the chrome-plated runners that extended in front of the room-long steam table. She considered the cucumbers and onions marinated in vinaigrette, then decided against it.

"When you said the cafeteria was the only place to eat at Fountainhead, I thought you were kidding." He pushed his tray past the large selection of attractively presented salads with barely a glance at them.

"Why?" Ariel indicated to the server behind the glass shield that she wanted the lamb. He cut three thin slices and passed the plate to her. She smiled her thanks and moved on. As she passed the offering of hamburgers, she smiled again, thinking of her conversation with Doris a week earlier.

"Why?" he echoed incredulously. "Because it's like being in the army. You have your little mess hall, and that's it."

"We have kitchens in our quarters. If anyone wants something not offered in the cafeteria, he or she can make it."

"Since when do you have time to cook? As I recall, you're always working."

She set a plate bearing a piece of cornbread on her tray. "That hasn't changed. But if I wanted to make something not served here, I've been given a place to do it."

She led him over to an empty table. Their meal was accompanied by small talk Ariel found excruciatingly dull, and she wondered what she'd done to deserve this evening of punishment.

Finally, the meal drew to a close, and they deposited their trays on the conveyor belt. As she and Nelson followed the lit walkway back to his quarters, she imagined what it would be like to have dinner with Jonah. They would have talked and laughed. Afterward they might have held hands while they strolled beneath the starry night sky. Time spent with Jonah would have been a joy, not this tiresome burden.

She fretted about Jonah not finding her note. Too clearly, she remembered the resulting turmoil last time she'd failed to show at the hedge.

Nelson droned on about how hard it had been to find a rental car when he'd arrived at the Asheville airport. The more time she spent in Nelson's company, the less she wanted to be around him. It seemed an unjust twist of fate that she could have dinner in the cafeteria with Nelson, and stroll Fountainhead's lamplit sidewalks back to Nelson's quarters for a glass of wine, but she was unable to do such things with Jonah. Because he was a patient and she a doctor. Because he would not leave the shadows.

Because he didn't trust her.

Jonah enjoyed her company, and he wanted her, but he couldn't bring himself to trust her. She wondered again what had caused his unrelenting caution.

They arrived at the hotel-style guest room, and Nelson unlocked the door, then preceded Ariel into the room to turn on the lights.

"It's not The Beverly Hills," he said, "but it'll do for one night." He went over to a small table and picked up a bottle of wine.

The accommodations looked clean, comfortable, and stylish to Ariel. Certainly nothing to be ashamed of. Or for Nelson to complain about.

He poured wine into two plain water glasses. "I wish I'd thought to bring one of the bottles from my private cellar," he said. "I'm afraid we're stuck with this little number that I picked up on my way to the Los Angeles airport. These amusing glasses are being furnished by your employer."

Ariel watched Nelson breathe in the wine's aroma. Then he rolled the voluptuous red liquid around in the glass. Finally, he sipped. He swirled the wine in his mouth, rolling his eyes consideringly. He swallowed.

"Not bad," he pronounced and took another sip.

Ariel sampled the wine in her own glass. Without looking at the label on the bottle, she knew this "little number" had probably been aging in a French cellar for the past ten years and had been liberated at no small expense. "Nice," she murmured.

"You were right," he said, sauntering over to the large picture window. He drew open the drapes. "This is a beautiful place."

Even from across the room, Ariel could see the rolling shadow of the mountains against the dark purple sky. Had Jonah found her note?

Nelson finished his wine and returned to the bottle on the table. He refreshed Ariel's glass, then his own. "When do I get my tour?" he asked.

Ariel studied him through her lashes as she took a swallow of the Bordeaux. Nelson was a handsome man. Now his evenly tanned cheeks bore a higher color than usual, and Ariel did not think it was caused by the wine.

She drifted over to stand in front of the window. Her eyes were drawn to the mountains. "Tour?"

"Of the clinic's facilities, of course. There must be something special that brought you here. It's got to be pretty damn good, because, remember, *I* know what you turned down."

She thought about taking Nelson into the hospital, of his walking down the halls, staring at the faces so desperate for repair. In his posh Beverly Hills practice, he would likely never see the ravages that were commonplace at Fountainhead. How would he view them? Would it be a freak show to him?

Sternly, she reminded herself that he was a reputable plastic surgeon. In his work environment, he had always presented himself professionally. She had no reason to think he would see the people who came to Fountainhead for help as anything less than the cases they were. Each one presented a particular problem that must be resolved. He would understand that. Still . . .

Oddly, she couldn't shake her uneasiness. This clinic was a temporary home for these people and Nelson didn't belong here. Besides, she thought, relieved to have a logical excuse, taking him on a casual tour of the Fountainhead facilities without Maitland's approval would be a breach of security. And it was too late to get the necessary approval tonight.

"I'm afraid I can't take you on a tour, Nelson. The Foundation is very strict about protecting patient privacy."

He looked surprised. "Well, I'm all for protecting the privacy of patients, but really. You can't even take me on a walk-through of the hospital?"

"You haven't been cleared."

"Who do you have staying here?" he asked incredulously. "The president?"

She laughed. "Maybe. I wouldn't know because he'd be assigned a different name."

Nelson walked over to join her at the window. "You're kidding?"

She shook her head. Her hair swayed around her shoulders. "No. Fountainhead is a nonprofit organization, but its costs are high, because here everything is first rate. So the movers and the shakers are allowed in. What they pay—and I understand that's plenty—goes toward the real purpose of Fountainhead."

He stepped closer to her. "And what would that be?" he asked, his gaze roaming her face.

He was standing too close. Ariel twirled her empty glass between her fingers as she eased back a step. "To provide help for those who can't afford it."

"Fountainhead is a charity?"

Ariel frowned. She disliked that word. "It's nonprofit."

"Which means you aren't getting peanuts out of this."

Hot color rushed up to flood her cheeks. She hadn't wanted any of her former associates to know. Pride demanded she succeed, that she go up in the world. She tried a bluff. "I get the experience." *Damn Renard. Damn him to hell.*

Nelson smiled faintly. "As if you needed more expe-

rience." He looked out over the moonlit mountains.
"I've always admired your brilliance, Ariel. You're
more than a skilled surgeon. You're an artist." He
turned his head and his gaze locked with hers. "You
are inspired."

This admission caught Ariel off guard. "I— Well,
thank you."

Nelson moved forward. Before she knew what was
happening, he kissed her. It was a pleasant kiss, as
kisses went. He was skilled enough to do it properly.

But he didn't have the power to drug her senses
with his presence. When he held her, her head didn't
spin, her body didn't ache for more. His kiss didn't
sweep away all common sense.

He wasn't Jonah.

Ariel placed her palms against Nelson's chest and
lightly pushed, but he didn't seem to notice the pressure.

"Haven't you ever suspected how I feel about you?
How I've always felt about you?" he asked, his lips
moving against her temple. "You're so beautiful,
Ariel, so talented. In medical school, I knew things
weren't easy for you, financially. Yet you were never
interested in my money. Other women were, but not
you. In fact, you never even seemed to notice me. I
always thought you were out of my reach." His fingers touched her hair, lightly, tentatively, as if he
feared that she might vanish at any instant.

Ariel blinked in astonishment. When had this all
come about? She felt as if she'd been blindsided by a
hurtling rocket.

"Nelson," she said, exerting a little more pressure

against his chest, "I never knew you felt this way."

With evident reluctance, he released her. "I didn't want to advertise the fact that the only woman I cared about probably didn't even know my name."

"I knew your name. Everyone knew your name."

Solemnly he studied her face. "I didn't care about anyone else."

"Nelson . . ." Oh, God, how did she tell him? She didn't want to hurt his feelings.

"When I got the call from Jeff MacDaid inviting me for an interview," he said, "I thought I'd died and gone to heaven. After all, Bendl and MacDaid is the most important cosmetic surgery practice in California. When I found out that *you* had recommended me . . . well." He smiled. "It was a dream come true."

Ariel needed some distance from this man who had just presented her with his heart. She walked over to the wine bottle and held it up, offering him a refill. He shook his head. She put the bottle back down.

"Nelson, I recommended you because you were right for the position." *Liar!* her conscience screamed.

He smiled sadly. "You and I both know that's not true. I'm a good surgeon, but I don't have it in me to ever be a star. I accepted that years ago."

Nelson had always been a glib, charming rich boy. At least, that's what Ariel, who had been so wrapped up in her own problems, had believed. Now she saw she'd been wrong.

There was more to Nelson Herrick than she'd supposed. She could only guess how hard, how very hard, it would be for him to accept such shortfalls about himself. Given his background and family expectations, they would be a bitter cup.

All his family's money could not buy him the gifts that she'd been given. Despite that, Ariel knew she had turned out to be no better than the other women he'd mentioned. His money had mattered to her. Or rather, the contacts it bought. Like all the rest of them, Ariel had sought to use Nelson. The only difference was, he cared about her.

"Nelson, you *are* a good surgeon. David Bendl and Jeff MacDaid are certainly impressed with you, or the partnership wouldn't be named Bendl, MacDaid, and Herrick now."

"Oh, I'm good enough for them," Nelson conceded. "But I doubt that they're quite as interested in my skill and knowledge as they are in my name and family connections. And the money, of course." His smile was derisive. "My partnership cost me considerably more than they would have asked from you, bet on it."

She suspected what he said was true, yet he seemed so calm about being victimized for his wealth. No, Ariel thought as she looked at him, not calm. Resigned. It would seem that Nelson had accepted this, too, as a reality of his life.

He walked over to her, took the wine bottle gently from her grasp and set it back on the table. He took her hands in his. "Ariel, it's you who have made me happy. And I came to see if maybe there was a chance for us."

Inside she cringed with guilt. She liked this new side of Nelson she was seeing. He was a realist. He saw things for what they were, and she respected that in him.

Ariel studied his face. It was as handsome as ever, but this close for the first time since medical school, she noticed the lines in his forehead, around his eyes, bracketing his mouth. They were deeper than they should have been. She spotted silver strands in his blond hair. His sky blue eyes were far too world-weary for his thirty-five years.

"Nelson." He deserved to hear the truth from her, to learn the real reason she'd recommended him to Jeff MacDaid. Didn't he?

Nelson touched her cheek. "Yes?"

But what purpose would the truth serve? It would only be hurtful.

She swallowed dryly. "Nelson," she said again, groping her way blindly into new territory. "I really did recommend you because I thought you were the best one for the position." A lie.

Some of the light in his eyes flickered and died and the muscles in her chest tightened in regret. "So," he said quietly, "I've come to Fountainhead on a fool's journey."

"No," she protested. "I'm glad you came."

He just looked at her, and she knew he expected her to elaborate. "You said you didn't think I even noticed you when we were in school, but you were wrong. I noticed you. I admired you very much." Another lie. "You were always so good with people. You liked them. And I remembered that when I had to turn down the partnership." Lie number three.

She eased her hands from his, and rested them

lightly on his shoulders. "You see, *you*, better than anyone else I know, realize that even the beautiful people have fears and troubles. That they need a doctor who won't be so in awe of them that he forgets they need comforting and reassurance, just like any other patients."

As she spoke, Ariel saw her opportunity to tap Nelson's wealth of important contacts sift away, like gold dust through her fingers. She had thought them essential, a way to find a good position when she left Fountainhead. But she found she just couldn't use him. Even though she felt certain that she would eventually regret this act of conscience, she just couldn't prey on Nelson Herrick.

He sighed. "So. You don't care for me." It wasn't spoken as a question, but there was something in his voice that asked.

"I do care for you, Nelson," she insisted softly. "As a friend." And she found she meant it. "In a way, we started out together. We've kept in touch, on and off, through the years. But maybe now . . ." She searched for the right word. "Maybe now we can better *appreciate* each other."

A flush tinted his handsome face. She knew he was embarrassed at having revealed his affection to her.

Somehow they managed to stumble through the rest of the evening. Ariel was relieved when she could finally walk to the door. Her hand was on the brass knob when he said, "I'm going to see if I can catch an earlier flight out of Asheville. There's no point in my staying here. So this is good-bye."

Ariel knew she might never again see Nelson without his carefree rich-boy facade, and she regretted that. On an impulse, she turned and kissed his cheek. "Have a good trip," she said, then opened the door and stepped out onto the railed, brightly lit walk that led to the elevators.

He strode to the door, bracing his hands on the inside frame on either side. "I'll call you."

She didn't believe that, but she helped Nelson to maintain the fiction. "I look forward to it."

Then, because there didn't seem to be anything left to say, Ariel left him standing there.

The next morning, when she called Fountainhead guest reservations, she was told he had checked out before midnight. A faint melancholy haunted her through her patient appointments, and by late afternoon, her blue mood had worked its way around into anger.

Last night would never have happened if Renard hadn't blackmailed her into coming to Fountainhead. *She* would have been the new partner at Bendl and MacDaid M.D., P.A. She would have contentedly performed rhinoplasties and rhytidoplasties and basked in the quiet glory that came of making superstars happy. Of course, banking large checks would have made *her* very happy. Nelson Herrick would never even have entered her mind, so her willingness to use him wouldn't have made her feel so rotten. It would never have been an issue.

But most important of all, she would have had the money to be in control of her life, the mistress of her fate.

Now the gray metal lamp on her desk glowed, augmenting the harsh fluorescent overhead lights of her office. Ariel slapped a file onto the growing stack. Another update completed.

She'd seen her last patient for the day hours ago. This small wing of the hospital had cleared out by six o'clock. When she'd come back after dinner, she hadn't seen any lights on in the other offices. Tonight she worked alone.

She glanced at her watch. Still two hours to go before it would be time to meet Jonah. She could go over a few more files and make it back to the bungalow to change clothes.

As she reached for the next folder, she noticed the hall outside her door growing darker by degrees, as if someone was turning off the lights. Just as she stood up, the hall light directly outside her door went out.

Every midnight creature feature she had ever seen flooded back to chill her. Her legs seemed paralyzed, her feet glued to the linoleum.

"Turn off your lamp," a man's voice commanded her.

A very familiar man's voice.

A second went by before she could breathe normally again.

"Ariel, turn off your lamp," he repeated.

She turned it off. Then, as she watched, a large, male hand curved around the doorframe and flicked off her office overhead light. Suddenly the room was plunged into utter darkness.

The old, too-familiar panic roared up inside her. "Jonah!" she gasped. "It's too dark!"

A few seconds later, a light came on in the hall. It was enough. Ariel's fear eased.

"Thank you," she said.

He stepped into the doorway, an onyx silhouette against blue-white fluorescence. His stillness couldn't mask the tension that vibrated around him.

"Did you find my note?" was all she could think to say.

"I did." His words were curt. He remained still, making no move to enter the room.

She sensed he had come there for a purpose. Quietly, she waited.

Finally, his harsh voice broke the silence. "Are you lovers?"

"Lovers?" she echoed dumbly.

He took a step into the room. Faint light slipped along the back of him, revealing the black cotton T-shirt that molded his wide shoulders and powerful torso and the black jeans that hugged his narrow hips and long, lean legs.

"You heard me," he said, advancing on her with feral grace. "Are you lovers?"

She didn't know why, but she backed away from him. "Yes, I did hear you. I just don't know what you're talking about." There in the darkened room, she could feel the tautness that hummed through his body. It filled the air and skittered under her skin like a thousand singing bees.

She came up against the wall. Before she could move, he leaned over her, boxing her in with an elbow placed casually on either side of her. As she knew he expected her to, she kept her eyes lowered.

"Now, exactly what part of my question confuses you?" His breath was warm against her forehead.

She straightened. Jonah wasn't going to get away with his intimidation tactics. She placed her palms against the solid wall of his chest and shoved. For all the distance she put between them, she might as well have been pushing against Stone Mountain. Then, with leisurely deliberation, he took two steps back.

Ariel glared at his chest. "I'll tell you what part of your question confused me. All of it. It doesn't make any sense."

"I'm not a fool," he said tightly. "I saw you."

A chill trailed up her spine. "Saw me?" The dark was Jonah's domain. Not for the first time, she wondered where he went when he wasn't with her, what he did. "Do you . . ." The words caught in her dry throat. "Do you spy on me?"

Jonah made a disparaging sound. "Spy? I didn't need to spy. The two of you were flaunting yourselves for all to see." He stepped closer to her and stopped abruptly, as if he were trying to control himself. He looked away, and in that moment she stole a glance at him. Shadows like liquid jet gathered beneath his eyebrows and under his high cheekbones. "Right there," he said, "in front of his window."

"That window faces the forest. Only a spy would have been out there to see anything. Not," she added stiffly, "that there was much to see."

"You let him touch you."

Ariel remembered Nelson had embraced her, kissed her in front of that damn picture window. The intimacy had left her cold.

But how had Jonah even known where she was?

Her eyes widened. "How did you find me?"

His hand sliced the air in a sharp gesture. "That doesn't matter," he said impatiently.

"Oh, but it does."

She could feel his gaze burning into her like a heat beam. "You forget that Fountainhead is a small community, Ariel. Your note said you had an unexpected visitor. Only one guest arrived yesterday. So I went to guest quarters." He shook his head in two short motions. "I don't know why. Curiosity, I guess. Then I looked up and there you were. With him." He drew a sharp breath. "Is he your lover?"

Under different circumstances, the idea of Nelson being her lover would have been laughable. Now it held no amusement for her. This angry man confronting her here, in this dark room, was Jonah. Proud Jonah. She saw the tension in the muscles of his arms, in the taut posture of his body. He'd seen her with another man.

And he cared.

A flurry of butterflies burst into joyous flight around her heart. Jonah had seen her in Nelson's arms and he had cared enough to risk exposure by coming here.

"He isn't my lover, Jonah," she said quietly.

Before she could draw a breath, he closed the space between them. He gripped her upper arms in a restrained hold. "You kissed him." She sensed he wanted to shake her.

"No," she said. If only she could meet his shadowed gaze. He would see in her eyes that she told the truth. "He kissed me."

Sarcasm edged his words. "I didn't see you resisting."

She frowned. "It was only a simple kiss." Unlike one with Jonah, which was never *only* a kiss. And certainly never simple. Nothing with Jonah was simple. "I wasn't going to hurt his feelings over it."

"A pity kiss?" Though his tone was sardonic, underlying it she heard the fierce, dark anger. He tugged her nearer, and she could feel the heat from his body. "Was that what it was, Ariel? Is that what ours have been?"

"I won't dignify your last question with an answer, Jonah. And I don't think I deserve that from you."

He was angry—that she could understand. What she couldn't fathom was the intensity of his emotions over a single, quasi kiss. She hadn't even responded beyond the effort required to save the poor man's pride.

She tried to see the scene as Jonah would have seen it. He would have been standing outside in the dark, maybe crushing her note in his hand as he watched her being kissed by a man of medium height, blond, handsome—

Realization struck her with an almost physical impact. *Handsome*.

How must Jonah have felt when he'd seen her being held by an attractive man? Someone who could move about freely, day or night, without incurring revulsion or ridicule?

Oh, Jonah, she thought, sorrow welling up to drown her annoyance with him. *It's you I want, not Nelson.*

She laid her palm on his arm. "No, it wasn't a pity kiss. Nelson doesn't need my pity. But he doesn't deserve to be needlessly embarrassed, either."

"How kind of you."

She moved closer to him, almost touching her face to the base of his throat, where the T-shirt skimmed over his pulse point. "I'm not feeling kind now," she whispered.

He stirred restlessly. "You're not?" But his voice had lost its hard edge. Now it sounded distracted.

"No. I'm not." She slipped one arm from his slackened grasp, and with the tip of her index finger, she nudged down the neck of the shirt to reveal that warm hollow. The pulse beneath beat fast and strong.

She pressed her lips to his skin and heard him draw in a long, slow breath. Encouraged, she touched the tip of her tongue to that same sensitive place.

He lifted his hands to frame her face, effectively stilling her. "It drove me crazy," he said, "seeing another man touch you."

Ariel thought she should be annoyed by such presumption, especially when he refused to commit to so much as telling her his full name. But his possessive words burrowed deep inside her, and the way he spoke them sent her blood singing through her veins.

"I'm glad," she murmured.

"Now," he said, "tell me who this Nelson is, and what he is to you."

Just who did he think he was, assuming she would obey his every command?

A small, quiet voice from the back of her mind answered her. This was a man who lived every day of his life at a severe disadvantage to people even far less fortunate than Nelson. This was a man whose only protection against the incredible cruelty of the world was his fierce pride.

This was the man she loved.

Ariel swallowed hard against the lump in her throat. She'd gone and done it. Despite all her resolutions and self-admonitions, she'd fallen in love with a patient. Not just any patient, either, but one who was certain to want to run away from dark memories once he was free to live a normal life. Unfortunately, she would be one of those memories.

"Ariel," he prompted.

She tried to gather her thoughts and return to the moment. This moment, in which she knew that Jonah cared for her. The damage was already done. She'd fallen in love with him. She would worry about the future tomorrow. Until then, she wouldn't complicate matters by telling him how she felt. All of her professional and personal experience told her he would leave her behind, the way that Patrick had left Vickie. She couldn't allow herself to believe things would be any different with Jonah. It was too late to save her heart, but she could at least keep her pride.

"Nelson and I were fellow students in medical school. In order to come here to Fountainhead, I was forced to pass up an offer of partnership in a prestigious practice in Beverly Hills. I recommended Nelson to them. It surprised him, after not hearing from me for years."

"What I saw didn't look like surprise."

She sighed. "He thought my recommending him meant more than it did."

For a moment she thought he would pursue his line of questioning, but he only nodded.

"Jonah," she said softly. "I missed our walk last evening."

He enfolded her in his arms and kissed her.

Her heart raced. A drugging light-headedness invaded her. Ariel curled her fingers into the T-shirt that covered his chest and kissed him back. She took deep satisfaction in feeling his heartbeat pick up its tempo, and his breathing grow rapid and shallow. He pressed her closer.

Footsteps sounded in the hall. Ariel ended the kiss, pulling away from Jonah slightly, listening. The sound of the footfalls faded and she was left feeling foolish for being so jumpy.

He lifted his head, his face turned up toward the ceiling. She saw his throat work as he swallowed hard.

"Jonah . . ." Her voice trailed off, leaving words unspoken. She wanted to assure him, but she knew there was nothing she could say that would make their situation better. Their time together—secretive and hidden as it was—would end when Jonah drove out the gates of Fountainhead, a new man. She was certain that he realized this. It was why he kept pulling back. She suspected that was why he wasn't willing to make love. Like her, he knew that final intimacy would make their parting infinitely more painful.

He touched her hair, his long, elegant fingers

brushing back a stray wisp from her cheek. "I'll meet you by the hedge at the usual time." His voice was low and husky.

She wanted to reach out to him, to smooth away the misery that she sensed lay under his controlled surface. But she suspected he would not welcome such concern, interpreting it as pity. Intolerable pity. So she simply said, "I'll be there."

Michael poked the purple stuffed dinosaur on its snout. A silly squeak rewarded him. Gauze and tape and the discomfort of the sutures from his latest muscle flap made smiling difficult for the boy, but his lively eyes twinkled with glee.

Lucy laughed. "Just what he needs. Another stuffed dinosaur."

Ariel squelched her disappointment. She'd been so certain Michael wouldn't have seen anything like it when she'd ordered the toy from the catalog. "You mean he already has one?"

"He has two. One from me and one from Dr. Sprague."

"Oh. But do they squeak?" Ariel asked hopefully.

Lucy grinned. "Yes. But yours is the only purple brontosaurus."

Ariel watched the child cuddle the soft plaything. When he'd come to Fountainhead three months ago, he'd been scarred, terrified, and poorly socialized. Since then, under the attention of his physicians and the maternal care of his nurses, particularly Lucy Norton, he had bloomed. He wasn't so afraid of strangers now, and he was even learning some manners. Best of all, he laughed frequently.

Her gaze shifted to the wooden chest next to his bedside table. She spotted the two other stuffed dinosaurs and smiled. Apparently roses weren't Kerwin Sprague's only soft spot.

She turned her attention to the tissue expander that she had inserted beneath a healthy section in Michael's scalp. As the balloonlike device was gradually inflated, the skin surface increased, producing a greater area from which she could take grafts to cover the place where his hair had been burned away. A brief inspection satisfied her that the expander was doing its job and that blood circulation remained good.

"I know the hospital kitchens change menus every so often," Lucy said, "but Michael doesn't like the new dishes as well as the old ones."

"You know he's on a special diet now. Make certain he eats his meals."

"He can be very stubborn." Lucy sighed, but her affection for Michael was clearly revealed in her face.

Ariel made a notation on her young patient's chart. "So can you, Lucy. And you're bigger and meaner. You shouldn't have any trouble with such a little fellow."

An hour and a half later, after Ariel finished her rounds, she went back to her office. She sat at her desk and tried to concentrate on finishing her notes. Her telephone buzzed and Ariel reached over the open file to answer.

A woman's voice greeted her. "This is Mrs. Lambert. Am I speaking to Dr. Denham?"

The title searcher. Excitement percolated through Ariel. "Yes."

"I'm calling at your request," Mrs. Lambert informed her officiously.

"Yes, I understand. Normally you just send the written report." Ariel tried not to sound as impatient as she felt.

"Which, of course, I will do in addition to this phone call," the searcher went on, apparently determined to follow some required routine. "You did agree to pay for the call."

Just get on with it, woman! Ariel wanted to shout. Instead she managed to rein herself in to agree calmly with Mrs. Lambert. "Yes, I did. So, the Mapping records on The Black Tupelo were finally located?"

Mrs. Lambert became more animated. "They were, and in the strangest place. A plumber found them when he had to go down into the basement to fix a leak. That log was smack-dab behind the row of file cabinets. The courthouse hardly ever uses that area. It's mostly for storage, you understand. And as an archive."

A current Mapping microfiche log behind old file cabinets in a basement? Ariel leaned her elbows on her desk. "How would the log have ended up hidden in the basement?" she asked.

"Pure deviltry," Mrs. Lambert said promptly. "No other reason. Maybe that new boy in the Mapping and Appraisal Department had a relative or a friend in the Farley area who hoped he wouldn't have to pay his taxes if the log disappeared." She chuckled smugly. "What he—or she—didn't know is that we're in the process of going on computer."

Ariel frowned. "Then why didn't someone in that office just pull up the records I needed on the computer."

Mrs. Lambert coughed delicately. "Well, the Mapping Department is a little behind. That's why they hired someone extra. For all the good it did them. No sooner had they hired him then— But the hooligan is gone now. Disappeared right after you asked for the information on The Black Tupelo." There was a short silence on the line, and Ariel thought Mrs. Lambert was probably shaking her head in disapproval of what the world was coming to. "It's sheer luck that log was found."

Ariel opened her mouth to ask if such record thefts happened often, when she remembered the clerk telling her the day she'd gone to the courthouse that a Mapping log had never gone missing before.

"I've done the search and have the information you asked for," the older woman said.

At last. Ariel picked up her pen and held it poised over her yellow tablet. "I'm ready."

"Well, there isn't much to tell. The property has had only two owners in the past seventy-four years, and you said not to go back more than twenty-five years. The property was owned for sixty years by a Jonah Albright. Until his death fifteen years ago."

The pen never moved in Ariel's still fingers. A chill rushed down her back. In her mind's eye she saw the form of a tall man standing in deep shadow, partially silhouetted by moonlight—a man she only met at night. *Jonah* Albright? She caught herself. Albright must be just a relative or a friend of her Jonah's family's. The Jonah she knew was too young to be Albright. Besides, Albright had died. . . .

"You said there'd been two owners," she asked, almost absently.

"Yes," Mrs. Lambert said. "Mr. Albright willed the property to Declan Stone."

"*The* Declan Stone?" Ariel asked. "The rock star?"

"The very one."

"Where does the trail go from there?"

"Nowhere. That's where it stops."

Ariel asked the title searcher a few more questions, and hung up. She sat still for a moment, absently staring at the telephone.

She'd expected The Black Tupelo to be a starting point, something that might eventually lead her to Jonah's true identity. Instead, she'd been left with a dead end.

Declan Stone, the young rock music superstar, idol of millions, had died twelve years ago.

12

Ariel bolted out of her chair and strode down the corridor. She didn't stop until she reached patient records, where she found Doris still at her desk. Everyone else had apparently gone home for the evening, even though it wasn't much past five.

Doris looked up with a smile, which faded when she saw Ariel's face. "What's wrong?"

Ariel dropped into the chair next to Doris's desk. "I just received the strangest information." Absently, she frowned down at her short-nailed hand that gripped the chrome-and-vinyl armrest. "From Mrs. Lambert, the title searcher I told you about."

Doris remained quiet, waiting.

"The Black Tupelo was owned for sixty years by a man named Jonah Albright. He died fifteen years ago."

"A relative, maybe. Seems Jonah might be your friend's real name after all."

"Maybe." Again, Ariel's mind conjured a picture of the tall, shadowed man. She thrust that memory back in its place, and focused on what she was telling Doris. "When Jonah Albright died, he willed the property to Declan Stone."

Doris's eyes widened. "Declan Stone?"

Ariel slowly nodded.

"I have every one of his albums. Do you remember *Winter Rose*? God, he was good."

"Yes, I remember." Stone had been called the poet laureate of rock, and he'd taken the world by storm. He'd given new scope to the word superstar.

Doris shook her head. "What a hideous way to go. Burned up in a car wreck."

"To die so young—" Ariel's eyes widened as a thought struck her. Could Jonah's brother, Tim, have been Declan Stone? It was a long shot, of course, but all the facts that she knew fit. He'd spent time in this area. He'd been musically gifted. He'd died young. She slowly straightened in her seat. And if Tim were Declan Stone, might Jonah have been in that blazing car accident with him? It would explain what had happened to Jonah's face. Except the scars on his face didn't look as if they'd been caused by burns or lacerations. Of course, the light had been dim, but she'd never seen anything like them before.

Doris didn't seem to notice Ariel's moment of preoccupation. "Jeez, she said, "small world, isn't it? Declan Stone owned property in little old Farley. So. Who did The Black Tupelo go to after Stone?"

"It doesn't appear to have changed hands. But then, the records might be incomplete."

"Can't those people in the courthouse keep track of their records? Jeez."

"I guess The Black Tupelo must have become part of the Stone estate."

"But Stone's been dead twelve, maybe thirteen years."

Ariel wearily rubbed her hand over her face. "Twelve, to be exact. It's hard to believe any probate process could take that long. Surely the estate was closed out years ago."

"I don't know. Declan Stone was known to be a 'live for today' kind of guy. I guess musical geniuses aren't expected to think about the future. Maybe he died before he got around to making a will."

"No, there was a will. There's a copy in the courthouse file—"

"You mean there's something they didn't lose?"

"Mrs. Lambert said it was in bad condition." Ariel's mouth tightened. "She said that it looks as if someone spilled something on it, then tried to wipe it off. The ink smeared in many places. One of the places it was smeared was over the part about The Black Tupelo. The name of the heir is illegible. That's the way it was when it was put on microfiche. But the documents that would indicate the estate came out of probate are missing. If, in fact, it ever did."

"If that's the case, I'd like to be the estate attorney. He's probably put all his kids through college on that estate alone."

Ariel pushed up out of the chair, suddenly unwilling to talk any more about Albright, or Stone, or The Black Tupelo. But most of all, the missing records.

"Well, I've got some files to go through and a journal to read. I'll see you tomorrow, Doris."

As she walked back to her office, Ariel couldn't stop brooding over what she'd learned from Mrs. Lambert's telephone call. She'd hoped her trip to Reavesboro and Mrs. Lambert's search of the records would answer her questions, but, in fact, the mystery had only deepened.

Despite her research, she wasn't any closer to learning Jonah's identity when she went to meet him that night.

He waited for her beneath the trees. A thread of faint moonlight wending through the branches exposed a wedge of bare chest, a sliver of jogging shorts, and a patch of cotton sock and running shoe. Ariel found it difficult to look away, not to stare at his torso. It was so beautiful. So manly. So *naked*.

Who was Jonah?

She wanted to ask him if he knew a person by the name of Jonah Albright and then watch his reaction. Silently she cursed the shadows. She wouldn't be able to even *see* his reaction.

"How was your day?" he asked as they fell into step along their parallel paths, separated by about six feet of lawn. They headed into the park, away from the ravine, on the route they took most often.

If she mentioned Albright's name, she thought, Jonah would know she'd been checking up on him. Maybe he already knew. Maybe that was why the information she needed had turned up missing.

"Good," she answered automatically, keeping her gaze trained to the walkway ahead of her with an effort. Then she made herself think about his question and what had happened during her day. "It was good," she affirmed.

His deep voice carried easily from the dense shadows cast by the rampart of trees and bushes. "What made it good?" Something in his tone told her he really wanted to know.

Why would the man who took a sincere interest in what made a day good for her, the man who had cradled her and comforted her in the dark, steal and conceal official county papers? How would he have done it? Did she really believe he had? That was the real poser, the one that made her feel more paranoid than logical.

If the courthouse had caught up to the latter twentieth century as it should have, Ariel thought darkly, and had already put everything on microfiche and computer, none of this would have been a problem.

She shuffled aside the problem for the moment. "Lots of little things made my day. A new patient came in, a young woman. Her parents have kept her sheltered. She's terribly shy, and I don't think she really believes anything can be done for her. But she wants a husband. Children. All the normal things. So she's willing to give this a try. And I feel very confident that she'll be happily surprised."

She thought of the times since she'd come to Fountainhead that she'd been privileged to share in the awed joy of patients when incisions began to heal and the swelling receded. It wasn't the critical pleasure she was used to from so many of her former patients who had inspected the results of a face lift.

Here she saw wondrous hope ignite in patients' eyes.

"And you?" he asked. "Do you want a husband and children? Or do doctors not have such common aspirations?"

She tried to bear in mind his opinion of doctors, but she found his question provoking nonetheless. "Doctors are quite human, I assure you," she said dryly. "We want the same things everyone else does. We just have to wait longer than most people to get them."

Jonah didn't respond immediately. "You didn't answer my question."

She frowned straight ahead, all too conscious of his presence, which lay upon her as surely as a touch, thrumming against her senses. Her eyebrows drew down farther as she thought of him striding along beside her, bare-chested, gradually working up a sweat, which would gleam upon his skin as it rippled over his athlete's muscles. "Of course I want a family," she said.

"Than why aren't you married?"

She looked over at him sharply. "Why aren't you?"

His chuckle held a harsh edge. "I should think that would be obvious."

Instantly she softened. Had his disfigurement cost him the love of a fiancée? A wife?

"You'll find someone else." The words were meant as comfort to him, but they nearly stuck in her throat. When he left Fountainhead, he would want all the things his scars had denied him. It was only natural. And she would be out of the picture. She must learn to accept that.

From the corner of her eye, she saw his hands tighten into fists, but she couldn't bring herself to voice any more encouragement. He might not believe her now, but he would learn on his own. The words echoed in her mind like a taunt. *On his own*. Without her. Perhaps with little or no thought of her. A cold, hard fact.

She must learn to accept, she told herself fiercely.

"So you're not only a surgeon," he drawled. "You're a psychic. How convenient."

Ariel ignored his sarcasm. "You don't have to be a psychic to see that a man will meet more women when he's out in the light of day than he will lurking about the shadows at night."

"I met you, didn't I?"

For some ridiculous reason she didn't want to examine too closely, his answer flustered Ariel. "Well, yes. That is to say—"

"You were telling me why your day was a good one," he interrupted smoothly.

She knew she should be only too glad for the change of subject, but Ariel couldn't help feeling a spike of annoyance at his assumption of control. Slowing her pace, she tried to release her irritation.

Jonah stopped and waited for her to catch up with him. When she did, he matched his pace to hers. "Your day," he said. "I'd like to hear what made it good. I'm tired of bad news."

"You've had bad news?" Ariel asked, concerned.

With a flip of his hand, he waved away her question. "Nothing that can't be fixed."

"Is it a medical problem?"

"No."

"So, it has nothing to do with your surgery?"

"Nothing."

And that, apparently, was all that Jonah chose to say on the subject.

"All right. As I was saying earlier, lots of little things made my day good. But mostly I think it's the progress of one patient in particular. Michael." Ariel shook her head, her amazement renewed as she thought of the little boy. "He could restore someone's faith in miracles. When I was given his file, I was surprised this kid had made it through the screening. He didn't seem to be a good candidate for all the surgery he needed. He has a history of infections. But blood serum workups revealed his liver wasn't metabolizing proteins properly. And his antibodies were down. So I had his diet changed and, along with the antibiotics being administered, the problem with infection has all but disappeared. There were some other problems, too, but infection was my most immediate concern."

Ariel glanced over at Jonah, who seemed to be listening to her. At least, he was quiet. So she slipped in a question that had been bothering her for a long time.

"When are you scheduled to begin your surgery, Jonah?"

When he didn't reply, she persisted. "It's been months now. What's the delay?"

"It's not your concern, Ariel," he said, his smoky voice underlaid with dark warning.

"I think it is."

He stopped. "Ariel—" He cut off what he'd been about to say. "Just back off, okay?" He raked his hand through his hair in a distracted gesture. "Just back off."

She faced him, her arms crossed over her chest. "I think I have a right to know," she said quietly.

He swore under his breath. Ariel stood there. Waiting.

"All right, " he said tightly. "I haven't decided if I'm going through with surgery."

Alarmed, Ariel immediately drew breath to object. But she caught herself before she could voice her objections. Instead, she studied the black-on-black shadow-man that was Jonah, trying to gain some clue to the cause of the resistance she felt coming from him.

His reluctance to discuss the matter of his surgery was clear, but she decided not to be so easily put off.

"Why?" she asked with a calmness that did not reflect the frustration churning inside her.

"I have my reasons."

"Will you share them with me?"

"No."

Ariel feared that if she continued to press him, he might think she was urging him to undergo surgery because she thought it was a cure-all. Or worse, because she wanted to change him for her sake. She thought of all the things he missed by confining himself to the dark. All the dear, common, everyday details that would forever remain beyond his grasp, if he never reached for them.

"What?" he said. "Not urging me to go under the knife, doctor?"

She smiled sadly. "No."

It was cruelly apparent to Ariel that Jonah was starved of hope. Her heart grieved for him. Oh, how she wanted to make everything right for this man! If only— She shook her head.

"This is a decision only you can make, Jonah."

Neither of them spoke as they walked back. But when they stopped beside the hidden cleft in the hedge, Jonah surprised her by taking her hand and coaxing her into the shadows and into his arms.

Ariel's heart tripped into a clattering dance as she gave herself up to the solid strength of his body. Eyes closed, she accepted his kiss. Delight swelled in her chest.

His palm curved around the back of her head, his strong fingers firm against her scalp. He kissed her forehead, her eyelids, her cheeks. She felt his heart pounding, felt his quick, shallow breath against her skin, and elation soared within her. Though she might try to deny it to herself, this was where she wanted to be. Here in Jonah's arms.

He moved his mouth over hers with fierce passion. When she parted her lips, he invaded that moist space in a greedy rush, as if he had been waiting too long for entrance.

She clutched his shoulders, every cell in her body alive to his warm, bare skin, to his every ardent caress, to his earth-and-evergreen scent. Under her fingers she felt powerful muscles ripple and tense.

He drew her more tightly to him, as if he feared she might slip away and vanish forever. Dimly, Ariel realized that tonight there was a ferocity about his embrace, his kisses, that had never been there before. But then his mouth moved back to hers and rational thought escaped her. She laced her fingers in his thick hair and lost herself to the magic of being held by Jonah.

After a moment more, he gently but firmly set her away. Even though his touch was temperate, she could feel the tension raging in him. "Good-night, Ariel," he said gruffly.

She looked at him a moment. Faint moonlight trickled through the leaves to gleam along his moist, bare shoulders. His chest moved with his labored breathing.

"Good-night, Jonah," she said and stepped through the hedge.

He was shaking. Jonah stared at his hand. Christ, he was *shaking*. Carefully, he breathed in a long breath, trying to calm his galloping heart. He'd been afraid the time had come. She'd demand answers or leave him.

She'd seemed finally about to push for explanations. And he'd steeled himself for the worst. God, he'd been sure it was the end of what they had together.

He wasn't ready to give her the answers she wanted, the answers he knew she deserved. His stomach roiled and clenched at the thought of what he knew would happen when the time came that she didn't pull back.

His temper blazed high again as it had earlier. She'd let him believe she thought of him as a man, a *man*, and he would not tolerate her trying to treat him as some reticent patient.

He *was* a man, he thought savagely. Her man. At least for now. For this dwindling time they had left to share their private world.

Walking a short distance from her bungalow, he sat down on the ground. Slowly he drew in a long, uneven breath. Just as slowly, he breathed out. He repeated the exercise a few times before he grew impatient and shot to his feet.

What the hell was he doing here, anyway? He never came this close to her quarters. Usually he contented himself with observing from the hillock until her last light went out.

He swallowed hard and stared longingly at the lit windows. One by one, he watched her draw the drapes, pull the shades, and shut off the lights, until she came to the last room. Her bedroom.

Jonah gazed at that brightly lit window. She came into view, catching the tasseled pull of the shade, and drawing it down, leaving him with only her dark, shapely silhouette framed by a bright rectangle. He would never be with her to pull that last shade before he turned to her in the light, kissing her soft lips, touching her sweet body. Seeing every endearing, exciting, haunting detail.

Against his will, he watched her, telling himself that he was only waiting for her to move away, and, finally, turn out that last light.

She reached up and took the binding from her ponytail. She tossed her head, and her hair fanned out and fell like a drapery of silk down her back.

His mouth went dry when she reached for the hem of her knit top. She pulled it up the length of her torso, arching her back slightly, her breasts out-thrust. She tugged the top over her head, and her hair draped back down. Then she hooked her thumbs in the waistband of her shorts and pushed them down.

He shouldn't be watching, he thought as his gaze remained glued to her silhouette. He was no better than a voyeur. But confronted with the sizzling temptation of her womanly silhouette, his resolve to do the honorable thing melted away.

He wanted her. God, how he wanted her.

Then she walked away from the windows, her delectably rounded hips swaying. The light in the bedroom went out.

He swallowed a groan of protest and thought of going to her door and knocking. Hell, that would take too long. He'd climb through her bedroom window. He took a step in that direction.

If he went to her now, would she welcome him? They could keep the room dark. He would make it good for her. Very good.

For a moment, he stood there, staring dumbly at her darkened window. The night air seemed oddly cool—until he realized he'd broken out in a sweat.

He whirled and stalked away from the bungalow, out toward the park. Madness! It was madness to think of making love with Ariel.

Because he couldn't risk losing her. He couldn't chance the loss of that precious belief that she saw him as a man, or that intimate sense of connection he had with her. Not now. Not yet.

But he must make his decision soon.

❖   ❖   ❖

Work was more hectic than usual the following day, and before Ariel realized it was past time to go home, the sun was setting. As she walked back to her bungalow she decided to call her father to see how he liked his new job. She poured herself a glass of iced tea, then dialed his number.

"Hi, Dad."

"Ariel! What a nice surprise!" Gerald Denham exclaimed over the telephone line. "I was beginning to think you'd forgotten your old dad."

The long cord of the kitchen phone allowed her to stroll to the edge of the living room. "You know I'd never do that."

"Oh, you wouldn't do it intentionally, of course. So, how is your work there?"

"Fine, Dad. Everything here is just fine. It's very pretty. I think you'd like it. There are trees and mountains. There's even a stream. We could get you a rod and reel and some tackle in Farley, and you could go fishing. The guest quarters are comfortable. Why don't you—"

"I'd love to, little girl, but I don't have the time. It's that bastard Renard, you know? There aren't enough hours in the day to get everything done. You wouldn't believe what's expected of a manager in this lousy chain of stores. And, of course, a man has to have a little time to relax. A card game now and then."

Ariel stared down at the toes of her bare feet as disappointment flooded her. "Of course." Nothing ever changed between them. Except now he actually had a job.

"You know I really want to visit you. It's just not a good time for me."

"That's okay. I understand." Just as she'd always understood. But for some reason she kept trying.

"Good, good." He paused, and she could hear him take a puff of his cigarette. "Has Renard been working you as hard as he has me?" He gave her no time to answer, but continued on as if he hadn't asked the question. "Every minute," he complained, "every goddamned *minute* is spent working. But I show him. I take an hour-and-a-half lunch hour. And questions! The fools that work in this store are always pestering me with questions. They can't figure things out for themselves."

"You're the manager, Dad," she said softly. "They're just deferring to you out of respect for your authority."

"Do you think so?" he asked, sounding slightly mollified. Then, as if he'd come to his own conclusions, he said, "No. They're just idiots. They can't do their jobs, so they take *my* time."

She twisted the telephone cord between her fingers. "Have you thought about talking with the other managers? Maybe they've encountered the same problem and have already come up with a solution."

"So you think the other managers are smarter than your own father? Well, that's just great. My only kid, and she thinks I'm too stupid to know what to do with lazy employees."

Her fingers twisted the cord tighter. "That's not what I said—"

"I heard what you said! I'll tell you, young lady, this is a problem you've always had. You think you know everything. But you don't. You haven't seen how these slugs constantly lean on me. 'What do you want me to do now, Mr. Denham?' 'Shall I check on the inventory, Mr. Denham?' 'The stock for the sale hasn't come in yet, Mr. Denham.' Like I have nothing better to do than to put up with them! Well, I'm going to fire their butts. The last thing I want around is people who hang on me, people who need me to make decisions for them."

The telephone cord tightened into a loop. *People who depend on you.* "I'm sorry you're so unhappy."

"Yeah. Well. It's not your fault, I guess."

She forced herself to release the cord before it tore out of the phone.

"I hear that Herrick fella you recommended to that ritzy practice you passed up is doing pretty good for himself."

"Yes." And she was stuck here. Her dream of being in control of her life was as far out of her reach now as it had always been. "Well, I've got to go now, Dad."

"Where to? It's eight o'clock at night and you live in an isolated valley." There was a pause. "Oh, I get it. Hot date, huh?"

"Uh, yes. A hot date."

After she hung up, Ariel walked into the living room, and gazed out the small panes in the French doors. The white moon was visible in the sky.

She shouldn't have called her father. Conversations with him always left her feeling depressed or inadequate. Or both. Nothing seemed to change, no matter how hard she tried to please him. She never quite measured up to his expectations.

Turning from the French doors, she glanced at the coffee table, and the single white rose she'd found on her desk that morning. The long-stemmed bloom towered out of the water glass she'd set it in, having left the crystal vase on her desk.

French Lace was the name Kerwin had given. He'd added it was a hybrid tea, and had won some kind of award. His usual discourse had been lacking its usual enthusiasm. Ariel had not missed the lingering looks that had passed between Doris and him.

Pleased for her two friends, Ariel now walked over to the flower. The petals were a perfect, snowy white, the edges of each curling back to reveal the petal beneath. Ariel smiled. Who came up with these names? French Lace. It sounded more like naughty underwear than a rose.

She continued to look at the flower. Why was Kerwin continuing to give her roses when he was clearly smitten with Doris? But wasn't that just like Kerwin? Tenderhearted. Maybe there weren't enough roses to give them each one daily. That was probably it. And he didn't want to hurt Ariel's feelings. Well, she'd have to have a little talk with him to let him know she wouldn't be offended if he gave the roses to Doris. Although—Ariel sighed—she had enjoyed receiving them.

Glancing at the clock, she hastened into the bedroom and changed clothes. Jonah had asked her to meet him earlier than usual tonight. She carefully looked around before she dashed down the incline from her terrace. It was still early enough for there to be people out and about.

Jonah was already at their meeting spot when she arrived. Without a word, he took her hand briefly, then broke into a light jog. She followed his example, and together they quickly, quietly made their way to the arch in the wall. Again he offered her his hand and led the way, ducking beneath the wall that separated them from the ravine and the forest beyond.

In the ravine they stopped. Ariel paced around, catching her breath. Jonah, she noticed, didn't seem winded at all.

"Where are we going?" she finally asked.

White teeth gleamed in the shadows. "I've planned a surprise."

He chuckled. It was a smoky, sexy, masculine sound that sent tendrils of awareness rippling through her middle.

"What?"

"If I told you, it wouldn't be a surprise." He held his hand out to her. It shone in the moonlight. His arm remained in shadow.

She took his hand. "Are there any ghosts?"

"Why? Do you want some?"

"No!" Ariel shook her head vigorously, sending her ponytail flipping from side to side. "No ghosts, please."

He started walking. "Some people. They have no sense of adventure."

She walked with him, still holding his hand. "Do I need one for what you've planned tonight?"

"No, I think not. Tonight is more a fantasy than an adventure."

13

They strode beneath the forest's tattered canopy, ducking low boughs, brushing aside willowy, leafy branches. Light from the summer moon formed beams of pale silver that slanted down to the forest floor like scattered spotlights. Pine and humus scented the air.

Ariel noticed how deftly Jonah sidestepped the columns of moonlight. He moved silently, while the carpet of fallen leaves rustled under her every step.

"How do you do that?" she asked, breaking the stillness of the woods.

"Do what?"

"Walk so quietly. You always move without a sound."

"Practice."

"But why do you go to the trouble of practicing?" she persisted.

"I don't want to be seen."

That, Ariel thought, was rather like Magellan's saying he'd go for a little sail. She tried again. "Where did you practice?"

"Here."

In her surprise, she almost tripped over her own feet. He'd never answered her so easily before. She managed to recover her balance, skipping a few steps to catch up with him. "Here, meaning Fountainhead? Or here, meaning this entire surrounding area?"

He spread his arms. "Here, meaning here."

She frowned, puzzling over his answer. "Just how long have you been 'here', Jonah?"

"The stock market went up today, did you hear? Thirty-six points."

He wasn't going to get any more specific about "here," that was certain. She decided to go with the flow. "The market interests you?"

"What do you think about them finding a new species of freshwater snail in Tennessee?"

So much for the flow. Ariel glared at his shadowy figure. "Freshwater snail?"

"Give it up, Ariel." She heard the warmth of a smile in his words. "Just enjoy the evening." He offered her his hand. She looked at it a second, then took it. "Tonight why don't we just relax? Let things unfold? Maybe we'll both learn something."

"Relax," she muttered. "Unfold."

"That's right, Sunshine. For tonight, just take things as they come."

Sunshine. He'd called her by the name before. It had been that night in The Black Tupelo. When he'd realized she was afraid. Now, as then, the word gentled on his tongue, becoming a lilt, a caress. An endearment.

Her heart beat just a little faster. "All right," she said. "I'll try."

To her surprise, he lifted the back of her hand to his lips and brushed a kiss against her skin.

After approximately three miles, gradually the forest thinned, and Jonah and Ariel emerged into what looked like a row of backyards. Ahead were well-spaced frame houses. Cheerful light spilled from a few windows.

As they quietly made their way between the houses to the brick street beyond, Ariel whispered, "I feel like a trespasser."

The dark form of Jonah's head turned. "You *are* a trespasser," he whispered back as he led her through the darkness under the old oaks that lined the street.

"I can see it now," she muttered. "The headlines will read 'Surgeon Apprehended Prowling Farley Residents' Backyards.'"

She heard the low chuckle in Jonah's throat.

They moved through the shadows of buildings and trees. Jonah glided soundlessly. Twice Ariel stumbled on roots and uneven pavement, but his firm hold on her hand always steadied her. The village was dark and deserted, and she thought that the old saw about small-town people rolling up the sidewalks early must be true.

Finally he led them to the back of one of Farley's few restaurants and opened the door. Watery moonlight flowing into the room partially exposed cabinets, a commercial stove, and a stainless steel worktable.

"Jonah, this is known as breaking and entering," she protested in a furious whisper.

"We're not breaking in," he pointed out. "The door's unlocked."

She looked back over her shoulder at the open door. "What kind of proprietor leaves his door unlocked? Does this have something to do with insurance money?"

He didn't answer her, but passed inside, taking her with him into the windowless room. Behind them the door swung shut, pitching them into absolute darkness.

Panic exploded in her chest. "Jonah!"

"I'm here, Sunshine. Hold on to me." He put his arm around her and drew her against his side. Instantly she clung to him. "That damned thing isn't supposed to close so quickly."

With rapid, sure steps, he guided her through the windowless, ink black kitchen. "It's just a room," he crooned softly. "Only one room, Sunshine. Then there will be moonlight for you."

They emerged into the dining area of the restaurant. Moonlight poured in through large windows hung with cafe curtains.

Jonah stopped. "Are you all right?"

She gulped air. "Fine," she managed.

"You're sure?" he asked. Anxiety rode his voice.

Ariel nodded.

He waited, one hand gently rubbing her back, her shoulders. When she had regained her composure, he said, "Is there enough light here?"

She looked around. "Yes."

Tables were covered with checked tablecloths over which glass had been set, to prevent the tablecloths from getting dirty. On each table was a clustered arrangement of a chromium paper napkin holder, a small, white dish containing packets of sugar and artificial sweetener, and a pair of white plastic salt and pepper shakers. The chairs and banquettes were upholstered in vinyl-coated fabric of a dark, solid color. Ariel thought it might be red.

In the corner of the dining room was a jukebox. It was an old one, from the looks of it. No trendy art deco trim, no spinning colored CDs. Just a good, old-fashioned, record-playing machine.

"Count to five, then join me around the corner," Jonah said, gesturing to where the room formed an *L*.

She counted to five, wondering what he was doing, wondering what they would say if the police arrived.

"Ready or not, here I come," she called softly, then walked around the corner.

And stopped in her tracks.

A table had been set with a white damask cloth and napkins. Moonlight gleamed on heavy silver flatware, antique china, and lead crystal. In the center stood a slim green malachite vase bearing two yellow chrysanthemums. On a side table sat covered silver platters and a wine cooler containing ice and a bottle of champagne.

The angle of the table to the windows had been carefully arranged, allowing her to remain in bright moonlight, while Jonah sat in thick shadow. Her chair, she noticed, had already been pulled out for her.

She swallowed hard. No one had ever done anything like this for her before. And Jonah—it must have been especially difficult for Jonah to make the arrangements this dinner would require.

"Oh," was all she could say.

He cleared his throat. "You'll excuse me for not getting your chair?"

She gave him a brilliant smile as she took her seat. "Certainly."

"I . . . uh . . ."

Ariel looked at his shadowy figure in surprise. He actually sounded embarrassed. She found it endearing.

"Jonah, am I being courted?"

He reached for her hand and drew it toward him. She watched as it disappeared into shadow. He pressed a kiss into her palm, and shivers of pleasure spun up her arm. Gently he closed her fingers over the place his lips had touched. "For tonight." His deep voice held something she hadn't heard in a while—that wistful, faraway note.

Her heart twisted with silent regret as she thought of what little time they had left together. Whether or not he underwent surgery, Ariel was certain Jonah's stay at Fountainhead must be growing shorter. There were so many people who needed the help Fountainhead offered, but only so much room at the clinic.

She managed a smile as she withdrew her hand, back into the moonlight. Her palm was still warm from the touch of his lips.

He lifted the wine bottle from its deep bed of ice, revealing that it was, in fact, champagne. He poured for them both.

She lifted her glass. "To tonight."

"To us, tonight."

As their glasses met, a crystalline musical note chimed and hung in the air. Ariel sipped the effervescent wine, letting it frolic on her tongue before she swallowed, savoring it as she did the moment.

Steam rose as Jonah lifted the silver dome from one of the platters. The mouth-watering aroma of beef Stroganoff filled the air like an exotic perfume.

Ariel breathed in the wonderful smell. "You've had help, I see."

"Oh? And how do you know I didn't make this all with my own two hands?" Amusement lightened his question.

She grinned. "Because it's still warm."

"Ah. I should have known you would immediately see through my flimsy efforts to impress you." He reached for her plate, his arm bisected by moonlight and shadow.

She handed it to him. "Jonah, I'm terribly impressed. And if you count all this"—she waved her hand to indicate the table and settings—"flimsy, I can only wonder what your serious effort would be."

He served the beef Stroganoff and the buttery egg noodles, then went on to dish up the delicate baby carrots and white asparagus concealed under two other silver covers. "Okay, I confess. This wasn't flimsy."

"Good. I'd hate to think I didn't rate a little higher than that." She took the first bite of Stroganoff, and closed her eyes in an ecstasy of enjoyment. The cafeteria's food was good, but it would never approach such sinfully rich perfection. "Mmm."

Jonah chuckled. "I'll convey your compliments to the chef."

"Oh, please do." Someone in town knew Jonah, Ariel thought. Knew him well, to trust him alone in the restaurant. She cut a bit of carrot as she said, with what she hoped was casual inflection, "I would like to meet this marvelous chef." She looked up through her eyelashes.

"André is much too shy."

"André? His name is André?"

White teeth gleamed in the dark, reminding her of the Cheshire cat in *Alice in Wonderland*, and she knew the chef's name was not André.

"Beef Stroganoff has always been one of my favorites," he said.

"Did your mother make it when you were young?"

"Every Sunday." He took a bite of the creamy stuff. "Did you ever have it as a kid?"

Ariel almost laughed. The ingredients were much too costly for her to have afforded. Besides, who would have made it? "No."

"What did you have? What was your favorite dish?"

"Ice cream."

"Desserts don't count."

"Then I'd have to say ravioli."

"That's funny, you don't *look* Italian."

"I'm not, but Chef Boyardee is."

His hands paused over the task of cutting asparagus. "Canned ravioli was your favorite food?"

"No, ice cream was my favorite food, but you said that didn't count."

She swallowed her champagne, in an instant comparing this moment of plenty to the many cold meals spooned from a can she'd eaten as a child.

They ate in silence for a moment. Then Jonah said, "Did your father ever make your dinners?"

She looked at Jonah, or rather the shadowy form that was all she could see of Jonah, and hesitated. She didn't like talking about her early life. It was filled with nightmares and loneliness. Jonah's, on the other hand, seemed to have been filled with family and love. He might not understand if she told him. Worse, he might pity her. Anything but pity. But if she refused to answer his questions, he might never answer hers.

"Rarely," she said. "Besides, I could open a can or box and make my own meals."

His hand stopped before his fork reached his mouth. "How old were you when you started, uh, cooking?"

"Seven."

He lowered his fork. "Seven?"

At his soft tone, she straightened in her chair, feeling her defenses slam into place. This communication thing wasn't easy. "It doesn't take an adult to open a can," she said evenly.

"It doesn't take an adult to turn on a stove, either. Or to lift a hot pan."

"That's right."

"And your father was away being an entrepreneur?"

She wanted to tell Jonah the truth. She really did. But this was a singularly difficult truth. So she told him the same lie she'd always wanted to believe. "He was working."

"Didn't you have a baby-sitter?"

"No," she said shortly. "I didn't have a baby-sitter."

To her relief he changed direction. "Where did you live?"

She wanted to sound airy, casual, but her words came out sharply. "Just about everywhere. We moved around a lot."

"Ariel," he said quietly, stroking her upper arm with one strong hand. "I'm not being critical. I just want to know. You've never spoken much about yourself, you know. Just your work."

"And what have you been willing to tell me? Damned little."

"I told you about my family. That's more than you've told me."

She was surprised to realize he was right. "I guess I don't talk about such things much."

"Why?"

She looked away, through the top of the window across the room. Outside, the leaves of a tree stirred in a breeze. "We were poor, Jonah. Desperately poor. And my father . . . I . . . he . . . We didn't see much of each other. I don't like remembering."

She felt his fingers thread through hers, exerting a reassuring pressure.

"Now you're a gifted, respected surgeon with a brilliant career ahead."

She listened carefully to his voice and found no trace of what she dreaded to hear. "And how would you know that?"

He grinned. "I took the trouble to ask around."

"Well, it's all true. I am brilliant."

"I said you were *gifted*. It's your career that's going to be brilliant."

She stuck her nose into the air in an exaggerated pose of grand indifference and flipped her hand a couple of times. "Gifted. Brilliant. Whatever."

Jonah cleared their dinner plates away, tucking them onto the second shelf of the side table. Then he lifted the last cover, to reveal two china dessert plates bearing slices of strawberry tart.

"It's glazed with a currant sauce," he said. "At least, that's what Chef André told me. I didn't have the heart to tell him that to me it didn't matter. All I care about is that it tastes good."

"And does it?"

He passed her one of the plates. "I'll let you be the judge of that."

It was heavenly. The rich flavor of the fruit burst in her mouth, and the sauce whispered a faint tartness, a lighter counternote to the sweetness of the strawberries. She was still enjoying that first luscious bite when Jonah asked, "Do you have any brothers or sisters?"

Ariel swallowed. "No. I was an only child."

She smiled. "What was it like, having a brother? Was he a friend or a nuisance? Did you do things together?"

"I'm two years older than Tim was. I always felt responsible for him, which used to drive him right up a tree sometimes. Especially when we started dating." He leaned back in his chair. "I must admit, sometimes I bugged him on purpose. We used to do everything together." He fell silent for a moment. When he spoke, his voice carried an underlying sad note. "He was my best friend."

Ariel's throat tightened with sorrow for him. She'd never know the joy of having a brother or sister, but she would never experience the terrible loss he'd suffered. She wanted to ask when Tim had died, and of what cause, but couldn't bring herself to voice the questions. They seemed too intrusive. Too cruel. She would wait until another, better time to ask.

"You said he was musically talented."

Jonah nodded. "Yeah. Music was Tim's life. Did I tell you that he'd been awarded a full scholarship to Juilliard?"

Ariel murmured that he had indeed told her.

"God, I was so proud of that kid. We all were. Mom and Dad all but took out an ad in *The New York Times*. Do you have any idea of the competition for a full scholarship at any school? Much less Juilliard?"

"Pretty fierce." She knew exactly how fierce. Scholarships had paid most of her way through college and medical school.

"Absolutely. He might have been"—Jonah's voice took on a suspicious roughness—"the greatest composer of our century." He fell silent, as if caught in the web of his memories.

After a few seconds, Ariel asked, "And what did you excel in?"

His cough of laughter was a bitter sound. "Trouble. I excelled in trouble. And, oh, I was good at it. So goddamned good."

Ariel studied him for a moment when he refused to say more. All that was visible was a shadow-shape.

Out of this entire room, romantic with moonlight, this man had chosen to sit in the very darkest place, as if he believed his face a blight on all this lovely fantasy. But now she saw the trouble went deeper than that.

Tears burned at the back of her eyes. She wanted to heal him, but she knew her scalpel could never reach his real wound. She wanted to comfort him, to wrap her arms around him and hold him close.

Pushing back her chair, she walked to the jukebox in the corner and plugged it in. Immediately, soft, colored lights came on. Jonah made a noise of protest. She pretended not to hear, and selected the only song on the country and western menu with which she was even vaguely familiar: "Tennessee Waltz."

She returned to the table and held out her hand to him. "May I have this dance?"

He hesitated, and she could feel his refusal coming. Then to her surprise he took her hand and left his seat. "I'd be honored."

Gathering her into his arms, he began to dance, moving with unconscious grace.

She disengaged her left hand from his formal grasp and wrapped her arm around his waist. She laid her cheek against his chest. His heart beat a steady rhythm.

"What did you excel in?" he asked. His athletic body might mask his uncertainty, but it lurked there, in his voice. She sensed that he thought he had gone too far, given away too much.

She would have liked to tell him that to drive her

away he'd have to do better than revealing just a glimpse of his deepest self. But feelings were not something Jonah seemed to be willing to discuss. So she said, "I excelled in stubbornness. Pure, bone-headed stubbornness. The more someone told me I couldn't do something, the more determined I became to do it." She laughed softly. "Not always the smart route to take, I'm afraid."

"It got you where you are today."

She lifted her head, careful not to look at his face. "Yes. Yes it did. And sometimes, it was all I had. That and pride." She wrinkled her nose. "Jeez, I sound like a thoroughly unpleasant person."

He chuckled, and her heart lifted at the sound. "I don't think you're unpleasant at all, Ariel Denham." He kissed the top of her head. "Not at all."

The music ended too soon for Ariel. She would have been content to dance in Jonah's arms for the rest of the evening. But when she dreamily suggested they deposit another coin, he hugged her—then unplugged the jukebox.

"I have another surprise," he said. His rich baritone failed to conceal the note of eagerness.

"Another surprise?" she echoed as he whisked her out of the dining room.

"Wait here," he told her. He went into the black-ness of the kitchen. Then a wedge of moonlight sig-naled that he had opened the back door.

She would have crossed the kitchen by herself—quickly—but he came back for her. Cuddling her in the curve of a protective arm he escorted her outside.

"Where to now?" she asked.

"This way." He grabbed her hand and gave it a little squeeze as he took the lead.

They kept to the shadows of the buildings that lined the street. The silvery lunar light and the profound stillness cast downtown Farley into a whole new perspective, Ariel thought. There was an eerie anticipation about the place. A watchful breathlessness.

Rubbish, she told herself sternly, trying to shake off such silly fancy.

Jonah finally stopped in front of the old, boarded-up movie theater. A few black letters remained in the marquee, an undecipherable cryptogram. The box office stood empty, its window clouded with almost a generation of dust and grime. A sheet of newspaper rustled in the night breeze, trapped in a corner along with an accumulation of dead leaves. Boards held by rusted nails crisscrossed over two sets of double doors.

Jonah went to the one on the right and tried the handle. The door, board and all, opened with a creak that soared up the scale like a ragged violin.

With the deftness of a magician conjuring a rabbit from a hat, Jonah produced a flashlight. He handed it to Ariel. "The place is big," he said. "And you have light. Will you come inside with me?"

The flashlight produced quite a bit of illumination, she noted as she aimed the beam into the darkened lobby. Burgundy carpet with a flowered print was revealed. Posters advertising movies long consigned to their cans were displayed in glass cases on the gold-painted walls.

"Why are we here, Jonah?"

He stood holding the door open for her. She saw him shift his weight from one foot to the other. "I wanted to take you to dinner and a movie," he said in a low voice.

His effort to accomplish something like normality touched her deeply. Tonight she would do her best to master her fear of dark, enclosed places. She couldn't disappoint Jonah. She just couldn't.

Standing on tiptoe, she tried to brush a kiss across his lips, but got his chin instead. "Thank you." Taking a fortifying breath, she walked into the lobby.

He stayed at her shoulder, slightly behind. Steering her off to the left, they took the stairs up to the projection room. There they found shelf after shelf stacked with movies in their canisters.

"These were the extra films they'd play before the main feature," Jonah explained. "You know, like cartoons, and episodes of *The Masked Marvel*. Pick out a couple."

They settled on *The Whispering Shadow* and a cartoon. She watched Jonah arrange the reel of their first selection on the old projector, then set about threading the ribbon of film.

Wait a minute. Why was the power on in an abandoned movie house anyway? Ariel wondered.

"Jonah, why is this theater closed?"

"Not enough business. It was built by a speculator in Asheville, who apparently thought the movies would draw viewers not only from Farley, which was never big enough to support it alone, but the surrounding area. It didn't. Probably because there weren't that many families living close enough to attend, and still fewer who could afford the admission. Marwood used to be the poorest county in North Carolina."

She flashed her light around the projection room, careful to keep it away from Jonah. Dust lay in a velvet layer of gray. Cobwebs draped the corners. "How long has it been closed?"

"About twenty years, I'd say. It was opened briefly during another attempt to do business, but the place is just too big and elaborate for such a small town." He finished working the film into its correct path. "There," he said with an air of satisfaction. "Let's go." He flicked a switch and the projector whined to life.

Cupping her elbow in his hand, he helped her rise from her sitting position on the floor next to the shelves. She brushed herself off and led the way out of the room, back down the stairs.

"Let's get our snack from the concession stand," he said.

"Okay." She headed back toward the lobby. "But won't they be a little stale by now?"

"That depends on what you choose."

The wide, U-shaped glass counter was long empty of its boxes of candies and nuts, but now two tall cups of cola and two striped paper bags brimming with hot, freshly popped popcorn had been set on top. The popcorn was warm. Ice cubes floated in the cool soft drinks. Hairs prickled on the back of her neck, and she swept the room with the beam of her flashlight.

Jonah lightly touched her ponytail. "They're gone

now, Sunshine. I just thought you might like a traditional movie treat while we watched the films."

She directed a smile toward him. "Is this the work of Chef André?"

"More like Chef André's cousin."

"Ah. So it's a family business."

He reached around her to pick up his popcorn and both their sodas. "Something like that."

She picked up her bag of popcorn. "Where to now?"

He lead the way into the theater proper. At the far end towered the screen. The projector was rolling. Numbers flickered over a test pattern. As they proceeded down the aisle, Ariel moved the beam of light over row after row of empty, burgundy velvet-upholstered seats.

Jonah pointed her to a chair, but instead of sitting next to her, as she'd expected, he took the seat directly in back of her. Of course, she thought with a small sigh.

The cartoon began. It was an old thing, something her father might have enjoyed as a youth. The film was scratched and the sound was a little raspy, but for Ariel the flaws of age only added to the cartoon's charm.

Jonah leaned forward. "The view is particularly good from back here," he said in a low voice. His warm breath stirred stray wisps of her hair, tickling her nape.

"It's much better from here," she insisted, awareness of his presence fluttering through her body.

"Ah, but all you can see is the cartoon," he murmured. "I have something prettier to look at."

She blushed at the compliment, then felt foolish for acting like a schoolgirl.

The black-and-white cat and mouse chased each other across the screen, stopping now and then for brief skirmishes that involved oversized mallets, trick mouse holes, and unreliable ladders. The mouse appeared to be the more intelligent of the duo.

Jonah laughed. It was a deep, rich, honest sound that prompted a smile from Ariel. The cartoon seemed much funnier when sharing in Jonah's enjoyment.

Finally, the cat gave up the chase, and the mouse triumphed, free to steal cheese for another day. The seat behind Ariel creaked softly.

"If I were that cat's master," he said, close to her jaw, "I'd invest in some good, sturdy mousetraps."

His nearness left her breathless. "Mm," was all she could manage.

"I'll be back in a minute," he said. "I've got to change reels."

She blinked at the credits scrolling down the screen. When she turned around, Jonah was gone.

Alone in the high-ceilinged theater, Ariel quickly switched on her flashlight, anticipating the end of the film, which came a few seconds later. The light on the screen went out. To divert her thoughts from the darkness that closed around her, encroaching on the solitary beam from the flashlight, she tried to learn more about the interior of the place. The narrow column of her light combed the walls, touching bright, apricot-colored walls, painted with lines of gold, stylized masks; gold, scalloped art deco lamps designed to cast the light upward instead of shining into the patrons' eyes; an orchestra pit, which Ariel thought a bit extravagant. Had one of the grand Wurlitzer organs held that place of honor?

"Are you all right?" Jonah called down from the projection room window.

"I'm fine," she answered. "This is a big theater." And she had a flashlight. A worrisome thought struck. "How old are the batteries in this thing?"

"They're new."

She breathed a sigh of relief. "Hurry, okay?"

Continuing her inventory, she found that heavy gold curtains flanked the screen, which was fronted by a stage. She guessed that the screen could be brought up, and the stage used for theatrical performances.

Suddenly the screen came to life. It remained white for a while, the only indication that film was running was the rain of black scratch marks, and the minute flickering. Suddenly the light vanished, leaving only white letters, stark against a black background. The words read: *The Whispering Shadow*.

Her hand holding her cup of cola stilled in midair as her imagination conjured the image of a dangerous phantom lurking in the shadows.

The weight of a hand fell on her shoulder.

14

Ariel jumped, a squeak escaping her throat. Cola sloshed over the edge of her cup, onto the floor.

"Did you miss me?" Jonah asked from behind.

She tried to recover her breath. "Don't *do* that! You scared me half to death."

"Sorry," he said, but amusement laced his voice.

She turned partially in her seat, glaring at his shoulder. "Being alone in this place is darn creepy, you know."

"I guess it might be."

"It *is,*" she grumbled, settling back into her chair.

The opening credits of the movie ended, and the story began.

The overacting in the movie was so bad they found it funny, but the notion of a mysterious phantom clung to Ariel. Behind her, Jonah leaned forward in his chair. His nearness so distracted her that she had

difficulty concentrating on what was happening on
the screen. Occasionally his softly spoken comments
turned into nuzzling, sending a shimmer of delight
through Ariel, who leaned back slightly to accommodate him. His breath smelled of buttered popcorn.
His lips were warm and inventive.

Still, the notion of a phantom gliding through the
night haunted her.

Before she was ready for the movie to end, the
closing credits were playing across the screen.

Jonah's lips brushed the curve of her jaw and Ariel
held her breath, focusing on that warm point of contact. No other man had ever had this power to thrill
her with his mere touch.

With a long sigh, he eased back in his seat. "It's
time to go, Sunshine."

Oh, not yet! But she knew he was right. She
couldn't go to work tired. She refused to shortchange
her patients. Or, as in the case of tomorrow morning's
surgery, put them at risk.

While Jonah went up to the projection room to
return the movie reels to their cases, she waited in
the lobby. Then they left the theater, pausing long
enough for Jonah to lock the front door. He pocketed
the key, and they walked the silent streets of the
town, back to the forest. Back to Fountainhead where
she would reenter her daytime life, and wait, once
again, for the coming night—and Jonah.

She was exhausted by the time she entered her
bungalow and went right to bed. Her dreams were
haunted by forests and phantoms, and the "Tennesee
Waltz." Morning came too soon.

When she opened the door to her office, she discovered that the rose on her desk was different from the others she'd received. Soft pink kissed the edges of white petals. When Kerwin saw it he told her its name—Escapade.

The two of them walked down the halls and took the elevator to the operating room where Ariel would begin rebuilding the face of a seventeen-year-old who'd been in a car wreck six years earlier.

Ariel scrubbed her hands and arms with the strong, antibacterial soap. The sound of running water splashing into the white enamel sinks filled the room. She thought about the name of the rose she'd received. Then she recalled her "date" last night. Now, *there* was an escapade. Romance and mystery with a dash of adventure. She sighed dreamily. Oh, why couldn't Jonah be the one giving her flowers?

"Something wrong?" Kerwin asked.

"Uh, no." Caught off guard, she resorted to a smile. She was being silly. She wouldn't spend another minute wondering who was responsible for the flowers she found on her desk each morning. They were there. That was enough.

But why couldn't it be Jonah?

She looked over at Kerwin, who already had his surgical mask on. Maybe she should just ask him. Just come right out and ask if he was the one who'd been leaving her the roses. That would settle the matter once and for all.

But what if Kerwin was the mysterious bearer of roses? What if he enjoyed the pleasant game? The man was very shy. Ariel remembered how he'd looked her first official day at the clinic, when he'd asked to sit at her lunch table. His face had flushed, he'd held his tray with a nervous, white-knuckled grip, and the poor fellow had stammered.

No, she decided. Straightforwardness probably wouldn't be the solution. This was a situation that called for a more delicate approach. She'd ask Doris if *she* could find out.

Those two were becoming quite an item, anyway. Doris's eyes sparkled whenever Kerwin's name was mentioned. And Kerwin . . . well, Kerwin seldom mentioned his beloved roses these days. He was much more interested in Doris. If Ariel hadn't been so pleased for her friends, she might have found this whole love thing vaguely nauseating.

Envy, taunted an inner voice. But she knew it wasn't envy that Doris and Kerwin's blooming love caused her to feel as much as an awful, gut-wrenching yearning. She and Jonah could have what her friends had found if only . . .

She cut short that thought, annoyed with herself. With more force than necessary, she thrust her hands into latex gloves. A teenage girl was waiting for her.

The operation went smoothly and, after speaking with her patient's parents, Ariel took a brief lunch break, then began checking on her other patients. But the question of just who was giving her the roses nagged at her. Finally she stuck her head into the patient records office. She spotted Doris hunched over an open file, looking as if she were ready to spit nails. "Got a minute?" Ariel asked.

Doris pushed her chair back from her desk and

walked out into the hall. "Thanks for rescuing me. This has been a day for messed-up files."

Ariel cleared her throat, feeling suddenly awkward. "Doris, would you . . . Do you think . . ." She felt her face growing hot. "Could you find out if Kerwin is the one leaving the roses?" she blurted.

Doris examined her flawless manicure for a moment. "You sound as if you think he might not be the one."

"I'm not sure. The more I've thought about it, the more I think Jonah might be leaving them."

Doris brightened. "That would be nice."

"For both you and me. But I don't want to hurt Kerwin's feelings, just in case he *is* the one. You know how shy he is." Ariel noticed the bright blush moving up Doris's cheeks, and managed not to smile. Maybe not *always* so shy. "And thoughtful. But if it is Jonah who's responsible, I'd like to know."

"Why don't you just ask Jonah?"

Ariel rolled the hem of her fresh blue scrub top between her thumb and finger. "I could ask, but I'm not sure he'd answer. I can't even guess where he'd get the roses."

"He probably got them from the same place Kerwin would get them. The rose garden."

Ariel's mouth fell open as she stared at her friend. Quickly she caught herself. "Rose garden?"

Doris raised an eyebrow. "How is it that you don't know about Fountainhead's rose garden?"

"How *would* I know?"

"You didn't read your orientation material, did you?" Doris accused mildly.

"Uh . . . no. I've been very busy since I got here. Very busy." She still hadn't told her friend about meeting Jonah in the park, but she suspected Doris probably thought they were lovers anyway. "Could you just do me a favor, and tell me where the garden is?"

"Well," Doris said, "I will admit that it's kind of in an out-of-the-way spot, so people tend to forget it's even there. It's not in the park. It's on the other side of the complex. Near the wall, next to the back gate."

"Back gate?"

Doris raised her gaze heavenward, as if applying to a divine source for patience. "Didn't you read anything Mr. Maitland gave you? The back gate isn't used very much. It's probably locked. I don't know. Most traffic comes and goes through the front gate because that's close to a main road."

Ariel sighed, silently kicking herself for not reading the orientation brochure Maitland had left her. "How come you never said anything about the garden?"

Doris leaned back against the wall and looked much aggrieved. "It never really came up. Besides, what was I supposed to do? Tell you that Kerwin was giving you stolen flowers? That would have been nice, wouldn't it?"

A warm flush washed up Ariel's face. "Okay, okay. I'm the one who goofed. I should have read the material. I'm off tomorrow, and I'd like to go see the roses. Now, will you tell me exactly where the garden is?"

They went back into Doris's office, and she drew Ariel a rough map. "Talk to Jonah about this first, okay?" she said as she handed over the paper. "If you can't get an answer, then I'll ask Kerwin."

Ariel had to admit that made sense. She thanked Doris, then hurried back to her office to try to catch up on her paperwork for the day. She was well into the third update when her phone rang. She recognized Mrs. Lambert's voice immediately.

"It occurred to me that you might not know the name and address of the attorney handling the Stone estate," the title searcher said. "Of course, it will be in the report you receive, but I just thought, since you seemed so concerned, that you'd like that information now. The report won't go out for another few days."

It appeared Mrs. Lambert wasn't as officious as she sounded, Ariel thought. "Oh, yes, please. I'd appreciate it."

After they hung up, Ariel dialed directory assistance for New York City and the operator supplied the telephone number for the law firm of Kramer, Vincent, Planck, and McGraw. Ariel's luck held, and when the secretary answered, she promptly put Ariel's call through to Philip Vincent.

"What can I do for you, Dr. Denham?" he asked. His voice was deep and resonant, but curiously bland, as if all trace of regional accent had been carefully tutored out.

"It's my understanding that you handle the estate of Declan Stone. Is that correct?"

There was a slight pause before he answered, "That is correct."

"Has the estate finished going through probate yet?"

"May I ask what your connection to this case is? I don't recall your name coming up before."

Ariel's mind raced, trying to come up with a valid excuse. She wasn't about to go into the real reason she wanted information, yet she hated lying. "I'm interested in The Black Tupelo."

"The Black Tupelo?"

"Yes. It's an old house in Farley, North Carolina. Actually, it's a bed-and-breakfast inn now. It's part of the Stone estate."

"A bed-and-breakfast inn, you say?"

"Yes."

"In North Carolina?"

"That's right."

"May I ask how you obtained my name?"

"It was on the copies of documents in the probate file."

"Ah, yes. The probate file."

Couldn't this guy do anything but echo things she'd already said? "Yes."

"If you have the file there, what are you calling me for?" he asked coolly.

"The file seems to be incomplete, Mr. Vincent. Did this estate ever finish going through probate? Or are you still working on it?"

"I hope you'll excuse me, Dr. Denham, but I'm pressed for time. All I can tell you about the case is that this firm filed the proper papers with the proper authorities in North Carolina."

"There seem to be papers missing—"

"Regrettable, of course, but these things sometimes happen."

Ariel wanted to reach through the telephone line and throttle Mr. Philip Vincent, attorney-at-law. She knew the bum's rush when she heard it. Before he hung up, she was determined to get at least a crumb of information from him.

"What do you know about Jonah Albright?" she asked, referring to the previous owner of the mansion. It was a wild card play, but she was running out of options.

"He's dead, I believe." His tone was so neutral that it was impossible for her to tell what might be going through his mind.

"I think that would be a safe assumption, since he bequeathed Stone The Black Tupelo." Ariel struggled to keep her sarcasm from oozing out over her words.

"It would seem you have all the answers. Now, really, Dr. Denham, I must go. I have clients waiting."

"One last question, if you please," she persisted.

He paused. "All right."

"Who owns The Black Tupelo now?"

"As I've said, the proper papers have been filed in North Carolina."

"Yes, but—" She was interrupted by a click, followed by the dull hum of the dial tone.

Philip Vincent had hung up.

Bright and early the next day, Ariel followed the directions on the map Doris had drawn for her.

The rose garden was located in a forgotten part of the valley, in a clearing about a mile from the complex

of medical and housing facilities. Just as Doris had
said, it was near the wall.

The place was deserted. Gravel paths intersected
the beds of lush bushes. Scattered throughout the
garden were wrought-iron benches, and classical
bronze statues covered in verdigris.

As Ariel strolled, she found pleasure in the full
green bushes, their delicate leaves and jewellike
blooms. Someone tended these plants with love, she
thought. There was no sign of disease and few spent
blossoms. Occasionally she bent to inhale the fragrance of a rose.

At the base of each bush was a small sign giving its
name. As she moved along the quiet paths she saw
American Beauty, Aloha, Pristine, French Lace, and
Escapade. Their sumptuous blooms were every bit as
lovely as the ones she'd received, only here they
blended into a rainbow.

She sat down on a bench, stretching her legs out in
front of her. Tilting her face up to the sun, she closed
her eyes and breathed in the perfume of this place.
Sweetly elusive, yet heady. No wonder perfumers
through the centuries had sought to capture the
essence. What woman wouldn't wish to anoint her
body with the scent of roses?

Though these flowers were delicate and all too easily damaged, their splendor was the embodiment of
passion.

Who had given her the flowers? Kerwin? Jonah?
Was there some significance to each different rose?

She recalled the different roses and their names.
American Beauty. Okay. That might be a compli-

ment, his way of telling her he thought she was pretty. Pristine. She'd received only one of these. What had been happening at the time? Ariel thought back, trying to set events in sequence, looking for the slightest nuances.

Pristine. Her eyes narrowed as she stared out across the surrounding lake of color. The night before, she and Jonah had— Ariel's face flooded with heat. That had been the night they had almost made love. The night Jonah had admitted that he wanted her, but insisted nothing could ever come of it. He had confirmed her belief—they had no future together. It was best that their relationship remain *pristine*.

She squeezed her eyes shut. How could she have missed the significance? It was so clear! How could she have continued to think Kerwin was responsible for her roses? Of course, so much had been going on. Her flood of patients, their problems, surgery. And the world of her nighttime dream lover was so different from her busy daytime life.

The next rose she'd received had been pink Aloha. Her mind raced backward through time. Of course! She'd received Aloha the morning after she had failed to meet Jonah at the hedge. Ariel squinted off into the distance as she tried to remember. In Hawaiian didn't *aloha* mean not only hello, but also good-bye? Jonah must have thought she didn't intend to meet him again.

So, that left French Lace and Escapade. She knew that Escapade was for last night, but what was the significance of French Lace? Ariel smiled. She would ask Jonah.

Ariel stood, looking toward the complex, but forest blocked the way, concealing the buildings from sight. She decided that this was the perfect place for the moonlight picnic she was planning as a surprise for Jonah. She considered it only fair. He kept surprising her.

Pleasure should be reciprocal.

If he wouldn't make love, at least he'd eat. She smiled as she recalled the old adage that said food was the way to a man's heart. As she headed back to the complex, she planned a menu.

By the time Ariel pushed her willow basket through the hedge in front of her, her kitchen was a jumbled mess, and she'd been through the cafeteria line three times. She straightened the gingham cloth that covered the prepared meal within and brushed off a few azalea leaves. Just knowing she would surprise Jonah with something she felt certain he'd like made it worth her trouble.

"What's that?" Jonah asked.

Ariel smiled, excited and pleased with her plan for a moonlight picnic. "It's your turn for a surprise."

He was silent for a moment, and she could imagine him taking in her announcement. Oh, she had been right to do this! He truly was surprised.

Jonah took a step toward her, stopping within the edge of the deep shade. "Mmm. Is that fried chicken I smell?"

"Yes, it is," she said, delighted at the hopeful note she heard in his voice.

The dark shape of his head bent slightly. He extended his bare arm from the cloak of shadow into the moonlight, toward her basket. His fingers plucked at the corner of the gingham. "What else is in there?"

Playfully, she brushed his hand away. "You'll find out soon enough. For tonight, I have a different route for us to take."

His shadowy figure executed a courtly bow. "Your wish is my command."

She headed in the direction of the rose garden.

"I told you I was receiving a rose a day, didn't I?" she asked.

There was a slight pause before he answered. "Yes, I believe you did. From another doctor, didn't you say?"

She stopped, and, a few paces beyond, Jonah slowed to a halt. But he didn't turn. He didn't look back at her.

Moonlight dabbled in the tops of trees, splintering to thousands of waxen shimmers among the leaves of hickory and sycamore, rhododendron, and dogwood. It glimmered like stardust over Jonah's hair, his sturdy shoulders and long back, fading into darkness.

Ariel walked up to where he stood, carefully maintaining her distance, marking her place on the path. It would not do to distract him at this moment.

"That doctor hasn't been leaving me the roses, has he, Jonah?" she asked softly.

"How would I know what doctors do?" he asked, a casual lilt to his voice.

She wished fervently that she could see the expression on his face now. The dark, curse it, could work to one's advantage. Jonah had learned all its tricks.

"You seem to have had a lot of experience with doctors," she said. "I should think that if anyone would know, it would be you." Impatiently she waved that subject away for discussion another day. "But we're talking about roses."

"I don't remember saying a word on the subject."

She tried another approach. "Some thoughtful person has been leaving me roses, and I just want to thank him."

When he didn't reply, she went on, her exasperation growing. "Of course, whoever it is has been breaking into my office to leave them."

"Well, you know doctors."

Was it her imagination, or was there a tinge of humor in his voice? Stealthily, she took a step forward, which put her at a better angle to see his face— or would have if it hadn't been so hidden by shadow. She squinted. Ariel would swear that he was grinning.

"What's that supposed to mean?" she asked.

"They're good with tools."

"Oh, right. We get that in medical school, you know. 'Lock-Picking with a Lancet' class one-oh-one."

"See? There you have it." There was definitely amusement in his voice.

She sighed. He wasn't going to offer her an answer. Which meant she'd either have to ask him point-blank or forget about the whole thing.

They made their way silently around to the other side of the complex. When they were well away from the clustered community, Jonah said, "You're taking us to the rose garden."

"Yes. I thought we could picnic there, under the trees." She gestured toward the stand of old oaks they approached. "Afterward we can go for a walk in the garden."

"There is no shadow in the garden."

"That's okay. I won't peek."

The spot she'd selected for their picnic turned out to be even more ideal than she remembered. She turned to comment on this to Jonah, but remained silent when she saw him looking out over the moonlit beds of roses. He stood so still she thought something in that place must speak to him, tug at him.

Suddenly feeling like an intruder, she busied herself with spreading the sheet she'd brought over the ground. Jonah turned away from his vision and helped her set out the dishes and the food. He opened the bottle of German white wine and poured, releasing the faint, fruity smell.

He reached out his glass for her to fill. "Do you plan to get me drunk and pump me for information?"

"Would it work?"

He laughed. "Probably not."

She made a face. "Then what's the use of trying?"

"Oh, I don't know." Jonah moved behind her and lightly brushed his lips against her temple, sending a delicious shiver of anticipation down her back. "Practice makes perfect?"

She deftly sidestepped him when he moved in for a second kiss. If she gave into her desire for his touch, this romantic picnic would fall to pieces, and all they'd have to show for their evening together would be more sexual frustration. That heart-deep longing that haunted her after leaving Jonah each night was hard enough to endure without adding to it.

"Let's eat," she said brightly, sinking to the cloth on the ground. She held up the container of chicken, hoping its mouth-watering aroma would draw him.

The tactic worked. He sat down across from her and began to dish up his meal from the containers she handed him.

Moonbeams slanted down through the overhead foliage in a crazy array. Ariel saw that Jonah wore a dark T-shirt out of which the sleeves had been torn. Tonight his jogging shorts were old, cutoff jeans.

"I thought fried chicken and buttermilk biscuits were on the list of forbidden foods," he said. "Oh, Lord, and apple pie, too. Is this heaven?"

She laughed. "It is. Forbidden, I mean. But every now and then I'm afraid I revert to the old ways. Besides, this was the most romantic menu I could find at the cafeteria."

He drew back, pressing a palm to his chest. "Say it isn't so! The very food you court me with was prepared by another's hands."

"Probably several others'."

"Okay."

Throughout the meal, a small, secret part of Ariel watched him, observing his gestures and movements, trying to learn *something*.

Maybe he didn't have anything to do with The Black Tupelo. Maybe he was just acquainted with the manager, as he said. Maybe he had friends or relatives in town who had arranged for the dinner in the restaurant and the movie afterward. Ariel could believe that. She wanted to believe that. Actually, it made sense.

What didn't make sense was that everyone in Farley she'd spoken to about Jonah had denied knowing him. Including Beryl, with whom he claimed an acquaintance. Then there was the matter of the hidden tax ledger. The missing probate papers. The brush-off from that attorney.

Jonah offered her his hand. She took it, and together they walked to the garden. Beneath their feet, gravel crunched, though secretly Ariel believed her feet made more noise than his. He stopped beside a bush loaded with pale blooms she thought might be pink. The sign at the base of the bush read Bewitched.

"Do you like roses?" he asked. He reached out to trace the edge of a petal with the side of his thumb.

She watched, mesmerized by the sight of his hand cupping the flower. "Yes, I do. I really enjoy the roses I receive." Unable to resist, she added, "Dr. Sprague brings them to me, you know."

"I think you know better," Jonah said softly.

She nodded, satisfied. He didn't need to elaborate. It was enough to know that he'd brought her flowers since their first meeting.

He soothed his index finger up the delicate outward curve of a petal, and her breath caught in her throat. She could almost feel his finger moving over her own skin.

"They're so lovely," he murmured. "So fragrant. So perfect."

She dragged her gaze from his hand to look up at the haze-enshrouded moon. Surreptitiously, Ariel drew a long breath. She had not missed his meaning. She supplied the words he'd left unspoken. "Unlike people."

"Unlike people." That sad, faraway note drifted through his low voice like a wisp of woodsmoke.

Ariel stood next to him and regarded Bewitched. "Roses have their faults, too," she said, reaching out to the tip of a bud.

Jonah's bare arm brushed hers as he plucked the rose, leaving several inches of slender stem. She felt the warmth of his skin and the friction of masculine hair. Afraid she'd lose what little caution she'd managed to hold on to, Ariel eased away.

"No," he whispered hoarsely, stepping toward her, eliminating the feeble distance she'd put between them. "Don't pull back from me."

She stared at the masculine column of his neck. The muscles there vibrated with tension. He was so close. Too close. She couldn't think coherently.

"You were telling me why you believe roses aren't perfect." He held up the rosebud she had touched.

She stared at it. "Thorns. They have thorns."

He moved around behind her.

"Would you say the thorns are an imperfection?" he asked, his breath stirring the stray wisps of hair at her nape.

"Yes," she said, her voice little more than a whisper. She tried again, more clearly this time. "Yes."

"But they protect the rose from her enemies. How could she survive without her thorns?" He caught her earlobe between his teeth. Gently, he applied the slightest pressure.

Suddenly, Ariel felt breathless. Oxygen seemed in short supply. She fought the urge to lean back into him, to be enfolded in his arms. His fingers were working in front of her face. Ariel willed herself to focus on the movement.

He was removing the flower's thorns, pressing them from one side, then the other, until they broke free of the moist green stem. One thorn proved more stubborn. Before breaking off, its point sank into Jonah's flesh. As she watched, a plump, dark droplet of blood beaded on his thumb.

Without thinking, moving as if she were caught in a dream, she brought Jonah's hand to her lips. Gently, she sucked his wounded thumb into her mouth. The pearl of blood tasted of copper and salt. His flesh bore the faint green bitterness of plant juice—the blood of the rose.

With his free arm, the one that held the rose, Jonah brought her back more fully into his embrace. On the tender backs of her thighs and calves, she felt the soft prickle of the hair on his legs. The hard, prominent ridge of his arousal pressed against her. A corresponding ache pulsed deep within her own body.

She released his thumb. Before she could capture his hand between hers, he reclaimed it. He hooked the tip of his forefinger through the straps of her tank top and bra and drew them down her arm. He paused over the bared curve of her neck and shoulder, as if savoring it. Then he lowered his head.

He feasted on her, plying hungry lips, tongue, and the edges of his teeth. Ariel leaned into him, nearly paralyzed with pleasure. Her blood sang through her veins like sweet summer wine.

His hand drifted down over her shoulder. Fingers spread wide, he brushed lightly over her breast, barely touching the tip. She gasped as lightning crackled through her body. Instantly her nipple hardened into a pink jewel. His hand continued, skimming over her abdomen, down to the elastic waistband of her shorts. With a broad sweep of his hand, he pushed the shorts down over her hips, down her thighs, leaving her bare. Hardly knowing what she was doing, knowing only what she wanted, Ariel stepped out of the shorts. He made quick work of her top and bra, which joined her shorts on the ground. Behind her, he stripped off his T-shirt.

When she would have turned to remove his shorts, he recaptured her in his arms. She felt the solid strength of his warm chest against her naked back.

Her first inclination was to cover herself with her arms. She was completely exposed to him, while he remained partially clothed and out of her sight. "Jonah, no. This isn't right. This isn't the way—"

He hushed her softly and stroked her arms to soothe her. "Let me do this. I'll make it good for you."

She could feel herself already melting in his arms. Sternly, she tried to hold on to her resolve. "I want it to be good for both of us."

"It will be." He stroked her cheek with the rose, a whisper of silk.

"I want to make love the regular way."

His reply was low and warm in her ear. "Lovemaking should never be regular or predictable." He trailed the rosebud down the top of her breast, stopping just short of the tip.

He kissed her ear and outlined the whorls with the tip of his adroit tongue. Her stomach quivered.

Ariel wanted him now, and she would have him—in a way. Jonah's way.

"God, you're beautiful," he whispered, splaying his hand over her throat and upper chest. "So beautiful." He cupped her breast in his palm. With the tip of the rosebud, he slowly circled the aureole. She pressed into his hand, seeking some relief for her tight, aching breast. But he granted her none. After teasing one breast, he went to the other one, repeating the maddening yet delicious caresses.

He slipped the elastic band holding her ponytail from her hair, and made a sound of approval when her hair tumbled about her shoulders. Then he parted the blond curtain and kissed her nape.

She arched in his arms as he possessed that sensitive part of her body. Shivers of delight coursed through her in waves.

He trailed the rose down between her breasts. He swirled it lightly across the plane of her belly. The pale petals were vaguely cool against her feverish skin. Jonah skimmed over Ariel's pubis with the rose, then followed the interior line of one thigh.

Her sense of balance spun out of control. She wanted . . . She needed . . .

"Jonah," she murmured. "Please."

He removed the few leaves from the rose stem, which was nubbed with those places where thorns had once grown. Then, lightly, he rubbed the stem across her sensitive nipple.

Pleasure ripped through her, sending her arching out, saved only by the embrace of his strong arm.

"That's right, my love. Let yourself go in my arms." Only then did she realize that he was breathing hard, that his body was moist with sweat. He dropped the rose onto the pile of their clothes.

Jonah learned with his hands those places of her body he'd touched with the rose. Then, when she thought she could not bear another moment, he slipped his fingers into her most intimate cove.

Oh, they were clever, his fingers. They sent her flying into a cosmic wind. Up and up she went. Energy vibrated around her, through her.

Time stopped. There was only wave after wave of golden sensation.

She was beautiful—God, so beautiful!—as she shuddered naked in his arms. Jonah thought he had never seen anything so glorious, so exciting.

He tried to concentrate on her, only her. His desire for her, the raging needs of his own body must be denied. If he gave in now everything would be ruined. The little time they had left in their secret, private world must not be squandered.

Ariel rolled her head back against his shoulder and sighed deeply. Jonah smiled. Tenderly, he kissed the top of her head.

"Now it's your turn," she said.

His body tightened painfully at the prospect of

being touched by her. Afraid he might weaken, his answer came out harsher than he'd intended. "No."

He saw her frown. She pulled away from him, apparently unconscious of her nudity. "What do you mean 'no'?"

How could he explain? Would she understand that he feared the moment he lost control she would see him as he really was—hideous? He wanted to be special to her. If it had been within his power, he would have made himself a prince for her, and swept her off to a castle in the clouds. But making that particular fairy tale come true was beyond even him. So he must settle for control. And right now that was strung to the snapping point.

"It's not a good idea, Ariel. I— It's just not a good idea." Christ, he was sweating.

She stood there a moment, looking down at the rose on the pile of clothing. She tossed her head, and pale hair shimmered into a cloak Eve might have envied. Then she walked away a few paces.

He filled his eyes with her. Ariel was surely Temptation incarnate. Would it really be so bad? Losing everything he had with her for the glory of having her touch him? It wouldn't stop there, he knew. Oh, God, he *knew*. But wouldn't it be worth anything to sink into her sweet, soft body, to become one with her for an instant of eternity? Just looking at her, naked, ready for the taking— Damn, it was difficult to think.

"No." The word caught in his dry throat, but he forced it out. And again, more clearly: "No."

She looked at him, but he knew she would not

allow her gaze to reach his face. "Jonah? What's the matter?"

"This can't be, Ariel. It just can't be."

"Why?"

Her question was simple enough. But he had no simple answers. He wasn't sure he understood the reasons himself.

"Is it . . . is it just me?"

"No!" He couldn't stand that note of hurt confusion in her voice, and he hated the knowledge that *he'd* put it there.

"Do you have a problem with making love?" she asked gently.

He stiffened. "I'm not some kind of deviant, if that's what you're implying."

Frustrated, disappointed, desperate, Jonah picked up his shirt and jerked it on over his head.

She began to dress. "That's not what I'm implying, and you damned well know it."

"I know." He shrugged the cotton knit down over his shoulders, then looked at her. "I know."

She flipped her hair out of the tank top's neckline. "Then what is it?"

He looked down at the ground. There, at his feet, lay the rose. It had been carelessly crushed beneath their feet. Something akin to grief twisted through his gut.

She lived in a world of light, where beauty was the desired goal. He was consigned to the dark, unable to consider looking even human, much less handsome. Ten years ago he'd been forced to accept the shattering fact that medical science could not help him.

What would she feel, looking at his face? Shock. Revulsion. Pity. Bitter experience had taught him that particular evolution. No woman wanted a monster for a lover. Especially one who could have her pick of handsome men.

"Jonah, you need help."

He cut her a sharp look. "Precisely, what you do mean by that?"

"Just what I said. You need help. We've danced around the subject, but I can't avoid it any longer. Until you make the decision to have surgery, nothing will change for you. You'll go on living your life in the dark. You'll refuse to let . . . someone . . . into your life. You'll back away from intimacy. You'll be alone."

Her last three words cut into him like a cold knife. He knew that she was right.

15

As they walked back to the stand of oaks to gather up what was left of the picnic, it seemed to Jonah that each of them moved within the silence of separate worlds. Regret sat like a cold stone in his chest. *Don't shut me out, Ariel!* He wanted to turn to her and voice his plea. Pride and hard-won control, ingrained after so many years, kept him walking a straight course, kept his words imprisoned inside him, where they echoed like a taunt.

They knelt on the ground and repacked the willow basket with unhurried efficiency. His fingers tightened on a paper plate, crushing it in the vise of his frustration.

"Jonah, I don't know what you went through before, or even how long ago—"

"Years," he said tiredly. "It was years ago."

She leaned toward him and rested her hand on his

wrist. "Medicine has made advances. There are new techniques. Jonah, you were screened before you were accepted at Fountainhead. All patients here have been. Even the paying ones like you." She paused, as if giving him a chance to deny that status, but he said nothing.

"I'm not your doctor," she continued, "so I haven't seen your file, but I know you wouldn't be here if the screening committee didn't think the chances of success were high."

"But not certain."

"That's true," she allowed. "There are no guarantees. But every available test that could indicate the outcome has been done." She gave his wrist a reassuring squeeze. "Jonah, I've worked with the other doctors in this hospital, and I'm impressed. They're the best in their fields. Fountainhead's facilities and equipment are excellent. Renard is a jerk, but the people he's hired know their stuff."

"Including you." He'd made inquiries about Dr. Ariel Denham.

"I'd like to think so."

He had no wish to say more on the subject. His memories of the operations he'd undergone, of the pain and the heartbreak he'd endured were, even after so many years, stark. But Ariel didn't know about any of that. She didn't know about his penance. And maybe he'd never find it in him to tell her. What mattered was that he'd finally accepted his mutilated face as his fate. This was his punishment.

But Ariel made him feel reborn. She was intelligent, beautiful, successful—and she chose to spend her evenings with him. Not with rich-boy Herrick, or that frigging Perry.

Jonah leaned forward and kissed her. When he would have deepened the kiss, she drew back.

She took a long breath, as if trying to draw courage from the atmosphere. "I think it's time we talked."

He froze. He'd feared this moment for months, feared that he wouldn't know the right way to handle it when it came. And he didn't. His brain seemed numb, unable to manufacture a suitable reply.

He would lose Ariel.

She sat so damnably still, her gaze fixed on her hands, clutched together in her lap. Jonah felt the muscles in his chest tighten, squeezing the air out of his lungs.

"I love you, Jonah," she said, her voice little more than a whisper. Her mouth curved in an unhappy attempt at a smile. "I love you, and I don't even know your name."

Jonah stared at her, at the pale crown of her head, dazedly trying to assimilate what she'd just told him.

She rose and picked up the hamper. "There's good in you. A tender streak a mile wide. Even though you try to hide it most of the time, I know it's there. Do you honestly think a mere face could ever change that for me?" She straightened and turned toward him. As always, she kept her eyes lowered, honoring his feelings. "We live in a world filled with hatred, and envy, and pain. What we've found together is . . . magic. It's so—" She broke off and swallowed heavily. "I can only believe it must be very rare." She looked away toward the garden and pressed her lips together. Moisture shimmered in her eyes.

When she finally spoke again, her voice was soft but level. "Are you so willing to throw it away?"

Ariel turned and strode off. Then she broke into a run. As fleet as a deer, she fled toward the complex.

Jonah leapt to his feet. "Ariel!" He started in pursuit, knowing full well that he could easily overtake her. Then he slowed to a stop. What good would catching up with her do?

She wanted answers, answers he wasn't willing to give.

He picked up the basket and followed her at a somber pace. Depression and uncertainty weighted his every step to her bungalow, where he found all the windows lit up from inside. Unlike most nights, he didn't wait until her last light had been switched off. Instead, he left the willow basket on her terrace and walked back to his own quarters.

He showered, letting the steaming water and soapy lather pour over his body. If only that purifying water could reach his soul, he thought. He'd scrub away the stain that haunted him night and day. Finally, he'd rid himself of the bloodstain.

Jonah shut off the water and toweled himself dry. He padded into his dark bedroom. Moonlight slanted through the crack between the curtains, flowing like a pale river over furniture and floor. For a moment he stood where he was, thinking.

She'd said she loved him. Loved *him*. Jonah chuckled bitterly. She hadn't seen him. Not really. Oh, she might have caught moonlit glimpses of him. But moonlight was kind. Full light would reveal every grotesque scar, each inch of jagged flesh that covered his face. How long could she stand the sight of that? Would she be willing to risk a lifetime with him if surgery were not successful?

Jonah slowly walked across the room to the dresser and knelt to open the bottom drawer. His hand paused over the knob. It had been years . . . He released a sharp breath and pulled the drawer open. Beneath the folded sweaters and sweat shirts, his fingers found the smooth surface of what he sought and reluctantly drew it out.

Moonlight glinted off the small mirror. Without looking, he knew it portrayed the desk, the chair, the headboard—all with impersonal accuracy. Jonah took a deep breath and held it for a moment. Then he slowly exhaled.

He looked into the mirror.

Oh, God. *Oh, God.* He lifted a hand, but stopped before he touched his skin. That skin. He dropped his hand to the bed.

"Oh, God."

But God remained silent.

Jonah knew the damage was too great. He was a fool to hope Ariel could change that. She was a surgeon, not a magician.

His agony echoed in his roar of denial as he hurled the mirror against the wall. The small looking glass shattered, exploding in a twinkling shower across the floor.

He was a monster, now and forever.

✧   ✧   ✧

Ariel sat staring at the pink rose on her desk without really seeing it.

Jonah had touched her naked body. She'd allowed him to touch her, thinking the moment had come when they would share intimacy and with it, their passion and ultimately, their dreams.

She'd been wrong.

There had been little shared between them. He had been in control, as always. When he'd refused to allow her to touch him in return, she'd been stunned. As she'd hastily dressed, wanting desperately to cover herself, to hide, she'd felt hurt and humiliated.

She'd thought he loved her, but, in the end, she'd been wrong.

Wearily, she brushed back a stray wisp of hair. Sleep had been impossible for her last night when she'd finally reached home. Ah, Lord, what a fool she'd been.

Doris tapped on the open door. "I came to see what kind of rose Jonah gave you today."

Ariel slowly revolved her chair around to face Doris.

Doris's eyes widened. "You look awful."

"Gee, thanks."

"What I mean to say is—" Doris seemed to cast about for an inspired kindness. When none came, she said lamely, "You've looked better." Her worried gaze searched Ariel's face. "You've been crying."

Ariel flushed. "Is it that obvious? I've splashed an ocean of cold water on my face since this morning, but it hasn't helped."

Doris shook her head. "You need an ice pack, doctor. When's your next patient scheduled?"

"In thirty minutes."

"Stay right here."

Doris strode away, down the hall. She returned in ten minutes with a disposable ice pack filled with crushed ice. Closing the door behind her, she instructed Ariel to settle back in her chair, then laid the pack across her eyes.

"Does this have something to do with Jonah?" Doris asked.

Ariel hesitated. "Yes," she said wearily.

"Did he tell you who he is? Is that why you're so upset?"

Ariel sighed under the soothing coolness. "If you mean did I just find out that he's public enemy number one, the answer's no."

"Well, he *could* be public enemy number one, for all you know about him," Doris said, fussing with the position of the ice pack.

Ariel was embarrassed to have Doris see her looking so pathetic, so she tried to play along with her friend's attempt at humor. "Why, he could be Elvis."

Doris straightened, instantly alert. "Does he look like Elvis?"

"No."

"Well, then." Doris frowned. "It's cruel to toy with an Elvis fan."

"I'm sorry," Ariel said. Doris was only trying to help. It certainly wasn't her fault that Ariel had ignored her own rule about falling in love with a patient.

Doris cleared her throat. "What kind of rose did he give you?"

"Kerwin told me the name was—" Her throat contracted. "Dream Dust."

Doris lifted the frigid ice pack. "The swelling is going down." She gently laid it back into place. "Now are you going to tell Auntie Doris what's wrong, or are you going to be your usual clamlike self and keep silent?"

"It's a long story."

Doris sighed. "It usually is. Well, if you feel like talking, you know where to find me." She patted Ariel's shoulder and quietly let herself out of the office.

Minutes after Doris left, Ariel heard a soft, almost timid knock on her door. She set aside the ice pack and glanced at her watch. It was too early for the patient yet.

"Come in," she called, straightening in her chair.

A middle-aged man whose hair was beginning to grow out from having been shaved stuck his head in the door. "Dr. Denham, do you have a minute?"

Ariel smiled warmly when she recognized her patient. "Bill." Here was a man whose fire-scarred face had kept him almost housebound for five years, yet not once had Ariel seen him lose his positive attitude. Now she took in his starched white oxford cloth shirt and navy blue suit. "It looks like you're ready to go."

He grinned and the faintly discolored graft areas curved on his cheeks. "Yep. I'm ready to return to the outside world."

"Well, that's good news. You won't forget your appointment next month, will you? If everything continues to go as well as it has, that will probably be the last one."

His eyes twinkled. "Wild horses couldn't keep me away. I want you to see the new me, hair and all."

She laughed. "That will be a change."

Bill laughed, too, as he lightly rubbed the bristly layer of short hair on the top of his head. "It sure will." He sobered. "At least I'll have hair now."

She glanced at the fine, but thick, crop of hair coming in. "We were lucky the grafts took. There was a lot of vessel damage in that area."

His solemn gaze met hers. "The only luck involved was that I got you for my plastic surgeon. You gave me back my life, Dr. Denham."

Warmth moved up Ariel's neck. "I think you may have a somewhat exaggerated idea of my abilities, but thank you, Bill."

He shook his head. "No. Thank *you*. I feel like a real person again, not a ghost people pretend not to see. I—" He paused as if he were carefully choosing his words. "You made me believe in miracles again. I won't forget it."

Ariel stood there, robbed of words. What could she say in the face of this man's declaration? She knew she was no miracle worker. The tenacious machinery of his body deserved the real credit. Or Mother Nature. Or God. Who could even say they were not all one and the same?

Bill gave her a nod, as if to indicate that he'd said what he'd come to say. He turned and walked out of her office.

She stood there for a moment, staring unseeing at

the closed door. Then she sank into her chair. It was a heady thing, this credit for performing wonders. More than that, though, she found that it was Bill's deep appreciation that touched her.

You gave me back my life. She had done something important. Bill knew it. And now she knew it.

Bill's words stayed with her through the rest of the day and into the evening. They reminded her that she was a physician, a surgeon, and she found herself taking a closer look at her reasons for having chosen her vocation. But she knew that her turmoil over Jonah was probably interferring with her judgment.

She was thankful for the full moon that night. She wasn't ready to talk with Jonah yet. He had hurt her. Embarrassed her. And she burned with resentment at the memory of being so manipulated. Now, as she looked back on the history of their relationship, she saw that he had always been in control. Control of location, of time, of situation.

Things would have to change. She could not, would not, tolerate even the idea of being controlled or in any way manipulated. There had been entirely too much of that in her life already. He couldn't have everything his way. No, things would have to change.

She had the next day free. It had been arranged, as with all her days off, to fall during the full moon. Just another instance of trying to accommodate Jonah, she thought as she drove toward Farley.

Summer lit the day, spreading its golden warmth over field and forest. Ariel rolled her windows down and felt her spirits lift with the wind. She promised herself she wouldn't think of how things stood between Jonah and her. She would do her shopping and enjoy the afternoon. Maybe she'd stop for an ice-cream cone.

Even as she parked the car along the curb in front of the picturesque shops, she knew her promise was an empty one. Everywhere she looked around this town she saw something that jogged a memory of him. This was his place, not hers. Here, like everywhere she'd ever lived, she was just a visitor. Only here she'd at least be staying a year.

Automatically, she locked the car, her mind not really on the movement of her fingers. *At least be staying a year.* When had she stopped counting the hours until she'd be free of Fountainhead?

She dismissed that thought as she adjusted her purse on her shoulder, then determinedly stepped up onto the sidewalk, her shopping list in hand.

Two hours later, she sat in the ice-cream shop with a chocolate ice-cream cone in her hand. She gazed out the plate glass window that fronted the sidewalk.

She knew what this street looked like when it was dark and empty of pedestrians and cars. Then footsteps echoed faintly, and the only light shone from the moon—

Ariel frowned. Streetlights. There were streetlights. But they hadn't been on the night Jonah had brought her here. Until this minute, she hadn't given the dark a second thought. Maybe streetlights were turned off here after a certain hour, to conserve on power bills. But she really didn't believe that.

Ice cream dripped on her hand. Absently she wiped off the chocolate blob. Then she turned her attention back to the restaurant across the street that she'd been studying earlier.

Dinner and a movie.

That was the restaurant to which Jonah had taken her. From the outside, it looked like many of the other buildings on the street. Built of wood, painted white, it was another tidy establishment. Cafe curtains hung in the large front windows, and a red-and-white striped awning hung over the front door. It bore the name André's.

André!

Quickly she ate the last of the sugar cone and wiped her hands on a paper napkin. Then she strode out of the ice-cream shop and across the street.

The restaurant was crowded. Conversation hummed just a few decibels below a jet engine, punctuated by the clink of silverware against plates.

"I'd like to speak to André," she told the hostess.

The hostess gave Ariel a subtle once-over, taking in, no doubt, Ariel's linen slacks and silk T-top. "Is Chef André expecting you?" the woman asked. "He's a bit busy now."

Ariel debated whether hauteur or a smile would get her what she wanted. She decided on a smile. "This will only take a minute," she assured the hostess. "It's important or I'd never disturb him while he worked."

The woman nodded, then turned and threaded her way between tables to the kitchen doors on the other side of the dining room. She was back in a few minutes.

"He'll see you in his office. Down the hall," she

said, then directed her attention to patrons waiting in line for a table.

Ariel found the office and tapped on the door.

"Come in." A short, trim man dressed in a chef's uniform sat behind the desk that dominated the small room. "You wanted to speak with me?" he asked with barely concealed impatience.

"Hello," she said. "I'm Ariel Denham. I wanted to convey my appreciation for the wonderful beef Stroganoff you prepared for Jonah and me."

His eyes widened in surprise.

"It was a delightful dinner. Thank you."

"I'm afraid I don't know what you're talking about," he said gruffly.

"Since we dined here, in this restaurant, and the food was freshly prepared and still hot when we arrived, you will perhaps understand if I find that difficult to believe."

André's face took on an impassive expression, but his fingers fidgeted with a pencil.

"There were a few other odd things I noticed that night," she continued. "None of the streetlights were on. And there was no one else on the streets. No one." She smiled. "The colas and popcorn were nice. Would you please thank whoever is responsible?"

She saw a flicker in his eyes. He was lying, of course. Of that she felt certain. She remembered her first trip to Farley, and how the townspeople she'd talked with had denied all knowledge of Jonah. What was he to the people of Farley that they would close ranks to keep his secrets?

"I'm afraid I don't know what you're talking about,

Miss Denham." A flush was nudging its way up Chef André's neck. He really was a very poor liar.

"Well, I just wanted to thank you personally. I'm sorry for having interrupted your work." Resigned that she would get nothing from him, she turned to go.

"Dr. Denham," André said.

She stopped and looked back at him in question.

"Do you love him?" There was concern in his gray eyes.

She met his gaze. "Yes. Yes, I do." Lord help her.

"Then trust him," he said. "Just trust him."

Trust Jonah? It seemed she was continually expected to trust him. When would he trust *her*? "Why won't anyone in this town talk about him?" She barely managed to keep the exasperation out of her voice.

André's smile was kindly. Maybe he guessed her frustration. "In Farley, we take care of our own."

Jonah caught himself staring out the window toward the hospital again. He plowed his hand through his hair. Things couldn't continue like this.

As if by a will of its own, his gaze moved to the telephone. He could call her. Talk to her. Maybe he could make her understand.

He bolted out of his chair and prowled through his quarters, noticing little of his surroundings. How could he make her understand? His feelings were so tangled that he wasn't sure of anything. Anything, that is, but the way he felt about Ariel.

He loved her.

And he would lose her if he did not make a decision.

Jonah spit a vile oath. Who was he trying to kid? There was a damned good chance he'd lose her anyway. There was only one certainty, and that was that he couldn't hide from her anymore. She was looking for answers, but he knew that was only normal.

Normal. There was nothing normal about their situation. Hell, there was nothing normal about his life. Yet she'd been patient. Persistent in her curiosity, but patient. What had he done for her? Christ, he'd taken what she'd given him, something good, something precious in its rarity, and twisted it to suit his needs.

Ariel deserved his trust. Hell, she *had* it. Now he must show her.

16

A misty cloud passed over the moon, and Ariel watched as it drifted by. Tonight was the first "safe" night after the full moon. Jonah would be going to the hedge soon, to meet her.

Only she wouldn't be there.

She drew the curtains over the terrace doors, over the windows that looked out onto the park. Then she walked into her kitchen. There, on the island, in an onyx vase, stood the last few roses she'd received. Kerwin and Doris had taken a few days off to visit Doris's parents in New Bern, but she didn't need Kerwin to tell her that all the roses were Dream Dust.

But it didn't matter, she thought. After tonight there would be no more roses.

She turned off the kitchen light and walked barefoot down the hall to her bedroom. She stood in the middle of her room, her arms crossed over her chest, her palms rubbing her upper arms, trying to massage out the cold that seemed to have seeped into her body, into her heart.

This was the best way. By not showing up at the hedge, tonight or ever, she was telling Jonah it was over. What they had together wasn't right, and without his help she was powerless to make it so. But the effort would be pointless anyway, she told herself sternly. They had no future together. She was doing the right thing.

But her heart was breaking.

If only they had met in a different place, a different time. If only . . .

There was a small, sharp tap on her window. Ariel blinked, trying to clear her thoughts. To her surprise, she found she had not turned on the bedroom light. The house was dark.

Another tap sounded. Someone was throwing pebbles at her windowpanes. A third tap.

Hesitantly, Ariel went to the window and lifted the shade to peer out. A tall shadow moved to her left.

"Ariel, let me in."

Jonah. His voice alone held a certain power over her. The deep-burning baritone beckoned her, enticed her, drew forth memories of laughter, of kisses.

Quickly, she backed away from the window, dropping the shade. Her bare ankle struck the leg of her dresser, but she hardly noticed.

He threw another pebble. "Ariel, I've got to talk to you."

She shook her head vigorously. "No!"

"Ariel," he said, close to the glass. "Please."

She swiped the back of her hand across her wet cheek. "Go away, Jonah. This isn't any good for either of us."

"That's not so. You know it's not." Was that a faint note of panic underlying his voice?

"Please, Jonah."

"Go open the goddamned door or I'll break it down!"

His voice softened. "I only want to talk to you. If you still want me to leave when I've had my say, I'll go."

She didn't want to hear him. She didn't want to see him. She feared her resolve wasn't strong enough to withstand the impact of his presence. But it looked as if Jonah was determined not to let her take the coward's way out. He was entitled to speak his piece, entitled to hear hers, face-to-face.

She threaded her way through the dark house to unlock the French doors.

He flowed into her living room on silent feet, a vibrant living shadow among the familiar inanimate. The door closed just as quietly.

Moonlight touched the room with fingers of silver, brushing across the couch, the coffee table, the carpet, outlining Jonah's inky hair, his broad shoulders and tapering back. His running shorts did nothing to hide the hard curve of his buttocks, the muscular length of his bare legs.

He stood still, and she had the curious sense that he was undecided on how to proceed.

Without speaking, he slowly knelt down at the coffee table and pulled something from his pocket. To her surprise, he struck a match and touched it to the wick of the centerpiece candle. The flame caught, fluttered, then gradually grew.

For the first time, Ariel saw Jonah's face clearly.

Golden firelight revealed ugliness. But she found beauty there, too. Beneath the ragged, disfigured skin elegantly formed bones gave his face shape and dimension, and she guessed that once this man had been stunningly handsome.

She knelt beside him and, with a tremulous smile, she reached up her hand and touched his cheek. It was as pale as the stars against the black night of his hair. She looked into his eyes.

"Brown," she murmured.

"What?" His voice was rough, as if his throat had gone dry.

She lightly traced one exquisite cheekbone, disregarding the seamed flesh. "Brown. Your eyes are brown." Her smile grew slightly wider, even as the surge of emotion within her caused it to waver. "I didn't know that."

His gaze moved over her face, as if he were drinking in the sight, locking it in his memory, unable to believe. Then frowned. Thick black lashes shielded his eyes from her view. "Do you think— I mean, could you—" Jonah raised his beautiful brown eyes to meet her gaze. "Ariel."

She saw the tension in his shoulders, in the tight muscles of his bare arms. His hands kept clenching, and opening, clenching and opening.

Without thinking, she leaned forward and touched her lips to his.

With a noise that sounded oddly akin to a sob, he

pulled her into his arms. His mouth over hers, he suffused the kiss with the wild essence of his desperation.

Ariel's plan to end her relationship with Jonah melted away like snow in spring. He had pushed his fears aside and come to her. She wrapped her arms around him and met his turbulent kiss with a soaring heart.

"Ariel," he whispered raggedly. "Oh, God, Ariel." He buried his face in the veil of her hair. She felt the warmth of his breath against the side of her neck.

She leaned back slightly, and cradled his face between her hands. She searched his eyes, his splendid golden brown eyes, and in their depths she saw a yearning that tugged at her, called to something deep within her.

"I love you, Jonah."

He looked at her for a moment, then slowly covered her hands with his. He placed a kiss in each of her palms, and she felt the uneven surface of his scarred flesh. Then he held her hands over his heart. Its beat was strong and true.

"You are so precious to me," he said, his voice husky with emotion. "You burst into my life like sunshine through a storm and refused to leave. You're caring, patient, nosy, stubborn, and I do love you, Ariel."

The candlelit room blurred as tears welled in her eyes. "I didn't refuse to leave," she said chokingly.

He drew her gently back into his arms, and cradled her head against his shoulder. "I was a fool. I drove you away. I was afraid."

She lifted her head and met his gaze and thought

how wonderful it was finally to look at him. "Afraid?"

"That you would see me. Afraid you would feel disgust, or worse, pity. I wanted you to think of me as a man, a man you could love. Not some repellent *thing*. And not a patient."

"How could you think looking at you would disgust me? I love you. But everything else aside, I'm a plastic surgeon. A reconstructive surgeon." And to her amazement, she found it was true. When had this happened? When had she begun to think of herself as working more with reconstruction than cosmetic surgery? She performed both here at Fountainhead.

"You're also a woman, Ariel," he said softly. "A beautiful, desirable woman. And I'm a monster."

She straightened instantly in his arms. "Don't say that! Don't even think it! You are *not* a monster."

He chuckled, and that warm, sexy, familiar sound made her heart flutter. "You're blinded by love."

"Will you tell me who you are?"

His smile faded, and he looked away.

"I don't even know your last name. There are no files under the name of Jonah, so I've been thinking you must be some sort of celebrity, to spend so much time at Fountainhead without undergoing surgery."

Jonah's dark eyebrows drew down. "Is that what you've been thinking? That I'm someone famous?"

Suddenly she saw where his reasoning was taking him. "Don't be a nitwit," she said shortly. "Celebrity has nothing to do with the way I feel about you. I've thought you were a patient from the first. When you wouldn't tell me anything about yourself I got curious. I checked around. There are no patient files under 'Jonah,' so I thought the name must be the alias of one of the paying patients." He said nothing. Now she frowned. "Well, what was I supposed to think?"

"You could have trusted me."

"Like you trusted me?"

He sighed. "You're right. And if anyone deserves to know who I am, it's you."

"Why are you making such a big deal out of this?"

"I'm Declan Stone."

She stared at him for a moment in disbelief. She'd thought it was his brother who'd been the most acclaimed rock star in history.

"I'm Declan Stone," he said again, defensively. He vented a sharp sigh of exasperation. "Look, put two and two together. I know you've been trying to discover who I am. You've asked the people in Farley. You've been to the county courthouse."

"How did you know that?"

"I got about three phone calls from people at the courthouse the day you showed up. Someone even took it upon himself to hide a tax ledger. But I figured you'd hit the dead end I'd created and would give up."

It gave her an eerie feeling, knowing that all along her activities had been reported to and observed by the very person she'd been checking on.

"Even my attorney called," he continued. "He said you'd spoken to him."

There had been something familiar about his looks, something that had nagged at the back of her mind.

But what was it? Her eyes widened. "You are Declan Stone," she said slowly. Now she recognized that magnificent bone structure. Stone had justly been acclaimed as one of the world's handsomest men. "I thought you were dead."

"That's what everyone was supposed to think."

"But the will, the probate—"

"The will was a fake, and the probate was started, but of course, never finished. The ruse was necessary in order to make my death convincing."

She nodded, feeling faintly dazed. "I see. I think. Where did you get the name Jonah?"

"From my uncle."

"Jonah Albright," she supplied.

"Yeah."

"So The Black Tupelo belongs to you, not Beryl." *Not to your brother.*

He nodded, his eyes never leaving her face, as if he were uncertain how she would take the news.

"Another lie," she said flatly.

"My life is made up of lies, Ariel," he said softly. "*I am a lie.*"

"You didn't trust me."

Again, he shook his head. "I can't afford to trust many people."

"Do you . . ." Her courage seeped away. If he gave her the wrong answer, the reprieve, the confession, her hope, would be for nothing. But she had to know. "Do you trust me now?"

He drew in a long breath and released it sharply. His eyes seemed to ask for her understanding. "I'm trying to trust you, Sunshine. I've already risked . . .

well, a lot with you. You're important to me. I need you, Ariel." He held her close, and she could feel the pounding of his heart. "God help me, but I need you."

Ariel's heart soared. She twined her arms around his neck and kissed him. Playfully, she nibbled his lower lip, and skimmed it with the tip of her tongue.

He splayed his fingers through her hair and cupped the back of her head while he indulged in a more serious exchange. His tongue entered her mouth, where it probed and stroked. His lips moved over hers with dizzying concentration. When he finally lifted his head, she made a small noise of protest. He smiled and settled her close against him, within easy reach for another kiss.

Then a question pierced the sweet glow of his kiss, and she knew she had to ask. "Why do you want people to think you're dead?"

He released her, and she watched at he rose to his feet in one lithe motion. Restlessly he paced, then stopped, staring into the dark kitchen, his back to Ariel, as if he'd lost his bearings.

"You remember I told you about my brother. About Tim."

He was going to tell her, she thought with a rush of relief. She nodded, then realized he couldn't see the gesture. "Yes, I remember." She smiled. "You made me wish more than ever that I had a brother or sister." There had been a deep, abiding love between the brothers. It had shone through every time Jonah had mentioned Tim.

"I killed him."

"What?" Ariel was certain she'd misunderstood what he'd said.

Jonah turned sharply to face her. "I killed my brother."

He stood there, soft candlelight playing over his disfigured face, his tall, hard body. Outside, a nightjar softly called. On the table in front of her, a drop of melted wax rolled down the side of the candle.

"Did you hear me?" he demanded harshly.

Ariel looked up, locking gazes with Jonah. What she read in his eyes, the gut-wrenching torment . . . She had to take a deep breath and let it out before she could speak. "I heard you say that you killed your brother. The brother I know you loved. Now I want to hear what really happened."

He glared at her a moment, and it seemed to her that he'd condemned himself with guilt and pain over his brother's death for so long that he couldn't believe there was someone who did not condemn him. She waited quietly.

"It was fourteen years ago," he began slowly, that faraway note haunting his voice. "I'd just finished my second European tour. My records were selling like crazy, the concerts were sold out, I'd just won another award." He began to pace. "I was on top of the world. When I got back to California, I was ready to party. So when Leland—"

"Who's Leland?"

"Leland Spivik. He'd just hit the charts. Do you remember?"

She made a face. "I remember."

"Anyway, he invited me to the bash he was giving, and I went. Leland's parties were wild, notoriously

wild. Taxis wouldn't even go out to his place." Jonah
halted in his tracks. "I should have known better.
Anyway, I drank too much." His short crack of laughter was filled with such bitterness that it pained her to
hear it. "Drank too much. That's the understatement
of the century. I got smashed. I couldn't have driven a
car on a bet. Hell, I was lucky to dial Tim's number
right." One of Jonah's hands clenched. "I wish to God
I hadn't managed. Just one more drink . . ." He drew
in a long breath. "But I did get the number right and
asked him to pick me up. I didn't want to stay at
Leland's. I'd overheard enough that evening to know
I'd better get out. Leland and his friends seemed to
be into some pretty weird stuff. Must've been something he'd started when I was in Europe."

"Drugs?"

He shook his head. "Satanism."

Ariel shivered.

"They were gathering for some kind of ritual at
midnight. I didn't want to stick around, but I was too
drunk to drive. No one would drive for me—they
wanted me there. So I called Tim and asked him to
pick me up."

Jonah roamed the room like a fretful panther. "He
was only a kid, for chrissake! He should have been in
bed. Instead, he was out on the road in the middle of
the night."

"How old was he?"

"Seventeen."

"So you were only nineteen."

"Old enough to know better."

She stood and walked over to him. She laid a hand

on his shoulder. "You were a kid, too, Jonah. One who'd rocketed to success in just a couple of years. One who'd suddenly had power and great wealth—and all that they bring—dropped on him. That must have been a heady experience."

"It was."

"And did you know how to deal with it? With the money? With all the people who wanted a piece of you?"

He walked away from her, across the room. "No. Hell, no. It scared me. And excited me. It was like some damned drug. The more I got, the more I wanted. My ego . . ." He looked up at the ceiling, as if a vision of the past was revealed there. "I think I must have gone a little crazy."

"You were barely older than your brother. Why do you think you should have been so much wiser?"

"I should have been, that's all," he snapped. "I just should have been."

"Why didn't you call your parents to come get you?"

"Let's just say we didn't get along. They didn't approve of what I was doing. They worried about my brother being contaminated by my music. He was destined for better things. They would have had a coronary if they'd known I'd called him to pick me up."

"What about all those backyard barbecues?"

"Oh, they still had them. But I wasn't invited." There was a strong note of scorn in his voice, but hidden underneath, as so much in his life had been hidden, was another note in the key of pain.

She wanted to hold him, to draw out his hurt and make it vanish. She didn't understand parents who tried to manipulate their children by the giving or withdrawal of love.

"I told Tim to meet me a quarter of a mile down the road, outside the gates. I didn't want him anywhere near a bunch of Satanists. I managed to slip out of the house—a damn miracle, considering I couldn't walk straight. The gates were locked, so I had to climb a tree to get over the wall. Nearly broke my neck, but I got away."

"And Tim was there to meet you?"

"Tim was there. He'd never fail me." His voice wavered. He swallowed heavily and paused a second before he could go on. "He paid dearly for his loyalty." Jonah looked out the glass panes of the French doors. The moon had risen high in the black velvet sky. "On the way to my place, a truck jumped the median and hit us head-on. Tim was killed instantly. I went through the windshield. The car caught fire." He turned back to her, his eyes haunted with old guilt. "And here I am."

But my brother is dead. The unspoken words hung in the air between them.

Ariel restrained herself from going to Jonah. He'd brushed her off before, and she recognized the behavior too well. He was hurting, but more than he wanted comforting he feared her scorn.

"What happened to the driver of the truck?" she asked quietly, not really interested, merely giving him time. It proved the wrong question.

Jonah laughed darkly. "He came off with only a few

scratches. Later I learned the guy was staggering drunk."

She stared at him, horrified. She wanted to cry for Jonah. For his brother. For his whole wretched family. But tears might be misconstrued as pity, so she struggled to hide them.

He stood there by the doors, alone. His brother was dead. His face was in ruins. His life had been shattered to dust. Never had she known a man who needed love, who needed the comfort love could bring, more than Jonah. Yet he kept his distance, across the room.

He was a proud man, that she knew. She'd recognized it in him from the very beginning. It was a strength they held in common.

But it had become their weakness. Pride imprisoned them in jails of ice. One of them must break through to free the other. And Jonah, she suspected, had gone farther for her tonight than he had gone for anyone in a long time.

If they were to have the freedom truly to meet, to touch more than mere flesh, it was now up to her.

Slowly, painfully, she opened her soul to him. She no longer held back her tears. They were a part of what she revealed to him in her eyes, in her face. The stark longing. The unbearable need. "Hold me, Jonah," she whispered. "Please hold me."

He looked at her a moment and for that span of time, their gazes met and measured. An expression of awe, of wonder touched his ravaged features.

Then he was across the room, sweeping her into his arms. They clung to each other.

"Oh, God, Ariel. Ariel," he murmured over and over, between the many kisses he placed on her wet cheeks, her mouth.

She said his name again and again. It became a prayer, a grace upon her lips.

Gradually they quieted, yet it seemed to Ariel that ease didn't accompany the surcease. Instead, a tentative anticipation hummed inside her, one that grew in intensity like a charging electric cell.

She looked up at Jonah. He was watching her with his golden brown eyes. He lowered his head. Her lips parted in welcome.

His mouth moved over hers tenderly at first, then with growing hunger, pressing, coaxing, demanding what she was desperate to give. His tongue plunged over her teeth, learning their shape and sharpness. He caressed her tongue with his.

Wild need coursed through Ariel's body, echoing the rapid beat of her heart.

Breathing hard, he shoved up her T-shirt. He bent over her and greedily took the tip of one breast into his mouth, laving it with his tongue, scraping lightly with the edge of his teeth.

Ariel whimpered and dropped her head back. Desire pounded in her veins. His name was a hot whisper on her lips.

She felt his hands tighten fractionally on her. He moved to her other breast. Through the lightweight fabric of his jogging shorts, the rigid evidence of his arousal pushed against her.

Jonah lifted her in his arms. "Your bedroom?" He followed the vague wave of her arm down the hall.

When they stood in the moonlit room, he stopped. "Are you sure?"

She knew what concerned him. Impatiently she drew his face down to hers, nose to nose. "Don't think you can worm your way out of it this time."

His eyes widened. "I'll take that for a yes."

"*This* time, we're going to do it my way," she said sternly.

White teeth flashed as he grinned. "That so?"

She nodded as she stood on tiptoe and struggled to pull his T-shirt up over his head. He obligingly bent down and all but took off the shirt himself. She flung it aside. "That is definitely so," she said. "Take off your shoes and socks."

He raised a dark eyebrow at her imperious tone, but sat on the side of the bed and complied. While he worked, she left the room, returning with the candle, which she placed on the dresser. He stood waiting for her.

Slowly, she pushed his shorts down over his slim hips, over the hard curve of his buttocks, down his long muscular legs. Along the way she touched him here, stroked him there. When she reached his feet, he quickly stepped out of the garment, and she tossed it in the opposite direction of his shirt.

He reached for her shirt, but she danced back out of reach. "My way," she reminded him. "We did it your way last time."

Jonah scowled.

She smiled. "Merely a small revenge, my love."

❖   ❖   ❖

Jonah would have granted her any request at that moment. She loved him. She'd seen him and still said she loved him. Hell, he would have climbed Mount Everest for her if she'd asked. He only hoped her revenge wouldn't be too painful or take too long. His body was ready for her now. But then, he'd been ready for her since that first night in the park.

She stepped back from him and slowly peeled off her clothes. Each movement was a provocative whisper that shot his blood temperature up ten degrees. Finally, she stood naked before him.

God, she was beautiful. So gloriously female. And she was his.

His heart hammered a rapid beat. He wanted her. Wanted to claim her in a way that could leave no doubt between them.

"Jonah." She made his name a moan of desire, and an answering sound clawed up his throat.

She came to him, her body silver in the moonlight, golden in the glow of the flame. Her breasts swayed. The patch of curls at the apex of her creamy thighs teased him. Fever burned in his blood.

She kissed his shoulders. Then his chest. Each of his nipples received special attention from her vixen's teeth. When she slipped her tongue over his tight belly the muscles there contracted involuntarily, and he heard her soft chuckle of satisfaction.

He held on tight to his control. It had been so long. He'd wanted her for so long . . . With an iron will, he kept himself in check.

Ariel went to her knees. She lightly stroked his thighs. He found it hard to breathe.

She touched him. She ran her fingertips down the length of his arousal. Blood pounded in his ears. His body screamed at his constraint. He shuddered as she curled her fingers around him. Oxygen grew scarce as he panted, struggling to fill his lungs.

Nothing mattered. Nothing but Ariel and what she was doing to him. Her hot, slow hands. Her warm breath. Her glistening mouth.

With more willpower than he'd ever thought he had, he pulled back from her.

She looked up at him with glazed eyes, and he scooped her up in his arms. "I—I'm not finished," she protested dazedly.

"We'll get back to your revenge later," he promised her as he laid her on the four-poster bed. He joined her there.

She smiled at him. Her lips were moist, and her eyes were nearly concealed by her lowered lashes.

He kissed her with searing, openmouthed carnality that brought her hands up to grip his shoulders.

He positioned himself over her and dipped his head to gently nip the tip of her breast between his teeth. To his intense satisfaction, she arched up under him, driving her head back into the pillow, catching her bottom lip between white teeth. He teased the sweet jewel with his tongue, then moved down to kiss the smooth plane of her belly. His hands learned the sweet feminine curves of her body.

His fingers were even more clever than she'd suspected, Ariel thought dimly as Jonah slipped his hand between her thighs. She gasped and automatically spread her legs a little farther as Jonah revealed precisely how clever his fingers really were. Warm, and strong, and— She cried out his name as the shudders rolled through her.

He entered her, pressing into her body slowly to accommodate the tight fit. His face was set, as if the gentle pace demanded great concentration. The muscles in his neck and shoulders corded. Under her fingers, the sinews in his back were as hard as granite. Sweat beaded his forehead and upper lip.

She arched up to meet him, welcoming him into her body with fierce joy, and he made a feral sound in his throat, and captured her lips in a hot, possessive, openmouthed kiss. "Yes." He thrust boldly into her. His eyes burned into hers. *"Yes."*

A great rushing tidal wave of sensation crashed through her, and she cried out, blindly gripping Jonah. A second later she felt him stiffen in her arms. A hoarse shout tore from his throat.

17

He gathered her back against him, spoon-fashion, his arms around her, warm and reassuringly heavy. He nuzzled her temple, and lightly kissed the curve of her ear.

"What should I call you?" she asked softly.

"Call me?"

"Jonah or Declan?"

He yawned. "Jonah."

She laced her fingers through his. "Good. I like Jonah better."

Against her temple, his mouth moved in a smile. "I like the way Jonah sounds when you say it."

Pleased, she cuddled against him more closely.

"Mmm. I like the way you do a lot of things." He turned her in his arms and kissed her more thoroughly. His hand moved across her ribs to splay against her back.

"Why did you give me the rose, French Lace?"

He sent her a wicked grin. "I watched you undress from outside your bedroom window."

"*What?*"

"Your shade was down. I only saw your silhouette, but it was enough to fuel some pretty torrid fantasies."

She regarded him with heightened interest. "Really?"

He nodded.

"Tell me about them."

He laughed. "Nosy wench. I don't have to. We've already acted them out—and then some."

She lowered her lashes and gave him what she hoped was a come-hither look. "I guess we'll just have to work on giving you some new fantasies."

"I'm all for that."

She planted a kiss on his chin. "Answer a question for me—"

"Another one?"

She made a face at him. "That cabin in the forest. You and your brother used to stay there, didn't you?"

"Camping there was the last thing we did together. We were in such a hurry to get out before a storm set in, Tim forgot his duffel bag."

"And the tape?"

"I composed all the music."

"It wasn't rock."

"I know."

"Do your parents know about that tape?"

"No."

"Why not?"

He lifted his head. "You said *a* question."

She decided not to press. Maybe someday Jonah

and his parents would be reunited, but clearly not today.

"Tell me what you do with your time," she coaxed. She wanted to know all the things he'd refused to tell her before. The things lovers wanted to know about each other. Every detail.

He wedged his muscular thigh between hers and propped the side of his head in one hand, his elbow buried in the pillow. "I'm a businessman. An entrepreneur, I guess you'd say. I've got my own record company now. Just a small one."

She drew an invisible line down the side of his neck, across his shoulder and along his arm. "So you're still in the music biz?"

He smiled lazily. "Yeah. In a way."

"What have you . . ." Her courage trickled away. Maybe this wasn't the right moment to ask. She looked at him stretched out beside her on her bed. Tall, marvelously made, blatantly masculine, Jonah appeared to be quite at home lying among her tangled sheets. Would he be willing to leave this room and walk into the daylight? She had to know. "What have you decided about surgery?"

He didn't answer immediately. "I haven't decided yet."

Her hopes plummeted like a stone. "Oh."

As if sensing her disappointment, he cupped her cheek in his palm. "Bear with me," he said.

"Will you tell me what happened after the accident?" She couldn't see any visible reason why Jonah's face had not been attended to after he'd recovered. True, he had keloid formations. Also true, fourteen years ago, silicon gel sheeting hadn't been in use. But most of the damage could have been corrected unless there had been some special problem.

"My manager and the record company wanted to keep the whole thing hush-hush, so it was announced that I'd withdrawn to meditate in a monastery in Tibet, for God's sake," he said. Bitterness saturated his voice. "They were scared shitless that my looks couldn't be saved. Or that my voice had been affected. So I was shipped off to one of my estates where a small hospital was set up. My manager retained a surgeon for me. Two years later it was announced that I'd been killed in a fiery car crash."

"What went wrong?"

Jonah lifted a lock of her hair. He stared down at it with an intensity that suggested his thoughts were centered elsewhere. "He put me through a series of operations, but I didn't look better at all. In fact, I looked worse. It seems my manager was terrified of losing his meal ticket, and had been desperate enought to believe the man who promised him that my skin could be made to regenerate."

Ariel frowned. "But that's crazy. Tissue regeneration is still in the experimental stages. No ethical surgeon would experiment on a live, unwilling subject."

"Unwilling? Unknowing is more like it. My manager didn't tell me. He forged the waivers and letters of permission. That lunatic thought he had a free hand with me! And my skin didn't even come close to regenerating. Instead, one of the concoctions he injected in me induced an allergic reaction. I almost died. When I recovered, I started asking questions.

When I was finished, my manager was unemployed. The mad doctor had already flown the coop."

"Are you sure he was a surgeon?" Ariel asked skeptically. " A plastic surgeon?"

"Yes. I had his credentials checked—too late I'm afraid."

"A demented one. He had no business practicing medicine."

"But he still had his license, and he was still operating on people."

"It was your manager who found him, Jonah."

"He was a doctor. I trusted him. Christ, I was in bad shape. I would have believed anything. Oh, God, I wanted my face back."

Horrified, Ariel wrapped her arms around Jonah. His life had descended into a nightmarish hell that was beyond her experience. The physicians that she knew were hardworking, conservative men and women who tried to do their best for their patients. Jonah's experience had been entirely different.

"He must have sensed how much I wanted to look good again, to look like I had before the accident." He drew a long breath. "What a fool I was. Finally, the lumps began to show up. And I knew there would never be any regeneration. Not for me."

"You got rid of him."

Jonah toyed with her lock of hair, smoothing it over and over again between his thumb and forefinger. "Yes. But I was thoroughly messed up by then. Another doctor was called in and now I feel kind of sorry for the guy. I didn't trust him an inch. Even had a detective check up on him. Well, he wasn't around long, anyway. Keloids formed. He tried pressure, then steroids, but when neither worked, he said there was nothing more that medical science could do for me." Jonah stared down at the piece of her hair that he held. "So I sent him home. A third doctor said much the same." His mouth tightened into a bitter line. "He declined to take me as a patient. Seems he felt the high chance of failure wouldn't do his career any good. I didn't try any other doctors after that. By then I knew."

It seemed to Ariel that his skin had grown chilled, so she tugged the covers up over him. He didn't seem to notice.

"Knew what?" she said, and kissed his forehead tenderly. When he didn't answer, she coaxed, "Won't you tell me?"

"I was sure that no doctor could save me from being a freak the rest of my life because . . . that was the way it was supposed to be."

She looked at him. He'd been living with this corrosive guilt for fourteen years. Had no one been able to make him understand he wasn't responsible for his brother's death? Had anyone ever tried? "You believe that you're being punished, don't you?" she asked quietly.

His brown eyes were haunted by remorse and loneliness.

She leaned forward and took his face between her hands. "Jonah, a drunk driver killed Tim," she said. "Your brother could as easily have been hit on his way to school, or coming home from a date. The guilty man is the drunk who ran into you. *Think*. If you'd gotten behind the wheel, you might have run into someone. Someone's teenage daughter. A mother and her children. A husband going home to his wife."

He looked away, toward the moon, which hung in the black sky like a disk of milky opal. "I know that."

She slowly shook her head. "No. I don't think you do. Or rather, I don't think you've accepted the fact."

"Yes, Dr. Denham."

Ariel punched him lightly on his arm. "Don't give me that. You know what I'm saying is true."

Jonah's lips curved up slightly. He released her hair and pressed a kiss in the space between her eyebrows. "I know. I'll work on it."

"You need to talk with a therapist."

"First a surgeon, now a therapist. According to you I'm a hopeless, useless ruin of a man."

She tossed him an impish grin. "Not useless."

His eyes lit with humor. "Oh, ho! We have a female chauvinist here."

Ariel squealed with glee when he lunged forward. She scrambled away, but he grabbed her, wrapping her in his arms. He rolled over with her, until she was on her back. He smiled down at her, and she smiled back. Then he dipped his head to hers and took her mouth in a long, slow, intoxicating kiss that tasted of unspoken promises and deep-burning desire. She reached up and laced her fingers through his hair, seeking an anchor in the spinning, breathless world to which only Jonah could take her. Only Jonah.

She woke to the rosy gray of dawn filtering around the shade at the window. Somewhere in her emerging consciousness, a tiny spark told her something about this morning was different from all her other mornings. Never before last night had a man filled her heart with such joy.

Ariel smiled as she lay there, on her side, the pillow beneath her cheek warmed by her skin. She didn't want to move, afraid she'd awaken him. For several seconds she managed to remain still, but finally she had to see him, had to touch him again. She turned over, reaching out to him.

But Jonah was gone.

"Dr. Denham!" Michael squawked with delight. He looked up at Lucy to make certain he had her attention, and his nurse smiled tenderly and smoothed back a short shock of his unruly hair—hair that hadn't been growing in that spot three months ago when he'd arrived at Fountainhead.

"To what do I owe the honor of this grand reception?" Ariel sat on the edge of his bed, and immediately Michael scooted over to lean against her. He rolled his cherub's eyes up to give her a coy look through his lashes. She chuckled and held out her arms for a hug. He launched himself into them. Laughing, she adroitly caught him before he cracked his head against hers. "Watch out, scout. You have to be careful of your stitches. We want everything to heal just right, don't we?"

He nodded enthusiastically, almost colliding with her chin in his enthusiasm. "I'm learning to read!" he announced proudly.

He was also learning to speak properly, Ariel noted. She'd noticed how his speech was increasingly progressing. She glanced at Lucy, whose affection shone in her eyes as she gazed at the child. Ariel knew who was primarily responsible for the healthy changes in the boy.

"Well, I'm impressed," she said solemnly. "Knowing how to read is very important. Not everyone can, you know."

"Dr. Denham, I can read about a cat and a hat," he told her breathlessly.

She hugged him, filled with a warm glow of pleasure in his personal achievement. "That's wonderful, Michael."

After satisfying herself that his latest grafts were doing well, she withdrew the usual fruit juice–sweetened treat from the pocket of her lab coat. "I think you deserve a reward, don't you?"

Lucy laughed. "He'll never say no to that."

Michael made quick work of the brightly colored paper wrap, then put the candy in his mouth. He wriggled out of Ariel's embrace and clambered down off the bed. He raced to his wooden chest, and reverently withdrew a book. "I'll read for you!"

"Dr. Denham has rounds to finish, Michael," Lucy explained gently.

He looked at Ariel expectantly as he clutched his book.

She found she was unwilling to disappoint him. She really did want to hear him read. "I'll tell you what. I'll take my lunch break with you. How's that? Then you can read to me about cats and hats." She smiled at Lucy. "I wouldn't miss out on this for the world."

"Why don't I make arrangements for lunch here?" Lucy offered. "We can have our own little recital."

Ariel nodded. "Great idea. Thanks." She turned to Michael. "That okay with you, scout?"

His eyes sparkled. "Okay!"

As Ariel walked down the corridor toward the room of her next patient, she reflected about how things were changing for her, how she was changing here at Fountainhead.

Jonah had left without so much as a note to her. Left alone in the gray of dawn, she had known despair. Until she'd walked into the living room and found the rose.

Purple with perfect pink-tipped petals, its sweet fragrance had helped to lift her spirits. She'd taken the flower to her office with her, where Kerwin had given her its name. Magic. Even as she'd held the perfect bloom to her nose and inhaled its perfume, she had thought of the floral language Jonah had been using.

Last night had been magic. Her heart beat more rapidly just remembering. His beautiful brown eyes. His intoxicating kisses. His passion. She'd drifted to sleep, certain that everything had changed, that now they had a future. But, without a word, he'd vanished like the night mists.

All she had to hold on to was one perfect, sweet-scented rose.

Tonight they'd have to sit down and have a serious talk about all this elusiveness. He didn't have to hide from her anymore. She'd told him that she loved him. He'd claimed to love her. The worst was behind them.

That thought suffused her with a happy glow, and she completed her rounds with a lighter step to her stride.

Before she went back to Michael's room, Ariel stopped in her office to pick up a few more sweets for him. The telephone rang as she stepped toward the door, on her way out. With a sigh, she answered it.

"Ariel, how is my daughter the doctor doing?"

"Fine, Dad. Is there something wrong?" she asked immediately, concerned. Her father seldom called her, and almost never at work.

"Wrong? Does something have to be wrong for me to call my only kid?"

His indignation caused her to feel ungrateful and mean. "Of course not," she protested.

"I just wanted to know how you were doing up there in the mountains. Is it cold yet?"

"No. Actually, the weather is quite pretty."

Ariel wanted to tell her father about Jonah, about her being in love. She yearned to share the wonder of her feelings with him. Oh, she knew there were some things she and Jonah had yet to work out.

"I met a man, Dad," she said hesitantly.

"That's nice. Have you heard about Herrick? I know the receptionist at Bendl and MacDaid and she told me."

She caught her bottom lip between her teeth, uncertain if her father was ignoring what she'd said, or if he was pursuing the point in a roundabout way. "I wasn't talking about Nelson Herrick."

"No, but *I* was."

"Oh." She picked up a pencil and began doodling on her calendar.

"He's rolling in money—"

"Of course he is. His family's rich."

"Don't interrupt me, my girl. As I was saying, Herrick is mingling with the stars and raking in the money since he became a partner with Bendl and MacDaid. You won't find anyone in *his* family working themselves to death in some damned store."

Ariel's fingers tightened around the handset. "You wanted that job. You insisted on having it. That job was your last hope—you said so yourself."

"I know what I said, but I was given to believe there would be prestige and power. No one told me I'd have to work like a mule." His voice took on a wheedling note. "I've been thinking. Maybe you were right all along. Maybe you should never have signed the contract with Fountainhead."

"A little late to think about that now, wouldn't you say?"

"It was just that I thought this was going to be a really good job. I was misled. I guess I should have trusted your judgment more. After all, you have more experience than I do with such things."

That was the truth, she thought, furious. *She'd* always worked. She reminded herself that he was her father. In his own way, he'd tried to do right by her. But, for once, the defensive litany failed to still the anger.

"You didn't have to work," she reminded him. "I invited you to move in with me. The condo had more than enough room for two people. Then you could have done whatever you wanted. You could have joined a country club and played golf. Or taken up a hobby. Or anything you wanted to do. *But you wanted that job.* And the only way you could have it was for me to sign a contract with Fountainhead."

"I didn't want to be your poor, hanger-on old man. Don't you see? I would have lost my self-respect." Gerald Denham vented a long-suffering sigh. "I could always have found another job."

She caught her breath, shocked at the way he'd twisted the facts. "No one else would hire you," she said bluntly.

"So *you* say. But I'm sure that if I'd had a little more time I could have found a better position. A man of my experience . . ."

Anger seethed through her. A dark voice from deep within her brain began the litany again. For the first time in her life, she silenced it. Someone was responsible for this horrible mess. Someone was to blame.

"It was Renard," her father insisted. "That bastard was the one who offered me this pie-in-the-sky job and blackmailed you into spending a year working for the Foundation. We were both swindled."

Ariel knew exactly whom to blame, and she didn't like it one bit. But she was finished making excuses. "It's not Renard, Dad. He's not really responsible for our problems. He offered you a great job, especially considering your track record, and you wanted it. You wanted it badly enough to blackmail me into giving up what I thought was the opportunity of a lifetime."

Her father sputtered indignantly. "Blackmail you! I never blackmailed you into anything!"

"Yes, you did. And even after a lifetime of living with you, even knowing how you operate, I let you do it. I gave up that golden opportunity so you could have what you wanted." She could see it all so clearly now.

"It was Renard, I tell you!"

Ariel slowly shook her head. "No. It was us. Ultimately, we're the ones who made the decisions. *We* signed on the dotted lines. All he did was make the offers."

"I can't believe you're talking to me like this," he said heatedly.

"We've been lying to ourselves, Dad. And I can't stand the lies anymore."

"I think you need to get out of that place. I don't know what they're doing to you there, but you don't sound like my little girl anymore."

She didn't reply.

He didn't seem to notice. "Do you think you can get out of your contract with Fountainhead? Maybe Bendl and MacDaid would like another partner in their practice. After all, they wanted you before. I could quit this job."

She felt inexplicably weary. "No, Dad. My attorney checked the contract looking for loopholes before I signed it. I'm here for a year. As for Bendl and MacDaid . . . well, I doubt they want another partner right now."

He gave another long sigh. "I don't suppose you could forward your old dad a little money?"

There was a light knock at the door, and Maitland stepped in.

"How much?" she asked her father. He told her and she promised to send him a check.

After she hung up, Ariel paused a second, trying to recover her composure. She resented Maitland's intrusion into such a personal moment. Finally she turned to him "Yes?"

"I'm here to take you to your next appointment."

She pushed herself up out of the chair. "I'm on rounds today. My next appointment is with a little boy."

Maitland smiled. "I'm afraid you'll have to postpone the rest of your engagements for a few hours. This next appointment is exceptionally important."

Ariel was so tired she wasn't even interested in what the mysterious appointment might be. "I don't want to disappoint Michael."

"You can make it up to him later."

Not moving an inch from where she stood, she unsmilingly met his gaze. "I'm not accustomed to breaking my promises, Robert."

"If you come with me, you'll understand why timing is important."

She studied him for a moment. Although he held himself with his usual ease, there was tension around his eyes and his mouth. It was important to him that she keep this so-called appointment.

With a short nod, she picked up the phone and dialed Michael's room. First she spoke to Lucy and explained the situation. Then she spoke with Michael. The child's disappointment was obvious, until she promised to listen to him read tomorrow.

"Who is this all-important personage?" she asked Maitland as they walked out of the hospital, to the parking lot where he opened the passenger's side door of the car for her. "A paying patient?" A movie star attempting to bring his career back on track? Or some foreign dictator?

Maitland walked around the car and slid behind the steering wheel. "You could say that."

In silence they rode through the valley until they came to the back gate. Ariel looked at the rose garden and remembered how Jonah had touched her, then had refused to allow her to touch him. With the perfection had come the pain.

To her surprise, Maitland reached under the steering column and touched a small remote attached there. The heavy wrought-iron gates slowly swung open.

"Where are we going?" she asked. "Just who is this patient?"

Maitland watched the road. As if he wasn't absolutely familiar with the deserted strip of asphalt, Ariel thought waspishly.

"This situation is a little different," he said. "And we try to accommodate our patients."

"Especially the paying ones," Ariel said snidely, and was instantly ashamed. Never had she seen favoritism at Fountainhead. Anyway, the doctors and staff rarely knew who paid and who didn't.

Maitland turned into a side road she hadn't even known existed, and arrived at another closed gate. With a touch to the remote, the tall metal gate opened, and they entered what appeared to be a compound. What was this place? It must be the best-kept secret in these mountains, because she'd never heard anyone speak of this place. It had a corporate look to it. She saw people wearing business suits.

Four contemporary-style, three-story buildings formed a square around a parking lot and a park area with benches and tables. Maitland parked the car, and led her into one of the buildings.

They walked through a lobby, past the receptionist, who greeted them with a smile, then down a corridor. The expensive paintings and furnishings reflected wealth and power.

Suddenly a thought occurred to her. "Are we going to see Mr. Renard?" she asked Maitland. "Did he finally return from his travels?"

Before he could answer, they had arrived in what appeared to be the anteroom of an important office.

A secretary in a business suit immediately rose to her feet. With a polite nod, she briskly strode to the floor-to-ceiling double doors behind her desk. "You're expected, Dr. Denham."

She opened one of the towering doors and stepped inside the room. "The doctor is here, sir." She gestured Ariel to enter, then closed the door as she exited.

A large leather executive chair was turned away from Ariel on the far side of an enormous walnut desk, which was loaded with papers and files and telephones. A collage of images moved across the bank of television screens set in the dark-wood–paneled wall behind the desk. There were no windows. The chair silently turned, revealing a tall man clad in a dark, exquisitely tailored suit.

Jonah stood. "Hello, Ariel," he said.

She stared at him. "Jonah, what are you doing here?" Why was he wearing a suit? He looked like a different person in those unfamiliar clothes. And why was he just standing there? Last night they had been lovers; why didn't he embrace her now? For the first time, she noticed how carefully he was watching her, as if he didn't know what to expect from her.

He came around the mesa of polished walnut that separated them. "Did you find my rose?"

"I would rather have found you."

He reached out and lightly, lingeringly traced the side of her cheek. "I had to go. I wanted to wake you to say good-bye properly, but you looked so beautiful sleeping there that I didn't have the heart."

"What is this all about, Jonah? Why are you in this"—she swept out her arms to encompass the room, the buildings, the entire compound—"place. What *is* this place?" The walls were hung with what looked to be original paintings by some of this century's most important artists. Even the desk was a monument to skill. Its simple style had required the hand of a master cabinetmaker. On the top of the desk, piled with neat stacks of files, correspondence and envelopes, she caught sight of a name that immediately gripped her attention.

T. J. Renard.

Frowning, she stepped closer, unashamedly reading labels and salutations. Renard Corporation. T. J. Renard. The name slammed into her perception, making her faintly dizzy.

"My God," she whispered. "You're Renard." She turned to face Jonah, wanting him to deny it, fearing he could not. The two terrible words echoed against the wood paneling to hang in the room like a curse.

"Yes," he said finally. "I'm Renard."

Ariel stared at him, stunned. Jonah, her lover, the man she'd trusted with her heart, was T. J. Renard.

His lies had been going on since the beginning, and now she knew that they hadn't ended last night.

Anger and hurt boiled up inside her, roiling in her stomach, clutching at her windpipe. She tasted the sourness of bile. "What exactly is your real name? Or have you made up so many of them that you've forgotten?" Her short, harsh laugh was empty of humor. "You said your life was a lie, that *you* were a lie, and I didn't believe you. But you were right. So horribly right."

Jonah stiffened. "My real name is Templeton Jonah Renard."

"Of course it is."

"Look, my parents hated the music I was playing, the songs I wrote. They were contemptuous of my success. In rebellion, I made my stage name legal. But later, after the accident, I took back my real name. I never lied to you, Ariel."

"Well you sure as hell left out a lot of details, didn't you? You knew how I felt about Renard, and you said *nothing*."

He regarded her for a moment. "By the time I discovered your feelings about 'Renard,' it was too late."

"Too late?"

"I already cared about you."

His words cut her like a blade. "How can I believe that, Jonah? How can I believe anything you tell me? After so many lies . . ." She thought of the roses he'd given her. She thought of the evenings they'd shared. "Everyone in Farley knew more about what was going on than I did—and I slept with you!" Humiliation washed over her. "André even told me to trust you." She spit the last two words, scornful that she'd been such a fool.

"I came back to my hometown because Farley had fallen on economic hard times. The townspeople had always been good to me, so I figured turnabout was fair play. I'd made millions as Declan Stone, and those had been parlayed into millions more. I bought land and established Fountainhead. This is the headquarters of Renard Corporation, which employs a lot of the people in the area. There are scholarships to put their kids through college. They don't care that I look like a nightmare."

"*I've* never cared what you looked like," she told him angrily.

"You didn't see my face until last night."

"Do you think you've been able to conceal yourself every minute? I've known for months. And it didn't matter to me. It didn't matter because I loved you."

His eyes widened. "You knew? And you said nothing?"

"It was clear you didn't want me to see. I didn't want to hurt you."

"I had to be sure of you."

Her eyes widened. "Sure of me? What for?"

Jonah shoved his hands into his trouser pockets. "I meant to be straight with you from the beginning—until I found out who you were. I've been a victim before. I'll never put myself in that position again. I wanted to learn more about you, about you as a person."

"To make certain I wasn't some unethical charlatan?" she demanded hoarsely, fury throbbing behind her eyes. How could he have believed that of her? "You brought me here. Why didn't you have me checked out?" She drew a stinging breath, trying to calm the turbulence inside her.

"I did," he said. "But my first doctor had been checked out, too, and look what happened. No, I wanted to get to know you."

She felt ill. "So after you read your report on me, you were still doubtful. But clearly not too doubtful to take me to bed," she flung at him, hating him for the lies, hating herself for believing them.

A muscle jumped in Jonah's jaw. "It wasn't like that, and you damned well know it."

She looked at him through the watery blur of tears. "No, I don't. Because I was clearly wrong about everything else. You see, I loved you—" Her voice broke, and she paused, struggling for control. "I thought you loved me."

He quickly crossed the distance that separated them and took her upper arms in his hands. "I *do* love you, Ariel. God in heaven, I love you more than I've ever loved anyone in my life! For fourteen years I lived in the dark. Then I met you." Jonah's face lit with a tender smile. "You weren't afraid of me. You talked with me. You even laughed with me. And you made me believe in miracles again. Don't you see, Ariel? You're my heart and my hope. I trust you. That's why you must be the one to perform the surgery."

She stared at him in shock. The blood drained from her face, leaving her numb. Her mind tried to assimilate his words but failed to make sense of them. Surely he hadn't said what she thought he had. She prayed that she had misheard him.

"Did you hear me?" he asked. "I want you to be the one to perform the surgery."

She pulled from his grasp. "I can't be your surgeon," she cried. Just the thought of cutting into Jonah's flesh, then having something go wrong, something beyond her power to correct, terrified her. Wildly, she shook her head. "I'm involved with you. It's impossible. I—I can't do it."

Jonah's face went white. "What?" he whispered, as though the breath had been knocked out of him.

Her heart felt as if it had been shredded to ribbons. He needed surgery. He'd never be whole without it. But envisioning Jonah lying pale and quiet on that sterile table . . . Ariel knew she couldn't perform the operations herself. "You can find another surgeon. There are several—"

"No." He sliced the air with his hand in a gesture of sharp denial. "I don't trust anyone but you to do what needs to be done." He stalked several paces away and stood for a moment, appearing to study the painting in front of him. Then he turned to face Ariel. "Please be my surgeon, Ariel." His eyes met hers in quiet appeal.

"I can't," she said raggedly. Then, before her tears could fall, she turned and fled from the room.

18

Ariel rose early the next morning, after a sleepless night. She shuffled into the bathroom and splashed several handfuls of cold water on her swollen face, then went to the kitchen to make coffee.

The message light was blinking on the side of the telephone, so she dialed the number of her electronic mailbox and listened, stunned, to the brusque, businesslike recording left by Maitland.

She was released from her contract with Fountainhead Foundation, he informed her. Her patients had already been assigned to other doctors, and she was not to see them again. He instructed her to vacate the bungalow by five o'clock that afternoon and to stop by the administration building to sign some papers on her way out. When the message clicked off, she sat numbly staring at the receiver in her hand.

She'd been dismissed.

Who was responsible for this termination? Was Jonah being vindictive? It didn't seem like him. But Maitland might be angry.

The punctuated whine from the telephone caught her attention, and she absently dropped the handset into its cradle.

Wasn't it enough that Jonah had taken her heart? Must it also be ground into dust?

Her patients. She feared they would suffer in this unnecessary reshuffling of responsibility. They needed her.

And, for the first time, she realized how much she needed them. Her work, her skills, had a profound effect on those who had come to her here at Fountainhead Clinic. In turn, they had given meaning to her life, meaning that transcended the financial gain she'd once thought so all-important.

Quickly she showered and dressed. Then she strode determinedly to the hospital. No one would keep her from saying good-bye to Michael and Lucy, Doris and Kerwin, to Mrs. Levy and all the rest of them.

But they did. Security met her at the door. Uniformed men she'd never seen before blocked her access to the hospital. She clenched her fists at her sides, trembling with rage and frustration.

"Dr. Denham! Over here."

Ariel swiveled toward the voice and found Lucy, Doris, and Kerwin standing outside, off to the side of the entrance. She hurried over to them.

"What's going on?" Doris asked, worry plain in every line of her elfin face.

Kerwin gestured toward the security men. "Everyone's received voice mail messages. You've been barred from the hospital. Ariel, all your patients have been given to other doctors. What has happened?"

She looked at her friends, suspicion taking form. "You aren't supposed to be talking with me, are you?"

"No," Lucy said. "But they couldn't stop us."

Ariel's throat tightened painfully. "I came to say good-bye."

"What happened?" Doris asked, taking Ariel's hand between her own. "Does this have anything to do with Jonah?"

Ariel smiled bitterly. "It seems he was someone important." She couldn't bring herself to talk about it yet. "I'll write you all later."

She turned to Lucy. "I guess I'll never get to hear Michael read now. Tell him good-bye for me, won't you, Lucy?"

The nurse nodded, biting her lip. Tears welled in her eyes. "I wanted you to know, Larry and I are applying to adopt Michael."

Ariel hugged her tightly. "I'm so glad," her voice hoarse with emotion. "I wish the three of you much happiness." She went on to hug Doris and Kerwin each in turn. "I wish all of you happiness. I expect wedding invitations." She laughed brokenly. "From you, Lucy, and"—she tried to level a stern look at Doris and Kerwin, but the effort fell short—"you, too.

"Now, go back inside. I don't want to make trouble for you." She managed a smile. "I'll miss you."

When she went by the administration office to sign the papers, she told herself that this was what she'd wanted all along—to be released from her contract with Fountainhead Foundation. But as her pen scratched over the signature lines, it seemed to her a terrible darkness had settled over her life.

Jonah had asked the impossible of her, but she couldn't find it in her to blame him. All she'd had left was her work, and now even that had been yanked out from under her.

She slid the papers across the desk to the secretary, who scooped them up.

"Please wait here," the young woman said, then disappeared down the hall.

A minute later, the door to Maitland's office opened. He stood regarding her for a moment, his face expressionless.

She rose to her feet, holding herself straight and proud. "Whose decision was this?" she asked. "Yours or Jonah's?"

"T. J. wanted you released from the contract you found so repugnant. He felt you should have a choice of staying or going. But I want you out of here before you do any more damage."

"And you are the official administrator of Fountainhead Foundation."

His lips moved slightly in the shadow of a satisfied smile. "Correct."

She opened her purse and drew out a piece of notepaper bearing a name and address. She held it out to him. After a second's pause, he took it from her.

"This surgeon can help Jonah if anyone can," she said. "He's excellent."

Maitland raised an eyebrow. "Don't concern yourself any further with T.J., Dr. Denham. Thanks to you, he probably won't have the surgery. He'll end up spending the rest of his life in this valley."

19

Gerald Denham swung the front door of his house wide at Ariel's first knock. "It's about time you got here!" he exclaimed, grabbing her in a bear hug. "How was your drive from Fountainhead?"

She hugged him back, trying to take comfort from the rare physical contact she had with her father, but nothing seemed to relieve the soul-deep numbness that had seeped into her. "It's good to be back."

He led her inside his new house. "I'll bet. I don't know how you stood living up in the sticks like that. Just one little hick town. Me, I like cities. Plenty to do."

"I guess I didn't really see it as the sticks, Dad." She followed him through a foyer, down a hall into the kitchen. "It's a pretty area," she said dully, "and the clinic is equipped with the best."

He beamed. "That would include doctors, too, of course."

She forced a smile for him. "Of course."

He went to the coffeemaker and poured a cup of coffee. He held up the pot and gave her a questioning look. She shook her head no.

"There are the fixings for a sandwich in the refrigerator if you're hungry," he said.

Exhaustion had suppressed any appetite she might have had. "No, thank you. But I could use a cup of tea."

"Tea bags are in the canister on the sink. There, to your left." He took a seat at the kitchen table, his steaming cup cradled between his palms.

Ariel thought about what she'd come to say to her father as she filled a mug with water and put it in the microwave oven. She punched in two minutes and pressed the start button. Neither Ariel or her father spoke, as if it were rude to talk while the microwave was busy.

"So, you got out of your contract after all," he said, breaking the silence that followed the oven's timer beep.

Ariel removed the hot cup and, with more care than was necessary, she selected a tea bag from the canister. What she had to tell her father would be unpleasant. She knew he wouldn't be happy to hear her news, but the time had finally come to settle things between them.

"I was released. I was also given until sundown to get out of Deadwood."

Gerald's head jerked up. "What? Why—"

"Call it a clash of personal philosophies, if you like. It had nothing to do with my skill or competence. But it may affect my ability to get the position I want."

"Bendl and MacDaid wanted you before, they'll want you now," her father said confidently.

This is where things would turn difficult. "I'm not going to contact Bendl and MacDaid," she said.

"Eh?"

"I said—"

Impatiently, he waved aside her repetition. "I heard what you said. Now I expect an explanation."

She turned to face her father squarely. This had been a long time, a lifetime in coming. "Why should I explain?"

He blinked, surprised. She waited, taking no pleasure in what she would have to say to him. She'd thought about it since their conversation earlier that day. And she knew she was right. This was the only way.

"Why?" he demanded. "*Why?* Because it's what's best for you! Because we had plans!"

"No, Dad. I don't believe going back to work as strictly a cosmetic surgeon is what's best for me, even if Bendl or MacDaid still wanted me, which I'm sure they don't. And we didn't have any plans. You had plans. You always have plans of one kind or another."

He scowled as he slowly rose to his feet. "I was going to quit my job."

Ariel took a deep breath and let it out. She said quietly, "I wouldn't if I were you."

"Just what the hell do you mean by that?"

"I mean that we don't have a healthy relationship, Dad. It's too one-sided. You make the plans,and I make the sacrifices. Because I've always loved you, you see? I've always tried so very hard to please you. But no matter what I did, it was never enough."

"That—that's completely untrue!" he sputtered. "You're the one who offered to support me."

She gave him a level look. "You were unemployed."

He glared at her. He opened his mouth to say something, then slowly closed it.

"If you'd moved in with me, at least I would have seen you once in a while," she continued. Probably when he'd wanted money, if their history was any indication.

He looked away, still frowning. The tactic was familiar. The Old Silent Treatment. This time it wouldn't work.

She dumped the hot water into the sink. "Well, you've got a nice job with benefits now, so that's not a problem anymore."

She jotted down the name of a hotel. "If you want to talk, here's where I'll be staying."

Over the years, she'd paid dearly in her efforts to win her father's love, and she still wasn't sure she had it. But this time the price had been too high.

She knew she would never get over Jonah. He had dragged her heart into the shadows with him, but when he'd wanted to come into the sunlight, she'd barred his way. He would never forgive her. She would never forgive herself. Now her future stretched before her, long and empty.

Ariel shouldered her purse and walked to the door, where she paused. Gerald Denham's stunned expression gave her no satisfaction. "I don't intend to be manipulated ever again, Dad," she said quietly. "Not by you, not by anyone."

Having said what she'd come to say, filled with a terrible loneliness, Ariel walked out of her father's house.

20

Ariel pulled into the driveway of her house and shut off the engine. As she gathered her purse and briefcase and got out of the car, she studied the front lawn. The sod that had been laid when she'd bought this place was almost finished growing into a smooth carpet. Maybe it needed more fertilizer.

She almost smiled. Who would have ever thought she'd choose a house over a more maintenance-free condominium? A year ago, she would have laughed at the idea. A lot of things could change in a year.

A lot of things could change in only eight months. It had been nearly that long to the day since that night she'd walked out of her father's house, after leaving Fountainhead. Her father had eventually called her, and they had begun the painful process of building a new relationship. Gerald had kept his job, and these days he rarely asked her for money. Occasionally they went to dinner or a movie together.

The envelope she'd received from Maitland's secretary had contained a glowing letter of recommendation. To her amazement, she'd received several offers, good offers, to join practices with excellent reputations. The experience acquired at Fountainhead had proved to be an asset, and she'd been able to negotiate a partnership in a reconstructive surgery group that interested her. Now every day was filled with the work she loved. It was work that made a real difference in the lives of her patients. She did her best to ensure that none of them would even think of retreating to the shadows.

It was the time away from her work that was hardest to bear. Nighttime was worst. Long, moonlit hours haunted her with the empty ache of regret.

She walked up the curved walk to her front door, pausing to admire colorful masses of impatiens. When she'd bought the house, she'd hired a landscaper to plan and plant everything except her large garden in the backyard. That pleasure she'd reserved for herself. Now she looked forward to spending time there every day—the real reason she'd bought a house instead of a condo.

Absently she sorted through the keys on her key ring. She stepped toward the door—and froze.

There, on the doorstep, sat a crystal vase bearing a single, long-stemmed rose.

With a trembling hand, she picked up the vase and its flower. The vase was the same as the one Jonah had given her, which she'd been forced to leave back at Fountainhead.

Quickly she looked around, but she saw no one about. The neighborhood was quiet at this dinner hour. A further search turned up no note.

She fumbled the key into the lock and somehow

managed to get the door open. Dumping her purse and briefcase on the foyer table, she hurried to her library, where she immediately pulled the guide to roses off its shelf. Then she went out into her backyard.

Ariel had carefully selected and planted each of the fifty bushes. She had tended them faithfully. Her reward was this rose garden of breathtaking loveliness. Perfect blossoms covered the many lush green bushes, creating a rainbow of pinks, reds, yellows and whites. An old sundial stood in the center of the garden, and from that circle wound brick paths. Here and there she'd placed a bench and over each she'd created an arbor.

She sat down on a wrought-iron bench beneath an arch of fragrant, white Silver Moon roses. Then she took the single, mysterious flower from its vase.

Its creamy yellow petals were tipped with pink. She brushed the curled edge of a petal softly across her lips and allowed her eyes to drift closed. Achingly sweet memories filled her, bringing with them a yearning that filled her with loneliness. She lowered the flower to her lap, holding it in one hand while she opened the book with the other.

"Its name is Peace," said a familiar, mellow-fire voice.

She stood so abruptly the book tumbled to the cedar-mulched ground.

A tall man stepped out of the shadows of the house, into the late-afternoon sun. His longish, raven-dark hair held a touch of wave, brushing the collar of his black leather bomber jacket. He wore a black T-shirt, and black denim jeans hugged his lean hips and long, muscular legs.

His golden brown eyes met hers.

"Jonah," she whispered, searching his face. His new face.

Gone was the ragged, discolored skin. While his flesh would never be perfect, it was much smoother now, more even. Black eyebrows—interrupted only by a thin scar that bisected the left one—slanted over his thick-lashed, expressive eyes. His high cheekbones, freed from the lumps and ridges that had covered them, were more elegant than ever. His nose was straight and finely shaped, above sensual lips that bore only three small scars. She thought he was beautiful.

He smiled, and her heart pounded. She'd missed him so much these past months. She'd grieved for the loss of what they'd once had together.

"Forgive me," he said, his voice low and burning. "Please, Ariel. I need you."

She remembered the terrible sense of betrayal she'd felt, standing there in his office, learning the truth. At the time, she'd feared it would destroy her. Yet as the weeks passed, she'd come to understand why Jonah had refrained from revealing his identity. Understanding his reasoning didn't make his actions right, but in the end being right had given her little comfort.

Tears stung the back of her eyes. Her throat constricted. "If you will forgive me."

His eyes widened. "Forgive you?"

"I refused to be your surgeon."

"I had no right to ask it of you."

"You were desperate."

"Yes. I was. So desperate that after you left, I even went to a stranger for help. Robert gave me the information on the surgeon you recommended."

He'd trusted her enough to submit to a plastic surgeon who was a stranger to him. She felt humbled by that knowledge.

Before she could speak he handed her another rose, light pink in color.

His gaze never left her face as he put a name to it. "New Dawn. It's what I'm asking for, Ariel. For us." Hope and regret, love and need, all were there for her to see in his eyes.

With a cry of joy, she flung herself into his arms. Instantly, he enfolded her in a fierce embrace. "Oh, Jonah," she said, "that's what I want, too. A new dawn. A fresh beginning. I've missed you so much. I thought I'd never see you again."

"I was wrong not to tell you who I really was," he said raggedly. "It was just—"

"I know, I know," she assured him softly, placing two fingertips over his lips. "I should have been more compassionate, more understanding. I was afraid you'd give up. Sometimes I even considered going back and agreeing to do what you wanted. But then I'd think about cutting into you, and I couldn't." She smiled up at him. "But you went through with the surgery anyway. You took another chance."

He lifted a stray wisp of her hair that floated at her cheek and examined it as if the blond strands were the rarest thing he'd ever seen. "I had to," he said. "I love you. But you're a child of the sunlight, and I knew that if I was to have any chance of winning you back, I must face the sunlight, too. I've repeated that to myself again and again over these past eight months. Each time I was wheeled into the operating room, each time I forced myself to look into a mirror."

She tried to swallow past the lump in her throat. Only Jonah had held the power to change his life. But she had the power to fill it with her love. Ariel touched his cheek. It was warm against her hand. "If we're to have our new start, we must make a promise that there will be only the truth between us."

"Yes," he agreed. "Only the truth." Then he lowered his head to hers and claimed her lips in a kiss of such shattering tenderness that she knew Jonah had at last opened his soul to her.

When he finally lifted his head and looked at her, Ariel was certain the joy that filled her must surely glow for him to see.

He searched her face intently for a moment. Then, slowly, he presented her with his last three roses.

Without being told, she knew. "Love, Honor, and Cherish."

He nodded, never breaking their locked gaze. "I want you to be my wife, Ariel. Will you take me as your husband?"

Gently, she eased out of his embrace. A muscle jumped in his jaw as he watched her go, but she walked only as far as a nearby rosebush, from which she plucked a creamy white bloom. Then she returned to Jonah and offered the flower to him. With a radiant smile, her heart soaring higher than the soft spring clouds, she told him the name of the bloom. "June Bride."

He swept her into his arms, and they claimed each other in a sweet, lingering kiss. Then, hand in hand, Ariel and Jonah walked through the lengthening shadows of the garden, into the house. Tomorrow a new sun would rise.

Let HarperMonogram
Sweep You Away

❧❀❧

AMERICAN DREAMER by Theresa Weir

Animal researcher Lark Leopold has never encountered a
more frustrating mammal than handsome farmer Nathan
Senatra. But Lark won't give up on her man until he learns to
answer her call of the wild.

BILLY BOB WALKER
GOT MARRIED
by Lisa G. Brown
A HarperMonogram Classic

Special Price only $2.99

Shiloh Pennington knows that Billy Bob Walker is no good.
But how can she ignore the fire that courses in her veins at the
thought of Billy's kisses?

SHADOW PRINCE
by Terri Lynn Wilhelm
A HarperMonogram Classic

Special Price only $2.99

Plastic surgeon Ariel Denham is working at an exclusive, isolated clinic high in the Smoky Mountains when she meets and
falls in love with a mysterious man who stays in the shadows, a
man she knows only as Jonah.

DESTINED TO LOVE
by Suzanne Elizabeth
A HarperMonogram Classic

Special Price only $2.99

In this sizzling time travel romance, a guardian angel sends Dr.
Josie Reed back to the Wild West of 1881 to tend to a captured outlaw. The last thing the doctor expects is to go on the
run—or to lose her heart.

Let Your Imagination Run Wild